Marooner's Island

By

F. R. GOULDING

Cherokee Publishing Company
Atlanta, Georgia

Manufactured in the United States of America

ISBN: 978-0-87797-370-6 Hardcover

ISBN: 978-0-87797-371-3 Paper

 Cherokee Publishing Company
P O Box 1730, Marietta, GA 30061

AUTHOR'S PREFACE.

AROONER'S ISLAND has been prepared as an independent sequel to THE YOUNG MAROONERS. The author does not approve of sequels; but so many and so urgent were the requests for the continuation of his former story, that he was allowed no option in the case.

The plan adopted in the former work, of imbedding in an interesting narrative as much information as possible of a permanently useful character, has been adopted also in this, and has been more fully carried out.

Visitors to the coast of Florida will probably bear witness to the life-likeness of the scenes described. Should any of them, however, look in vain for the beautiful island which afforded so pleasant a refuge to the heroes and heroines of our adventure, they are requested to remember that extensive *land-sinks*, caused, probably, by the action of subterranean currents, are not unusual in that remarkable country. Indeed, the sudden disappearance, in this way, of several acres was announced in the newspapers while Chap. XXIV. of this book was in the process of publication. It is, therefore, not to be expected that all the places existing in the year 1831 are in existence now.

To the kindly hands of those who have expressed so lively an interest in the "YOUNG MAROONERS," as to compel the hazards of a Sequel, the author commits the present work, with the hope, that, although it may not equal the other in pathos, it may not be behind it in utility.

CONTENTS

CHAPTER XVI.

CHAPTER XVII.

CHAPTER XVIII.

CHAPTER XIX.

CHAPTER XX.

CHAPTER XXI.

CHAPTER XXII.

CHAPTER XXIII.

CHAPTER XXIV.

CHAPTER XXV.

CHAPTER XXXIII.

CHAPTER XXXIV.

CHAPTER XXXV.

CHAPTER XXXVI.

CHAPTER XXXVII.

MAROONER'S ISLAND.

CHAPTER I.

THE CAUSE OF THE SEARCH.

OON after sunrise, on the morning of October 26th, 1830, a scene of wild excitement occurred upon the edge of a bluff that overlooked the pure and tranquil waters of Tampa Bay.

A gentleman, thirty-five or forty years of age, stood for a moment gazing with anguished face over that beautiful expanse of water, then fell upon his knees and wrung his hands with grief.

A few steps behind him stood a man in the garb of a United States soldier, holding a horse by the bridle, and apparently awaiting orders; and close, on either hand, were negroes, who, in eager sympathy, had thrown themselves beside their master, and were mingling their sorrows with his.

Upon the surface of the bay, at the distance of half a mile, was a pleasure-boat, containing four persons, passing rapidly towards the sea. Without sails, or oars, or any other sign of a propelling power, it moved with such velocity as to raise before it a sheet of spray, and to leave a train of whitened water in its wake.

The kneeling figure, in the foreground, was Dr. Gordon, a gentleman from Georgia, who had recently come to Tampa to prepare a winter residence for his invalid wife. The persons in the boat were his children and a nephew, the son of his sister, who had come with him as companions and pupils for the time.

Five minutes before, no group could be found on earth with brighter faces or more hopeful hearts ; now, none could be found more miserable. They had all taken their seats in the boat, ready to start on a marooning expedition to one of the wooded keys at the mouth of the Bay, when the Doctor was called by a sudden messenger to his house, and in the interval the anchor of the boat had been tripped by a Devil-Fish, and the young voyagers were dragged seawards under the grasp of one of the most powerful and most dreaded monsters of the deep.*

* It is neither unusual nor unnatural for those who are strangers to sea-board life to regard all stories told of the Devil-Fish as so many draughts upon the imagination. But

Overwhelmed, and for a moment paralyzed by this accident, Dr. Gordon was nevertheless too much of a man to remain long inactive. Springing to his feet, and issuing a few rapid orders to his servants, which sent them running in different directions, he turned to the soldier, who had been a silent though not unmoved spectator of the scene, and said to him:

"Sergeant, you have seen what has happened. Hurry back to Fort Brooke. Tell your commandant of my misfortune, and ask him from me to send without delay a boat and boat's crew to go in search of my children. I know he will do what he can, for he is not only a man of humanity, but he is my relative and friend. Lay your horse to the ground, good soldier; I will be responsible for damages."

"Had you not better give me a line in writing?" suggested the soldier.

Dr. Gordon drew from his pocket a book, and pencilled the following words upon a blank leaf, which he tore out, folded, and gave to the soldier. The language was informal, but to the point:

that the uncouth monster known as Devil-Fish has a real existence, can be attested by the author himself, who has seen it with his own eyes; and that it is in the habit of playing just such wild pranks as those alluded to in the story, is too well known to be doubted by any who frequent the waters where they abound.

"BELLEVUE, TAMPA, FLORIDA.

"For mercy's sake, send me a boat with hands, to be absent for several days. The bearer of this will tell you the dreadful reason, and will give you all necessary information.

"Yours,   CHARLES GORDON, M. D.
"To MAJOR BURKE, Commandant at Fort Brooke.
"*By Sergeant Tomkins.*"

The soldier, with a respectful touch of his cap, received the paper, mounted his horse, and dashed away at full speed along the hard, smooth beach, in the direction of Fort Brooke, which was distantly visible at the head of the Bay.

Dr. Gordon then turned to his negroes, who by this time had come to report progress in obedience to his orders. The only boat at his command, besides the one to be expected from Fort Brooke, was a canoe lying at the landing, badly damaged by an accident. This he determined to refit in all haste, and to dispatch in pursuit of his children. Stimulating and systematizing the labors of his people, who were as willing as they were unskilled, he had the pleasure, in less than two hours, of pronouncing the boat seaworthy. Then calling his body-servant, William, a black quadroon reared in the family, also his black-skinned carpenter, Sam, who, though many years older than the other, was far less intelligent, he gave them his instructions.

"William," said he, "I put you in charge of this boat; and, Sam, do you also listen well to what I say. Make for the island at the mouth of the bay, which you can see from this place, marked by a clump of tall palmettos. Beyond that clump you will find the house of Riley, the Indian, whom you know. Go first to him. Tell him what has happened, and say to him from me that if he will find and bring back my children, he may ask for anything in my power to give. If he needs either of you to help him, do you, Sam, go; and do you, William, return, to go, if necessary, with me. Should Riley not be at home, you may leave word with his wife, while you yourselves push on as far as you judge best, to learn what has become of the children. Another thing: if you hear anything about them from Riley or his wife, make a big smoke upon the beach. I will watch for it. And if you learn anything good, make two smokes — one on each side of the palmetto grove. And now, my good fellows, good-bye, and God bless you!"

He extended to each of them a hand, which they most reverently took, saying, —

"Mossa, ef de Lord help us, we 'll bring dem chillun back."

Tears flowed on both sides, and for a moment or two no one could say a word. But Dr. Gordon,

2 *   B

with a strong effort, commanded his voice and said, —

"Boys, I have no doubt that you and Riley will, of your own hearts, do for me all that you can. But remember now, as you go off, that I make to you the same promise I make to Riley. Bring back my children, and you may ask me for whatever you will."

With these words, Sam looked into his master's face, and, with great earnestness, replied, —

"Mossa, we don't want nutten, but to bring dem chillun back. We got ebery ting else a'ready."

Dr. Gordon kindly shook them off, and saw them to the boat, in which they were soon skimming over the water, where, in a very short time, they became reduced to a speck in the distance. He then returned to his now desolate home, pondering upon the change which one short hour had wrought, and whispering to himself, —

"It is as true of our happiness as it is of our persons, that 'In the midst of life we are in death.'"

CHAPTER II.

PREPARATIONS AND DELAYS.

HEN Dr. Gordon returned from the bluff to the house, his first effort was to devise for himself some employment of mind as engrossing as possible. It was no part of his faith or practice to mope or mourn needlessly over misfortune. He believed that he could best serve his God, his loved ones, and himself, by cultivating at all times and in all things a cheerful spirit. True, he could not always *be* cheerful, sometimes by reason of sickness, and sometimes (as now) by the pressure of misfortune; but he could always *try* to be so, and in the effort he would be apt to find a refuge from disturbing thought.

Alas for him, however, on the present occasion his preparations for leaving home with his bright-faced children on their proposed maroon of a week, had been so complete that it was not easy to devise anything more that was suitable to his circum-

19

stances. All that he could do was this: he called
before him his two remaining servants, Judy and
Peter. Judy was his cook. Her skin was almost
as black as the tea-kettle and the pots that she so
skilfully used, and her face was as homely as Afri-
can faces ordinarily are; but she was as faithful and
loving as she was black, and no one could hear her
soft musical voice, or see her face, all radiant, as it
usually was, with native kindliness, without feeling
drawn towards her. Peter, her husband, was some
years her junior, and was also a good and faithful
servant, but he was decidedly stupid. At their
home in Georgia he had been only a " field hand,"
and he had accompanied the party to Tampa as a
servant of all work, only because his master was
unwilling to separate husband and wife.

" Judy," said Dr. Gordon, " you know that I
expect a boat from the Fort this afternoon, to go
with me in search of the children. We may return
to-morrow, or may be absent for a week or more.
No doubt the men aboard will bring their rations
with them ; but we must not depend on that.
They are going on my business, and it is but right
that they should go at my expense. I wish, therefore, that you would provide for them out of my
stores, as well as you can, and especially that you
would try to have something that you think
soldiers would like to eat. Remember that all the
provisions intended for my own use during the

marooning party have gone off with the boat.
Call upon Peter for any help that you may need
in this service."

Peter, in the meantime, stood listening, until
his master beckoned to him, saying, " Until Judy
needs your help, come with me, and let me show
you what work may be done between this and
my return, should I be gone more than a day or
two."

He then marked on the ground the line of a
light picket fence which he knew Peter understood
how to make, and also gave him instructions about
other matters in connection. During these occu-
pations, however, he could not resist going every
few minutes to the bluff to see whether there was
any sign of the returning company, or of the boat
expected from Fort Brooke.

Anxiously, too, did he look for the promised
signal by smoke from Riley's Island. So long as
the boat containing William and Sam was in sight,
it seemed to him to move very slowly over the
water. Then as the hour of half-past eleven drew
near, at which he calculated the boat should reach
the Island, it seemed that the sun as well as the
hands of his watch had become tardy. Time and
again he had looked for the expected signal, when
at the hour of noon, just as he was beginning to
lose hope, he saw a little blue haze curling from
the right-hand side of the palmettos on Riley's
Island, and soon resolving itself into a smoke.

The sight made his heart beat, for its meaning was "There is news of the children." The next moment, however, his fears gained the mastery, for he said to himself, "There is but *one* smoke. That is the sign of bad news; at least of none that is good." But as he looked on and indulged these troubled thoughts, his attention was caught by another curl of blue that arose from the south side of the palmettos, and he joyfully clasped his hands, exclaiming, "That is the sign of good! Perhaps my children are recovered. Perhaps they are on that Island. Perhaps they are even now returning home."

He kept a close and almost incessant watch, both by the eye and by the help of a pocket spy-glass — the larger glass having been put aboard the ill-fated boat; but no object appeared from sea-wards until late in the evening, when he saw at the mouth of the bay a dark speck that slowly increased in size. In the course of time this speck was developed into a canoe, manned by a solitary boatman, who wielded his paddle as if weary with long exertion. Long before he reached shore, Dr. Gordon knew by the glass that the boatman was William, his body-servant, returning alone from Riley's Island. It was, therefore, highly probable, nay, almost certain, that the children had not escaped, and that Sam had remained to accompany Riley on a cruise in pursuit of them. This con-

jecture proved true. William reached home at
dark, and reported that the canoe had arrived at
the Island in due time, and that he had learned
from Pancheta, Riley's wife, that a boat answering
the description of Dr. Gordon's had passed the
Island about an hour and a half after sunrise—
that Riley had recognized it, conjectured the state
of the case, gone off instantly in pursuit, and had
not returned; that they then gave her Dr. Gordon's message to Riley, and set off in pursuit of
him, first instructing her to make two smokes, as
agreed upon; that in the course of an hour they
met Riley returning with the news that he had
tried in vain to overtake the boat or even to keep
in sight of it; that when they gave him the message about going in pursuit, he assented, saying,
however, that he must return home for a larger
boat and for provisions, and that he would leave
with Sam the next morning at daylight, and follow down the coast as far as necessary. He also
said that Riley spoke of the boat as moving with
great stiffness and steadiness upon the water, and
that when last seen she was about four miles from
land, moving as fast as ever.

This account greatly cheered, at the same time
that it troubled, the mind of the anguished father,
because it proved that, although all was well with
the abducted party when last heard from, there
was no prospect of their release from the deadly
grasp of the devil-fish.

Later still in the evening there was the measured sound of oars from the northeast, and at last came the expected barge from Fort Brooke. It was manned by six able-bodied oarsmen, and was commanded by no less a person than Major Burke himself, who being a kinsman of Doctor, or rather of Mrs., Gordon, felt a special interest in the family misfortune, and stretched his prerogative of office so far as to leave the command of the Fort to the officer next in rank, while he accompanied his cousin in the proposed cruise along the coast. The men were furnished with rations for ten days, and they had on board a good supply of arms and ammunition in case of hostility from the lawless denizens of that wild and unfrequented shore. The delay in coming was occasioned by the absence of the Major until late in the day, on business of the garrison.

Besides the Major and his men there was on board a warm friend of Dr. Gordon's children in the person of a half-breed Indian boy, who was known by some as Willie or William Morgan, but who preferred to be known by his Indian name of Wildcat. His father was an unfortunate white man, who having offended hopelessly against the laws of his country, had fled from justice and sought refuge among the Seminoles, where he married the beautiful daughter of a Tustenuggee, or sub-chief, by whom he had several children. The boy had formed a strong attachment to Major Burke; and, his father and the chief being both dead, he had asked and received from his mother permission to come and serve his military friend in any capacity in which he might learn more of the science of war, and fit himself for being a "sense-carrier," or interpreter, between his people and the government. After having served for about six months in the capacity of a page or honorable body-servant, he formed the acquaintance of Dr. Gordon's young people. This occurred about a month before the accident spoken of in the preceding chapter, and during a visit made by them to the Fort.

His admiration had been excited to a very high degree by the "book-learning" of Robert Gordon, and by the wild-woods knowledge (or, as our forefathers called it, the wood-craft) of Harold McIntosh, the son of Dr. Gordon's widowed sister. The two cousins and Wildcat were nearly of the same age, a little more or less than fourteen; and they had been so well educated in their respective spheres — although in many respects these spheres were as diverse as if they had lived on different continents — that they were well prepared to enjoy and to be benefited by each other's company. He had often enchained their attention by recounting, in his simple broken English, the arts and expedients of Indian life and the wild lore of his peo-

3

ple; while they had as deeply interested him by lessons given in the white man's arts and white man's learning. No one at the Fort felt a more lively interest than he in the fate of his young frier ls, and he could not be satisfied until he had obtained from his patron and employer a promise that he should be one of the exploring party, to be sent out for the recovery of the unwilling fugitives.

The barge and its company reached Bellevue, Dr. Gordon's place, about nine o'clock, in the brilliant light of a moon, half at the full, which shed its sweet radiance far and wide over the gleaming surface of the bay and upon the dark-green foliage of the bluff. The night was so inviting that the question arose whether the expedition should not be commenced at once; but as nothing could be gained and much might be lost by passing Riley's Island in the night, it was concluded to remain safely moored at Bellevue until such time in the morning as would allow them to reach the Island about sunrise.

The company embarked an hour before day, just as the morning star, rising amid the darkness left by the departed moon, began

"To flame upon the forehead of the dawn."

A light breeze from the east filled their expanded sails, and they went skimming over the water at so rapid a rate as to reach the Island at the very moment when a long and narrow pathway of golden light, streaming from the farthest extremity of the bay eastward to a few oars' length of the barge announced that the sun was peeping over the water.

The two gentlemen in charge of the expedition went immediately to Riley's house, accompanied by Wildcat, to know if any further tidings had been received. They learned from Pancheta, whom they found to be a young and pretty squaw, that Riley and Sam had left about two hours before, in a large canoe, with provisions for ten days. She said that Riley did not think it would be safe for him to go very far down the coast, because his friendliness to the whites had made him many enemies there. But that he knew that Dr. Gordon, besides being a great "Medicine-man," was his good friend ; and that he would do for him and for his young folks all he could.

While they were listening to this account, a messenger from the barge came to announce that a vessel, apparently a Revenue Cutter, had appeared beyond a small island at the south, beating up against a head-wind.

CHAPTER III.

NEWS BY THE CUTTER.

N O doubt, the cutter Jackson," said the Major, as with rapid steps he and Dr. Gordon made their way to the beach. "She is expected with Government dispatches and supplies for our garrison. And, since she is direct from both Charleston and Savannah, it is possible, Doctor, that she may have letters for you as well as for me."

"I shall greatly prize my mail," responded Dr. Gordon; "yet I have an interest in the cutter at this moment paramount to any reasons connected with news from home. She has probably passed over the track pursued by my fugitives; and if she has not been fortunate enough to have given them a passage back, I cannot but hope that she is able to tell us something about them."

"Why did I not think of this myself?" rejoined the other, in a tone of self-reproach.

By the time they reached the low bluff, the approaching vessel had passed so far to seaward on her larboard tack as to present to their sight her full broadside, with black hull, raking masts, and well-defined port-holes. Every one recognized her as a cutter, the cutter Jackson.

"All aboard! Shove off!" were orders issued in rapid succession. Officers and men were in their seats, except the two belonging forward. They were standing in the water until the bow of the boat had been lifted from its bed in the sand, and was clearly afloat, when they leaped lightly in and also took their places; and then the short and sharp "Give way, men," brought the oars to work with such vigor and concord as to make all feel the successive impulses with which they shot along the water, until they had rounded a projecting shoal, when the sail was again raised, the oars were unshipped, and they glided noiselessly and swiftly on their way.

Less than an hour's time brought the two parties together. The topsails of the cutter had been backed by a signal from the barge, bringing her to, and a ladder of rope had been thrown over the vessel's side, by which Dr. Gordon and the Major ascended to the deck, and received a cordial greeting from Capt. Randolph and his courteous lieutenants in command.

The question was not asked whether the wanderers were aboard; they were not to be seen, nor

8*

was the boat aboard or in tow. The captain and his lieutenants, however, who became instantly interested in the case, gave an account of what they had seen.

"About two o'clock, yesterday," said the captain, while we lay becalmed about fifty miles south of this, the watchman sang out, 'Signal ahead!' and soon afterwards added, in a tone of wonder, 'Sail-boat running without wind or oars!'

"We all gathered to the starboard to see this strange sight, when, sure enough, our glasses showed us, about three miles ahead, between us and shore, a masted boat heading south and in rapid motion. There were four persons aboard, one of whom was a female and another a little boy. Something white had been run up to the mast-head to attract our attention, and we could see the smoke of several guns, though the distance was too great for the sound to reach us. Lieut. Somers said he saw the little boy holding out his hands, as if begging us to help them.

"I instantly ordered a boat to be lowered and manned with six strong oarsmen, to intercept and help them as they passed, and at the same time nad a signal run up and two cannons fired, to show them that they had been seen.

"We were for a while at a loss to account for the mysterious motion of the boat, until an old salt belonging to these waters explained it by sayι ς ἀλαί the anchor had probably been tripped by a devil-fish, which had dragged the boat to sea. Now, we are all familiar with this trick of that stupid fish, and we know that it abounds in these waters, and that it is strong enough, too, in many instances, to run off with a boat of that size, (for I myself harpooned one of a school in St. Joseph's Bay that measured twenty feet across the wings,) but we doubted whether they were ever seen so late in the season. Moreover, we could not but wonde, why, if this surmise of the sailor were correct, the people aboard had not freed themselves by cutting the cable."

"The cable was a chain," Dr. Gordon explained, "strongly linked and firmly stapled to resist robbery. The young folks had no tools aboard that could cut or break it. But pray go on with your account."

"From the time we first saw the signal until the time the yawl started in pursuit, could not have been more than ten minutes; yet it was manifest by the change of place that the boat was moving through the water at such a rate that our only chance of intercepting her was by keeping well ahead and nearer shore. Unfortunately, however, for the help intended, there came down a shower of rain, attended with thunder and lightning—"

At this moment the captain observed an expression of great anxiety overspread the face of his listener, who at the same time noticed a significant glance exchanged by the lieutenants, and he hastily added,—

"There was no wind though; at least none that a boat so steady as that would feel; only the little *outrider* that you may always see, on land and water, preceding a shower, and which seems to be a blast caused by the fall of rain. I am pretty sure that, although the rain was quite heavy all around the cutter, it did not extend half-way to the boat. What do you say, Lieut. Somers?" he asked, addressing the pleasant-looking young man at his side.

"I am as sure as I can be of anything two miles away," he replied, "that not a drop of rain reached the boat; and as for wind, there was barely enough to shake our sails for ten or fifteen minutes."

With these assurances Dr. Gordon seemed relieved, and the captain continued:

"By the time the rain cleared away, the boat had passed beyond reach, and, indeed, beyond sight, for there was a slight mist or fog sufficient to conceal everything at the distance of a mile. We, however, did not give up the boat and its crew for a long time after it disappeared, but every once in a while we fired a gun to show where we were, and to let them know that we were ready to do what we could for their relief.

The last that any of us saw of them was about four o'clock in the afternoon, or later. The mist which still hung over the sea near us had cleared away in the south, and the man in the foretop said he saw, far away down the coast, something that looked like the spread of a small sail glancing in the light of the almost setting sun

"Sorry I am, Doctor," the captain said, in conclusion, "that I can give no better account of our attempt to succor your young folks. I feel almost certain, however, from what was reported by our look-out in the foretop, that they succeeded at last in getting loose from the devil-fish, and that long before night they had safely landed (for they were not more than five or six miles from shore), and that by this time they have again spread their sail on their return home."

"God grant it may be as you say," Dr. Gordon ejaculated. "And most sincerely do I thank you, captain, and others of your vessel, for these humane efforts, although they did not accomplish all that you wished."

"I have another fact to relate, which may have some bearing on the case," resumed the captain. "This morning, soon after daylight, a canoe passed us about two miles to the eastward, just inside a reef or shoal that extends from this island to the key below. It was going south, and seemed to contain a light-colored Indian and a negro."

"These were Riley, the owner of this island, and one of my servants, going in search of my children," Dr. Gordon responded.

By this time the purser came forward with letters and despatches for the two gentlemen, and for some of the boat's crew whose names had been mentioned. After opening and glancing at a few of the despatches, Major Burke turned gravely to the Doctor and said,—

"I am sorry to inform you, my friend, that the orders just received require my immediate return to Fort Brooke. This, however, need not interfere with your expedition, for you are welcome to the barge and to the use of the men so long as they are necessary for your purpose. I am only sorry that I am denied the pleasure of accompanying you in person."

Dr. Gordon expressed the greatest obligation for these kind intentions, and a regret for the loss of his friend's company; still he said he h⌐ⅰ no doubt that in so plain a work as simply exploring the coast, he and the crew were perfectly competent to all that was necessary.

While this sequel in the conversation was going on, Wildcat, who had occupied a respectful distance within hearing, began to show signs of great uneasiness, especially for one trained as he had been to the sobriety and stoicism of the Indian; ne shifted hastily his position, and looked with searching glance deep into the eyes first of his employer, then of Dr. Gordon. Finally, he watched the opportunity of a moment's silence, when he glided modestly up to the Major and whispered a word in his ear, who replied, —

"Certainly, Wildcat, I shall be glad to do so, both for your own sake and for that of the others. You are one of the last I should think of stopping."

The boy's face flashed with delight. He murmured gratefully one single word of his tribe, "Enk-lis-chay!" * then quietly resumed his place. Not perfectly understanding the language used, he had been uncertain whether his going depended upon the contingency of the Major's going too, and had come to inquire.

Resuming now his conversation with the Doctor, and talking in an undertone, the Major said:

"You will find that boy a perfect treasure. Not only is he true as steel in his courage and fidelity, but he is quick in his perceptions of an exigency and in his device for meeting it. I can commend him to your confidence as well as to your care. The crew are picked men and have a character to sustain. I doubt not they will prove themselves orderly and obedient. Sergeant Tomkins, whom I appoint in command, under your direction, is skilled in the language and habits of the Seminoles, generally — they being composed,

* Good.

as you know, of refugees from several different
nations. He lived among them so long that he is
almost half Indian in his own ways. Corporal
Wheeler, the man next him in position and capa-
bility, has seen a good deal of wild life in Mexico
and the Rocky Mountains. Should you be so
unfortunate as to have any collision with the Indians, these men will be invaluable. Of the rest
I know little, except that they are well-behaved
soldiers, and that they have been selected by Tomkins with express reference to their fitness for this
work. Yes, Simpson, that swarthy-faced man
with black hair and with a down look, that I confess I do not like, lived for some years among the
Eufaulas of Alabama, and not only speaks the
Muscogee language, but can also understand and
make himself known in the grunts of the Uchees,
of whom there are quite a number scattered along
this coast.

"And now a word in your ear about the Indians
you will probably meet, if you meet any at all.
Some are friendly, but the greater part are restless,
dissatisfied, and ready at any time to break out
into hostility. My advice to you is that you have
as little as possible to do with them ; but if forced
to communicate, let your dealings, and those of the
men, be at the same time bold and conciliatory ;
for there are no people who more admire manhood,
and it is to be supposed that they are not insensible to kindness."

Then lowering his voice to a whisper, he added, "I trust, however, that these seemingly imminent hostilities may be averted ; for the despatches just now received inform me that a ' big talk' with the chiefs is proposed to be held at Payne's Landing, to the northeast of Tampa, for which I am ordered to make immediate preparations."

At this point, Captain Randolph approached, saying, "I have a proposition to make. It is this : that, unless your instructions, Major, require my presence, I will leave Tampa day after to-morrow and sail close along shore, keeping a look-out for the young folks, or standing ready to take the Doctor as far as Key West or the Tortugas, if he so desire ; at either of which places he can engage wreckers to scour the coast with or for him from Cape Sable to Tampa Bay."

Major Burke replied, that he had seen nothing in his instructions, so far as they had been examined, to interfere with such an arrangement, and that he would esteem any assistance of the kind rendered to Dr. Gordon, in his efforts for the recovery of his children, as a favor done to himself.

Dr. Gordon thanked both these gentlemen for their evidences of good will, and said that, although he was unable to form an opinion as to the desirableness of such a measure, he would esteem it a kindness if Capt. Randolph would sail as close in shore as convenient and keep a look-out for any

signals that might be given, either by flag or
smoke.

And so they parted — Dr. Gordon, with Wildcat in company, going aboard the barge, while
Major B. remained on the cutter for the purpose
of returning to Fort Brooke.

CHAPTER IV.

THE CRUISE BEGUN.

URING the conference recorded in the
preceding chapter the cutter had re-
mained with backed topsails, or else had
sailed in short curves around the spot
where she was first boarded. It was near mid-
day before the barge pushed off and spread her
sails to the now freshening breeze. She had
scarcely got into motion before the boatswain of
the cutter was heard piping all hands to starboard, where fifty caps soon waved over the gunwale and fifty voices cheered the departing voyagers, while a flag was run up the mast in token
of honor and good will. Dr. Gordon bowed his
acknowledgments with uncovered head, while his
men waved their caps, and Wheeler, who was sailing-master, ran up to the masthead, in reply, the
only piece of bunting at his command.

This day was Wednesday, and although the hour was too early for regular dinner, the captain of the cutter, with great hospitality, had ordered, through the steward, a plentiful lunch for all his visitors, both in the cabin and at the vessel's side, so that the departing crew was saved from all delay and inconvenience on account of rations before night. For several hours the cutter and the barge continued in sight of each other—the one making due east for the bay, at the north end of which lies Fort Brooke, and the other seeking a passage around the north end of Riley's Island, in order to pass between it and the main, and thus to keep down the coast in the smooth water that prevails inside the long chain of reefs, shoals, keys and islands that skirt the western coast of peninsular Florida.

In passing the sheet of water known as Manatee Bay, the exploring party delayed only long enough to look in and certify themselves that the missing boat was not there. They then continued evenly between the shore and the reef so as to keep a safe lookout on both sides. All that afternoon the land showed little more than a low, sandy bluff, surmounted every now and then with a heavy breastwork of sand blown up by the wind and ornamented at intervals with clumps of tropical-looking palmettos, or with groves of wide-spreading liveoaks, while patches of large-leaved cactus, high as a man's waist, and crimsoned with beautiful pears the size of a pullet's egg, occasionally adorned the spaces between.

Perhaps no opportunity more convenient than the present can be found for gratifying the desire of those who may wish to know more of the peculiarities of the western coast of Florida, to which our story confines us, and of which we seldom see any accounts.

The Bay, known as Tampa, extends from Egmont Key to the town of Tampa, about forty miles distant, and varies in width from eight to twelve miles. Extending east for fifteen or twenty miles, it bends suddenly northward and divides into two tongues, the western of which, a shallow lagoon, is called Old Tampa, and the eastern Hillsborough. The part which is common to both these tongues is called Spiritu Santo, or Holy Ghost bay, being the name given to it by De Soto when he landed here on his famous expedition in 1538.

Of all the beautiful inlets and harbors on the Gulf coast, this is the easiest of access, and the best protected from storms. Its mouth is land-locked by the small low island, or key, called Egmont, on which is a light-house, and between which and Mullet Key, (another low island to the west,) is a pass or channel having a depth of twenty-three feet at low water, while to the southeast is another pass not quite so wide or so deep.

From Tampa, as far south as Punta Rassa, at
the mouth of the Caloosahatchie river, the coast is
double, having a chain of keys and shoals extending, with scarcely an interruption, the whole distance. These keys are composed of sand and
broken shells, some almost wholly of one, some
of the other, and some of a mixture of both, and
are covered with mangroves, cabbage palmettos,
live-oaks, and various other trees and shrubs; and
are inhabited by wild turkeys, deer, raccoons,
bears, and other denizens of the forest, and, in
some instances, by wild hogs and cattle that have
strayed there from the main.

The palmetto is a tall, beautiful tree of the class
known by botanists as *endogens*, because its growth
is by additions inside the trunk, and not, as in
ordinary trees, by successive layers of wood on
the outside. It has neither limbs nor bark, but
grows by means of a single terminal bud at the
top, which is always tender and edible, and being
in flavor not unlike cabbage, has caused the tree
to be called by some the cabbage-tree, or cabbage
palmetto. The fruit is a small berry growing in
clusters. The leaves, of which there are sometimes as many as fifty, are all at the summit and
constitute each an immense fan, from three to six
feet in diameter, expanding from a flat stem a
yard long and two or three inches wide. The
trees grow singly or in immense groves, according

to circumstances. The wood is worthless as timber, being only a dense pith, hardened on the
outside by exposure to the weather, and strength-
ened within with long, tough threads, which run
longitudinally with the trunk, and often project,
like sharp needles, through the surface.

The mangrove is a growth of the salt marshes
and quicksands, requiring frequent overflow from
the tides. It is a shrub, with a woody stem that
is close-grained, hard and knotty, and when dry
makes a quick, hot fire. The leaf resembles somewhat that of the lemon in shape and size, being
thick and of a dark green color, so that a mangrove marsh at a little distance is a lovely sight.
Its growth is peculiar : it has quite as many roots
branching from the trunk towards the ground below as it has limbs branching towards the air and
sun above. These limbs begin near the ground
and extend laterally a great distance, sending out
roots, like the banyan tree, to form new trunks,
and to support the weight of the foliage above.
These branches and roots interlace so densely that
a mangrove swamp is almost impenetrable.

When the declining sun approached the tree-
tops of a pretty key to the west, the bow of the
barge was turned towards a creek or cove that set
deeply inland, bounded by a luxuriant mangrove
marsh upon one side, and by a sandy bluff densely
wooded with cedars and stunted pines upon the

other. Here they prepared to spend their first
night. Two tents were pitched—one for Dr.
Gordon, Tomkins, and Wildcat, the other for
Wheeler and the four men. A few armfuls of
dead wood soon produced a crackling fire, and
caused the merry kettles to sing the welcome song
of supper; and the odor of some delicious tea
which Dr. Gordon had given as a treat to the men,
in addition to their ordinary rations, appeared to
exert a refreshing influence, even before it was
tasted.

And now, as they gather round their ruddy fire
to enjoy their evening meal, the group is so pic-
turesque that we are tempted to pause a moment
and look at it.

Seated on a camp-stool, and marked as the only
one of the company habited in citizen's attire, is
Dr. Gordon, a man of ordinary height and middle
age, with a countenance of thoughtful, habitual
cheerfulness, but pale now from distress, and wearing at times an expression of anxiety. He occu-
pies a place near the door of his tent, listening to
the lively jests of the men, and occasionally throwing in a kindly word to make them feel more at
their ease. Near him, on a log rolled there for
the purpose, is the stalwart form of Sergeant Tomkins. No one who looks into his calm gray eyes
will doubt that he is a man of courage, and the
quick, merry twinkle of that same eye proves that

he is good-natured, too, and can enjoy a joke as well as any of them. But Sergeant Tomkins is withal a martinet in his ideas of order, and can never for a moment forget that the military command of the company devolves on him, and that a certain degree of persistent dignity is necessary to discipline. Standing respectfully beside and somewhat in the rear of Dr. Gordon is Wildcat, whose intelligent face is lighted up with pleasure at a remark just addressed to him by his patron. His dress is neither that of the soldier nor of the citizen, but of the Indian. The materials are of dressed deerskin, buff-colored and profusely ornamented. A hunting-shirt, with a broad cape over the shoulders, and with a deerskin fringe on all its edges, covers his body and reaches half-way down his thigh. Leggings of the same, and fringed in like manner, cover his legs from hip to ankle, while moccasins, heavy with small, bright-colored beads, enclose his feet, and a flap or apron, still more adorned than the moccasins, and having pockets, protects the stomach. His head is enveloped in a handkerchief worn as a turban. This dress was prepared by the skilful fingers of his mother, and Wildcat would feel denationalized if he doffed it for any other costume. At the moment we look upon him, he is starting from his position by Dr. Gordon to the men beside the fire, where he is to take his share of supper.

Wheeler and his men are seated on the clean sand, each with his tin plate and tin cup in hand, preparing to enjoy the contents. He is a man of well-knit frame, and in his aspect it is hard to determine which predominates, the soldier, the sailor, or the hunter. Of the other men, the swarthy visage, heavy figure and down look of Simpson are in striking contrast with the open, laughing face, light complexion and agile figure of a pleasant-looking man beside him of the name of Jones. Thompson, (Swan Thompson he calls himself,) an Irishman but recently imported from the Green Isle, acts as temporary cook in place of Magruder, a raw-boned, sandy-whiskered Scotchman, who treads the margin of the bluff as sentry over both camp and boat.

On the edge of the bluff, within a few paces of the fire, glisten the bright muskets of the men, stacked according to military rule, while the barge, within full reach of the firelight, tilts heavily upon the sand, where she lies aground ; and the shelly beach stretches like a broad white belt between the sleeping waters of the cove, on the one side, and the dark forest of pines and cedars on the other, illumined from below by the rich red of the resinous fire, and from above by the silvery light of a moon, nearly overhead, and more than half at the full.

CHAPTER V.

THE FIRST NIGHT ASHORE.

MERRY crowd they were, and many a harmless prank was played off under the grave yet complacent eyes of those sitting at the door of what some of the men called the *marquee*, for soldiers released from duty are like boys let out of school.

Dr. Gordon, who made it a rule to cultivate cheerfulness under all circumstances, and whose habit it was to watch the different devices by which the various acts of life are accomplished, interested himself in observing the men while they enjoyed their tea.

"I say, Pah-thrick," said Jones, addressing Thompson, and trying to imitate the brogue of a south of Ireland man, "how do people in ould Ireland manage to dhrink their tay out of tin cups when it is scalding hot, and there is no saucer to cool it in?"

"We drink it so," replied Thompson, suiting the action to the word, and pointing to his cup,

which had been placed on the ground to cool.
"And, moreover," he retorted in a fair English
tone, which he could assume at will, being a mid-
country man and having less than usual of the
national accent, "my name is not Patrick any
more than yours is Sambo. My mother called me
Swan because I was so white and pretty, and I
have been called so ever since."

"That must have been when you were a baby,"
returned Jones, "for you are a very different-
looking swan now."

"Do you want to know why?" Thompson
inquired. "When I was only a little boy, my
mother married a man by the name of Jones, and
after that I stopped taking after my own father,
and got to looking like the Joneses. That is the
reason I am no better-looking.

This preposterous statement — more decidedly
American than Irish — completely turned the laugh
against Jones, who, nevertheless, persisted in his
original purpose, for he and Thompson were excellent friends, and they enjoyed themselves much
in their rough jests upon each other.

"But," said he, "if there are such things in
Ireland as hot tea and tin cups, I should be glad
to know how they manage them together, that I
may judge whether our American plan is not
better."

" We have plenty of tea in Ireland," Thompson replied, "and plenty of tin cups too, but we are too wise to use them together hot. We wait till they are cool."

"That would be too slow for us fast Americans," said Jones.

"I'll tell you how we manage out thar in Georgy, whar I come from," chimed in Simpson, who perceived from the signs that there was some fun in prospect, "we pour in plenty of cold milk."

"Don't you?" said Thompson, smacking his lips at the thought; "and would n't we do the same if we had it?"

"But as you have n't it, what would you do to save time?" said Jones, persisting in his persecution; but Thompson seemed to be tired of the joke and ceased to answer; Jones, therefore, addressed the question to Wheeler, who replied:

"I would do as I am doing now; break into it my bread, and then eat with a spoon; by the time my biscuit is soaked and eaten, my tea is cool enough to drink."

"And now, friend Sambo," said Thompson, "after having asked so many times, it is only fair that we should hear what you would do."

This question was exactly what Jones had been all along trying to draw out from Thompson, for, knowing well his habits, and seeing that he was preparing as usual to toast his bread at the fire, he had used the intervals when the other's back was turned, to play upon him a practical joke. He had slyly emptied Thompson's canteen of water on the ground, then poured the tea into the canteen, and finally placed the empty tin cup on the wet earth to appear as if the *tea* had been lost.

"What would I do?" he replied; "why I would pour my tea into my empty canteen, and then pour it, little by little, into my cup; just so."

Jones was about to give an illustration of his mode of procedure, but was brought to a sudden stop. His own cup was missing. Wildcat, who was passing, with noiseless tread, to the rear of the group at the moment when Jones' attention was engrossed, and whose quick eye discerned the trick about to be perpetrated, resolved to add to the amusement of the company by a little prank of his own. He carried off Jones' cup, and, with a sly wink, put it into the hands of Magruder, the sentinel; after which he came to the tea-pot and soberly poured out his own tea, just as Jones, discovering his misfortune, called out, "Where's my cup?"

"That ere's hit, ain't hit?" said Simpson, laughing and pointing to Thompson's forlorn-looking cup.

"Blessed Saint Patrick!" exclaimed Thompson, looking ruefully at the wet ground and the capsized cup; "that's mine! me own darling tea! and lost it is forever!"

D

"Lost? no!" rejoined Wheeler; "I heard you say yesterday that a thing is never lost when you know where it is. But poor Jones' tea *is* lost, for it is gone where I dare say he will never find it again."

Jones' face by this time had stretched to such length that Thompson burst into a laugh, saying:

"Come, Jones, let's be content with water in place of tea. People say that misery loves company, and sure we both have reasons to be thankful for having each a neighbor as bad off as ourself."

With this remark he put his hand upon his canteen, and, perceiving from its changed temperature the harmless nature of the joke played upon him, he said, merrily,—

"Feel in your canteen, Sambo; I suspect somebody has been cooling the tea for you too."

Jones felt there, but in vain, then said resignedly to his companions,—

"Well, fellows, I have got only what I deserved, for not *watching* while in such company as this is. So I'll drink my water, and say nothing more about the tea."

While thus making the best of his misfortune, (for Jones was a dear lover of the beverage, and that lost cup had emitted a most delicious odor,) Wildcat came gravely forward, and presenting his own smoking cup said, in a tone of mock compassion, but with his Indian order of words,—

"Here! half of mine take! Your cup, hand it to me."

"Be off, you bundle of mischief!" stormed Jones, while his face relaxed into a manifest smile, for he and Wildcat also were excellent friends, and he was convinced by the other's officious pity that the tea, although for the present missing, would soon be forthcoming. "Be off, and bring back my cup. You know where it is; I see it in your eye."

"Cup too much big to be in my eye," Wildcat replied, at the same time pulling down his lower eyelids with his fingers. "Tea not in here; tea too much hot."

"Nobody said that the tea was in your eye, though I will put some sand there if you do not bring back my cup," Jones threatened, grasping, as he spoke, a handful of sand. Wildcat pretended to be dreadfully alarmed, and fled to Thompson for protection; then whispering in his ear, "Fight him for me," he slipped around to Magruder, obtained the missing cup, glided noiselessly to the rear of Jones, who was warding off some witticism of Thompson's, and put down the cup near Jones' heels, saying, —

"Ees-ta had-kin * must take care! Tea will burn his foot!"

Gladly did Jones turn at this hint, to find his

* White man.

tea lying close within reach; and finding also that
it was now cooled down to the exact temperature
he liked best, he sipped it with great complacency;
then looking at Wildcat's smoking cup, he resumed
his old question, and asked, —

"How does the Ees-ta chat-tee * drink his hot
tea from a tin cup?"

"So," replied Wildcat, taking from his pouch
a joint of reed, open at both ends, and with great
comfort sipping the hot tea through it.

"That joint of reed," said Jones, looking with
admiration upon his little friend, "is a perfect
wonder in that boy's hands. I have seen him get
water with it, where without it you could get
none; I have seen him drink through it when the
water was so muddy or so wormy that without it
you could drink none; I have seen him kindle a
fire with it, when without it you could kindle
none; and I have seen him find game with it,
when without it you could find none."

Jones' enthusiasm produced a laugh, but he
continued: "I am telling you the truth. I saw
him use it one day as a turkey-call; he put it
between his lips and made a quick jerking noise
through it that soon brought a gobbler strutting
towards us from the bushes. I saw him use it
again for a blow-pipe; we had only a spark of
fire that we were afraid would go out, but he put

* Red man, or Indian.

the spark between two dead coals, and blew upon
it through his reed until both coals were in a glow.
I saw him use it to obtain water one day on the
beach when we were fishing; our canteens had
given out, and the sand was so spongy that, although there was fresh water in it, we could not
separate it from the sand. He took that same
reed, tied a thickness or two of woollen cloth
around the end, buried that end in the sand, and
then sucked the pure water through it. In the
same way he used it as a filter, when the water
was full of wiggle-tails, or full of mud or moss."

"It is a wonderful reed," said Thompson,
stretching his eyes wide, as if in great admiration, "and some of these days I think I shall get
it and put it to another wonderful use, as the stem
of my pipe."

"Pipe-stem!" said Simpson, "I'm a-wantin'
one na-ow," and he stretched out his hand and
clutched at it, but his motion was not quick
enough for the nimble boy, who suddenly with-
drew himself beyond reach, and with a murmured
"Catch me first," went to sip his tea at another
part of the semi-circle.

They thus amused themselves until nine o'clock,
when Tomkins ordered the men to quarters, soon
after which every man, except the sentinel, was
wrapped in his blanket, and most of them wrapped
also in slumber; though several were to be ob-

served tossing restlessly about, being kept awake
long after a soldier's hours by the combined influences of moonlight and green tea, co-operating
with the effects of the preceding merriment.

CHAPTER VI.

SCOUTING AND FISHING — A PROPOSITION.

ARLY next morning, when the men had
gathered around their fire, in prepara-
tion for breakfast, they were perplexed
at the non-appearance of Jones and
Wildcat. No one could tell how, when, or why
they had so unceremoniously taken their departure. Simpson, who was the last on guard duty,
said that just at daybreak, when his face was
turned toward the sea, he heard the hollow tread
of some one walking, but he saw nobody, and
had no suspicion that any one wished to desert.
Indeed, no one supposed that either of the missing
ones were guilty of *desertion,* for Jones was too
good a soldier to think of it, and for Wildcat
there was no motive. While they were engaged in
discussing the probabilities of the case, they saw the
two emerge from a little recess in the cove, each
bringing a mess of delightful-looking fish, sheephead, whiting, and cavally, strung by their gills on
a stalk of marsh-grass, knotted at one end.

Wildcat came with his to Dr. Gordon, and pre-

sented them with a look and manner of undoubt
ing satisfaction. Jones brought his to Tomkins,
whose brow was somewhat clouded, and said to
him in a free and easy way, betokening a clear
conscience, " I was sorry, Sergeant, to go off with
out asking leave, but you were all asleep, and I
concluded, as we were not on strict duty, and I
was certain of doing what you all would like,
that it was best to take leave first, and ask for it
afterward, and I shall feel much obliged if you
and the Captain here" (looking at Dr. Gordon)
" will grant it to me now."

"So far as I am concerned," said Dr. Gordon,
" you have it from the time you left."

" It was not soldierly," Tomkins rather sternly
replied, " to go off without leave, and I hope none
of the men will do the like again. But as no
harm was done this time, we will let it pass."

The fine mess of fresh-looking fish excited Dr.
Gordon's admiration, and he remarked it was a
great pity they had not been brought a few minutes earlier, as they would have made a pleasant
addition to the breakfast of the men.

" If you will allow me ten minutes' time," said
Jones, " you will not say that they have come too
late."

The Doctor and Tomkins exchanged looks,
and the latter answered —

" We will give you a trial. But you must not

neglect your own breakfast, for we are almost ready to sail."

Jones gave a nod of invitation to the others, who followed him to the fire, where he distributed the fish among them, selecting several of the finest, which he wrapped in the green leaves of the palmetto, and thrust fluttering under the embers. In a very few minutes he took them out, put them on a clean palmetto leaf, stripped off their skin and the scales attached, skilfully separated from the bones the white flesh, which he transferred to a hot plate, and bore smoking and steaming to be enjoyed by Dr. Gordon, who pronounced the cookery capital.

Just before the tent was taken down, preparatory to embarking, Wildcat came to Dr. Gordon, who was alone, and said,—

"Jones and Wildcat been on a *scout*. Tell Tomkins call Jones and hear what he say."

Dr. Gordon hesitated a moment, when Wildcat earnestly reiterated,—

"*Call Tomkins.* Moccasin too near."

Tomkins came, as requested, and summoned Jones, who, as soon as he was freed from the presence of the other men, went on to say, "Sergeant, I had another object besides fishing, in going out this morning. Just at tattoo last night, Wildcat came and whispered in my ear, 'Eestachattay* in the bush.' I asked him why he thought so.

* Red man.

He pulled me along to the edge of yon cedar-thicket, where we heard something moving off very slowly and softly. I told him to say nothing about it to the men, but to join me at daybreak this morning, when we would kill two birds with one stone, by going both a-scouting and a-fishing. As soon as it was light, we went to the spot where the sounds had come from, and saw there the print of two pairs of moccasins in the sand not forty steps from our fire."

"Did you follow the trail?" asked Tomkins hastily.

"I did," Jones replied. "It came from the south, and it ended on the beach, where the persons seem to have gone off in a canoe."

"How do you know they did not go along the beach in the shallow of the tide-water?" inquired Tomkins.

"Because I followed the beach to a muddy creek, and saw no signs of a trail coming out. The persons must either have gone off in a canoe or taken to the water."

Tomkins looked grave. "I will go and see for myself. Jones, you may return to the company; but say nothing to them about this. Doctor, can you spare Wildcat for a little while, to go with me?"

"Certainly," replied the Doctor, "and go myself, too, if you have no objection."

On arriving at the ground and looking about,
Dr. Gordon could not but admire the ease and
precision with which the keen eyes of Tomkins
and Wildcat enabled them, not only to discover
human footprints in the soil, where to his unprac-
tised sight there was scarcely a visible impression,
but also to distinguish the tracks from each other
by their difference in size and shape, and also to
decide how many hours had elapsed since they
were left. As he was in the act of making some
remark upon the subject, an expressive Indian
grunt from Wildcat, (for which we have no suitable spelling unless it be Ugh ! or Umph !) called
their attention, and they saw him bending over
an impression in the sand, which Tomkins instantly recognized as the mark left by the butt
of a rifle.

The barge was by this time ready for sailing ;
and when Dr. Gordon and Tomkins, on their return, came within ear-shot of the conversation
there, they could scarcely avoid laughing to learn
the device of Jones for averting the suspicions
of the men. He had given them a very interesting account of the curious object which the two
superiors had gone out, under Wildcat's guidance,
to examine, namely, the skulls of two large bucks
that had engaged in a fight in which their horns
had become inextricably locked, and they had,
consequently, perished from starvation, or had

been drowned — a fact in natural history that does sometimes occur, but which, on the present occasion, had its existence only in the fertile fancy of the narrator.

The lively conversation with which the voyage of that morning commenced, and which Dr. Gordon and Tomkins not only permitted but encouraged, from policy, began to flag in the course of an hour; and Dr. Gordon, who was ever on the alert for opportunities to make the time of the men pass pleasantly and usefully, proposed that they should relieve the tedium of the voyage, and at the same time increase their mutual acquaintance, by each giving to the company so much of his private history as he felt perfectly willing to do.

"We always feel more interest in those we know than in those we do not know," said he. "Indeed, an intimate knowledge makes us feel sometimes almost akin."

In making this remark he observed an expression of pleasure and at the same time of uneasiness overspread the countenances of most of his auditors, and divining the reason, he continued,—

"In the history of all persons there are portions which they prefer to keep to themselves. But there is much besides of common interest, especially that which contains useful information, showing how to help one's self or to help others in a time of need. No doubt every one present sees much in his own life which interests himself; and he may set down as a good general rule that whatever interests himself will interest others also."

This piece of philosophy brought a smile to the faces of the men. They evidently assented to its truth, and no doubt they reflected that, coming together as they did from such distant parts, and having had such different experiences in life, there would be some rare scenes presented in the accounts to be given.

"I do not, by any means, insist upon it," he continued. "I only propose it. Suppose, now, that as we quietly sail, you all talk over the matter among yourselves, and let me know the result when you are ready."

"I am ready with my say, na-ow," said the sombre-hued and drawling Simpson.

"And what is that?" inquired the Doctor.

"That I never had no eddication," he replied. "And though I am willing to tell of what I have seen and heern, I hain't never seen or heern nothing that I think anybody would care to hear about."

"I think you speak of yourself more disparagingly than you have a right to do," said Dr. Gordon. "Will you allow me to ask a question or two?"

"Yes, sir, to be sure," was the answer.

"Well, where were you born and raised?"

"I was born on Kiokee Creek, in Columby County, Georgy," Simpson answered; "and when I was a boy, I lived at Wolfskin, not far from the Cherokee Corner; but as for raisin', I wasn't raised nowhar; I jest growed up so."

"And who were your parents?" Dr. Gordon inquired.

"My father was a preacher," Simpson responded. "And as for my mother, though she was an oncommon fine-lookin' ooman, nobody never knowed her name, for she was stole from home when she was a baby, and she lived among the Injins tell she was about sixteen ye'r old, when my father found her thar and married her."

"Really, I feel interested in your story, already," said Dr. Gordon. "But allow me to ask a question or two more. You say your father was a preacher; of what denomination was he?"

At this question Simpson stared, not being able to understand what the word "denomination" meant. His questioner enlightened him by asking, "What was his church?" to which Simpson replied,—

"Oh! he was a Baptist—an Old-side—a Primity—(Primitive)—a *Hard Shell*—a *Two-Seed*."

The listeners could scarcely avoid a smile, for although the very large and respectable denomination designated by the general title was, of course, known to all, it was evident that the *load* of titles just given was intended to point out and dignify some very small concern. Tomkins looked for an explanation to Dr. Gordon, who replied in a subdued voice,—

"The Hard Shells, as they are called in burlesque, or the Old Sides, or Primitives, as they call themselves, are that part of the great Baptist family celebrated in Georgia for their opposition to Sunday-schools, missions to the heathen, Theological Seminaries, and religious education generally, for which sake they refuse fellowship with the modernized and more active brethren of the church at large. They occupy a very large part of our piney woods, and other dark corners of the State. The *Two-Seed* Baptists, of whom I believe there are few—at least I have never met more than two or three of them—are the extreme wing of this party, and are remarkable for nothing except for certain bigoted notions, the result of ignorance, concerning the *"two seeds,"* between which they suppose the whole family of mankind to be divided—the good seed and the bad." *

With this explanation, Tomkins looked towards Simpson with a compassion which he should not otherwise have felt, for he perceived that many of

---

* Let it be remembered that the above dark picture dates from the year 1831—backward

the poor fellow's faults must have been, to a great extent, the result of the influences under which his early days had been spent. This was soon made manifest by the question next addressed to him.

"You remarked at the outset that you had no education," said Dr. Gordon. "Do you mean to say by this that you never went to school at all, and that your parents did nothing to instruct you?"

"Well, now, you see," he replied, "the only eddication my mother had for herself was what she got in an Injin's lodge, and as for my father, I believe he only knowed enough to spell out his text in the Bible when he went to preach, and to line out the *hymes* for singing. The only school in my neighborhood, when I was a boy, was kept by an Englishman named Gunter. He teached about half of one winter, and I went to him and larnt finely, he said, as far as b-a-g, bag, c-a-g, cag. But he drunk pretty hard, and did more whipping than teaching, and so we all quit his school. I remember that, of cold days, when our fire-wood was scace, he used to make us join hands in a ring, and run around, and he would follow us up with a switch, and laugh and holla, and hurry us around with the awfullest sort of licks. That was all the eddication I had. I don't think it was much."

While this conversation was in progress near the stern, (for Simpson was next to the stroke-oar,) there was kept up a quiet side-talk among the others, which was concluded by the appointing of Wheeler to say to Dr. Gordon that his proposition met the approval of all, unless it might be of Simpson.

"And I'd be mighty proud to jine in it too," he quickly responded, "sept that it *oneases* me so to think how little I've got to say."

"Why, my good fellow," said Dr. Gordon, "you have interested the whole boat's crew already in trying to prove that you have nothing to say. I'll warrant there is not a person aboard but wishes to hear more."

"Well, sir," said Simpson, half pleased, half reluctant, "ef that's what you want, I've got plenty more behind and will give it, sich as it is."

"Since it is settled that each shall give some account of himself," continued the Doctor, "there is one thing more to be agreed upon, and that is, the order in which the persons shall be called for. Shall it be alphabetically, or by age?"

"I move it be by age, beginning at the youngest," said Thompson, looking mischievously at Wildcat, who during the past few minutes had appeared much excited, and who had uttered some imploring words to Jones about having him excused, and who now nervously ejaculated, —

"Wildcat can't talk white man's talk."

" But he can talk through a linkster,"* argued
Thompson, "and there is no better *sense-carrier*
for Muscogee than the Sargeant there, or than
Simpson. I should like, above all things, to hear
a real Injin story."

" I hope Wildcat will be excused, unless he
chooses to unite," said Tomkins. The poor boy
turned towards his unexpected advocate a look of
unmistakable gratitude, and with an almost laugh
of pleasure said, in his own language,—

" Enk-li-tum-ma-hitz-chay!"†

" Now," said Jones, looking maliciously at
Thompson, " I, too, vote that the order go by
age. But I think that the first person in this order to be called upon is Thompson; for, although
Wildcat came here from 'tother world about thir-
teen or fourteen years ago, Thompson came here
from Ireland only last year. He may be old as a
man—he looks as if he were—but, as a countryman, he is the youngest of the crowd. I hope he
will be called upon first."

" I am ready to obey orders when they come
from the right mouth," Thompson retorted; " but
I think it is only fair that Simpson, who began
his story first, should end it first."

---

* *Linkster*, though not found in our dictionaries, is a word
in common use in many parts, being a corruption of *linguis-
ter*, (probably from the Italian *linguista*, if not the English
linguist,) and means *interpreter*.

† Good, good as it can be.

"Simpson! Simpson!" was called by several voices.

"You hear the call, Simpson," said Dr. Gordon. "I hope you will answer as the Turks do, 'To hear is to obey.' If I were called upon for a vote, I should give it as these have done, for I have no doubt that whatever your *schooling* may have been, you have seen some rare sights."

"And so I have," he answered, while his brow relaxed from its usual half scowl as he listened to the call, which implied a flattering interest already in his life; "and I'll be proud to tell of 'em, too, as well as I kin."

"That is bravely spoken," said Dr. Gordon. "And now, the only rule I would suggest to govern what is to be related is, that each one shall aim in what he tells to give us something useful as well as entertaining."

"I have n't much in that line," Simpson modestly replied; "but such as I have I'll try to give."

With that he began and narrated a story, in which he committed horrible outrages upon all the rules of language and of elocution, but in which he gave some new and interesting sketches of rough life. This story, improved somewhat in style, and retaining only a few of its barbarous peculiarities, will be found recorded in the following chapter.

CHAPTER VII.

SIMPSON'S STORY.

HEN I was a " big chunk of a boy," my father moved from Kiokee, where I was born, to a place called the Cherokee Corner, where he farmed and preached. My time was divided between working on the farm during the busy season, and helping in a store in which my father had an interest, and which kept up a pretty brisk trade with the neighbors and the Indians. I do not mean to say that the Indians were *living* there at the time, for that part of the country had long been settled by the whites, and the red men had been pushed off towards the sunsetting; but the store *used* to be a famous place of trade with them when the Cherokee line cornered at that place,† and they would come a long way to trade at their old-time stand.

Some of the Indians came as much on my

† The passages in this story of Simpson's marked thus, are historical, or rather traditional, being parts of the unwritten history of the places and parties concerned.

mother's account, as on account of trading, for she was a great favor*ite* with a large part of the tribe. You remember I told you she had been captured when a wee-baby, and had lived among them all her life until she married my father. The truth is, the "Injin" in her was so strong that to the day of her death she was never able to give in entirely to the ways of the Unaykas, as she called the white people; but she loved her red-skinned brothers and kinsfolks, and they loved her to the last. The name they had for her showed their feelings; they called her O-see-u, which is the Cherokee for Good morning, because her face always brightened on seeing them, as if she was saying in her heart, "Welcome! I am glad to see you." And the name she gave me showed her love for Indian ways, for she did not give me a Christian name, as might have been expected of a Christian man's wife, but one in Cherokee, the same as if I were to belong to the tribe. People know me as Joe Simpson, and suppose that I was named Joseph for my father; but this is not so; the name my mother gave me was Yonah-steeka, which is the Cherokee for Little Bear; and my father, who thought the world and all of his pretty wife, but who did not "give in" to all her ways, humored her so far as to tell the people that my name was Jonah-Stephen, the nearest sound in English he could find to my Cherokee name; while, for short, he called me Joe, after himself.

I do not think that my mother's love for her
adopted people is to be wondered at, when her
history is known. She was brought up in the
family of an old warrior, who, after her parents
had been killed, had taken her from her home and
adopted her as his own child, in place of a daughter that had been killed by the whites. He was a
very great "brave;" no one in his nation stood
higher, or could stand higher than he. I will tell
you why.

As long ago as two life-times, — maybe more,—
there was a big war† between the Cherokees and
the Coosas—these are the same that are called
Creeks, on account of the many streams that per-
vade their country.† The Creeks, who wanted
more land, tried to force the Cherokees beyond
the Blue Ridge Mountains, and the Cherokees
who loved their hunting-grounds, and the graves
of their fathers, tried to keep the Coosas back to
their old limits. After a long and bloody war, in
which many lives had been lost, and the Cherokees
had been forced almost to the Blue Ridge, and the
Creeks had settled as far as the Coosa-wattee river,
(Coosa-wattee means the settling-place of the
Coosas,) it was agreed by solemn oath between the
parties to leave the question in dispute to be settled by a fight between twelve men selected from
each side. If the Creeks were successful, the
Cherokees were to give up all their hunting-

grounds south and east of the Blue Ridge Mountains; if the Cherokees were successful, the Creeks
were to be content with their former boundaries.
The place selected for the battle was a mountain,
which has a level top, containing about forty acres
—a beautiful place for a fight—away up above
the world.   There they met and fought, those
twenty-four men, while all the rest of the two nations, assembled on that high table land, looked
on without striking a blow.   Of the twenty-four
men who went into the fight, only one came out
alive.   That was a Cherokee, my mother's adopted
father.   The Coosas kept their word, called back
their warriors, broke up their settlement at Coosa-
wattee, and established the boundaries as they
were before the war.   The place of the fight keeps
the name of " Blood Mountain " to this day ! †

This old warrior had three sons, one of whom,
named Yonah-steeka, was my mother's playmate
when she was a child.   He died young.   The
others grew to be men, and were quite famous in
their day.   One of them was named Nung-noh-
hut-tar-hee, (he who kills the enemy in his own
way,) and the other Kah-nung-da-ha-geh, (the one
who walks on the mountain ridge.)   These men
my mother taught me to call uncle; but as their
names were too long to be pronounced by any one
except a Cherokee, the first was called by the
white people, Way, and the other was called Ridge.

My uncle Way was a great sportsman, both by land and water, and was skilled in all the arts practised by his people for taking deer, bears, raccoons and wolves, and also for spearing and shooting fish.

My uncle Ridge was a " medicine man," or doctor the most famous in his tribe, and not only did people come to him to be cured from all parts of the *nation*, but many also from the white settlements.

Whenever these two men made a visit to the *Corner*, they would ask my mother to let me return with them, and she was almost as ready to consent as they were to ask ; and I would go and spend one, two, or even three weeks at a time at their lodges, living just as they lived, and enjoying myself more than you would suppose in that wild kind of life ; and when I returned home, nothing pleased my mother more than to hear me recount what I had seen and done.

It seems to me, now I look back, that I learned more and more that was useful, among them, than I did at home. May be this was because I did not expect it, and because what I learned at home came to me natural like.

Among the useful things I learned at uncle Way's were two in one day. The first is that *clear water is much deeper than it appears to be.* I was in a canoe with him and a son of his, about my own age, spearing fish. There was a fine trout near my end of the boat, in water that seemed only knee deep. I begged him for the spear, and tried at it, leaning over the side of the boat and expecting to find myself supported by the resting of the spear upon the sandy bottom. I missed the fish, however, and found myself soused head and ears, in water beyond my depth. My uncle never laughed aloud, he was too much of an Indian for that, but inwardly he laughed as heartily as any one, and when I was floundering in the water, I saw his sides shake until the tears came into his eyes. The other thing I learned was, that in shooting at an object under water you must aim much lower than the place where it seems to be—how much lower is to be learned only by practice, or by seeing how much a spear or arrow is bent by being dipped in the water.

His son was a great trapper of squirrels and opossums, oftentimes bringing home six or eight from his traps in a day; and though I admired the contrivance by which he did this, I never could bring myself to practice it. He would fasten an ear of corn to a nicely set trigger at the end of a rail, and just at the place where the animal must sit to nibble he suspended a thin loop of tough wood, attached to a weight. The pulling or nibbling at the ear let fall the weight, by which the poor creature was squeezed to death between the loop and the rail

One day I went with my uncle to his bear-trap when it had caught a bear. It was a large, hollow log, inside of which were set spikes of tough wood, sharpened and arranged so that although it was easy for a bear to push his head into the log, he could not draw it back, because the spikes pressed close behind the ears. The trap was baited with wild honey, which the bear could smell but could never reach. On the same plan he caught wolves and panthers, baiting with a piece of fresh venison.

But what amused me most at uncle Way's, although it was a small thing of its kind, was his plan for catching terrapins. Whenever they were to be seen in any number floating on the surface of a pond, he and his son would swim or wade towards them, pushing a screen of leafy twigs before them until they were near enough to grasp the terrapin by one of its outspread legs, and secure it in a bag.

My other uncle, as I told you, Uncle Ridge, was a great "medicine-man." He studied no books, and learned under no doctor. He followed his own head, and took to the work by nature, but he would sometimes work cures in which the white doctors had failed. A case of this kind occurred during one of my visits to him. A white man, who had been for a long time ailing with a dreadful ulcer, and whose life the doctors despaired of, came to him and asked if his so e could be cured?   My uncle looked at it, asked various questions, and finally answered,—

"Yes, if you will let me *tie* you."

"I will let you do anything and will pay you anything you ask, if you will only cure my leg" the man said.

"Very well," my uncle answered; "come to-morrow as soon as your shadow lies your own length on the ground.   I will promise to cure you, or I will take no pay."

The man came next day, as directed, bringing with him a friend, and found my uncle seated on a log by a fire, on which was a pot of herbs stewing in deer's tallow, and close to it lay a piece of iron, with one end in the coals.   Besides these nothing was to be seen, except some thongs of deerskin.   After allowing him to rest, my uncle asked, "Are you ready?" and he answered, "I am."

"You consent that I shall tie you, and do what I think to be right?"

"I do."

"You promise, if I cure you, to pay me twenty dollars?"

"I do."

"Then come to this post and put your arms around it."

The man looked a little pale, but he did as directed, and was then tied fast, hand, foot and head, so that he could not move, nor look at the fire

behind him. My uncle then took the iron which
was heated not quite red hot, came softly up and
applied it to the ulcer. The poor fellow roared
and tried to break loose, but in vain. My uncle
kept moving the hot iron up and down and around
the ailing part, until it was burnt as deep and as
far as it was sore. He then poured on some cold
water to allay the pain, and anointed the part
with a salve which had been prepared, and said,
as he loosed the man,—

"I did not know what the sore was yesterday;
but it is a burn to-day, and I can cure a burn." †

In the course of a week or ten days the man
felt so well that he paid his twenty dollars and
returned home.

I learned many other useful things from my
uncle Ridge in the way of wildwoods physic; how
to cure chill and fever, by pills of black spider's
web; how to stop a trouble of the bowels by
chewing the leaves of the sweet-gum,* or a small
piece of a green persimmon, and how to stop a
heart-burn by chewing the young buds of the pine,
and other things of the sort, which you would tire
to hear of. There was one thing I learned, however, not in his line—his way of managing a balky
horse. My uncle's wife was a good farmer. The
Indian *men*, you know, never work; they will
fight, and hunt, and trap, and spear fish, and doc-

---

* Known to botanists as Liquid Amber.

tor people, and manage generally, but anything
like work, and bearing burdens, they leave to the
women. Well, my aunt had a beautiful pony
that would do anything except drawing a cart.
One day it was necessary that several loads of
corn should be brought from the field, and the
pony refused to pull. My aunt tried coaxing, and
then switching, but in vain. Then she applied to
her husband. He came out and I came with him
to see what was to be done. The pony had a stub-
born and mulish look. His ears were laid back,
and his whole manner said, as plainly as pony
could say, You may do what you please, but I
will not pull one step. The first thing my uncle
did was to quiet him by a little patting and gen-
tling, and by whispering a word or two in his ear.
Failing in this, he applied three or four tremen-
dous whacks with a switch. But this only made
matters worse. He then put in each ear a corn-
cob, and tied it tight around with a string. This
stopping of the ear made such a buzzing and con-
fusing sound that the pony hauled one load without difficulty, but refused to haul any more. My
uncle then locked the wheels so they could not be
turned, fastened the pony by a halter to the tree,
and left him in the shafts all night, without food
or water. The next morning there was no gentler
pony to be found, nor one more willing to do his
duty. He never was known to balk again. My

uncle said that if ever there was another balk he should try the effect of some unpleasant *physic*.

Before I was quite grown my good mother died, and I happened to a great misfortune. While on a visit to the Indian nation, there arose a quarrel between me and the son of a chief, and I hurt him so badly that he was likely to die. I returned home the next day, and it was not long before a message came that made me go still further. It was the picture of a fish-spear, painted red, and under it the word "Conagatee." The fish-spear was the sign of my uncle Way; the red paint meant danger; and the word "Conagatee," (which he had caused the trader who brought me the picture to write,) was the Cherokee for "Go away!" From these hints I learned that the chief's son was dead, and there was no time to lose, for an Indian never forgives. I, therefore, made some excuse to my father for visiting some of his kinfolks in South Carolina, and there I staid until he wrote me word that he had removed from the Cherokee Corner to the western border of the white settlement, near the Coosas, whom you call Creeks.

As soon as I was of age, my father gave me a pony and a little money. I bought some trinkets and went among the Coosas on a trading expedition. In this I succeeded so well that I was soon able to enlarge my business. Money came in upon me very fast, for I had no love for the Coosas, and did not hesitate to cheat them on all occasions, because they were themselves such cheats and liars. They had no mercy on a white man, and it was not fair to expect a white man to have mercy on them. You may judge of what I say when I mention a few facts.

I once called upon a very old Indian woman to learn her age. She was quite free-spoken, and seemed ready to tell anything I asked her about. As for her age, she said that she had seen so many "moons" she had long stopped counting them, for the want of numbers. This did not surprise me, because I knew that most Creeks could not count beyond *Parli-parlin* (ten tens). But when I asked her to tell me something that she recollected in early life—some war, some work, something that happened—she told me with solemn face, and tried to make me believe that she recollected the time when *her people first dug out the channel of the Chattahoochee river.**

About five or six years ago a white man (who lives near that little town I hear people begin to talk about by the name of Columbus,) went over the river to attend a big gathering at a ball-play. He rode a horse that he kept purposely very poor-looking, but which was nevertheless one of the

* This incident and the one next succeeding are still related in Columbus, Ga., as part of the early history of the neighborhood. The "little town" of 1830 is now a city.

swiftest nags of its size. His object was to draw
some rich red-skin into a race on a large bet, and
by this means to win back some of the money that
he had lost in former bets with them. He picked
his man, persuaded him into a race, and bantered
him to a very high bet. They went to the ground,
stationed the judges and started. Barnet, for that
was the white man's name, was fond of fun as
well as of money, and was so confident of the
speed of his horse that he allowed the Indian some
distance the start, in order to enjoy seeing him dig
into his pony's ribs and try to keep ahead. At
the close of the race he let out his horse to full
speed and came out far in advance.

"Now," says he, turning with a laugh to his
competitor, "pay me your bet."

"Umph!" says the other, "will pay you when
judge say so."

"What's the use of the judge saying anything?"
Barnet asked. "Didn't I win the race?"

"Will pay when judge say so," the other repeated.

"But did I not give you the start, and then
come out ahead?" Barnet asked again.

The Indian still said, "Will pay when judge
say so."

The matter was then referred to the judges.
They went off to themselves and soon returned,
saying—"*Injin beat.*"

Barnet was amazed at their impudence, and asked :

" Did I not give him the start ?"

" Yes."

" And did I not come out ahead ?"

" Yes."

" How then can you say that he beat ?"

" Injin beat *most*," they answered.

" Beat most ! What do you mean ?"

" White man beat at the two ends ; Indian beat in the middle."

And with this decision they put the stakes into the Indian's hands. Barnet returned home a wiser man than he came. He never, after that, trusted a Coosa.

And I had a touch of that experience once my-self. While I was keeping store near where Columbus is growing up, a young hunter, who had often traded with me, and who had been as fair as any Coosa is known to be, came in, offering to purchase a few articles, and to pay for them with a very fat deer which he said he had just killed, and which he offered very low, on condition that I should send for it. I had no misgiving in the case, for I knew the young man, and knew the very spot where he reported the deer to be hang-ing, (on a sapling, near a large poplar, the other side of a pond, not a quarter of a mile off,) and moreover I had heard the report of a rifle in that direction only a few minutes before he came in.

He got what he asked for and went off. I did not see him again for months, nor did I ever see the deer. A long time afterwards he came to my store to trade, looking as innocent as if he had never done me a wrong. I immediately ordered him off, and forbade his coming to me any more.

" What for?" said he, looking mightily taken by surprise.

I answered: " For lying about that deer when you were last here. There was not a word of truth in what you said."

"White man wrong. Did he look wnere Indian tell him?"

" I did."

" And did not find any *pond?*" he asked.

" Pond? Of course I did. I knew of that pond before," I answered.

" Ah, well, that is *one true* I tell. And white man did not find the *poplar?*"

" Certainly I found it. I knew of that also before."

" Ah, well, that is *two true.* And white man did not find the deer?"

"No, I did not; there was no deer there, and had not been."

" Ah, well, that is *one lie.* Two true to one lie. But," said he, turning to me with a laugh, " don't you think that two true to one lie is pretty good for Iniin?"

F

I am bound, however, to say of the Coosas that they had some good in them, as well as much evil In the first place, they are a very modest people — much more so than the whites — for in all my dealings with them for years, I seldom saw or heard an indecent thing in men or women, old or young. The men were brave, and the women generally correct in their behavior.† The mothers, too, were *real* mothers; and it almost won my heart to them, Coosas though they were, to see, as I often had seen, mothers pale with hunger, staggering as they carried their chubby children, that looked as if they had never known what hunger was.† Both men and women, too, were very hospitable. If ever you went to the door of their wigwams, you were asked to come in ; and if ever you went in, you were bound to partake of their sof-kee.† There were seldom any quarrels, and such as arose were almost always made up at their green-corn dances, at which time it was customary for all, and especially for those who had quarrelled, to meet together and shake hands in their large council room, which was always kept so dark that they could not *look into each other's eyes.* *

After I had traded long enough among these Indians to gather a pretty little property, I lost it all in one day by standing security for a fellow-

* Sof-kee — hominy made of pounded corn.

trader. I would have commenced business again, and gone on the same way as before, but I had nothing to start with, and, more than this I had so offended some of the chiefs that it was not safe for me to remain in the nation. I wandered about the country for some time, and finally, about three years ago, enlisted in the United States army, hoping to be sent out west. Instead of this, however, I was put on different posts, first in Charleston, then in Savannah, and now here. My time will be out next month, and then I shall be a free man, but somehow I feel very indifferent to it, as if my freedom were hardly worth the having.

That's my story, with all the useful things I could think of worth the telling.

CHAPTER VIII.

FISHING FOR SHEEPHEAD—A CHASE BY WATER

"VERY much obliged to you for your interesting story," said Dr. Gordon to Simpson, when he had concluded. "I doubt not that every person aboard unites with me in saying so." He stopped and looked around. Tomkins nodded his approval as cordially as could have been expected from one of his stiff habits while on duty, and from the men there came a general murmur of assent. The swarthy face of the narrator almost revealed a blush of pleasure on learning that his rough rehearsal had met with such unexpected favor, and he stammered out, —

"I had'nt no idee that I'd a had so much to say, or that any body would a-cared to a-heern it."

"Your story has interested us all," said the Doctor. "In truth," he continued, "*every* person has an interesting history, if he only knew it, and knew how to tell it; and the secret of making it so to others consists in presenting those portions

84

only which may prove instructive or entertaining.
I trust that, after the good example set us by
Simpson, no one will hesitate to do his part, and
I propose that we call for a story from some one
every day. But who is to come next?"

That point had been already settled, for, during
the recital of Simpson's story, Jones had exchanged
words with several of the men, and now, on a sly
wink from him, they all cried out,—

"Thompson! Thompson!"

"Mr. Thompson," said Dr. Gordon, in a serio-
comic tone, assumed as best suiting the temper of
the man, "the company express the desire that
their next entertainment shall be furnished by a
son of 'the Green Isle.' It is their hope and
expectation that you will honor them by your
response to-morrow about this time, unless it is
called for sooner."

"The honor of ould Ireland will not let me
say nay," replied Thompson, "and our friend
Backwoods (nodding towards Simpson) has done
so much better than he expected, or than we either,
that I must say I feel encouraged."

"You had better say *dis*couraged," Jones added,
in a teazing spirit, "for what can you bring us
from the bogs of Ireland to compare with what
has been given us by the Georgia *cracker*." *

* The term "cracker" is a derisive epithet that has been
applied, from time immemorial, by dwellers upon the sea-

To this taunt Thompson retorted by some allusion to " pitch, t'yar, and turpentine," these
being the staple products of Jones' native State,
North Carolina, and " t'yar" being the corrupt
pronunciation by the uneducated of that State, for
the word " tar."

This friendly pass of arms was soon interrupted
by Dr. Gordon saying to Jones, —

" Do give us some little account of your fishing
excursion this morning ; particularly that part of
it," he added with a smile, " which occurred after
you had passed the locked horns of the deer."

Jones' eye twinkled at this allusion, but he perfectly commanded his countenance, and went on
to say, —

" We fished, as we ordinarily do, from shore.
Here is my fishing-tackle."

He drew from his bosom a line of great strength,
but of delicate proportions, wrapped into an oval
mass by oblique crossings around a nicely trimmed
stick. It was forty or fifty yards long, and was
armed at its lower extremity with two strongly
built hooks, each of which was attached by a snell

board of Georgia to the rough denizens of the piney-woods,
and afterward to all other backwoodsmen. Its origin is
obscure; but it probably originated with the early Scotch
settlers, in whose dialèct "a cracker" is a person who talks
boastingly ; this kind of talk being very natural to the sturdy
sons of the foiest, to avoid being overborne by the preten-
tious refinements of the city

of more delicate line, so as to hang about a hand's breadth apart from each other, and from the sinker, which last was a wedge of lead, several ounces in weight, attached to the extremity of the line.

"You know," said he, "that for sheephead we fish in about four feet of water, next the bottom, and that on this shallow shore you must throw your hook ten or fifteen yards before it finds depth enough. The fish, however, are very plentiful, and you do not have to wait long for a bite; indeed, I hooked my first fish (the same you ate for breakfast this morning) before the lead reached bottom."

"You seem to have had no net or other convenience for catching shrimp; I should like to know what you used for bait?" Dr. Gordon inquired.

"O, as for bait," Jones replied, "you need not be very particular, for however shy sheephead may be elsewhere, they are so tame here, and so plentiful, that people say you may walk along shore any morning, and *kick* out enough for breakfast. But I did not rely upon kicking them out. I used bait, the best to be had, barring the shrimps, and that was black fiddlers * and clams. I filled my pocket with fiddlers, after breaking off their legs

* Fiddlers are a small species of crab, seldom an inch long, having one large and one small claw, and burrowing in the muddy sand of our salt-water beaches.

and claws, and the clams I broke open and cut into pieces suitable for bait. The bait was not the best, to be sure, but good enough to bring the two strings of fish you saw this morning. We were fishing not over half an hour."

Dr. Gordon was so much pleased with the intelligence and skill of the man that he said, —

"If Sergeant Tomkins approve, I hereby appoint Mr. Jones fishing-master for the rest of the excursion."

Tomkins readily consented, and Jones looked as if he had gained a pleasant point for himself and for the men.

The barge continued all day its steady cruise along the coast, turning its bow shorewards whenever there was a possibility of the lost boat being concealed behind any of the points of marsh or beach that marked the frequently occurring creeks and inlets.

About the middle of the afternoon they witnessed quite an interesting chase. In one of those intervals of perfect stillness which often prevailed, broken only by the measured thump of the oars against the thowl-pins, Dr. Gordon was aroused from his meditative attitude by hearing a sharp, quick call from Tomkins, "Look yonder!" He looked in the direction indicated by Tomkins' eye, and saw, at the distance of less than half a mile, a noble buck, with fine branch-

ing antlers, making for a precipitous bluff of about
ten feet in height. His head and tail were proudly
erect, and he was moving along in an easy, graceful lope, while not a hundred yards behind him
followed three dogs in hot pursuit. On reaching
the bluff, the buck leaped sheer off into the air,
showing against the distant sky his whole profile,
with out-spread legs, and with his head thrown
back to watch his pursuers. He alighted upon
the beach, full twenty-five feet distant from the
base of the bluff, and immediately plunged into
the water. Soon after him came his panting
pursuers, with mouths open and tongues lolling
out, and while one of them made the leap from
the bluff, in faint imitation of the deer, the others
scrambled down the steep declivity, and all of
them plunged into the water also.

In the course of a few minutes more, two canoes,
each containing two Indians, shot from behind
the projecting bluff and paddled rapidly after the
dogs. By this time the deer had gone so far to
sea as to be scarcely visible, except perhaps to the
keen eyes of the Indians, although the dark heads
of the dogs were plainly to be seen rising and falling upon the swell of the gently moving waves.
Whether guided by the sight of the now distant
deer, or of the dogs, the hunters did not hesitate,
but pushed right out to sea. The dogs, after
swimming about half a mile, seemed to fail, either

in strength or courage, and returned to shore, passing the canoes at the distance of a few rods, and on reaching land shook their dripping coats, and lay panting upon the sand, with their eyes steadily directed to the canoes, and seeming to anticipate what they knew was to be the end of the chase.

Dr. Gordon observed that while one of the canoes paddled rapidly in the direction from which the dogs had come, the other followed leisurely in its wake. Soon the head of the foremost canoe was turned south, upon which the one in the rear moved with all possible rapidity in the same direction. The deer, having exhausted the swimming power of the dogs, had turned also towards land, and it was the plan of the Indians to intercept and capture it. The struggle, on the deer's part, to escape was long and obstinate. It made a wide detour to pass its dangerous-looking enemies; then swam with all its might to win the race to shore; failing in this, it made desperate efforts to pass, now to this side, then to that. Its efforts, however, were all in vain. The other canoe came up; the poor brute seemed to lose heart; it began to swim feebly, then almost at random; at last its branching horns were entangled by a lasso-like thong thrown around them; its head was pushed under the water and held there until life was nearly extinct when it was drawn alongside the canoe and its throat cut; after which it was taken aboard, just in time to save the carcass from several immense sharks which had scented the blood from afar, and whose black fins, projecting a foot into the air, seemed almost to make a fizzing sound as they hurried fiercely to the scene of slaughter.

When the barge came to the spot from which the canoes were now departing the disappointed sharks could be plainly seen, staring with their green, hungry eyes at the crew, and looking as if they were meditating a leap at them over the gunwales.

As the canoes were moving off Tomkins hailed them and congratulated the leading Indian, an elderly, fine-looking man, on his skill as a hunter. No answer, however, was returned, except a grunt, expressive certainly of indifference if not of disgust. Thinking it possible that none of them understood English, Tomkins repeated what he had said in Indian, and at the same time inquired if any boats had been seen passing on the coast. Still there was no reply, nor even a turning of the ear, or a movement of the eye to intimate their consciousness of any presence except their own. The elderly Indian alone gave one searching look into the faces of the crew, then with a scowl of hate and a murmur of command he turned his face toward the shore, and they paddled silently away.

Tomkins turned anxiously to Dr. Gordon, and whispered,—

"I am afraid, Doctor, there is trouble in the wigwam. I never knew a redskin look that way, yet, but mischief was sure to follow.'

Dr. Gordon also became very grave, and sending a sad, far-reaching glance down the coast, replied,—

"I fear the same. And my poor, poor children! how are they either to escape or to meet it?"

The faces of the men reflected instantly and unreservedly the feelings which they saw so plainly depicted in his, while Tomkins, acting as spokesman, said,—

"These men may not be fair samples for the rest; and, supposing they are, why, what we have to do is to push on as far and fast as possible in search of your children. If there is a storm gathering, we may be able to save them, and to return to Fort Brooke before it bursts."

To these words the men responded by looks of hearty approbation, all except Simpson, whose usually *down*-look was more down than ever, since the appearance of the Indians. But creditable as they were to the soldierly spirit of the men, they conveyed little or no consolation to the heart of the father. The quick ear of Tomkins, who sat next him, caught the sound of a stifled groan, and his eye detected an expression of countenance

which convinced him that not only was the mind
of the sorrower far away, but that his heart was
holding communion with One who is not of this
world. Soldier though he was, and accustomed
to deal fearlessly with dangers and dangerous
things, the sight awed him into reverential silence.

The shadow that fell thus suddenly upon the
spirits of the group was not wholly dispelled that
day. Dr. Gordon made various attempts to rally,
in which he was well seconded by the native live-
liness of Jones and Thompson, and by the assumed
cheerfulness of the rest; but although to the eye
of an observer all was pleasant enough, each was
conscious of a foreboding that the cloud which
had begun to gather was not to be dispersed until
they had heard its thunder and felt its force.

Late in the evening the bow of the barge was
turned shorewards, in search of a place of encampment for the night. Before leaving the open water
the spy-glass was brought into requisition and the
whole horizon swept by it. No sign was discovered of the missing boat, but far away to the
north a dim speck, barely visible to the naked eye,
was developed into a canoe, manned by two Indians, and moving south.

CHAPTER IX.

*WATER! WATER!—BRACKISH WATER CORRECT-
ED—SALT WATER CONVERTED INTO FRESH—
SUBSTITUTES FOR WATER—MODES OF ALLAY-
ING THIRST—SIGNS FOR FINDING WATER.*

THE encampment that night was in **a**
nook of the coast, where the soft shell
rock, which underlies a great portion
of peninsular Florida, had been worn
into the proportions of a mimic bay. The surrounding bluff was higher than usual, being
withal surmounted by hillocks of sand blown
up from the beach, and by a clump of thick,
dwarfish cedars and small bushes; while beyond
these, for a quarter of a mile, the country was
perfectly clear of growth, even of the cactus. In
a military point of view, no better place could
have been selected, for while it gave to persons
or the spot every advantage for concealment and
defence, it furnished none to persons approaching.

But there was one serious deficiency attending
it—the water which oozed through the sands of

94

the beach was all brackish, while the runlet on
board the barge was nearly dry. In this emergency two suggestions were offered. One was by
Jones, who said that in the part of North Carolina from which he came, it was common to correct the brackish taste of water by the use of the
Yupon.*

"I see several bushes of it growing among
these cedars," said he, "and although the water
we have found is too brackish to be pleasant, it
will be made pleasant enough if boiled or steeped
with a few leaves of the Yupon."

The other suggestion was from Wheeler, and,
by way of authority, was prefaced with a short
narrative. He said that while aiding once as
escort to a company of learned Frenchmen, under
the lead of some one by the name of Nickoly, or
Nicolay, they were all saved from suffering, and
perhaps from death, by the happy device of one
of the corps.

"We were passing through those horrible salt-
prairies out West," said he, "where there is oftentimes water enough in pools and lakes, but which

* The Yu-pon, or Cassena, (spelt also Cassina, or Cassine,)
is a beautiful evergreen shrub, growing to the height of
eight or ten feet, and adorned in winter with berries of a
brilliant red. It abounds along the coast, and is known by
many as "North Carolina tea," being often used as a substitute for the better article of commerce.

is all as briny as the ocean. For several days our horses' feet had been crunching through the salty crust of the prairie, which looked all the while as if covered with frost, when by an accident we lost our supply of drinking water.

"The faces of most of the party turned pale at the sight of the empty kegs, for no one could tell how many days it would be before fresh water was to be had; but one of them spoke up cheerily, and said, 'We shall do very little credit to our education, if, with our camp-kettles and with the wood around us, we suffer long from thirst, because the water happens to be salt.'

"I saw Mr. Nicolay's eyes brighten as if there was life in this remark, and so did the faces of the others; but how it was possible to turn salt water into fresh by means of a kettle and wood, was more than I could imagine, for I knew that the longer salt water is boiled the more briny it becomes; nor did I know how, until I saw it done. But I have practised it several times since, and if the Doctor and the Sargeant say so, I will do as I saw the Frenchmen do, and make some of this sea-water fit for use."

Tomkins had a high regard for Wheeler's good sense, as well he might, but at this suggestion he looked rather doubtful, until Dr. Gordon remarked,—

"Wheeler is right. The great Author of nature

has endowed water with such laws that it can be compelled to part with its salts, and most other impurities, by either of two methods, the very opposites of each other, and fitting, too, the two extremes of heat and cold. One is by freezing, and the other is by boiling. Those who visit the Polar regions tell us that the icebergs are all fresh, though composed of sea-water. *The act of freezing forces out the salt.* And the same is true of water that is evaporated, though in a different way; the heat forces out the water in the shape of steam or vapor, leaving the salt behind. Now, if we can catch and condense that steam, we shall have fresh water; and all that we need do to condense it, is to bring it into contact with something colder than itself. This is the philosophy of the case, expressed in a simple way; but I am curious to learn Wheeler's process for this, which must be simple, indeed, since it can be practised on a salt-prairie or a sandy sea-beach."

It was then agreed that a trial should be given to both plans, and as both plans required fire, and as it was expedient, for the sake of concealment, to avoid, as far as possible, all flame and smoke, the fire was committed to the Indian skill of Wild-cat, who selected a place amid the dense growth of the thicket, which he made still more private by a screen of bushes, and then made his fire of small dry twigs, which soon produced a strong

G

heat, with very little flame or smoke. The result of the two experiments was, that the party enjoyed a comfortable supper, and had some water left, over and above their evening's necessity, for break- fast next morning. Jones' Yupon did not alto- gether destroy the brackishness of the water; it only modified and disguised it to such degree that the water, which was wholly unfit for tea and other purposes before, was *endurable* now. But Wheeler's plan, although liable to the serious ob- jection of being very slow, was perfectly successful.

His whole apparatus consisted of a camp-kettle for his boiler, a tin bucket for his condenser, and a tin cup for his receiver. The kettle was filled only about half-full, leaving a perfectly free pas- sage for the steam through the spout when most vigorously boiling. As soon as the steam began to issue freely, the tin bucket of cold water was suspended, in a tilted posture, near the spout and to the windward of the fire, so that the steam, un- mixed with smoke, should pour upon its cool side, where it instantly condensed into the form of dew, and then trickled, drop by drop, down the side, and then down the leaning bottom of the bucket into a cup set for its reception. The process was so slow, that one kettle would scarcely distil a quart in an hour, and the water, besides, was flat to the taste, as water always is after being boiled; still, *it was perfectly fresh*—it could quench thirst—it could save life in time of need.

Dr. Gordon expressed himself highly delighted with the simple contrivance. When the water thus produced was cooled and handed to Tomkins, he tasted it, then looked very sad, and finally surprised every one by brushing away a tear.

"Excuse me, sir," he said to Dr. Gordon, "but this water carried me to a time when I saw people die for the want of it, or rather, I may say, when I saw an angel of a child starve to death for the want of water, when, if we had only known this simple plan, we might have saved her life. She was not my child, sir, nor any kin of mine, but the daughter of a passenger, who was so unfortunate as to lose his wife at the same time. It was years ago, but all is as fresh to my mind as if it happened yesterday. We were on a wreck at sea, off the coast of North Carolina, where we floated for four mortal days without a mouthful to eat or a drop of water to drink. You know people suffer more from thirst, and die of it sooner, than they do from hunger. Well, this child died in her father's lap the third day of our misfortune. She had cried for water and for something to eat several times during the first day and a half, but when her father said to her, 'My darling, there is none to be had; you must try and not ask for it,' she never cried again. She suffered and died, but the word 'water' never passed her lips. Oh, sir, she was an angel! and when I think of her, the

tears come up in spite of me.   Now, we had wood
enough on the wreck for fire, and matches, too,
and vessels sufficient to distil what that poor child
needed, and perhaps others, too, that died, but nobody knew of this way of producing it.   Oh, if
we had known ! "

"Did you adopt no plan for quenching your
thirst?" Dr. Gordon asked.

"Oh, yes," he replied ; "we tried many plans,
but the only one that proved of any avail was
keeping our clothes wet with sea-water.   It seems
that the skin has some of the power that you as-
cribe to both freezing and evaporation ; it can separate the water from the salt, and, as it were, suck
the water into the system.   We who kept our
clothes wet, and who kept wet cloths around our
necks, lived in tolerable comfort, while those who
drank the sea-water sickened, and raved, and died.
We lost five out of eighteen."

These last remarks led into quite a long and
interesting conversation on the various expedients
for allaying thirst and for obtaining water.

Wheeler gave it as his experience that, in long
and thirsty marches, such as he had made in
Mexico and the Rocky Mountains, it is better to
drink well at the start, and to drink no more
until the halt, and at the same time to keep the
mouth shut during the march, breathing only
through the nostrils.

Thompson said that his experience was like Wheeler's, and that whenever his thirst became great, he found it better to quench it by drinking a teaspoonful at a time, very often, than by swallowing large draughts at a time.

Jones remarked, that on a march, his own habit had been to keep a bullet or a pebble in his mouth, or to chew a leaf or straw; and that, according to his experience, a small piece of clove kept in the mouth will create moisture for a long time.

Dr. Gordon said that a little vinegar mixed with the water will greatly allay the sensation of thirst, and so will any sub-acid fruit, and that the mucilaginous leaves of the sassafras and of the prickly pear are often used for the same purpose.

Tomkins added that he had once carried with him to the battle-field a canteen of cold tea, and found it to have the effect of both food and water, and that he had no doubt a canteen of cold coffee would do equally as well.

"When I was crossing the ocean," said Magruder, "our water became very stale, and the ship's company began to suffer, when our captain gave us a treat in the way of drink that none of us will be apt to forget if we live to the age of Methuselah — it was a drink of ice-water fresh from the clouds. There came up a hail storm in the midst of our distress, and the captain stretched several large sails to catch it. The water soon

began to collect into the middle of the sail, and
to pour through it in a perfect stream. We
caught more than two bar'ls of it, though the
captain did not allow any of it to enter the
bar'ls until the salt had been all washed out of
the sails."

"I was present once," said Wheeler, "when
some thirsty men, for the lack of sails, spread
their own clothes in the rain, and then wrung out
the water into cups to drink. I confess I preferred to starve a little longer for water than to
drink what was wrung from dirty clothing."

"A cleaner mode," added Dr. Gordon, "would
have been to collect the rain-drops from the trees
by means of a sponge or cloth. Even dew-drops
may be collected in this way, and it is surprising
to know how much water they will afford."

Wheeler said he had once tasted water from the
paunch of a newly-killed deer, and it was fresh,
but unpleasantly sweetish. He had also heard
fishermen say that the water to be found in a
little sac around the heart of the sea-turtle is
fresh enough to quench thirst, but he had never
tried it.

Wildcat, who had been silent through all this
colloquy, now whispered modestly to Jones that
he had often quenched his thirst, during the
spring and early summer, from the vine of the
wild grape, which, on being cut or even bruised,

will emit for days a quantity of very palatable water.

" While we are talking about fresh water," said Tomkins, " there comes to our ears the sign of it not half a mile away. Do you hear the cawing and chattering of those sea-birds going to roost? They are cranes, and herons, and gannets, and water-turkeys, that wade in the salt water, and feed upon salt food all day; but I observe that they always try to sleep over a fresh-water pool at night."

Wheeler stated that hunters among the wild mountains and boundless prairies of the West would often die for want of water, were it not for knowing that the paths worn by wild beasts almost invariably lead to water, of which they are next to certain when they can find two of them converging to the same point. He said there was one fresh-water sign which had never yet deceived him, and this was the growth of grasses with a three-cornered stalk; wherever these were to be found, on hill-side or valley, there was sure to be water near the root. Another sign, he said, was nearly as good, though by no means so precise, and this consisted in dancing companies of mosquitoes and other gnats, for these troublesome insects being born and bred in water, and laying their eggs in water, cannot afford to travel very far from it. He also described the process of trying for water in moist-looking places. An iron ramrod is first shoved into the ground as deep as it will go, and if it comes up moist, there is water there. It is usual to commence digging by first sinking a hole not larger than a man's arm, and afterwards to enlarge it. After the hole has been sunk beyond the reach of the hand, it is easy to loosen the dirt by means of a sharpened stick, the point of which is hardened in the fire, and then the loosened dirt can be taken out by means of long, tough splinters tied around the end of a rod, so as to leave a hollow in the midst. With a sharpened stick and a dirt-lifter, it is easy to bore into soft earth to the depth of ten, or fifteen, or perhaps even of twenty feet.

With this lively chat about water, which interested all by its promise of usefulness, they passed the evening from sunset to bed-time, when, just as they were preparing to turn in for the night, they were aroused by an incident which will be recorded in the next chapter.

CHAPTER X.

HE encampment for the night and all things pertaining to it, had been effected with an eye to concealment and defence. Not only had the fire for distilling their water and cooking their supper, been kindled in a concealed place, and been fed with dry sticks and twigs which gave the greatest amount of heat with the least of smoke and flame, but the barge was concealed behind a pile of sea-weed and other stuff, brought in from sea and lodged against a mass of hardened shell-rock on shore; and the two tents, pitched in the very heart of the cedar thicket, were covered with a coat of leafy-branches so thick as to conceal so much of the white canvas as peered above the dwarfy growth around.

Soon after the animated conversation recorded in the preceding chapter had subsided, and when the men began to listen for the command, "All to quarters!" the hoot of an owl was heard from the

105

neighboring forest, followed a few seconds afterwards by an answering hoot from the coast above,
each seeming to be at the distance of a quarter of
a mile. The sound was so perfectly in keeping
with the country that it would probably have passed
unnoticed had not Tomkins, in a casual glance at
Wildcat, observed his eye fixed upon him with
glistening, uneasy gaze. Its meaning was too plain
to be misinterpreted, and yet the basis of its intended report was so slender that Tomkins resolved
to trouble no one with it but himself. He simply
announced to the others that we was going out to
reconnoitre a little before " turning in," charged
the Corporal with the command during his absence, and asked Dr. Gordon to allow him, in the
meanwhile, the company of Wildcat. Then shouldering a musket, and motioning his young companion to do the same, he thrust a night-glass into
his bosom, and passing the sentinel, who was
posted in a concealed place on the bluff, he moved
rapidly, but silently, along the beach in the direction from which the last hoot had come.

"So you think those were not owls we heard?"
he said interrogatively, to Wildcat, in a low murmur, as soon as they were alone.

" Not owl," was the reply, " but red man in the
bush, and red man by the water."

" You think the men in the canoes are on our
trail?" he asked again

"Think so," was the laconic answer.

"I should like to find out how many of them there are," Tomkins said.

As he spoke, there was another hoot from the woods back of the encampment, followed by another reply from the beach.

"Can make canoe *come here*, if Sergeant say so,' Wildcat intimated.

"How?" Tompkins asked.

"Wildcat will talk like red man in the bush," he replied.

"Did you notice the difference in the two cries? and can you hoot like each?"

Wildcat grunted assent in true Indian style, then, in a low tone, imitated the two cries, saying, "Red man in bush say, Oo-oo-uh-oo-oo! and red man by water say, Oo-oo-oo-oo-uh!"

"That is well done," Tomkins said in admiration of the boy's power of imitation.

"I will tell you very soon if it is best to bring them."

During the walk they frequently stopped to reconnoitre; at which times Tomkins, with his night-glass, would search every visible point; but, although the light of the misty moon, almost over head, was sufficient to reveal objects to the naked eye at the distance of eighty or a hundred yards, and to the glass at double that distance, he could discover nothing amiss, or even suspicious. Reach-

ing at last a part of the bluff where the concealment suited his purpose, amid some hillocks of
sand blown up frcm the beach below, he seated
himself with Wildcat by his side, and said to
him,—

"Now see if you can bring the canoes."

Wildcat first rehearsed to himself in very low
tones the cry he wished to imitate, then putting
his hands before his mouth to deaden the peculiarities of the human voice, he gave utterance to
his "Oo-oo-uh-oo-oo!" in tones so owl-like that
Tomkins looked around, almost expecting to see
a pair of big eyes staring at him.

Not many minutes now elapsed before two canoes appeared moving boldly down the const, within
easy gunshot of shore, one of them containing two
persons, the other only one, the companion to the
last being probably the hooter in the woods. Tomkins kept his place of concealment until they had
passed, waiting to see whether others were to follow. Then, seeing how insignificant the force
was, he motioned Wildcat behind the breastwork
of sand, along which they both hurried back to
camp.

Scarcely, however, had they come within earshot
of the sentinel when they heard the peculiar voice
of Simpson, who was on duty, sing out three several times in quick succession, first in English,
then in Indian, "Who comes there? Halt, or I'll
shoot!"

The canoes did not halt, but with an exclamation, seemingly of surprise and wrath, hurried rapidly on.

"Halt, or I'll shoot!" Simpson was heard to say again, and immediately upon his words came the flash and roar of a musket. Tomkins ran as fast as he could, halloing,—

"Stop your shooting!" but, before his command could reach its destination, another musket had jarred the night air, quickly succeeded by a *third*, while from the canoes came what sounded like a muttered curse,* then the whistle of balls, accompanied by the sharp crack of three successive rifles.

"Them fellows come mighty nigh a hittin o' me!" said Simpson, in a deprecating tone to the Sergeant, on his approach, pointing, as he spoke, to a white spot on a cedar which had been barked by a ball within a foot's range of his head.

"What on earth possessed you to shoot?" asked Tomkins sternly. "Do you wish to bring the whole nation upon us?"

"I thought," replied Simpson, "you put me h'yur as sentry, to shoot ef people don't stop when halted."

* To the credit of the American Aborigines, and especially of the Cherokee tribe, it is said that they have or rather had no "curse-words" in their language, and that before they could be profane they had to learn English.

"That is his duty in time of war," Tomkins answered; "but it is not a time of war yet, unless your attack on the canoe has made it so. But how come you with *three* guns?"

"I was a' mos' sartin the red skins would be upon us to-night; so I borried the guns to be ready," Simpson explained.

Tomkins was exceedingly annoyed by this unfortunate termination to his harmlessly intended ruse in decoying the Indians from their concealment. But the deed and its consequences were now past recall, and all that he could do was to confer with Dr. Gordon on the increasingly serious aspect their affairs began to assume, and on their duty in the premises.

"If blood has been shed by that foolish firing," said he, "I am afraid our cruise along the coast will not reach much farther, for blood is an offence which no Indian can either forgive or forget."

This caused Dr. Gordon to ponder long and anxiously. Eager as he was to proceed, and all the more so in consequence of that day's experience, he questioned the propriety of endangering, in his private cause, the lives of men who had no interest in it beyond that of common humanity, and who had been kindly lent to him by an officer whose account must be rendered to a higher and it may be an unsympathizing authority. While he was silently meditating his duty, Tomkins,

whose quickened eye gave evidence of some re-
lieving thought, continued and said —

"It is ten to one that no blood has been shed;
for though Simpson is a capital shot by day, he
had poor chance for a telling aim to-night. And,
even supposing the worst, that the red skins come
upon us in force, why here we are in a boat, which,
though called a barge, is strong as any sea-boat
need to be; in her we can easily put to sea, where
their little periwinkle canoes dare not follow. All
that I fear is for your children that we come out
here to save, and I think we soldiers are now
more bound than ever to do what we came to do."

Dr. Gordon could not help admiring the soldierly spirit of the man, at the same time that he
was gratified with the kindly interest manifested
in his unfortunate children; but he yielded his
assent so slowly and doubtfully to what was said
that Tomkins energetically reiterated:

"I will leave it to the men whether it would be
manly in us to hesitate in such a case as yours, for
the sake of a little danger. Why, sir, if we were
to give it up so, and the matter were known at the
Fort, we should never hear the end of it, and I
think we should deserve to be cashiered and
drummed out of the garrison. No sir, we must
keep on now, unless you order us back, for your
orders we are bound to obey."

"I certainly cannot take that responsibility, if

I am to judge of your duty by my feelings," replied Dr. Gordon. "We will, therefore, continue our cruise until that duty is made plainer."

With this conclusion, Tomkins, and the men too, seemed satisfied. They turned in to rest, while he went out to give instructions in case of further disturbance. There was nothing more, however, to mark the history of the night, except that the hoot of the owl, coming from the woods back of the encampment, was in the course of time cautiously repeated, and was answered by a hoot from the coast below, accompanied by the screech of a panther.

CHAPTER XI.

FOG—"GANNET-VENISON" — DESTROYING RATS—
FRESH SUPPLY OF WATER—MAN POISONED, ANL
WHAT WAS DONE TO RELIEVE HIM—BIVOUAC—
ISLAND A-FIRE—EFFORTS—LOSSES AND UNWEL-
COME VISITORS.

HE next morning (Friday, October 29,)
dawned an hour later than usual, for so
heavy a mist had settled on both sea and
land, that not a ray of light was visible
in the sky until it was time by the watch to look
for the rising of the sun. Every leaf and twig
around was loaded with a drop of moisture—rain
it could not be called, since none had fallen, and
neither was it dew, yet everything was wet. The
mist did not lift itself until the sun was far above
the horizon.

So far as the work of exploration was concerned,
it was worse than useless to leave shore, because
it was not possible to *see* more than a few boat-
leagths away, and as for *hearing*, the sound of
passing oars could be better detected by their keeping perfectly quiet. About nine o'clock, however,

the fog began to rise, the sun shone out, and the day was pleasant as usual. They then weighed anchor, and sailed in the still water that prevailed between shore and the almost continuous chain of reefs and shoals, and low sandy islands and mangrove marshes that lay at the distance of a mile or more to seaward, and that broke or wholly arrested the waves from the open gulf.

This advantage to them of still water, which certainly was very great, was, however, almost counterbalanced by a corresponding disadvantage, for while they were exploring the shores of one side of an island, the boat of which they were in search might pass unseen on the other side. Another inconvenience, of a similar character, began to be sorely felt this same day—the bays, creeks and inlets occupied so much of their time that they were able to make very little progress southward—the close of the day finding them scarcely twenty miles from their previous night's encampment.

During their inland excursions large numbers of gannets flew past them overhead, so low as to be within easy gunshot. These are large birds, crane-like in shape and habits, only more heavily built, with white body and wings tipped with black. After several gangs had passed, Wheeler, who had observed them with some interest, turned to Dr. Gordon and inquired :

"Captain, are you fond of venison steaks?"

On being answered in the affirmative, he added:—

"I can obtain a nice supply for you, if allowed to shoot."

Dr. Gordon looked to Tomkins, who replied rather doubtfully:

"No objection to his shooting, on condition that he brings the venison."

"If I do not bring real deer's meat," answered Wheeler, "I will bring something so like it that no one can tell the difference."

"Well, shoot away," Tomkins rejoined.

Wheeler drew the ball from his musket, put in its place a load of large duck shot, waited until a flock of low-flying gannets appeared, and until two of them were in a range, when he brought them both down, shot through the head and neck. He laid them upon their backs, ripped open, with a sharp knife, the skin upon their breasts, and then, with *another knife*, cut large slices from the red fleshy muscles thus exposed, which he immersed in strong salt and water, to be kept there till wanted.

"I shall be very much disappointed," said he, "if, at dinner time to-day, or whenever else we have a chance for broiling, you do not all declare that you have been eating venison steak. The only difference any one can perceive, is that of a slightly birdy taste.

"You have tried it, then?" Tomkins interrogatively remarked.

"Often enough to know what I am talking about," replied Wheeler. "Indeed," said he in continuance, "the only secret in making venison steaks of the gannet consists in avoiding to touch the flesh with anything (hand or knife) that has touched the skin. You must butcher your meat as the market-man prepares his mutton; for in mutton, as in the gannet, the rank taste resides in the skin, and it is kept from the flesh by the same plan — rolling the skin so as not to touch the parts to be eaten."

Several of the men testified to the excellence of "gannet-venison," and Dr. Gordon remarked:

"The fact that the fishy taste of most sea birds is confined to the skin, is not new to me; and the plan that Corporal Wheeler has just practised is founded in sound philosophy. It is said that burial in the ground for several days will also remove the fishy taste. The Indians have a mode of freeing the flesh of skunks and pole-cats, even, from their disagreeable odor, so that they can be used for food."

"I have seen them so, *alive*," said Jones.

"Indeed!" said Dr. Gordon; "how and where?"

"In North Carolina," replied Jones, "in the house of a wealthy old gentleman in our neighborhood. His house and plantation were so over-

run with rats, which bred and multiplied in spite
of all the cats and traps he could command, that
he at last resolved to try snakes and pole-cats.
First, he obtained a number of pole-cats when
they were young, and dissected out the little bag
under the tail that holds all the unpleasant stuff;
the pole-cats then had no more of a bad smell than
a common house cat, and were far better mousers,
or, as I should say, *ratters*. They were most beautiful creatures, too, with their large bushy tails,
and parti-colored coats."

"But what about the snakes?" asked Thompson. "Ye're not going to forget to remember
about them."

"O, no," replied Jones, "I hadn't come to them
yet. The Doctor—I mean the old gentleman,
for he was a doctor—soon found, that although
the pole-cats killed all the rats to be found above
ground and in the open places, there were many
that burrowed and bred underground, and in the
walls, where the pole-cats couldn't get. He then
tamed about a dozen black snakes and chicken
snakes, and kept them about his house and barn.
These are excellent mousers, too, and they have
this advantage over a cat, that they can go into
every place where a rat can go, and devour the
young ones in their nest, as well as the old ones
in the burrows. The Doctor soon had the pleasure of seeing that his rats had disappeared; but

people say that he had a great *dis*pleasure along
with it. He was fond of company, and used to
have his house full and lively by day and by night.
But his snakes drove them away, for a gentleman
who staid there one night, found the next morning
that one of the Doctor's long-bodied mousers had
been his bedfellow. The story got wind, and from
that time people were afraid to come where they
were liable to meet such company."

While Jones was giving the above account, the
barge passed a fine bold bluff, and Wildcat, without saying a word to interrupt the narrative,
signed to Wheeler, who was sailing-master, to notice the beach, which glistened under the bright
sky as if wet with oozing water. Wheeler called
Tomkins' attention to it, and the boat was headed
shorewards.

Jones uttered the last words of his story just as
the bows grated upon the sands of the beach, and
the whole crew were immediately ordered ashore
to look for fresh water. An abundant supply of
this was soon found, and very good it was, but
how to get it into the runlet was a question, for
the sands were so quick that they instantly filled
any basin that was scooped. After having tried
many times and places in vain, Wildcat ran to the
barge and brought thence a closely woven cane
basket, such as is found in every Indian's lodge,
washed it clean, and sunk it in the sand where the

best water was to be obtained. It proved an excellent curb, and kept back the sand sufficiently long for the keg to be filled.

On returning to the boat, all observed that Simpson looked very pale and sick. Indeed, he was seriously ill, being afflicted with an incontrollable nausea, and wearing an expression of great distress. No sooner had he reached the boat than he addressed Dr. Gordon, saying :—

"Captain, unless you can do some'n to help me, I'm afeerd you will soon have a dead man aboard."

"Indeed," returned the Doctor ; "what is the matter ?"

"I'm afeerd I'm pisoned," he replied.

"Why do you fear so?" the Doctor asked.

"You know," said Simpson, " I haven't been myself since yesterday midday. When we landed for water, I thought I would take a dose of physic that I carry in my money wallet, that always helps me. But thar's a paper of *rat pison* there too, exactly the same in looks, and put up in exactly the same way as the other ; and I'm afeerd I have taken a dose from the wrong paper, for besides this dreadful sickness and vomiting, thar's a burning pain right h'yur," laying his hand on his stomach, "and it gets wuss and wuss every minute."

Dr. Gordon saw that the case was urgent, and

therefore adapted his means accordingly, for the man had swallowed *arsenic*, and any means adopted to save his life, if that were possible, must be used without delay. He, therefore, ordered a fire kindled, and made the man swallow pint after pint of melted lard, (this being the only oily matter on hand,) then of flour and water, and of mustard and salt, all tepid, until he had taken enough to have satiated an ox, had it not been rejected from the stomach almost as soon as received. In the course of half an hour, he pronounced him free from immediate danger, though still liable to severe effects from the irritation of the poison.

Tomkins thanked him for his prompt assistance, and for the information furnished them by his treatment of a case which, though rarely occurring, is always possible, and which few people know how to manage.

" My success," said the Doctor, " is attributable in part to the action of the poison itself, causing its own expulsion. It is said to be for this reason that while a small dose of arsenic will kill a dog, a large dose will seldom harm him."

" What was your object in giving him the lard ?" asked Tomkins.

" For the double purpose," he replied, " of coating the stomach with grease, and of acting as a quick and powerful emetic. It has been often noticed that *fat* hogs may swallow arsenic in doses

either large or small, and may even be bitten by
rattlesnakes, with impunity. Its grease, when
abundant, seems to protect the parts from poison."

"And would you treat all cases of poison in
this way?"

"Were I required to answer Yes or No, I should
answer Yes," he replied, "for this is the almost
universal rule, but some cases require particular
treatment.* The truth is, poisons are curious
things. It is said by those who have tried the experiment, that *milk*, which you know is perfectly
harmless to most stomachs, will produce death if
injected into the veins; and that the poison of a
rattlesnake, which is deadly enough when mixed
with the blood, may be received into the stomach
without injury. More than this, there is nothing
more necessary to life than air received into the
lungs; yet if a bubble of it were introduced into
the veins by careless bleeding, it would produce

* In all cases of poisoning, the first aim should be to *rid
the system of the offensive matter*, then to neutralize the poison
that remains, or to sheathe the parts against its action. In
protecting the stomach, the chief resort is had to oil or
grease, white of eggs, paste gruel of flour and water, sugar
and water, etc.

In poisoning from opium, the emetic should be followed
by *very strong coffee;* constant motion, under compulsion, if
necessary, and dashes of cold water on the head and breast.

For strychnine (nux vomica) in poisonous doses, **camphor**
is used.

instant death. So, you see, poisons are not always poisons, and wholesome things are not always wholesome."

Simpson was a decided invalid for several days, and never recovered his looks, bad as they were, so long as he and the others were together. The men seldom failed, on fair opportunity, to rally him upon his love of physic, and from that day forth they dubbed him Doctor.

No sign as yet appeared of the missing boat, and no clue could be obtained of either its passage or its fate. The spot was now passed abreast of which it had been seen by the cutter, and Dr. Gordon began to feel very uneasy at discovering how unbroken the shoal was to seaward, and how heavily the surf rolled over it under all winds from the Gulf. He feared that if his young people had reached land at all, they had been compelled to continue much farther down the coast. To these apprehensions, however, he gave no expression, except by an occasional interchange of thought with Tomkins or Wheeler, who, in return, said all they could to fill him with hope.

A little before sunset that evening they came to anchor at the south-eastern extremity of a little wooded key, which was about one and a half miles long, by a half or a quarter of a mile broad, and which was densely covered with dwarf palmettos, and other small growth, with an occasional tree of

larger proportions. A pleasant location for en-
camping was selected under a wide-spreading live
oak, whose umbrageous canopy was so thickly lined
with masses and long flowing streamers of grey
moss, that the tents, though brought ashore, were
not pitched, all being satisfied with the leafy shelter of the tree, and the mild and steady dryness
of the air.

So little work remained to be done, that four
of the men were dispatched to the seaward side
of the island to reconnoitre, and to learn the
probability of water for their next day's supply,
namely: Wheeler and Jones to the north-western
end; Thompson and Wildcat to the south-western.
They returned about dark, reporting, "No water
to be had;" but Wheeler and Jones reported
quantities of wild turkeys, of which they said
they might have brought back a shoulder-load if
it had been right for them to shoot; and Thompson and Wildcat each brought a turtle, which had
been caught on the south-western beach.

The night was magnificent. A splendid moon,
almost at the full, hanging over the mainland and
the intervening belt of water, gave to everything
around a soft and cheerful beauty, while Jupiter,
the brightest star of the sky, except Venus,
shot his silvery rays through the crevices of the
oak with a persistent glory that seemed to convey
hope and courage by its very steadiness.

By nine o'clock all were abed, except Thompson. He had been for sometime watching, without being able to understand it, a tinge of red light ir the north and northwest, which kept increasing until its lurid glare eclipsed the brightness of the moonlight. Not liking the appearance, he called for Wheeler, (who was sailing master by day and corporal of the guard by night,) and pointed it out to him,—indeed it needed no pointing out only that a person should be in a position to see it, for the whole northern and western horizon was a-blaze with light.

"It is fire!" said Wheeler. "The whole island is on fire, or soon will be."

All hands were immediately roused from their incipient slumbers, and called to the duty of fighting the approaching foe. So rapid had been its progress within the past few minutes, that when the men came out, they could distinctly hear the roar, like that of distant surf, or of a coming storm, and see the live flames leaping into the air and dancing among the tree-tops. The island was in a fearfully combustible state. The fallen and half decayed herbage of the palmetto, apparently untouched by any previous fire, covered the earth, like so much tinder, to the depth of one, two or more inches, while the green, fan-like leaves rose to the height of three or four feet above it, and waited only a few moments' heat to make them as inflammable as the stratum below, and the wind, rising, as it usually does with a fire, stimulated the flames to a fury indescribable. The men who came out at the call of Tomkins were first astonished, then fascinated with the terribly beautiful scene, and would have looked at it longer in eager admiration, but for the voice of command—

"To your work, men! You have no time to lose. Two of you—Magruder and Thompson—carry back to the beach such things as are liable to be hurt by the fire. Wheeler and Jones, do you help me clear a ring around the oak. Doctor, do, if you please, take charge of the sick man, and of anything else that may seem to you necessary. Wildcat may render his assistance to either you or me."

The men went to work with a will, and had nearly accomplished their several parts, when Tomkins, after a few words with Wheeler, returned to Dr. Gordon, and said,—

"I had intended to fire the outside of our cleared circle as soon as it was ready, so as to have a belt of burnt ground between us and that roaring giant yonder. But Wheeler reminds me that if we start a fire here, we may show our enemies on the main where we are; and as we probably have time enough, I propose to fire first the western side, just across the island from us, that it may seem as if the fire from our camp comes from a

spark blown from the other side. Will you let
Wildcat go with Wheeler for this purpose?"

" Assuredly," was the reply; and in less than a
minute, the two were forcing their way through
the tangled undergrowth. They had not made
half the distance ere they had impressive evidence
of the progress of the conflagration. A whizzing
sound overhead caused them to look upward, and
they saw a large gang of wild turkeys, that had
been running before the fire, rise on meeting them,
and take refuge in the trees; after which a tram-
pling announced something on the ground, and a
herd of deer passed careering wildly through the
undergrowth, and behind them they heard the
whine of a pup, and saw a she-wolf bearing in
her mouth a crying, and, no doubt, half-burnt
whelp.

" Poor brutes," said Wheeler, " there is many a
one suffering to-night, particularly of the young
deer and squirrels. Who would have expected so
much loss and suffering from so small a spark."

The fire, beginning at the north end of the
island, and driven by a wind from the west, had
spread rapidly east and slowly south, until it
appeared like an immense *seine of fire* stretched
across the island, driving everything before it that
had life, and swinging round upon its right staff.

Observing the progress southward to be much
more rapid on the east than on the west side of

the island, Wheeler took advantage of the first open place to start his fire, then called to Wildcat to unite with him in a speedy return to camp by way of the southern beach.

On their way, and while yet a quarter of a mile distant, they heard the voice of the Sergeant giving orders, then a confused sound of several voices together, in the midst of which came the report of one, then of two other muskets.

"I'm afraid," said Wheeler, "there is trouble in camp. Let us run."

They came at full speed, which was not slackened by observing that the light at the camp flashed up into a momentary glare, attended with another confusion of voices. On arriving, they saw that the fire had overleaped the clear ring which had been made, and had extended down to the beach, where the articles had been sent to be out of danger, but where, unfortunately, there was a little patch of tall grass that took fire and conveyed it to the tent and some other combustible materials heaped together on shore. This was not the result of carelessness, but of accident—a sudden whirlwind, created by the heat of a burning tree-lap, (as the head of a fallen tree is called,) had carried some cinders beyond their usual bounds, and set on fire the part supposed to be safe.

On the alarm being raised, the men rushed back

to save their goods, but not in time for the tents and some valuable articles of clothing. A stack of muskets had also been reached by the fire, and were so badly scorched that one of them was discharged, throwing down the others, so that they exploded also, together with a cartridge-box or one of the men.

To increase the confusion, a blind wolf — rendered so by the heat and smoke through which she had passed, or else by the discharge of the muskets (for she appeared at the moment they exploded) — sprang in among the men, snarling furiously and snapping at their legs, until she was arrested by being pinned to the earth with a bayonet.

The loss, however, which was most seriously felt at the moment by the men, thirsting intensely from their hot work, was that of their drinking-water; for Thompson, in his Irish haste to extinguish the burning tents and clothing, had emptied the contents of the runlet by bucket-fulls upon the flames where most needed.

For a time, the smoke, prevailing from the north and west, threatened to drive them all from the island; but, at last, the land-breeze, gaining the ascendancy, enabled them to breathe freely, and to think of resting. And it was time, for midnight had now come, and in five hours would arrive the light of another day, and the call for renewed labor.

All assembled under the oak, which was now their only shelter, and, as soon as they were sufficiently composed, the Sergeant said,—

"There are two points of business requiring our attention before we go to sleep: one is, to determine what we shall do for water; and the other is, to learn how that fire in the woods got out." To which Wheeler promptly responded,—

"I wish, Sergeant, that I could speak to the first point as certainly as I can to the second. I have seen no signs of fresh water on the island, though I suppose, from the deer and turkeys we met, that there must be some somewhere. As for the fire, I am pretty sure it came from my pipe. When Jones and I got to the nor'west end of the island last evening, we felt pretty tired; so we lighted our pipes and sat on a log to rest. My pipe had in it only tobacco enough for a few whiffs, so when it ceased giving smoke, I knocked out the ashes on the log, not dreaming there was a live spark in it. And that is how the fire got out."

"A costly smoke," said Tomkins, "but one that we shall have to excuse."

"It was a bigger one than I intended when I struck * my match," rejoined Wheeler; "and sorry

---

* We use the word "*struck*" in deference to the present mode of originating fire. No doubt this term will change in the course of time, so as to express some other mode, not

I

enough I am for it. But it is only a circumstance compared with what I saw once on the
prairies."

"We must remember that, and call for it some
other time," said Dr. Gordon. "In the meantime,
we must inquire about water."

"I have a canteen full of it, in the boat," said
Thompson, "and the company are welcome to all
of it, except one drink."

"I have a canteen of it, too," added Magruder;
"I'll save one drink and give the rest away."

"I, too," said Wildcat, with a merry laugh, in
which everybody joined, and in the midst of which
Dr. Gordon observed, —

"I do not know how fair it would be in us,
who have no canteens of water, to accept the offer
of those who have, for this would be giving us
three drinks apiece to their one; for I see that
Simpson also is supplied."

The question about water was settled for the
night. It was understood that the next day's
supply should be sought in the morning. But
the adventures for the night were not quite over.

"I have often heard," said Magruder, "that it

as yet in vogue. In the year 1831, the most approved
matches, known as "Lucifers," were "*drawn*" through a
fold of sand-paper; though many people continued still to
"*dip*" in a vial of sulphuric acid, or of phosphorus, according to the nature of the preparation. Flint and steel, with
tinder, were also in common use.

is an ill wind that blows nobody any good; but
I'd like to know what good is blowed to anybody
by the fire to-night?"

"This good, at least," said Wheeler, quickly,
"though I am sorry to buy it at such cost, that
we shall have no trouble from *mosquitoes*. There
were plenty of them when we landed."

"And another good," added Jones, looking
rather mischievously at Thompson, and alluding
to a peculiarity he had boasted of his native isle
in being free from the annoyance of serpents, "is
that we shall not have any trouble from rattlesnakes."

Scarcely had he said this, however, before
Tomkins sung out: "Take care, men! *there* is one
now!" and, sure enough, there, within a yard of
Thompson, lay a huge rattle-snake, drawn up in
his coil, and shaking his rattles at a most significant rate. He had been driven from his hole
under a burning log, and had come into the
cleared circle to escape the fire. The scared Irishman, with an exclamation of horror, leaped instantly away, and was barely in time to escape the
fangs of the venomous reptile, which threw itself
forward a full yard and a half to strike him. The
next moment, however, it lay motionless under a
well-timed blow across the neck from Jones' ramrod—for it is very easily killed by a blow on
that part. On being examined, it was ascertained

to be five and a half feet long, and to weigh about ten pounds. Its tail contained fourteen rattles.

This incident closed the history of the night. All hands, worn out with unusual labor and late hours, were ready for sleep, and all slept soundly, except Thompson, whose occasional movements and muttered exclamations proved that he was dreaming of snakes.

CHAPTER XII.

DETAIL TO LOOK FOR WATER AGAIN — THE RAC COON — WILDCAT'S MERRY PRANKS — THE CAP-TURED SQUIRRELS — HABITS OF THE RACCOON — NEWS FROM THE YOUNG MAROONERS, AND POS-SIBLE NEWS OF RILEY AND SAM.

T was a weary-looking company that arose from their bivouac under the oak on the morning of Saturday, October 30, 1831. But a sense of weariness soon gave way to merriment, on seeing how oddly each looked in his last night's costume of dust and smoke.

"Our first duty this morning is to obtain water to drink," said Sergeant Tomkins. "If we can-not obtain it on this key, we must at once seek it elsewhere. Corporal Wheeler will please choose some man to accompany him on another tour along the western beach; and Mr. Morgan * has proved himself so expert in water-works, that, if Dr. Gordon permit, I will send him with a companion along the eastern shore, (Dr. Gordon bowed assent,) and he will also pick his man for this purpose. Neither party must be absent over an hour."

Scarcely had the sergeant ceased speaking before Wildcat, in response to a sly wink of invitation from his friend, said, "I pick Jones."

"And I choose Thompson, my comrade in misfortune last night," said Wheeler.

The parties immediately separated, each having several extra canteens for water, slung over their shoulders, and also furnished with some woollen and fine linen as a filter to the mouth of the canteens, in case of need. In the meantime, the party at the tree prepared breakfast and reloaded the barge ready for departure. The explorers returned within the limited time, bringing a supply of water, it is true, but none which they could report as being more than barely endurable.

Wheeler and Thompson, in addition to their supplies of water, bore upon their shoulders a pole, on which hung a very large turtle, tied by

---

* Willy Wildcat would hardly be recognized under his official title, without some notification.

the legs with silk grass,* the long, tough leaves of which, an inch wide and one or two feet long, form excellent wild-wood ties, capable of supporting each from one to two hundred pounds' weight. This turtle was laid comfortably on its back beside the others taken the evening before, and promised an abundant supply of delicious steaks, and stews, and broils, which the most fastidious epicure might envy.

When Jones and Wildcat came into camp, there were exclamations of another sort. On the shoulders of the first sat demurely what Thompson, at first, took for a fox, then for a wildcat, with a sharp face strongly marked with black stripes, then for a kind of ring-tailed monkey, but which proved to be, what he had never before seen, a young raccoon. Jones had espied it perched in the fork of a small persimmon-tree, looking very disconsolately on the sea of ashes and cinders around, some of which still smoked, and seemed to keep the poor brute in mortal fear. On being approached, it made no attempt to escape, and offered no resistance to capture, but seemed to hail with delight the approach of deliverance. A few leaves of the bear-grass (silk-grass) were woven,

---

* Known also as *bear-grass* — the *Yucca filamentosa* of botanists — having filaments of thread stretching from end to end of the leaf, and almost equal in toughness to the sinew fibres of the deer

as they walked, into both collar and cord, by which it was for the time made secure.

Some of the men thought it was a shame that Jones did not give to Wildcat the pet which seemed so much better suited to a boy than a man. But when one of them was preparing to express himself to this effect, there appeared a mysterious commotion in Wildcat's pouch, (occupying a place like a Highlander's, over the pit of the stomach,) which caused him to press his hand hastily there, saying as he did so,—

"Wy-gus-chay!" (the Muscogee for "quit that!")

Then turning to Thompson a face that seemed to be writhing with pain and pleading for sympathy, he exclaimed, with a terrible groan, "Oh! he bite! I feel him gnaw!"

The Irishman began to be seriously concerned for his dusky friend, and was about to call Dr. Gordon, when the artful boy, satisfied with this exhibition of his powers of acting, threw off from his countenance the mask of pain, and bursting into a laugh at the success of his joke, so well suited to a young savage, he added,—

"He bite! he gnaw! but he don't hurt!" then, putting his hand into the pouch, he drew thence a beautiful squirrel, nearly half-grown, which he proceeded to place upon his shoulder, ard to supply with a piece of cracked hickory

nut. The graceful little thing, after one start of
surprise, and a quick dash under the fold of the
buckskin hunting-shirt, to hide itself from the
unexpected crowd, took its place with a perfectly
home-like air upon Wildcat's shoulder, curled its
tail upon its back, in the shape of the letter S,
and proceeded composedly to eat its nut.

While thus engaged, Magruder who had been
absent, came from the beach and joined the company, when there began to be another commotion
in the pouch, another pressing of the hand upon
it, and other exclamations and writhings as before,
with the eyes turned now towards the new-comer;
but the Scotchman was too wary to be caught by
such appearances. He merely smiled a grim
acknowledgment of having detected the snare,
and then Wildcat, inserting his hand into the
pouch, drew out another squirrel, the mate of the
first, and placed it with a piece of nut upon the
other shoulder.

Upon inquiry by some of the lookers-on, it was
ascertained that soon after the capture of the *Coon,*
the squirrels were discovered by Wildcat on a
small tree, from which they evidently wished to
escape, but dared not, on account of the terrible-
looking bed of ashes. The two explorers went to
the tree, and standing one on each side, held out
their hands in an inviting way, saying, in soft,
encourag'ng tones, "Bunny! Bunny! Petty!

Petty ! ' when the little, trustful things, seeming to understand the language of tone and gesture, actually came down the tree, smelt of the extended hands, and allowed themselves to be taken * and placed in Wildcat's pouch. As soon as their thirst was relieved, for they are large drinkers, and seemed to have suffered much for the want of water, they were supplied with a handful of sweet acorns from the live-oak, poured into the pouch, after eating which, at their leisure, each rolled itself into a ball, and slept until the captors returned to camp.

Both these varieties of pets became great favor ites with the men, and friends to each other. The squirrels enjoyed the full freedom of the barge, and would chase each other up and down the rigging, and from shoulder to shoulder of the men, and dive into their pockets after nuts and other eatables. The raccoon, being naturally of a more staid and dignified demeanor, was at first annoyed at having the little frolicsome squirrels leap upon its back, and clamber on its head, and showed some signs of displeasure, but it also soon became reconciled, like a good philosopher, to what it could not help, and finally began to toy with its little companions in return. It soon

* This is not a mere sketch from fancy. The writer witnessed a similar scene only a few days before this paragraph was written.

learned the way both to the supply of crackers
and ship-bread, and to the water-can, and, according to its peculiar habits, would always soak its
dry food in water before eating.* Nobody's
pocket, and no box nor little hole where anything
could be kept, was safe from the sly intrusion of
its paws.

On leaving their fire-marked and thirsty island,
the boat's crew made directly for the main, and
they had not sailed many hours along its beach
before the now raging thirst of the men was
allayed by a large supply of the sweetest and
coolest water they had found since leaving Tampa.
Ah, how delicious is good water! We, who live
in this land of fountains and of rivers, can no
more appreciate it than most people appreciate
the blessed light of the sun and the free breath
of heaven. None but asthmatics can properly
estimate the last, and none but the temporarily
blind, the first. Yet Solomon knew how to value
good water. With all his wisdom and his wealth,
he must, some time or other, have been thirsty, or
he could not have penned the words : "As cold
water to a thirsty soul, so is good news from a far

---

* It is this peculiarity which caused the raccoon to be
known by naturalists as *Lotor*, or washer, *Ursus Lotor;* for
it was classed by Linnæus in the general family of *bears*,
on account of its carnivorous and frugivorous habits, and
its *plantigrade* foot, which means its habit of walking flat-
footed

country." * The man who wrote that must have drawn his picture from experience. We almost partake the enjoyment of the royal writer as he lifts to his eager lips a jewelled cup, filled with water from David's well at † Bethlehem, and dewy with cold from the snows of Hermon.

Nothing more of special interest occurred till late in the day. The key, inside of which they were then passing, stretched its low, sandy barrier so far southward, that Dr. Gordon was apprehensive lest the missing boat might pass them unobserved upon the Gulf side. He, therefore, requested that some one might be sent to the western beach to reconnoitre; and Wheeler, who was regarded by all as being peculiarly fitted for duties of this sort, on account of his keen observation, was detailed for the purpose. He was gone much longer than was expected, and though he could be occasionally seen ascending some wind-raised hillock of sand, and directing his spy-glass down the coast, the only answer he gave to the signal of inquiry made from the barge, was a wave of the hand, signalling in return that the barge should pass slowly down the inside beach.

For a time the hearts of all beat high with hope that he had spied the lost company; but this was dissipated under the inquiry, "If so, why not come and report the fact?" No, he was mani-

* Prov. xxv. 25.   † 2 Samuel, xxiii. 15.

festly detained by some other reason, and their curiosity was excited to a pretty high pitch when, after a longer disappearance than usual, he was seen walking with rapid steps towards the barge, having something in his hand covered with a large bandanna handkerchief, as if for concealment.

With a grave, yet highly pleased expression of countenance, Wheeler went directly to Dr. Gordon and said, —

"Captain, what would you think of my bringing you a message direct from your children?"

Dr. Gordon turned somewhat pale, and his voice almost choked as he asked, —

"Are they here?"

Wheeler was troubled to see how much more of hope had been excited by his words than he intended, and he hastily replied, —

"No, *they* are not here. I wish they were; but here is a message from them which I doubt not will give you joy."

He then unwrapped from its envelope and put into Dr. Gordon's hands a little vessel, nicely carved out of a piece of white cedar, and ballasted with buckshot so as to right itself upon the water, even after being upset. The little sails were so rigged that whenever she "yawed," as sailors call the turning of a vessel out of her course, she would "luff up" into the wind, or run before it as the case might be, but always keep moving. On its

tiny flag of white silk was the word " Hope," and
on the smooth white deck were deeply pencilled,
in a female hand, the words :—

" SCHOONER HOPE.

Harold McIntosh, Builder ; Robert Gordon, Rig-
ger ; Mary Gordon, Sail-maker ; Frank Gordon,
Captain and Supercargo.

Bound from Marooner's Island to Bellevue, Tampa, with a full freight of love and good wishes."

This precious little toy Dr. Gordon took into
his hands, and, with all the composure he could
command, examined in every part. Not a word
was exchanged between him and the rest, only a
few whispers and low murmurs of the voice, beginning with Wheeler, conveyed from man to man
the general fact that the young marooners had been
heard from. Unable longer to control his feelings,
Dr. Gordon drew back as far as possible from observation, covered his face with both hands, and
trembled with emotion, while the men, who used
every excuse for looking in an opposite direction,
could not help seeing an occasional tear trickle
through his fingers.

As soon as the Doctor had finished his examination, and had laid the little vessel on the seat,
Tomkins took it up, scrutinized its various parts,
then passed it to the men. Poor Wildcat, who
could not read, and who was, beyond comparison,

the most powerfully excited person aboard, except
Dr. Gordon, looked pleadingly to his friend Jones
to read and explain to him every word. Then the
men began to talk, first in low whispers, then in
an under-tone, and at last more freely, until they
had exchanged thoughts upon all the points connected with the little vessel and its launchers
The conclusions at which they seemed satisfactorily
to arrive, and which Dr. Gordon was much interested to hear, although he had not as yet allowed
himself to say a word, were : —

1st. That the missing company had reached
land in safety ;

2d. That the land they had reached was an
island ;

3d. That this island could not be very far away ;

4th. That when that vessel was made and
launched, the young people were at leisure, in good
spirits, and in no fear ;

5th. That this toy had probably been made
and launched within the past two days.

These conclusions, which tallied closely with
those of his own mind, were very comforting to
the grief-stricken father, and caused him to feel
very near to his lost ones. There were some
other questions also discussed by the men on which
there was a strong division of opinion. These were:

1st. Whether that island lay to the north or
the south of their present position.

2d. Whether the young people were most probably then upon the island, or had left it and returned to Tampa.

3d. Whether, therefore, it was worth while to continue their search down the coast; and whether it were not better to turn northward, and to search the coast on their way home.

These several points were freely discussed, and some important facts adduced about currents and counter-currents in the Gulf; but when, after discussing the third point, some one appealed to Dr. Gordon to know whether he thought best to return to Tampa, or to keep down the coast, his reply was—

"To keep down the coast. My impression is," said he, "that they are still below us."

This decided the question about the voyage.

In addition to what had been said, Wheeler took occasion to remark that one reason why his exploring tour upon the Gulf side of the key had been so much prolonged, was that he could catch occasional glimpses of some object far south which seemed to him like a canoe with two persons aboard. Thinking that they might be Dr. Gordon's negro man, in company with Riley, he had tried, by ascending the most elevated points of the key, to obtain a better view of them, but the curvature of the earth hid from him all but the head and shoulders of the men, if indeed they were men, as he supposed.

Towards sunset they approached another low island of pines, where they landed and prepared to encamp for the night.

CHAPTER XIII.

THE EMERALD ISLE AND ITS INHABITANTS — AT-TACK AND DEFENCE — MUSQUITOS AND GALLI-NIPPERS — INGENIOUS DEVICES — MUSQUITO KEY —PLANS FOR THE DAY—ADIEU TO MUSQUITO KEY —CAPTURE OF FLYING FISH — SIMPLE SERVICES — WORSHIP — WHAT IS IT?

F all the places for encampment which they had found since leaving Tampa, the one selected this evening seemed for a time the most promising of comfort. At a distance, its dense growth of low, stunted pines, and its glassy surrounding of shining water, made it appear like a great emerald set in a surface of crystal. And when they landed, the balsamic fragrance of the trees was refreshing, and the measureless profusion of straw-like leaves overspreading the ground, and drifted here and there by the wind into soft luxurious beds, promised all that men, wearied as they were, could ask for a night's repose.

They landed early, and early made ready for orders to "turn in," but they received at the same time decided information that no sleep was to be enjoyed there that night, except by the use of some uncommon means. For with the increase of darkness, increased also the swarms of musquitos with which the island was in no ordinary degree infested. Whether numbers made them bold, or famine made them desperate, they did not come with the usual modest song of the musquito of other places, serenading first their intended victims, then timidly alighting on some exposed part, and seeming, by their hesitation, almost to ask the privilege of sucking an evening's meal of blood; these gave no concerts and asked no permission, but with the " Whing!" of a rifle ball, and with the directness of one, pitched at once upon the spot selected, and then, quick as thought, pushed their little poisonous bills into the rich fountains underlying the skin.

It has been remarked by some one as a great pity that these insects cannot draw their coveted supplies of blood without first diluting it by the injection of their painful poison;* for most persons would submit patiently to a mere loss of

* It is said that the stinging musquitoes are all *females*, that the blood they suck is necessary to the production of their eggs; and that each female asks but *one full meal* to enable her to fulfil her course. The males, distinguishable by their slender bodies and delicately plumed heads, do not sting.

blood sufficient to feed a regiment of them, rather than keep up the constant fight necessary for defence. But, no, the first intimation of their stealthy phlebotomy given after their complimentary serenade, is a sharp, stinging pain in the spot attacked and a constant itching and burning for minutes afterwards. True, if let alone until the meal is finished, each musquito will suck out most of its own poison along with the blood, so as to leave scarcely any trace of its visit; but few persons have fortitude enough to endure the torment.

The musquitoes of this island were as remarkable for their energy and adroitness as for their boldness and numbers. They not only attacked those parts of the person where the skin was exposed, but the larger variety, known as *gallinippers,* pushed their probosces through the thinner parts of the clothing, and some of the men declared with all seriousness that they had been actually bitten through the pores of their boots.*

The annoyance was so great that every available means was used for defence. First of all, there were several bright fires kindled and kept up at some distance to the leeward of the bivouac, for the purpose of decoying the insects thither to their destruction. The expedient, however, was of doubtful utility, for though many were thus

* This is no exaggeration of the powers of the gallinipper, as many persons can testify.

led off, and some of them destroyed, many more
were attracted from a distance that probably would
never have come but for the light. Another plan,
much more effectual, was that of a smoke to the
windward. A quantity of gray moss, and of green
pine-leaves, was amassed, and a small pile of it
was heaped upon a thoroughly burning brand and
renewed whenever necessary. By this means was
produced a dense, continuous smoke which was
tolerable, if not pleasant, to the men, but intolerable to the musquitoes. There were three such
smokes kept up within ten feet of the sleep-
ing-places. Yet neither was this device effectual,
except in part. These being the only plans of a
public character that could be thought of, the Sergeant announced to the men that each must now
exercise his own ingenuity in devising modes of
individual defence. And it was almost laughable
to see some of the plans adopted.

Simpson, who by this time was nearly well
again, took from his private stores a lump of deer
suet, with which he gave a heavy coating of grease
to every portion of his skin exposed to attack, remarking, —

"They can stand smoke, but they can't stand
grease."

Jones had been thoughtful enough just before
dark to gather several handfuls of pennyroyal, a
strongly aromatic plant, with which he rubbed
his face, neck and hands, saying, —

" I know it will keep off fleas, and I reckon the musquitoes will not fancy it much."

Before the company had gone to sleep ~e was heard to laugh rather merrily, and on being asked the reason, replied, —

" I am laughing at the musquitoes. Not a fellow of them has yet had a bite of me. I can feel them alight on my skin, but the moment they smell the pennyroyal they rise with a kick. It makes me laugh to think how disappointed they must be."

With all his boasting, however, Jones' face and hands the next morning looked as if he were suffering an attack of measles. The perfume of his pennyroyal was a good defence so long as it lasted, but it needed renewal every half hour.

Wheeler's device was, to appearance, as ineffective as it was novel. He took the shrimp net, of which the meshes were at least half an inch square, and selecting a spot shaded from the light of the fires, he spread it over a ridge pole so that it should cover his face and hands without touching them. He said that musquitoes would never pass through a net, even when the meshes were much larger than these, unless they could see light on the other side. He slept without complaint through the night, though neither was he without marks the next morning.*

* Herodotus describes this mode as practised by fishermen ρ Egypt more than 2000 years ago.

Sergeant Tomkins, who was fortunate enough
to have a large tough newspaper, shaped it into a
helmet for head and neck, having cut a V-like
orifice for breathing, and leaving the point of the
V to cover the end of his nose. His hands were
well protected under his blanket.

Wildcat stripped his deer-skin hunting-shirt
wholly from one arm, and partly from the other,
doubling the loose end of the partly filled sleeve
to cover the enclosed hand, and spreading the body
of the shirt over all other parts exposed, except
his head, which he closely enveloped in his turban,
leaving only a small orifice for breathing.

Dr. Gordon, well knowing the reputation of the
coast for musquitoes, had provided himself, before
leaving home, with a yard or two of musquito
netting, by means of which he was perfectly safe
from attack.

Poor Thompson and Magruder resorted first to
one device then another, and were satisfied the
next morning, (at least Thompson said that *he*
was,) that they had received their full share of attention from their nimble little visitors. But
when they came to talk the matter over, Magruder, looking at his swollen hands, said,—

" You, who were born and raised in a musquit
country may know better than I how to keep from
being stung, but — every man to his trade! — I have
an advantage over you all, as cook, in curing the

bites after they have been made," and with this he took from the cook's stores a spoonful cf soda, which he dissolved in a little water and applied to the swollen places, remarking that wet soda, or even strong salt and water, would relieve the sting of any poisonous creature, whether gnat, wasp, or scorpion.

To which Dr. Gordon added: "That is true, for animal poisons are said to be powerful *acids*, and the best corrective of these are alkalies, such as hartshorn, soda, potash, or even lye or soap suds."

And Thompson also said: "If we are to take Magruder's rule, 'Every man to his trade,' I must not slight mine, for I carry with me a cure for every sting I have tried yet. It is the oil to be had from the stem of my pipe. It is awful bad-smelling, but it is as good to cure as it is bad to smell." *

By unanimous vote, the island was named Mus-QUITO KEY.

This day being the Christian Sabbath, Dr. Gordon called the crew together at the close of breakfast, and said to them:—

"It has been my custom, as a Christian man, to honor the Sabbath by making it, if possible, a day

* This oil, however it may be used with impunity by tough old hunters, cannot be applied with equal safety in all cases. It is said to have produced fatal effects, once, when applied to a raw place on the skin of a child.

of rest and of worship. Such was my intention to-day, and when, last evening, we selected this island, which looked so beautiful at a distance, I said to myself, 'How delightful a spot it will be for spending the Sabbath!' But you perceive how impossible it is to carry out this intention. We are forced to seek some other place. I propose, therefore, with the consent of Sergeant Tomkins, to resume our voyage, and continue it until we find a place suitable for stopping; and in case we do not in time, that we spend a season on board in the exercise of worship."

The smile of pleasure which overspread the faces of the men showed that the proposal accorded with their preferences. A half hour, or more, before embarking, was allowed them to pay such extra attention to personal appearance as was possible; then they took their places aboard and bade a joyful adieu to the deceitful beauties of Musquito Key. For hours they sailed along the coast, looking in vain for some place to stop, and greatly delayed in their onward progress by a broad sheet of water stretching inland, studded with low hummocks, covered with mangroves and sea-myrtles, which it was necessary for them to explore before passing.

The only incident of interest occurring as they sailed this morning, was the capturing, or rather the self-deliverance, of a number of flying-fish. Quite a large school of these timid little creatures, alarmed by vonitnes or some other object of terror in the water, arose from their native element, and flying frantically through the air, plunged into the water about one hundred yards beyond. Four or five of these struck the sails of the barge and fell between the gunwales. Their immense pectoral fins, expanded into wings, were quite a curiosity to those who were not already familiar with their peculiarities.

About eleven o'clock Sergeant Tomkins announced to the men that having not yet found a place on land suitable for the purpose, they would have religious service aboard. Each man retained his accustomed seat, and was ready to fulfil any duty that might be necessary, while the boat was under easy sail, and while every needless labor was avoided; but the moment the beginning of service was announced, the head of each was uncovered in token of reverence for that Presence which is always recognized in the act of worship.

Before they commenced, however, and while Dr. Gordon was making ready, one of the men, possessed of a fine voice, began a familiar hymn, set to solemn, wild music, in which the others united, particularly in the chorus. This voluntary, well suited in sentiment and air to their circumstances, floated softly over the waters, and was an excellent preparative for what came after. The

vcices of the men were rich and strong, but, having
no surrounding objects to cause reverberation, they
sounded weak and child-like on that wild surface
of water ; thus illustrating practically their lonely
condition, and causing them to realize more than
otherwise was possible the fact of their depend-
ence, as recognized in the words soon after to be
repeated, " Our Father who art in Heaven."

The exercises were few and simple. Without
any book but the Bible, Dr. Gordon repeated from
memory two suitable hymns, (leaving the tunes to
the taste of the men,) read several portions of
Scripture in a style of unaffected reverence, made
a few simple remarks, and offered prayer to the
best of his ability, in language suited to their circumstances, then announced the services concluded.
Brief and artless as they were, they seemed to
touch deep chords in the hearts of the men, and
to bring out some of their best feelings. Magruder,
who was usually a man of few words, but who
had shown throughout the services a reverentia!
spirit, took occasion, as soon as the men had begun
to talk freely, to say, in a tone of great sincerity,
to Dr. Gordon,—

" Captain, I do like that free-and-easy way of
yours in conducting our worship to-day. It made
me feel at home."

" I am not sure that I understand you " returned Dr. Gordon.

"What I mean is this," Magruder said; "that oftentimes when we attend Divine service, the preacher or chaplain makes us feel by his manner that the services are *his, not ours;* but you made us feel to-day that the service was ours, too. Rough as I am, and little reason as I give any one to suspect it, I do love to worship sometimes."

"It is pleasant to hear you say this," Dr. Gordon rejoined, "and no doubt others feel so at times, whose ordinary conduct gives no sign of it."

"I do, for one," said Wheeler.

"And I, for another," said Jones.

And all the rest (except Simpson, whose dark, impassive countenance seldom gave token of sympathy) looked as if they were ready to say the same.

"Worship," continued Dr. Gordon, "is one of the noblest acts in which any creature can engage, and, in some form or other, it is suited to the capacity of every right-minded being — simple enough for a child, sublime enough for an angel."

"You do not believe, then," Sergeant Tomkins interrogatively remarked, "that the church and the pulpit are necessary to it?"

"As much so as tables and chairs are to our daily food," replied Dr. Gordon. "They are a part of the *decencies,* and will be provided by all persons, according to their means, who cultivate a proper respect; but they may be dispensed with in time of need, (as was the case just now,) and, therefore, they are no part of the essentials."

"What is worship?" Tomkins asked, and Dr Gordon was about to reply, "The homage of the heart," when, observing the eye of the young Indian fixed on him in eager gaze, he replied,—

"It is the *talking of the heart with the Great Spirit*, whom we are taught to call 'Our Father in Heaven.'"

Then pausing a moment, and observing that all were waiting, as if for more, he went on to say,—

"Any person who can come before God, in any place, and in any language, or even without a word spoken by the lip, and say, with a loving and trustful heart, 'Our Father who art in Heaven,' is, in some sense, a worshipper. He may not have attained a very high grade as such, but he has attained a *grade*—he has learned the first letter in the alphabet of Divine knowledge— he has begun to use the language of heaven."

"And beautiful language it is!" ejaculated Thompson, with strong emotion. "When I kneel down, (for I do kneel sometimes,) and say, 'Oh Lord!' or 'Oh God Almighty!' it scares me. I want to get further off, for I doubt whether I know Him; but when I say, 'Our Father in Heaven!' I feel somehow as I used to feel when

I was a boy, and was coming to one that I knew, and that cared for me."

"You express yourself very naturally," said the Doctor, while his eye kindled and his heart warmed towards the free-spoken man. "I am no preacher, and therefore cannot speak with authority, but it is my opinion that of all the feelings which have come down to us from the Garden of Eden, the least impaired by the Fall are those of the parent to the child. They are those of the purest and most perfect love known on earth — a love that does not measure its gifts with a stingy hand, but which takes pleasure in giving pleasure, and which knows no limit except its own power and the other's good. Now, this is the feeling which Jesus Christ teaches us to recognise in God whenever we can come to Him and say, 'Our Father in Heaven!' I confess," he continued, brightening with his theme, and raising his voice with a gesture of earnestness, "that sometimes, when I catch a glimpse of what is implied in those first words of the Lord's Prayer, I am almost ready to cry out, Halleluia."

For more than half an hour afterward, it was observable that there was little conversation among the men, and what there was partook of a serious character. It was easy for a reader of the human face to discern in theirs the renewal of old and long-neglected lessons, learned perhaps at the paternal home, and perhaps also at the mother's knee.

CHAPTER XIV.

HE afternoon was spent in sailing lei-
surely among the multitude of small
islands which dotted the coast, of which
there was not one, however, which was
eligible as a place of sojourn for the night, or even
for a few hours' rest; and when the sun began to
decline, there were some apprehensions lest they
should be compelled to seek their next stopping-
place upon the main, which they preferred to avoid
on account of possible hostilities from the Indians.

More delightful weather for their excursion
could scarcely have been desired than they had
and were still having; yet about three o'clock in
the afternoon, Wheeler, who had been observed to
look repeatedly at the rigging, and also at the sky
in their rear, was heard to say anxiously,—

"If we were in Texas, or even in Northern

Louisiana, I should say that we are about to have what the people out there call a norther."

"What makes you think so?" inquired Dr. Gordon.

"Yon cobwebs," he replied, pointing to something like gossamer that could occasionally be seen floating in the air and caught upon the rigging. "I never expected to see it so far east as this, and across the Gulf too, and therefore I do not know exactly how to calculate upon it, but in Texas I should have no doubt."

"No doubt of what?" asked Tomkins rather abruptly.

"That we ought to make for shore at an early hour, and prepare for rough times to-night," Wheeler quietly answered.

"I never neglect warnings of that kind," said Dr. Gordon, "and you have my consent to land at the first place that promises safety. But do inform me, as you seem to know, what are the signs and circumstances of a Texan norther?"

"One of their worst signs," Wheeler returned, "is that they have no signs at all, but come upon you with all their force before you know it. At this season of the year, and after a spell of just such weather as we have been having, and when men have been wearing their summer clothes, all of a sudden comes a cold, dry wind, (not always dry,) from the Rocky Mountains, and in less than three hours, often in less than half an hour, it is so cold that you can hardly get clothes or fire warm enough to keep you from freezing. It may be expected any time from October to April, and it lasts usually from one to four days, though I knew one once in the Gulf that lasted nine days."

"No one, to look at the bright sky overhead, would prophesy rain or change of weather soon," said Magruder, "but I have an old bone in my back that generally gives warning of bad weather, and since we have been talking I heard it very plainly say, 'Look out!'"

"Then we *will* look out," added Dr. Gordon, "for bright as the skies are, it would be folly in us to neglect such signs, especially at this time of the year, and of spring-tide on the coast."

It was fully an hour by sun when Wheeler turned the bow of the barge into a snug little bay made by a tongue of land, (whether island or not they could not determine,) which promised a safe protection in its smooth water against any violence from seaward. The bluff, too, was unusually high for that part of the coast, and there was a convenient level just below its highest part, where they could encamp for the night, with the advantage of having their sleeping-place protected in a measure from wind, and the light of their fire concealed from observers on the main. Here the barge was at first moored, and the flukes of the anchor were sunk amid the roots of a stump high upon the beach. The tarpaulin of the boat was rigged up as a tent for Dr. Gordon, and while some of the men looked rather rueful at the prospect of spending a night exposed to the cold predicted by Wheeler, and the rain predicted by Magruder's "old bone," Wildcat said cheerily to them,—

"Make *house*—make *Injin* house. Palmetto plenty."

The suggestion was valuable, for palmetto booths are easily made, and when properly constructed are as impervious to rain as the roof of a house. By Sergeant Tomkins' order, the men immediately dispersed to obtain the materials necessary for this purpose, consisting of poles, silk-grass, and the fan-like leaves of the palmetto, and long before dark they had the comfort of seeing a substantial shelter for their persons * in case of need, and of having all needful things from the barge stowed there also.

---

* Shelters of this kind are so cheaply constructed wherever the palmetto abounds, and are withal so useful, that a brief description of the mode of making them may not be amiss. Horizontal poles, about a foot apart, are fastened to the rafters. Three or four (sometimes half a dozen) fans of the dwarf palmetto are laid flat together, and tied to these horizontal poles, stem-end up, by means of strips torn from the side of the fans. The stems are tied *under* the pole next above, while the leaves lie smoothly *upon* the supporting pole

It is oftentimes the case that, after having worked hard to protect ourselves against anticipated evil, we find that the evil does not come, and we feel as if there has been labor lost. So it seemed to the crew in the present instance. Wheeler and Magruder had croaked so loudly about wind and rain as to have induced them to convert the close of the " day of rest" into a time of labor ; yet when the sun had set, and the twilight had begun, there was no more evidence of a coming storm than there had been during the day. The men were beginning to feel almost disappointed, when, soon after supper, Wheeler, pointing to the film of mist in the sky that rushed wildly overhead from west to east, as if, scared at something in the Gulf, it were hurrying to the land for protection, said, —

" There comes our norther."

To which Tomkins replied : " I do not know why you should call it *norther*, for, from the scud-ding of that mist, a more suitable name, it seems to me, would be *wester*. But whatever the name you give, there is no doubt of a gale close at hand, and our business now is to be ready for it. Come, let us look after our boat."

" She is already as safe as I know how to make

below. The work is begun, shingle-fashion, at the bottom of the roof, and each tier of leaves above overlaps a part of the tier below. A well-made roof of palmetto thatch will last many years. They are frequently to be seen upon our seaboard.

L

her," Wheeler said, " lying there safe from shore, with head to sea, anchored at both bow and stern, with a good length of cable-tow, and having a nawser to command her motions, made fast ashore. But as you seem anxious, I will go and show you."

They descended to the bluff together, and Tomkins called his attention to a peculiar and ever-changing curve in the shore-line of the water, indicative of the undulation of a very broad, flat wave; to which Wheeler responded : —

" That is a ground-swell from sea."

" I know it," said the Sergeant, " but it was not there when we landed. It is one of the forerunners of the gale, and it makes me feel queer to think that a wave should out-run the wind that makes it."

" It is no more strange than the *sound* you can hear at this minute," replied Wheeler. " Hark to the *moan* that comes in from sea. That is from the storm, too, and I have heard it sometimes when the storm was too far off for any sound to travel from it." *

---

* There are some facts connected with storms which, like other strange facts, have a mysterious aspect, simply because we do not know how to account for them. One of these is, that our severest storms oftentimes *begin to blow in a direction opposite to that in which the storm is travelling.* For instance, a storm which begins to be felt first in the West Indies, and day after day extends along the Atlantic coast till it reaches Newfoundland, oftentimes begins with a gale from the *northeast*

With all Tomkins' anxiety, there was nothing more to be done to the boat, and though he left it reluctantly, as if oppressed with some presentiment of evil, he said, "All right!" and, with his companion, ascended the bluff to look after things at the camp.

The eastern sky was now brightening with the light of the rising moon, while the western, overhanging the sea, looked black and portentous. Soon

Another singular fact about them is, that, although the *wina* of a storm moves at the rate of eighty or one hundred miles the hour, as tested by an anemometer, the *storm itself* may travel at the rate of only fifteen or twenty miles the hour. For instance, the storm that begins in the West Indies on Monday, and reaches the coast of Georgia on Tuesday, and of Connecticut on Wednesday, and spends itself at Newfoundland on Thursday or Friday, evidently travels at a rate necessary to make that distance in that time, which is from fifteen to twenty-five miles an hour. These facts have been accounted for by the theory that all storms, so characterized, are immense *whirls*, of several hundred miles diameter, in which the wind moves with great rapidity around its centre, while the centre itself moves with far less rapidity in its northeasterly direction. The cause of Tomkins' wonder (viz: that a wave should out-run the wind that raises it) is to be accounted for by knowing that ocean-billows are esti- mated to move sometimes at the rate of forty miles the hour, while the body of the storm that causes it moves only at the rate of twenty or less. And Wheeler's mysterious *moan from the sea* is explained by the fact that sound travels much far- ther and more rapidly through water than through air, and thus a coming storm often sends its voice of warning far ahead of its winds and waves.

a sigh was heard, followed by a little puff of wind,
then another sigh, and another puff. The moan
from sea deepened every moment, as also did the
darkness. Every puff of wind became more decided, and it was not long before a deep darkness
settled upon everything visible, and there was such
a roar from sea and sky as almost drowned the
feeble voices of those who tried to speak. It was
fortunate that the tarpaulin tent and the palmetto
booth had been located under the partial protection
of the bluff, and also of a mixed mass of herbage
and sand near its margin; otherwise they would
have been prostrated at the very beginning of the
gale. Assisted, however, by some sails from the
barge, which were firmly staked, the inmates were
screened against wind and rain, and it was not
long before they needed protection against both.
With the driving of the rain, and of the spray
from sea, came also the rising of the tide, which
in half an hour's time had covered the whole slope
of the beach, and had lifted the waves so that
they were beating heavily against the bluff above
high-water mark. The unexpectedly serious aspect beginning to be assumed by the storm, caused
Dr. Gordon to recall with painful distinctness the
scenes of wild disaster which he had witnessed at
his home upon the Georgia coast, just seven years
before,* when so many lives, of both whites and

* The hurricane of September, 1824, in which some of the

blacks, were lost by the overflow of the sea. He, therefore, said to Sergeant Tomkins,—

"I am sorry we did not select a higher spot for our encampment. If we are to judge of the present storm by one I witnessed a few years since, we may be compelled to change our quarters before morning. I propose, therefore, to take Jones, if you will let me have him, and my young friend Wildcat, and ascertain, by going a little way into the interior, whether there is not higher ground to which we may go in case of need."

"This will be dangerous work, Doctor," replied Tomkins. "You will lose yourself in the darkness, I fear."

"There will be the light of your fire; I cannot mistake that," Dr. Gordon said.

"That might guide your return, but not your going out," argued Tomkins, "for, whichever way you incline, (and it is almost impossible to keep any given course in the dark,) the fire behind you will look just the same; and while you think you are going due south, as you intend, you may sidle to the right, and be falling over the bluff into the sea before you expect it."

"You are right," Dr. Gordon replied; "I pro-

islands were totally submerged, and all the inhabitants destroyed, and in which many houses upon the main were overwhelmed, not only by the wind, but by the fearful tide that rushed in from sea.

pose, therefore, that while we are gone, you keep *two* fires, about four rods apart.   We can use them as sailors use beacons on the coast."

"That is well thought of," Tomkins returned with a brightening look.   "The two* fires will give you all needful guidance both going and returning."

The two fires being made, and the course carefully laid down which they were to pursue, Dr. Gordon called his two companions, and set out upon his gloomy reconnoissance.   For mutual support and guidance, as well as to avoid separation, they took each other by the hand, Dr. Gordon being in the midst, and Wildcat upon his right; and it was well that this expedient was adopted before they left the fire, for each soon became perfectly invisible to the others, and the loudest halloo could not be heard the distance of ten paces.   Another important aid was also provided on the suggestion of Wheeler, (who said he knew what it was to grope in the dark,) without which the explorers would probably have lost their lives: — it was a rod, or *groping-stick*, six or eight feet long, in the hand of each, with which to feel the way.

Accoutred and supported thus, they began their

* For that purpose, *three* fires, arranged triangularly, with a long apex pointing the way, would have been better than two; but perhaps Dr. Gordon knew that there was not wood enough for them all.

march, stumbling over a drifted hillock here, and
running foul of a stunted cedar there, until they
had gone some two hundred yards, and had satisfied themselves that several of the spots over which
they had passed were a yard or two higher than
the place of their encampment. They were conscious, however, that, notwithstanding their attempts to guide themselves by the two fires, their
course had been very uncertain, for the reason
that the driving rain and mist had so obscured the
distinctness of the fires that at a short distance
nothing was visible of them except their com-
mingled light. In doubt, therefore, whether they
were in the midst of the tongue of land, or upon
one of its edges, they faithfully plied the groping-
sticks before them at every step; and it was well
indeed they did, for as they were about to turn, at
the end of their course, Wildcat suddenly uttered
his Indian grunt, " Ugh!" then griped fast hold
of Dr. Gordon's hand, crying out, " Hold fast!"
and immediately began to sink. The company had
groped their way to the crumbling edge of the
bluff, below which the dark waves from sea were
beating in their fury, and so undermining it that,
at the moment Wildcat's stick warned him of his
position, the brink gave way beneath his feet. It
was as much as Dr. Gordon and Jones could do by
their united strength to brace themselves against
this sudden pull, while Dr. Gordon held on to the

imperilled boy and called to Jones to draw them both back.

And now a new danger presented itself. The light from the encampment, which had been growing dimmer and dimmer, disappeared entirely, ere they had walked two minutes on their homeward way—the fires having been extinguished by the rain. They were deeply impressed with the diffi·culty and peril of their situation; nor did they hesitate to warn each other of the necessity of keeping an arrow-like directness in their route, if they hoped ever to reach the camp. On they went, so slowly stepping, and so carefully feeling their way before they stepped, that it seemed as if they had gone double the distance; and Dr. Gordon and Jones, having no guide on which to rely ex·cept their consciousness of moving at a certain angle to the wind, would long before have come to a full stop, confident that they had veered from their course, and were in danger again, had it not been for Wildcat's cheery voice: " We right ! we right! keep on !" when, at last, Jones gave Dr. Gordon's hand a grip, such as Wildcat had given it before, and with a cry of " Hold fast !" lurched forward, dragging the others along with him. Te-naciously did poor Jones cling to Dr. Gordon, and manfully did the Doctor and Wildcat struggle to save him and themselves from being precipitated into the boiling waters below. It was impossible, however, to resist the downward impulse. They went together, nor did they stop until Jones found himself lodged against an obstruction that first gave a hasty movement, then a cry of—

"Murder! Help!"

They had fortunately kept so straight a course, under Wildcat's Indian guidance, as to have come to the camp itself, and falling down the little declivity above it to have lodged against Simpson, who had stepped out for a moment to see what progress the storm had made. Jones' cry of horror, as he thought himself plunging into the sea, was arrested, and in place of it came such a ringing laugh of merriment at discovering that Simpson had mistaken him for a hostile Indian trying to murder him, that he was joined in it by Dr. Gordon and Wildcat, and soon after by all others in the camp.

CHAPTER XV.

THE merriment excited by Simpson's alarm was as short-lived as it was boisterous. Serious as affairs had been for the past few hours, they were every moment becoming more so. The tide, always high a day after the full moon, and now higher than usual in consequence of the gale from the west, was rising with fearful rapidity. Dark and dirty billows were rolling in from sea, angry at being made to overleap the sandy barrier which they met a mile or two from shore. With all the care which Wheeler had taken to moor the barge securely, she was at times lifted by the waves with a force sufficient to drag her anchor, and then brought so near the bluff as to be in imminent danger of being staved; yet what more to do in insuring her safety no one could tell.

170

The storm continued until past midnight. The tide, however, did not continue even-footed with the gale. It commenced to subside before the violence of the wind abated. Two feet more of rise would have brought the waves sidling upon the level of the encampment, and have compelled them to seek higher ground. But those two feet they were spared; and as soon as the promise of this fact was sufficiently certified, all who could, gave themselves up to sleep. Dr. Gordon sought it, like the rest, but his visions were so troubled that wakefulness proved more refreshing than sleep.

Between two and three o'clock in the morning, after the extreme violence of the storm had abated, but while the surf was still rolling heavily from sea, the sentinel on duty announced hastily to Wheeler that the bluff above the place of anchorage had given way, carrying with it a large log, to the great danger, as he supposed, of the boat. Wheeler instantly aroused Sergeant Tomkins, and the two hurried to the place, where, by the light of the scarcely living camp-fire, they had evidence enough of the slide, but where all was pitchy dark in the chasm beyond. Vainly did they try by torches of resinous pine to illumine that darkness; the flame did not live a minute. And as vain was their attempt by means of a kind of lantern which one of the men extemporized out of a three-

pronged branch, inclosed by a white handkerchief
—the light in both cases was extinguished. Excited the more by these failures, they gathered upon
the edge of the bluff all the wood at their command, and placed in the midst a few burning
brands protected from the rain, while exposed to
the wind; its lurid light soon flickered over the
edge of the bluff and glanced upon the rolling
waters below; but no sign of the barge could be
discovered. In the meantime, Wheeler had cautiously groped his way to the place where his hawser had been made fast, and returned to Tomkins
with the disheartening intelligence that the hawser had been snapped, and that the boat had been
evidently torn from her moorings.

With this unpleasant discovery they were compelled to content themselves, for, far as they could
peer into the stormy gloom, by the light of their
fire, and by the help of their night-glass, nothing
could be seen but foamy, tumbling water. The
men, who, though nearly worn out by labor and
unrest, had been aroused from their fitful slumbers
by the unusual light upon the bluff, and by the
excited movements of Tomkins and Wheeler, came,
one after another, to the place of observation,
looked, each for himself, upon the signs of the recent slide, then upon the dark water, imperfectly
illumined, where no boat was to be seen, and
finally returned to the palmetto tent to sit upon

some wet box or bag and talk over their now dismal prospects. In this way they spent the rest of that gloomy night, without much sleep, or much comfort either of body or of mind.

By three o'clock the gale had ceased, and by half-past four the almost setting moon peeped through a large, clear rent in the western clouds. Encouraged by the momentary flood of light poured upon the water by the slanting rays, the men hastened to the place of observation, and strained their eyes to discover traces of the missing boat, but, with the exception of seeing something that looked like a buoy lying upon its side, and tossing on the swell, they looked in vain. At last the dawn struggled through the still clouded east, and revealed to them that which sent a pang to every heart—their beautiful barge an utter ruin. By what means they could not conceive, it had been severed wholly in two. Part of it was hanging, buoy-like, to the dragged anchor, and part of it was swinging in the tide, afar off, detained by the killick * which had been thrown out astern.

Fortunately for the company, the Texan experience of Wheeler and the aching bones of Magruder had prevailed upon them to take out of her, and to bring safely ashore, all that was most needful, and even her oars and some of her sails.

* A small anchor.

But what were sails and oars without their boat ?
And what were they now to do? It was manifest that the *cruise was over*, and a failure. Their
thoughts instantly turned to Tampa; must not
their faces turn there too? Yet how were they to
get back? Not by water, for they had not the
means; not by land, for a swarm of hostile savages
lay between. Were they destined to lie here
indefinitely, upon this barren coast, hemmed in by
impassable waters on one side, and by still more
impassable Indians on the other?

Thus ran the gloomy thoughts and queries of
the men when the light of day revealed the extent
of their calamity. But from them all they were
soon called by the voice of Tomkins, who ordered
first a fire, then breakfast. The comfort of the
one to their stiffened limbs, and of the other to
their craving appetites, soon imparted a more
lively tone to their conversation, and a more
cheerful aspect to their affairs; for oftentimes our
spirits are as much affected by the *view* we take of
things, as by the things themselves. At the
earliest convenient moment, Dr. Gordon summoned all to meet him in what he called a "council of war," recapitulated briefly the state of affairs,
and asked what was to be done.

"Before asking your opinions, however," said
he, "I think it is right to state some facts that
may not be known to you.

"Any day after this we may expect the passing of the revenue-cutter Jackson, as near shore as possible, having some one on the look-out for signals from us, or from others on the coast. By stopping her and getting aboard, we may either obtain passage direct to Tampa, or to Key West first, and thence to Tampa by other means. So that our case is not so hopeless as at first sight it may appear.

"Moreover, as to the reported hostilities of the Indians, there is reason to hope that whatever these may have been, they are passing away. I have not felt at liberty to tell you, until now, that the day we left Tampa orders were received from Government to prepare for a friendly talk with the chiefs at Payne's Landing. No doubt the notice has reached them by runners ere this, and whatever may be the result of the Talk, there will pretty certainly be no outbreak until after it, if there is at all. And, as confirmatory of this, you have yourselves noticed that although we had some signs of hostility the first two days after we left Tampa, we have had none since.

"I, therefore, think we may hope for good things yet."

This little harangue had so tranquillizing an effect upon the spirits of the men that they actually gave Dr. Gordon an unexpected cheer. He went on to say, —

"I think the questions to be discussed by us are substantially these, —

"First. What order are we to to take in reference to the schooner Jackson? Shall wo wait for her here, or elsewhere? or shall we act independently of her?

"Secondly. If we resolve to leave this place, what shall we aim to do? Shall we try to return direct to Tampa? or return by some other way?

"Thirdly. If by either way, how shall we attempt it, by land or by water?"

The points thus systematically and lucidly arranged, enabled the men to enter with spirit on the discussion, which was both free and full. Each was called upon in turn, and each had something sensible to say; and all persons noticed particularly the ready devices of Wildcat, the travelled experience of Wheeler, and the quiet but resolute courage of Tomkins.

In consequence of the discussion it was unanimously agreed, — First, to wait, where they were, the coming of the cutter, and if possible to return by means of her to Tampa, and, secondly, in case it were not possible to return by her, to make their way back by such means as might yet be devised.

Upon this last point, Wheeler said,—

" With the sails and oars saved from the barge, it might be possible for us to go from island to island of the group through which we passed yesterday, by means of a long light raft, made up of dry logs. And if the weather continues good after this, I am not sure but that we might thus pass all the way to Tampa."

Wildcat offered to make his way into the interior, if it were desired, and, on one pretext or other, to obtain canoes enough to carry them all back. A few silver dollars, he said, would obtain as many as they wanted. But he insisted that, if he went, the company should keep in perfect concealment on the coast.

On the subject of concealment, Simpson suggested that a close watch should be kept; that all Indians who came to the place should be seized and kept in confinement until the company departed; and that their canoes should be impressed for the company's service.

To which Tomkins added — "Being well paid for first." Then he went on to make a statement which exceedingly interested his listeners.

"A few miles below this," said he, "I think not half a day's sail — perhaps not two hours'— there is an island which no Indian dares to visit. Is it not so, Wildcat?" he asked, turning to his young companion, who answered,—

"So? yes — Great Spirit Island."

"I know it," said Tomkins. "People say that it is enchanted, and that no one, except some great Medicine-man,* or other favorite of the Great Spirit, can set foot on it and return alive. For this reason it is never visited by the red men, although it is crowded with game. If we are driven

M

to the necessity, that is a place which we can cer
tain'y reach, and where we may remain unmo-
lested as long as we stay. A friend of mine, who
was left there once by mistake, and who afterward pointed out the island to me, as we were
passing up the coast, informed me that he had
spent two months there most delightfully, among
the deer and turkeys, and fish and oysters, with
an occasional visit from a bear or a catamount;
but that in all that time he had never seen a human face, white, black, or red.

* Doctor, or Conjurer, being the same in Indian fancy.

CHAPTER XVI.

NAVIGATING BY RAFT— SAIL OR SEA-BIRD?— COUN CIL OF WAR, SECOND— AN INDIAN CAMP-FIRE— SIGNS OF DANGER— DARING INTRUSION.

N the course of the morning it was discovered that the supposed tongue of land where they had experienced the terrific gale which had deprived them of their boat, was virtually an island, inclosed on one side by the sea, and on the other by a miry marsh overflowed daily by the tide. They were thus as secure as they could expect to be from hostile approach, but they discovered, also, after a short search, that they were likely to suffer for the want of fresh water. Unwilling to leave a spot so well suited, in many respects, to their circumstances, they not only explored the beach, and even attempted distillation, as they had practised on a former occasion, but, under Wheeler's direction, they bored * the island in several places

* For the details of these processes of boring and distillation, see Chapter X.

to the depth of the ordinary tide mark upon the beach, but in vain. It was manifest that they must remove to some other point.

Several miles to the northward was a bold, sandy bluff, which they had noticed in passing the day before, and which they could still see, that promised both a better look-out upon sea, and the precious fluid, of which they were beginning already to feel the need. By Dr. Gordon's advice, the men were set to work to make the best raft they could out of the poor material furnished by the island. A number of the longest logs to be obtained were fastened firmly together, with all the length and with the least breadth possible for the load to be carried; and to this rude structure were attached the gunwales, row-locks, and seats of the barge, with whatever else could be of use; so that, although appearing in very different shape, and possessed of vastly inferior qualities, almost every portion of the wreck was consumed in the work.

The next day, (Tuesday, Nov. 2d,) about three o'clock in the afternoon, they embarked with all the stores they had saved, and by vigorous plying of the oars they worked their sluggish way against wind and tide, until they reached a low sandy key, covered on one side with saw-palmettoes, and on the other with an impenetrable growth of mangroves. While toiling heavily un-

der the lee of this little island Jones suddenly
sung out, " A sail ! "

" Where away ? " asked Wheeler, who had
temporarily given up his place at the stern to
Jones, and who looked seaward with a vain attempt to penetrate the dense intervening foliage.

" Through the opening in the palmettoes we
have just passed," answered Jones, " and right
over the clump of oaks on the island beyond."

" Back water, men ! back water ! " was Wheeler's order to the oarsmen.

The raft was backed until it reached the spot
indicated by Jones, but nothing could be discovered toward sea except a mixed flock of gannets, gulls, and curlews, and Wheeler impatiently
remarked,—

" I gave you credit for a better eye, Jones, than
to mistake a flock of birds for the sails of a vessel."

" Those were not birds I spoke of," Jones
quickly replied ; " I saw the birds, and saw the
sails, too.   It was but a glimpse I had, it is true,
but if that was not a vessel, you and the men may
laugh at me all the rest of my life, and never trust
my sight again.   I tell you *it was* a vessel.   She
had all her sails spread, was at least four miles
away, and seemed to be sailing very fast."

This earnest reiteration on the part of Jones
stopped the laugh that had arisen, when Wheeler
added,—

"We must run no risks about the cutter. Pull away, men! and all of you keep a sharp look-out for some opening through these mangroves. We must get ashore and raise a smoke, even if it is to be seen only by gannets and curlews."

They made all the speed possible, until they found a place where the mud was hard enough to bear their weight, and the mangroves open enough to allow a passage through; and no sooner had one of the men pushed his way to a point where he could see, than he cried out, —

"Jones is right. The cutter is passing!"

"You had better say she has passed," said Tomkins hastily; then with a shout, "All hands to work to raise a smoke. Quick! quick! before our chance is gone!"

Each man sprang to his duty, and with pocket-knife, hatchet, or axe, severed and brought together so large a pile of green foliage from the mangroves and palmettoes that, ere Tomkins had his fire of dry twigs ready, he had to say to the men, "Hold! enough!" Wheeler, meanwhile, had tried other signals. Asking the assistance of D-. Gordon and Wildcat, he had brought ashore the boat's flag, and then waved it high as they could reach by means of two oars lashed together. The loaded muskets of the men had also been brought ashore, and as soon as the flag was ready for waving, he asked a moment's use of the men.

who not only fired their pieces simultaneously, but also discharged them *upwards,* that their smoke as well as sound might serve as a signal to the cutter.

Eagerly did they watch the effect of these signals, and afterwards of the dense smoke from the pile of green herbage, rising obliquely in the wind until it had attained its equilibrium, then stretching like a streamer for miles over land and water. None of them, however, seemed to have reached the eyes or ears of any one on board. The white canvas, distinctly visible behind the low growth of a distant island, continued spread and set as before, until it passed wholly out of sight. They had seen the cutter just a few minutes too late to arrest her attention.

With her disappearance, the men looked anxiously into each other's faces, and asked, by expression of countenance, if not by so many words, What shall we do now? But this question they were not allowed many minutes to discuss, for Tomkins, observing their dejection, ordered them all to the raft, saying, "The first thing we have to do is to reach yon point and quench our thirst."

The wind being now somewhat in their favor, Wheeler raised the sail, remarking he had no doubt that their deep-lying craft would obey the helm, the same as if it were a keeled vessel. "In-

deed," said he, "she is *all keel*." This expectation
was not wholly disappointed; they made a great
deal of lee-way, because their craft was too heavy
to slide through the water, and, therefore, with
the wind abeam, they drifted sideways almost as
much as they went forward. Still the sail was a
great assistance, when co-operating with the oars,
to obtain headway, and they made such comfortable progress that Wheeler expressed himself
much encouraged, although Tomkins laughingly
remarked about their change from the barge to the
raft that they had "gone from a stage-coach to an
ox-cart."

The bluff, which they reached in due course of
sail, furnished them plentifully with what they
needed,—fresh water of an excellent quality, with
which they filled every canteen, kettle and pot, as
well as the runlet. It had been the intention of
Dr. Gordon and Tomkins to leave the main after
supplying themselves with water, and seek a lodging for the night on some of the islands, as usual;
but the sun was now so near the horizon, and
their craft so slow-motioned, that they were con-
strained to abandon the purpose. Calling a halt
at so early an hour resulted, however, in two advantages—it enabled them to select at leisure
their place for encampment, so situated that it
could be easily watched and as easily defended,

and also to hold another "council of war upon the subject of duty in their present change of circumstances.

The discussions which now arose were far from being animated or hopeful; for, as a sailor would say, the sheet anchor of their hopes had been lost with their chance of return by the cutter. The questions proposed by Dr. Gordon were simply these: "Shall we attempt a return direct to Tampa? and, if so, how?"

On the first of these questions there was but little difference of opinion. No one thought of remaining where they were, and no one thought that any place yet seen offered them any special inducement to abide. The only division of opinion was, for a time, in the preference expressed by Jones, and supported by Wheeler, to seek a refuge on that enchanted island of which Tomkins had spoken, the same that Wildcat had called " Great Spirit Island;" but when they came to analyze their motives for this preference, it was manifest that they had been influenced more by their love of wild-woods life than by any advantage arising to the expedition. Moreover, Jones observed, during the discussion, such an expression of distress on the countenance of his young friend, Wildcat, who, with all his good sense, evidently sympathized with the superstitions of his people, that he not only ceased to express his own preference on the subject, but prevailed upon Wheeler to do the same.

Upon the question, which incidentally arose, whether it would not be better to work their way southwardly to the Florida cape, and thence over to Key West or the Tortugas, it was decided that the distance to those places was probably as great as it was to Tampa, while they were far more inaccessible on account of the open sea between. The unanimous verdict was, therefore, that they should return to Tampa.

Upon the second question—How? there was a long and careful comparison of views, and the decision was that they should continue to use their raft until they had passed the waters of the Caloosahatchie River, and of Charlotte Harbor, (which extended too far inland to allow the hope of heading them in safety,) and then that they should make their way on foot along the beach as far as Manatee Bay, if not to Tampa itself.

These discussions occupied them until deep twilight, when they prepared for supper, and after that for bed. The weather had been cool ever since the storm, and the men felt the need of fire. To this, however, Wildcat objected very strongly, on account of the exposure to observation which it would occasion, and finally went to Dr. Gordon to say,—

"Tell men make *little* fire; tell men *hide* it

Injin hear too much gun," alluding to the volleys fired that afternoon. " Injin see too much smoke. Will come, see who's here."

In the excitement caused by their great calamity in losing the help of the cutter, no one had thought of the probable effect which the signals intended for the vessel might have had upon the people on shore. Wildcat's remonstrance was, therefore, indicative of more than usual shrewdness, and his carrying it to Dr. Gordon showed also his sense of propriety, for he knew it was the habit of the officers to keep from the men all intelligence of a discouraging character. Dr. Gordon was very much pleased with these traits in his young friend, and after a moment's conference with Sergeant Tomkins, he said to Wildcat,—

"Go, say to the men from me, that they must have very little fire, and that they must let you manage it."

Wildcat went to the men, delivered his message as well as he could, and added : " Much fire don't need ; Injin fire *never big;*" then with a laugh at the picture he was about to give, he continued. " White man make big fire, and stand way off in the cold. Injin make little fire, get close over it, and is warm."

Being instructed to manage it, he first selected a spot as much concealed as possible by the growth of bushes, then increased that concealment by

planting a screen of thick bushes in places where
they were lacking. After which he took two of
the men and brought a number of thoroughly
dried saplings, of which he put the ends of four
or five together, and set them to burning at the
point of contact, for an Indian seldom *heaps* his
fire, or makes it of large logs, but uses long, small,
dry wood, with which he keeps up his fire by
shoving the burning ends together. Having thus
obeyed orders, he called the men and made them
get as near over the blaze as they could, while he
squatted with them, Indian fashion, and encouraged the warm air of the fire to come under his
leer-skin clothes and next his flesh.

Thus sat or stood the men, talking freely and
hopefully of their prospects. Laugh, jest, and
story went merrily around, and they were certainly
a more cheerful-looking set than they were only
a few hours before; yet why? No doubt it would
have been difficult for any of them to say; but the
secret was this: they had now a definite aim, and
a definite plan by which to accomplish it. This
is all that a man, who is *a man*, needs to prove
that he is one. Suspense or inaction may paralyze
him, but give him something to do and he will
soon animate himself with hope.

While the men thus circled cosily around their
Indian fire, there occurred an incident which
hushed every laugh and jest, and threw a tem-

porary gloom over the company. The site for the encampment had been selected in a sharp angle of the bluff, peninsula-like, where the men might lie at ease among the thick-growing myrtles and cassinas, and where the sentinel could keep easy watch over the whole camp, front and rear, by treading his path across the neck of the peninsula, and, at each end of his beat, looking down the bluff, first on this side, then on that. At this hour Wheeler was on duty, and as the warning of Wildcat had suggested that danger might be apprehended from enemies on the main, he and Tomkins had agreed upon a private signal—a low, short cough.

The moon had not yet risen, though the eastern sky was brightening with the promise of her coming, and the red embers threw a lurid glare upon the faces of the men, as they warmed themselves in preparation for sleep, each with his blanket in hand, or spread like a cloak upon his back. The lively talk had ceased in momentary expectation of the order to "turn in," when Dr. Gordon heard a low, short cough from Wheeler, the sentinel. He then observed Tomkins look downward, as if in deep thought, saying, "Hist!" then turn his ear toward the bushes and listen in an attitude of seeming carelessness, but, as his expanded mostril and quick-moving eye indicated, of profound attention. Looking now at Wildcat,

Dr. Gordon observed him also with an uneasy air endeavoring to appear unconcerned, but evidently on the alert for sounds from a distance. Simpson's posture was however the most noticeable of them all, sitting with his face toward the sentinel, and with his head enveloped in his blanket, so that he could scarcely be recognized, he was not only listening like the other two, but had his feet and legs bent under him ready for an instant spring. Dr. Gordon was surprised to see how keen were the senses of those who had lived much among the Indians. Soon Tomkins' voice was heard in a very low whisper from behind his hand, which hid the motion of his lips,—

"Hist, men! Don't move, any of you. There is an Indian in the bush. Jones, rise; move slowly as if going to bed, then quickly throw your blanket over the fire, and jump out of the way. As he does this, do you all leap from your places, seize your guns, and be ready to obey orders."

Jones did as he was ordered, and so did the men, with as much promptness as if this Indian movement had been a part of their ordinary drill; but as it was taking place there came from a thicket about fifty paces beyond the sentinel, the sharp crack of a rifle.

"Missed that time!" Simpson was heard exultingly to exclaim, in a voice barely loud enough to reach the ears of the men, when he added, in a somewhat louder tone, " No, by Jacks! he has hit *me!* "

Instantly the musket of Wheeler darted its expanding volume of fire and smoke toward the hostile intruder, and his voice followed it, saying, " There's but one, and I think I have stopped him."

" Charge, men!" shouted Tomkins, seizing a musket and rushing toward the spot. All who had muskets went with him, but everything there was quiet, and no enemy was to be seen either dead or alive. Ordering a halt, and calling for perfect silence, they could hear afar off the quick, soft tread of a moccasined foot moving rapidly away.

" There was but one red-skin," said Wheeler ; " he must have been a daring fellow !"

Soon after this the moon arose. " We will have no further disturbance to-night," said Tomkins. " Indians never attack by moonlight if they can have darkness."

CHAPTER XVII.

SOON after this the whole camp was in a state of repose. Nothing was to be heard but the hard breathing of the sleepers, and the footfalls of the sentinel whose quiet tramp upon the appointed beat was as regular as the ticking of a clock ; for Tomkins was so sure there would be no further disturbance from Indians after the rising of the moon that he encouraged all to go quickly and soundly to sleep. A little past midnight, however, he himself was called from his bivouac. The sentinel on duty at that hour was Simpson, whose hurt, a mere scratch on the temple, needling only the staunching influence of a little cold water, did not at all disqualify him for service. Having been instructed to give the Sergeant private warning in the event

192

of anything unusual, he came and with a gentle shake said—

" I hear something in the bush !"

They went noiselessly to the concealment of a leafy evergreen, where they listened, and became convinced that there was either a human being or some large animal stealthily moving through the underbrush   They could distinctly hear the rustle of leaves displaced, and the gentle crush of a soft foot on grass and brittle twigs. They pressed cautiously forward to reconnoitre under cover of a screen of vines, and peeped between its openings to catch a glimpse of the intruder, when Simpson, whose sense of hearing had been cultivated to an unusual degree, said in an undertone—

" Too much noise for Injin. It must be some sort of varmint—a *bar*, maybe, or a *painter*. Yes, thar he is now !" pointing to a little glade on which the moonbeams brightly shone.   Tomkins looked and almost shuddered to see an enormous panther passing slowly, and as he fancied, reluctantly, away from the neighborhood of the sleepers.

With the first peep of day, Wheeler, the sailing-master, caused all to be aroused, saying that the tide was moving northward, and that it was important they should avail themselves of its assistance to carry forward their clumsy craft.   The toilet of a soldier on bivouac does not usually occupy many minutes ; he has only to shake him-

N

self, and is ready for breakfast r for service
General ablutions, hair brushings, and other acts
of civilized life, are not always observed. Breakfast was soon dispatched, the raft loaded, and the
company afloat. A fine breeze, directly astern, assisted the tide, and kept it company for eight*
hours, during which they made the distance of
twenty-four miles, when it ceased and the raft
made such slow progress with the scarcely moving
water that, although the sun was an hour or more
above the horizon, they resolved to encamp where
they were, and await the expected renewal of wind
and tide next morning. All were much encouraged
with the success of the day, and the sailing-master
strongly insisted that, slow and uncertain as their
progress had been, it would be safer and better for
them to use the raft all the way to Tampa.

"No·doubt we shall readily agree to it," the
Sergeant replied, "if you will provide us all the
way with wind and tide."

"I can try," said Wheeler laughing. "Let us
see what shall be our success to-morrow morning."

They had stopped at a prettily wooded island,
which promised a pleasant, and perhaps safe, resting place for the night. On landing and looking

---

* Persons accustomed only to the Atlantic tides may regard this statement as made by mistake ; but they will find
upon inquiry that from Tampa Bay to Punta Largo there is
but one tide a day, and that not very high, having a rise and
fall of only about three feet.

around, nothing was seen worthy of note except the fresh signs of deer in such abundance as to arouse in the hunters of the company a desire for game. A short conference with each other resulted in a determination to ask permission for Wheeler, Jones and Wildcat, to go upon a fire-hunt that night.

"Our time for going out must either be now, before sunset, or at nine o'clock to-night, when the moon rises," said Wheeler to Tomkins. "But there is so little time before dark, and we know so little of the haunts of the deer that I propose to spend the hour of daylight that is left in looking out the deer paths; and then to take Jones and Wildcat with me on the hunt after moon-rise, when the deer are pretty sure to be on foot, either feeding or going after water."

Permission to this effect was readily given by Tomkins, especially with the encouragement of Dr. Gordon, whose sympathies were ever ready.

Wheeler returned from his exploring tour about sunset, and reported every encouragement for expecting a successful hunt that night, at the same time turning over to Magruder a fine wild turkey which he had shot upon the way. The two expectants of the sport, who had remained in camp, had occupied themselves in hunting a supply of the richest pine to be had, and now spent the interval between sunset and dark in reducing it to small splints, and tying it into a fagot convenient for carrying. Magruder, the cook, was solicited for a frying-pan, which he lent on condition that it should be returned in good order, or with an equivalent for the trouble he should have in cleaning it. With these preparations, the hunters were ready for their departure, and then waited only for the moon.

Gradually the eastern sky brightened, and when the first silvery tip of the moon was seen, they set out, Jones bearing the fagots of resinous pine, and Wildcat balancing upon his shoulder the frying-pan, from which the burning splinters threw a strong light forward, illumining the backs of the hunters and the forests before them, but leaving their faces in shadow. Another provision was as necessary as fire, which was to get and "keep the wind" of their game; but the air was so still as to leave them in doubt which way it blew. To determine this important point, Wildcat practised the Indian device of wetting his finger in his mouth, then standing still and holding it perpendicularly in the air to discover which side was coolest. He pointed due north, and as he did so, Jones called attention to the smoke from their frying-pan, which, after rising a few feet, inclined steadily toward the south. With these indications they went to the southern end of the island, and struck their course northward. Having walked about half a mile, Wheeler suddenly stopped the others, saying, "I see a deer."

Jones and Wildcat looked in the direction indicated, and saw a bright red spot shining in the far-off darkness.

"That spot," said Wheeler, in a very low tone, "is made by the eyes of a deer, blended by the distance. It is at least eighty or a hundred yards away. When we have come within sixty yards, that spot will become a *stripe* of light. The eyes then begin to divide; but you will not see them shine as two until you have come within forty or fifty yards, or perhaps less. Then we must get ready to shoot. A cow's eyes have a light and watery appearance, and divide at the distance of eighty yards."

"But look!" said Jones, "there are two or three more spots shining in the dark."

"I expected that," answered Wheeler. "Each of us now can have a shot. We will move on softly until these eyes have fully divided. Then, Wildcat, you must set down your light behind you, and we must all prepare to shoot. Do not aim at the eyes, but a foot below. A deer when feeding never turns his body, but only his head, and when you shoot by firelight you can seldom tell whether he has turned toward you his side, his breast, or his tail. You only know that a foot below his eyes you are most likely to give him his

death-wound. Jones, do you take the rightmost
deer ; I will take the buck to the left, and Wildcat
may choose one between. As soon as we are all
ready, I will give a low whistle, then we must
take aim ; after that I will give another, when we
must fire together."

They moved forward until the red spot of light
had become elongated into a stripe, showing that
their distance was sixty yards or less; then a little farther, when that stripe had divided into
two distinct sparks of light. Here they began to
look about for some place on which Wildcat and
Jones might deposit their respective burdens.

"The deer will not run," said Wheeler, " until
we approach within twenty steps or less, but we
had better not try them too far."

Wildcat's fire-pan was set upon what Jones
called a " harry-cane " * root, and beside this mass
Jones also deposited his burden of light-wood.

At a slight whistle from their leader, they all
levelled their pieces, and at another signal they
pulled trigger ; then snatching up the light, they
ran to see what execution had been done. Wheeler's buck lay dead in its tracks, having leaped
spasmodically upward, then fallen where it stood.
Jones's fell about twenty steps away. Wildcat's

---

* Hurricane-root, meaning a mixed mass of earth and
roots upturned by a gale.

was nowhere to be found, and his disappointment seemed to be very great. Indeed, his mortification caused him to be almost loquacious.

"I not used to musket," said he; "I used to rifle I kill, though; when daylight come, you find mine too, if no wolf here." And the others kindly encouraged him in this hope.

As a company they had reason to be satisfied with their work, notwithstanding poor Wildcat's failure, for there, upon the ground, lay as much venison as their united strength would enable them to carry back to camp, encumbered as they were with guns and other things. Tying the legs of the buck and suspending it upon a pole, Jones and Wildcat lifted it between them, while Wheeler took the other upon his own brawny back.

Loaded thus, they were about to start home, when the whole plan was altered in consequence of a pleasant and unexpected discovery made by Wildcat. The pole proving too slender, they were seeking another, at some distance from the scene of slaughter, when they were surprised by the sound of a rustling in the bushes, accompanied by a long, deep sigh. Wheeler and Jones looked wistfully at each other, but Wildcat, with a joyful "I say so!" rushed toward the place of the sound, saying to the others, "Come see!" Crouched in a thicket, lay a half-grown buck, with broken leg and wounded side, just in the act of expiring.

They bled it, like the others, by severing the blood-vessels of the neck. And now, the load being wholly beyond their strength, they resolved to leave the greater part of it till morning, protected from wolves by the usual device. They bent down two strong saplings, and trimming a forked branch at the upper end of each, inserted it into a hole cut in the abdomen of the two smaller deer and let each fly back to its place.

"Now let us travel!" said Wheeler, and soon they were on their way, Wildcat leading the van with his pan of fire, and the two men bearing the large fat buck between them.

It was past ten o'clock when they reached camp, and by ordinary rule every man ought to have been in bed and asleep, but their labors that day had been light, and their sympathy with the hunters had kept them awake; in addition to which, the sound of the three guns had raised their expectations, and they were waiting to see the result of the expedition. It must be confessed, too, that the wakefulness of some of the men was greatly increased by a vivid conception of the odor and taste of broiled venison. When the hunters came in, they threw their game upon the ground, leaving to the others the pleasure of skinning and quartering it, and they watched with interest the nice tit-bits which were soon frying upon the coals, and the larger and more luscious pieces that were thrust under the embers to roast, after having been enveloped in a thick coating of green leaves. Whether it were that the venison killed that night was uncommonly fat and tender, or that the smoke and ashes of the fire imparted a peculiar flavor, both Dr. Gordon and Tomkins declared that never had venison tasted sweeter.

At daybreak four men were detailed to bring in the game left in the woods. There had evidently been some hungry visitors at the spot, as was manifest from the disappearance of the offals, which had been thrown upon the ground, but the bodies suspended in the tops of the saplings had been untouched.

A rich breakfast of venison steaks, broiled ribs and fried liver awaited their return, and a plentiful supply of the same was prepared also for their midday meal, and by the time they were ready to embark, the wind and tide were inviting them to go. They made for the northern shore of Charlotte Harbor, which was in full sight, but towards which their progress was not so rapid or so encouraging as it had been the day before. Not only was the northward tendency of the tide impeded by its flow sideways into the harbor, but the raft lay more heavily in the water, being saturated by several days' submersion, and therefore less buoyant. It began to be certain that either they must work their way to Tampa by land, or provide something more manageable than the raft.

CHAPTER XVIII.

T was during the laborious voyage of
this day that Dr. Gordon, for the pur-
pose of enlivening the spirits of the men,
said to Wheeler, —

" You remarked the other night, when our island
was afire, that you had witnessed a grand fire-scene
of some kind, out West. I, for one, will be glad
to hear the particulars, and I have no doubt that
others of the company will too."

"Oh, it was only a fire on the prairies, a common thing enough out there, and a grand thing,
too," the other replied; " yet it was a small matter
in itself, as compared with a trouble that came
along with it."

"Indeed!" said Dr. Gordon; "do tell us all
about it.

Wheeler seemed gratified with the request, and
after a little premising, went on to give the following account : —

202

"I was travelling once as leader to a company of traders returning from Santa Fe, in New Mexico. We had had a merry time of it, for most of the men were as much hunters as traders, and had enjoyed themselves greatly in chasing the buffalo as we passed their feeding-grounds. It was not uncommon for a hunter to kill four or five a day, and there was one of them who said that he had one day killed as many as nine. This was a great waste of life; for, though we had over a hundred persons in the company, and at least forty wagons in the train, we could neither eat nor carry all the meat that was killed; the hunters contenting themselves with cutting out the tongues, tenderloins, and humps, and leaving the rest to be devoured by wolves. You, Doctor, and the others know that I am not particularly superstitious, but I confess that this waste of life troubled me. I was almost afraid that some judgment would come upon us for it, and so I told the hunters. They, however, laughed at me and kept on.

"Well, one day, as our oxen toiled over a wide prairie, browsing as they went, I observed, far away to the north and west, a dingy look in the sky, which rapidly increased. Any one accustomed to prairie life will recognize a smoke twelve or fifteen miles away, or farther, if the wind sets toward him, and he will make his arrangements accordingly. But most of the hunters out that day had no experience of this sort, and I doubted whether they would notice the signs until it was too late to help themselves, for they had gone off in squads, east, west, and north, and a few had even made a detour to the south to get the wind of a herd of antelopes in that direction. I was greatly concerned on their account, for I foresaw we should soon need their help, and that they would need ours; yet we had no means of signalling them beyond the hearing of our guns, or at most beyond the sight of a flag, which we sometimes hoisted on a fifteen-foot pole 'stepped' on the lead wagon. There was no time to be lost in getting the train into a place of safety. I do not mean safety from the fire,—that was easy enough, for we had only to burn the grass to the windward, and drive upon the ground,—but safety from the buffaloes that would come rushing upon us in countless thousands ahead of the fire, and against which it is sometimes impossible to erect a barrier, especially if anything should put them upon a stampede. The prairie was wide enough to allow a hundred times as many to pass us, if they would, but unfortunately we were in the pass-way between one feeding-ground and another, across a long and deep canyon,* which the buffaloes could approach only

* A canyon is a precipitous, tunnel-like passage for water, common in the Mexican and Texas prairies, and sometimes hundreds of feet deep.

at that point, and where they would, almost of necessity, crowd and excite one another.

"There was a Butte, or sharp, lonely hill, about
six miles ahead of us, and I knew that if we could
reach it in time we should be safe, both from fire
and buffaloes. Every teamster was therefore ordered to push his team to the extent of their speed,
consistent with our keeping together, and I thought,
for a time, we should accomplish our purpose, but
when we came to rising ground about a mile and
a half from our place of refuge, we saw that this
was hopeless. Five miles away, east, west, and
north, far as the eye could reach, the sky was black
with smoke, and the earth red with fire. But that
which we had to dread was nearer still : a long,
broad belt of buffaloes — how long we could not
tell, for the two ends were out of sight, and how
broad we could not tell, for they did not stretch in
an unbroken line, but in great squads of a wedge-
like shape, from a furlong to a half mile or more
in length, each squad having its leaders in front,
and the thousands and tens of thousands of the
herd following hard after them. This black, irregular belt of buffaloes was moving upon us at
the distance of not two miles, and beginning to
crowd and jostle each other as they neared the
crossing place of the canyon, miles below us.
Even while we were looking on, they got into
some disorder, then into more, and finally into a

stampede, which brought them towards us with
the rush and roar of a hurricane.

"We had not a minute—no, not a second—to
lose   Giving up all hope of reaching the Butte
in time, I ordered ten of the foremost wagons to
be halted in a line, end to end, close as they could
be jammed; then a second ten to be halted side by
side with them, "breaking their joints," as car-
penters and masons say, or covering the gaps between wagon and wagon; then another line of
wagons, and another still, until there was a bul-
wark of wagons, four in depth and ten in length.
And as fast as they were brought into position, the
teams were taken out and placed on the southern
or safe side, where they were fastened as securely
as possible in the very little time left us.   While
the teamsters were engaged in this duty, all other
hands were called to firing the grass.   This was a
difficult and perilous work, for although the mes-
quite grass, which grows only about a foot high,
is easily manageable, the prairie grass, in the midst
of which we were, grows as high as a man's waist,
and it was as much as we could do to burn it on
the outside of the imperfectly cleared ring, without
at the same time firing our crowded wagon train.
It was done, however, and in a few seconds the roar
and rumble of our fire, which burned against the
wind with a high flame and intense heat, was as
loud as that of the blaze coming down upon us.

"For a while there was reason to hope that our fire would compel the herd to divide and pass us to the right and left, but whether the leaders did not regard the fire, or could not help themselves, we saw them leap right through and hold their head-long course, until they saw that there was an obstruction before them which they could not surmount. Then their confusion and terror became intense. They looked wildly around, and attempted to pass to one side or the other, but, being pushed forward by those behind, they planted themselves to withstand the pressure, until overpowered, some endeavored to break through the gaps between the wagons, but became entangled and were shot by our men, and some, over-ridden by the others, were trampled and smothered to death. The most dreadful part of that scene was at the line where they met the fire, and where they could neither go forward, on account of the stoppage in front, nor go back on account of the pressure behind. Poor wretches! their roar of pain, as the fire burned slowly under their bodies, and passed from one to another, was horrible, mixed as it was with the groans and gaspings of the smothered ones next the wagon-train.

"At one time it seemed as if the number crowding and pressing against us would be such as to enable those behind to climb over them, and over our rampart of wagons, and trample us to death

Fortunately for us, however, the herd vith which we had to contend was comparatively small, and our wagons were so closely set that, although some of them were pushed a little out of place and jammed against the line next to them, not the first buffalo was able to get across. The only serious accident to which we were exposed was from the fire. In spite of all our care, a little flame had straggled off from the rest and got to blazing under our wagon-train. One of our wagons was actually on fire, and what added to the seriousness of the case was the fact, that, while the buffaloes were pressing and jamming upon us in their greatest fury, this wagon was burning *next to that which contained our gunpowder*. For a while it seemed as if we were doomed to be blown to atoms if we remained, or to be trampled to death if we attempted to escape.

"In ten minutes or less, perhaps in five, the whole herd had passed. I do not know how long the time was, measured by the watch. I only know that no ten *hours* of my life seem to me so long, or so crowded with horrors as those minutes. About a quarter of an hour after they had passed the fire came, but we were by this time well protected, for the fire kindled just around us had spread so as to leave us untouched by that which came from above. And now, Doctor, I think you will agree with me, that, however large the fire on

the island was the other night, and however much
I regretted it, it was only a circumstance compared with one I had seen on the prairies."

"I do agree with you," Dr. Gordon replied ;
"yet let me ask whether in all that horrible melee
of fire and buffaloes there was nobody hurt?"

"Nobody seriously," was the reply, "though
there were some very narrow escapes. When the
cry of Fire! at the ammunition-wagon was given,
there was a boy so badly frightened that he attempted to run. We judge, from circumstances,
that he had no eye nor thought for any danger except that from the gunpowder, for he was seen to
run, and was afterwards picked up, breathless, just
inside the track of the buffaloes; and it is supposed that one of these beasts, finding him in his
way, took him on his horns and flung him back
within the line."

"What became of the hunters who were out at
the time?" Dr. Gordon inquired.

"They had a pretty rough time of it," replied
Wheeler. "One of them must have perished, for
we never saw or heard of him afterwards, although
we remained two days at the Butte and searched
for him in every direction. He and his horse must
have been trampled to death. Of the different
squads that went out, the only one that came in
was that which had gone west. They came at full
speed, with their horses in a lather, and joined us

barely in time to save themselves, but not in time
to help us.   Another party made for the Butte and
sheltered themselves behind it from both buffaloes
and fire; and so did another party by getting down
into the canyon.   But the squad that went south
perceived no sign of danger until it was too late
to return.   The first thing they knew, the buffaloes and the fire were upon them, and they had to
run for their lives.   They got together, all but one
man, and made for a high rock they had seen in
their hunt, and thus escaped.   The missing man,
who had strayed miles away from his companions
in following a bull, saw no chance for life but to
run his jaded horse ahead of the buffaloes, as a
sailor scuds before a storm under bare poles.   He
kept ahead of them mile after mile, when just as
his horse's strength was failing, he saw a mass of
iron-rock * sticking out of the ground like a
stump, about a yard in diameter and two yards
high.   Behind that he dismounted, threw his lariat
over it, drew up his horse as near it as possible to
leave himself room, and there abode his fate.
When the buffaloes came and the earth began to
shake under their tread, his horse became so frantic with the noise, and struggled, and struck at
him so violently with his hoofs, that after hesitating whether to risk death by the horse, or death

---

* These singular masses are said to be *meteoric.*   One of
them forms quite a little hill

by being left afoot on the prairie, he chose the latter, cut the lariat, and set the frightened brute at liberty. It was well he did so, for the moment the horse was free he recovered his senses, crouched up trembling to his master, and there kept perfectly quiet until the herd passed by."

"Do not these terrible fires cause great destruction of life among the poor brute creatures inhabiting the prairies?" Dr. Gordon asked.

"Of course, a good deal," replied Wheeler, "but, so far as we could see, not so much as you might suppose. You know that most of the small creatures that live there burrow in the ground. When a fire comes they have only to go into their holes, and are safe. It is so of wolves, foxes, prairie-dogs and rabbits, and even of owls and snakes. All the larger animals seem to know, as well as we do, that their safety consists in being on the burnt side of the prairie, and I have seen them, when the fire came near, rush right through the flames, and scamper to where the ground is cool. And not only they, but even the grasshoppers, when the flame is not too high, as is the case in the low grass, which they prefer to inhabit, will rise in the air and pitch over the flame into the burnt ground beyond."

CHAPTER XIX.

MARCHING — RAIN — AMBUSH — DETOUR, HIDING
THE TRAIL — CONCEALED ENCAMPMENT — WILY
SCOUT — IMPROVISED ARMOR — WELL-AIMED SHOT
— DANGEROUS PASSAGE — BLOOD ON BOTH SIDES
— CHINNOBEE.

T was nearly midday when, wind and tide both failing, the company landed on a smooth, hard beach, convinced, after a long and laborious tug, that the raft must be abandoned and the passage home attempted by land. They arrived very slowly at this conclusion, both on account of their ignorance of the necessary route, and of what they had reason to believe concerning the unsettled state of the country.

Far as the eye could reach along the coast, the way was open and easy upon a level beach, but in the dim distance was a blue streak in the horizon, a little off shore, indicative of one or more islands; and they knew that in such cases the margin of the coast was apt to be more or less marshy and broken by creeks, if not by rivers. Yet what else

212

could they do? It was useless to stay where they were, and it was possible that the hostility they had experienced was confined to a very few, — at least this was Tomkins' opinion, for which he could give no better reason than his favorite one that he "felt it in his bones."

With this hope they prepared themselves for travel, by each putting up five days' rations, dividing among themselves the cooking utensils, and other necessary things, and concealing in a large hollow log such articles as were too valuable to throw away, and too cumbrous to carry. They then broke up their raft, turned its parts adrift, to leave as few signs as possible for the prying eyes of the savages, and then took up their line of march, Tomkins in the lead, Wheeler in the rear, and Dr. Gordon (by compliment) in the middle. At the same time a scout was kept one or two hundred yards in advance, with orders to reconnoitre every suspicious-looking place and report by concerted signals the appearance of danger.

Their march, during the afternoon, was accomplished without interruption; and, about sunset having reached a spot upon the bluff where was a semicircular wall of sand thrown up by the wind, encompassed by ground free from all coverts within range of ordinary rifle-shot, they determined to complete the breastwork thus half made to their hand by nature, and make it their camping-place

for the night. A fallen tree in the edge of the
forest supplied them with the few sticks needed
for the fire they kindled under the bluff, and a
thicket of palmettos and myrtles furnished the
materials for a shelter. This last they built with
care, being warned by Magruder's never-failing
token that rain might be expected that night; and
it was well that they acted upon the hint, for ere
midnight there commenced a cold drizzle, which
continued far into the next day.

The discomfort of the morning was more than
compensated by reflecting that the cold rain would
probably keep most of the Indians at home, that
its steady fall would interpose a veil between them
and all distant observers, and that the dampness
would materially interfere with the use of the flint
and steel gun, such as the Indians then had. Encouraging themselves, therefore, with these important advantages for a secret march, they pushed
forward as fast and far as possible upon their un-
comfortable way, keeping ready for defence at a
moment's warning.

A drizzling rain upon our coast usually ceases
with the turn of the day or of the tide; and so
they found, for by three o'clock the sun began to
make itself known in both light and heat. Their
success in travel so far had been very cheering,
and several expressed the hope that their annoyers
had been left behind, when the scout was seen to

descend hastily from the bluff and wave his cap
as a token to halt. He reported three armed Indians, apparently in ambush, half a mile ahead.
He said that he had discovered them by means of
his spy-glass, from behind a cover of bushes,
where he himself had watched them unobserved;
that he had attentively regarded their motions and
was confident they were in concealment watching
for something or somebody to pass the beach.

"How lies the coast beyond them?" Tomkins
asked.

"So far as I could see, it bends sharply to the
west for a little way, then trends northward," replied the scout.

"Then we will give our expecting friends the
go-by," said the Sergeant. "We will make a circuit through the woods, and leave them where they
are, to watch for us until they are ready to go
home."

The sluggish tide was still rising. The greater
part of the beach was so firm with shell and sand
as scarcely to receive an imprint of their feet, and
their line of march had been near the water's
edge, in order that their trail might be soon obliterated by the coming tide. The company was
now marched back to a place where the shell extended partly up the bluff. Here they left the
immediate coast, covering with sand and herbage
neir tracks from the water to the top of the bluff,

then making a wide detour around the supposed ambush, they came to the beach at a place beyond sight, and once more resumed their journey.

When the sun was about an hour high, Tomkins ordered a halt, preparatory to encampment. He had already gone ahead and looked out the ground. It was a thick growth of oak and other saplings, where a person in the centre was invisible to any one without, yet was of such narrow compass as to be easily watched by a single sentinel. He did not allow the men to approach this place directly.

" I have a mind," said he, " to try a turn upon our red-skin brothers that may bother them a little. There is our camping-place," he continued, pointing to it from the distance of a quarter of a mile, " but if they come upon our trail to-night, we will make them believe we have gone farther."

Halting them by a well-marked tree, he detailed Simpson to conceal himself near by for the purpose of seeing whether any enemies were upon their trail before dark, and Dr. Gordon remained with him. The others went half a mile farther, to a place where they cooked and ate their supper, Wildcat being dispatched by a circuit with the rations intended for Dr. Gordon, Simpson, and himself. From the fire there made the men dispersed, each a different way, then re-assembled at the appointed tree, and thence marched in single file *to* their sleeping-place. In this last movement each was instructed to step exactly in the track of his file-leader, as Indians do upon the war-path, and the last man of the file, skilled in such work, walked backwards for a short distance, carefully obliterating all signs of the trail. As soon as they were safely lodged within the little grove and a sentinel posted, Tomkins said,—

"Men, if you will keep perfectly quiet, you may all take a sound sleep to-night, all except one for keeping guard, and unless some of you snore uncommon loud, I think Johnny Redskin will be bothered to track out our sleeping-place."

The men smiled their approval of his device, and being weary with a long day's march, gave themselves up very soon to the comforts of their leafy bivouac. Of course no fire was permitted, and no one was allowed to go beyond the limits of the covert.

The peep of day, next morning, saw the camp in motion. Nothing had disturbed their repose during the night, not even the prowling of a panther, nor the howling of a wolf, and an examination by Wheeler and Wildcat, who made a wide circuit around the encampment as soon as it was light, revealed no signs of a moccasined foot in pursuit. There was reason to hope that their oft-baffled pursuers, unless urged on by uncommon earnestness of purpose, would be discouraged from further attempts.   Provision enough for the day's necessities were cooked at the morning fire and by the time the sun had shed his full beams on land and water, they were once more upon their way.

About ten o'clock that morning, however, the scout was seen again to wave his cap, and on making his report he said that he had observed a large bunch of moss hanging rather unnaturally from a tree within fair gun-shot of the beach, and that, after a time, not liking its looks, he had dropped behind a hillock of sand and levelled his gun at it, as if about to shoot, when the bush was evidently shaken as if by some one standing behind.

On this report, the Sergeant dispatched Wheeler and Wildcat, his two keenest observers, to go with the scout and examine the spot more carefully, being supported by the rest, who ensconced themselves behind the ramparts of sand and levelled their guns ready to fire upon the hidden enemy, if he dared to show himself.   The reconnoiterers returned, confirming the report of the scout, and adding that behind the tree on which the moss hung, as if placed there for the purpose of enlarging the screen, the ground had been trampled, but by what or by whom they could not conjecture, unless it had been by some one who had worn a pad of moss tied under the foot to hide the track, for they had seen what answered to a man's tracks,

thus disguised, making off from the tree in a
straight line with the position of the scout, and
leaving small fragments of moss behind.

" More trouble ahead !" Tomkins muttered as
he listened to this report. " More Indians dogging
our trail."

Before, they had marched with due circumspec
tion, but after this their watchfulness was redoubled. There was not a bush, nor hillock, much
less a thicket, within gun-shot of the beach, capable of concealing a foe, that was not examined
before passing. All observed, too, that Simpson's
mode of adjusting his load was such as both to
conceal his face and to act as armor to defend his
vital parts. A bag of biscuits was balanced on
his right shoulder and kept raised as high as his
cap, while a broad-bladed hatchet was stuck under
his vest, on a line with his lungs and heart ; and
a camp-kettle that he volunteered to carry for one
of the men, was hung on his left arm, so as to protect his hip and the greater part of his side.

After travelling thus for about an hour, they
came to a point of woods so thickly grown up with
palmettos and other low shrubs that examination
was perilous as well as hopeless. They, therefore,
moved by with all possible celerity ; but while
doing so, there was heard the sharp crack of a
rifle. Simpson staggered and fell at the water's
edge, and there came from amidst the palmettos a

yell of triumph from at least three voices, which, however, were so broken into short shrill notes as to sound more like the yells of an hundred. Tomkins instantly ordered a charge, and heading the men, who dropped everything except their arms, they rushed up the bluff and into the thicket. Nobody, however, was to be seen, not even the sign of a footprint, although they went to the very spot from which the smoke and the yells seemed to have proceeded. Such, however, was the size and impenetrableness of the thicket — capable of concealing a thousand men in ambush — that Tomkins deemed it prudent to withdraw his little force to the beach, from which he dispatched two of them to a point where they could command the ground without being themselves exposed to danger. They watched a few moments, and saw in the distant underbrush a movement which satisfied them that the foe had retired. To the surprise of every one, Simpson, who they supposed had fallen dead, rejoined them on their return from the charge, and said, with a ghastly attempt at merriment, —

"I thought them red varmints had got me this time. But, unless they have better luck, I hope to die in my bed yet."

"Simpson," said Tomkins earnestly, "what have you been doing to these Indians? They are after you, not after us."

"Not a thing," answered Simpson. "1 never harmed a har o' their heads, so far as I knows. in all my born days. But see, all o' you, wh t a dead aim they tuck at me."

He showed a bullet-hole through his coat in deadly range with his heart, and a bullet battered to the shape of a thin biscuit against the hatchet, which he had worn flat against his side.

"The ball hit me so hard," he continued, "that it knocked the breath clean out of my body, and I was sure for a while that I had got my ticket to t 'other country."

Tomkins mused a moment, then walking aside with Dr. Gordon, said in an undertone : "They singled him out the other night, when he was less in their way than any one else; and, to-day, when there were three of them in the bush, and they might just as easily have picked off three of us as one, there was only one gun fired, and they singled him out again. Simpson lies. He has done the Indians out there a wrong, somehow, and now he is going to get his pay. Take my word for it, he is a dead man, and he knows it."

They resumed their march, and proceeded without interruption for several hours, when they reached a marshy bottom, which they were compelled either to head, by going far into the interior, or to cross at a particular place. There a log lay across the narrow channel, now nearly filled with tide-water, and a blind trail led to it and beyond through a wilderness of mangroves, while on the other side a level strip of hard sand, leading to the beach, lay between the mangrove marsh and the dry land, which was covered with trees and shrubs. Such places are always dangerous to those who are liable to attack. The leaders of the company eyed it for some time and deliberated gravely before they ventured to cross.

But perilous as the passage promised to be, and unpleasant too by reason of the mud, they resolved to attempt it. It was after most of the men had worked their way through, and were luxuriating in the privilege of walking upon firm sand, and Tomkins was lending his assistance to Dr. Gordon through the most miry part of the pass, that three rifles were discharged in quick succession from the edge of the woods. All looked around to ascertain what damage had been done, when poor Simpson was seen to sink like a bag of sand upon the earth. The three men nearest the enemy dropped their loads, and without waiting for orders, rushed forward to the charge, and fired their muskets in the direction from which the shots had come. This was followed by a commotion in the bushes The heads of two or three Indians were seen moving toward the same point, and then there was a disturbance of the undergrowth, as if they were engaged in bearing off a wounded person.

The whole company, with Dr. Gordon among them, now pushed forward to support their advance, who were stopping to reload, and came to the ground supposed to be occupied by the enemy. But on reaching it they had again disappeared. Nothing human was visible. No sound of footsteps was heard among the palmettos or in the open ground beyond. Not a twig snapped, nor leaf rustled. To all appearance, the assailants had, by some magical power, sunk into the earth.

But Tomkins and Wheeler, versed in Indian warfare, were not to be thus eluded. They followed a scarcely discernible trail, marked in one place by a crushed leaf, in another by a newly broken twig, and in another by a spear of grass, bent beneath a softly shod foot, and it was not long before one of them exclaimed, —

"Here is blood!"

This they followed, tracing it, drop by drop, until they reached a place where they saw an elderly Indian crouched behind a thickly leaved vine, and appearing to be severely wounded. One of the men drew his gun to his shoulder, and was in the act of pulling trigger when Dr. Gordon struck up the piece, with the command, "No firing on a prisoner!" and caused its contents to be discharged into the air.

The Indian, who had raised himself on his elbow, and was handling his gun with the show of fight, although the piece was empty, uttered a grunt of surprise, looked approvingly at Dr. Gordon, and dropped his gun beside him in token that the fight was over.

"Why do you shoot at us?" Dr. Gordon earnestly inquired.

The Indian looked fiercely around and answered, "Bad man."

"But we have done you no harm, and wish you none," Dr. Gordon remonstrated.

The Indian looked him full in the eye, as if to gather from his looks what he could gain only in part from his language, and pointing to the beach, said with emphasis, "Bad man there. Bad man kill."

"Do you mean to say that you intended to kill only him?" Dr. Gordon inquired.

"Kill *him,*" the other responded in a tone of assent.

"But why? What has my man done that you should kill him?"

The eye of the Indian flashed with a fierce glare, and he replied in his own language, of which Dr. Gordon could understand nothing except the words, "Holly-woggus-chay," (bad — very mean,) uttered with scorn as he pointed down the bluff. Tomkins, however, who had returned from looking after his own wounded man in time to hear what was last said, remarked —

"I knew it was so. These men were after Simpson, not after us. He has done this old man and his family a wrong, for which they were bound by Indian law to kill him. I don't blame them at all."

On hearing this, Dr. Gordon waited no longer, but, learning that nothing could be done for Simpson, he stooped kindly towards the Indian, whose dignified and fearless bearing had deeply interested him, and said in gentle tones, —

"I am sorry you are hurt. Can I help you? I am a doctor — a medicine man."

The old man pointed to his thigh, which was bleeding profusely from a flesh wound. The ball, as Dr. Gordon ascertained by using a smooth, narrow pencil-case as a probe, had passed nearly through the leg, and lodged within an inch of the other side, severing one or two small blood vessels in its passage.

"I can take out this ball, and you will soon get well. Shall I do it?"

On this being repeated by Tomkins in the Muscogee dialect, the Indian nodded and uttered the half-grunted syllable "N'Cah!" in assent.

Dr. Gordon began at once to prepare for the operation, while Tomkins, after the exchange of a few words in Indian, went in the direction indicated by the old man's finger, and shouted in the same language, —

"So-massee! Moheta! Come! Chinnobee call."

P

CHAPTER XX.

EXTRACTING A BALL FROM A WOUND — NEWS OF
THE MISSING ONES — INDIAN REVENGE — SIMPLE
HAND-BARROW FOR CARRYING A WOUNDED PER-
SON — CONFESSION OF CRIME — PREVALENCE OF A
MOTHER'S TEACHING — MISERABLE END OF A LAW
LESS LIFE.

WO fine-looking young men, sons of the
elder, arose from their concealment,
within half gunshot of the place, and
came fearlessly forward. The proposed
operation was explained to them, and they were
asked to assist. Not a word was exchanged between them and their father, only a look of inquiry and a smile of approval, when they knelt
affectionately, one on each side of him, and watched
with eager interest the entrance of the knife and
the expulsion of the ball. The only instruments
at command were Dr. Gordon's pocket-knife, and
his silver pencil-case. Of course the incision
through the skin and an inch into the flesh, with
so dull an instrument, must have been painful, but
the old man gave no indication of pain. He

226

talked with his sons as serenely as if the operation were performing on some one else; and when it was over, and the wound washed with water and bound up, he turned to Dr. Gordon with a look of gratitude, and said, —

"Enk-lis-chay!* Chinnobee will not forget."

Dr. Gordon then delivered him to his sons, with a few simple instructions, the substance of which was to depend mainly on cold water and cleanliness until the ninth or tenth day, which is the usual crisis with gun-shot wounds. The young men, as well as their father, seemed perfectly to understand the character and treatment of such wounds, and with grateful looks expressed their thanks in broken English, which was pleasant to the ear, not only for the novelty of its tones and combinations, but as a token that the tomahawk was buried, although Dr. Gordon could scarcely maintain his gravity when one of the young men, wishing to express his sense of obligation in a more civilized way, perpetrated a most awkward bow, and accompanied it with the words, " Welcome, thankum ? "

The Doctor then proposed to visit Simpson in person, and suggested that while he was gone Tomkins should inquire of these new acquaintances the best route to Tampa, and whether they could give any tidings of his missing ones.

* Good! very good.

Tomkins promised to do as he was desired, but Dr. Gordon paused before leaving, and asked in an undertone, —

"Do you think they can be trusted? You will bear in mind that they are Indians, and that the little we know of them is ' their consummating an act of deadly revenge."

"Trust them?" echoed Tomkins. "Yes, certainly. Chinnobee is a chief, not very high, it is true, only a Tustanuggee; still he is a man of character, and he and his sons have been on Simpson's trail for nearly three years, dogging every step, and watching their chance to kill him."

"And you give this as your reason for trusting them?" Dr. Gordon musingly inquired.

"I do," the other replied, "for I have always observed that Indians who are most faithful to avenge a wrong, according to their law, are also most faithful to remember a favor."

Dr. Gordon pondered this last remark. There was a deep philosophy in it, and it coincided with his own observation of Indian character. Still he hesitated to entrust the precious interests of his children to the partial keeping of Indians of whom he knew so little, and that little an act of deadly feud. But would it not, after all, be best to inquire of them? He drew a long breath, then said to Tomkins, "Yes, go on!" and went to look after Simpson.

To these inquiries Chinnobee replied that he and his sons knew little of the country, being themselves not residents, but only visitors from the Creek nation in Alabama; that there was an inland route to Tampa, which they might travel with safety, since most of the hostile Indians lived farther south, and the minds of all had been much mollified by the news of a proposed council at Payne's Landing; still, that the route was so greatly interrupted by creeks and swamps that it would be much more easy and desirable to return by water, if canoes could be obtained. He said, too, that about ten days previous a sail-boat, containing several persons, had been seen upon the coast near an island which the Indians never visited, and which they called *The Island of the Great Spirit*, but whether they landed, or where they went, he never learned. He also stated that, two days after the recent gale, a half-breed Indian, answering to the description of Riley, had been picked up in a marsh near that island so nearly dead from cold and starvation that he could give no account of himself; but that he was now doing well. Of the negro man, Sam, he had heard nothing.

On being asked whether canoes could be obtained from the natives in the neighborhood, he replied that he did not know, for the people there were not Creeks, as most of the Seminoles were, but a colony of Choctaws, with whom he did not feel so free, but that he would cause inquiry to be made, and report the result two days from that time.

Dr. Gordon, returning now from his visit to the wounded man on the beach, authorized Tomkins to say, in his name, that he was ready to pay any reasonable price for canoes, and also to say to Chinnobee and his sons that if they would bring back to Tampa his children, and Riley, and Sam, he would give them his hatful of silver money.

When Tomkins made this last offer the old man's eyes glistened with pleasure, but he raised himself into a more erect posture, and said, with an air of dignity,—

"Tell the medicine man that his words are good, and no doubt his money is bright. Tell him, that Chinnobee and his sons will do all they can for him, but that they can take no money from the man who saved Chinnobee's life."

In making their preparations to depart, the young men cut two light stiff poles, capable of bearing a man's weight; then stretching their father on his blanket, they laid these poles close by him, one on each side, and fastening it securely to them at full length, they kept both blanket and poles distended by means of three cross-bars lashed firmly to them, one at their father's feet, another just under his head, and a third over his stomach

These side poles projected far enough beyond his head and feet to be used as handles, which the young men grasped, and raising their father gently from the ground, they bore him off with ease, having his rifle laid beside him in the hand-barrow, and their own tied to their backs.

When Dr. Gordon made his first visit to Simpson, he found him lying, propped against a tree, near the place where he had fallen, with three ball-holes in his body, each of which was mortal. He was writhing in great pain, and asked for nothing but water and a speedy death. He was so plainly beyond the reach of help from medicine or surgery that Dr. Gordon ordered simply his removal to a spot beyond the reach of tide-water, where he might pass, without disturbance, the few hours that remained to him. On his second visit, perceiving that he had recovered from the exhaustion attending removal, and casting in his mind for some mode of relief, he concluded to try upon him the effect of a few words of sympathy. Seldom is a sufferer, and especially one conscious of approaching death, insensible to kind words. They refresh the soul as cool water refreshes the body. Simpson listened, at first impatiently, and without reply, as was to be expected from one of his dark and ungenial spirit; but soothed by the gentle tones of a person whom he believed in his heart to be a g od man, he finally said :

"Captain, I want to make a clean breast of it afore I die. All the trouble that has come on you and the rest by them Injins, is on my account. They didnt mean nothing agin you; it was all agin me. When I was detailed at Tampa to come with you, I would have got off if I could, for I knowed them'ar fellow had been hanging about the neighborhood for a long time, watching a chance to kill me. The moment we met them in their canoes at sea, on that deer hunt, I knowed ther was gwine to be trouble."

Here he writhed again, suffering apparently as much in mind as in body. Dr. Gordon asked no questions, preferring to let him confess just so much as he pleased in his own time and way.

"I know who they were that shot me, the same if I seed their faces when they fired, " said Simpson. "Old Chinnobee is as good a man as a Coosa ever gits to be. I haven't a word to say agin him or his sons for doing what they did. By Injin law they were bound to kill me, if they could. It was in hopes to keep out of ther way that I enlisted in the army, after losing my property; but this only tied me hand and foot, and throwed me in ther way."

Pausing awhile, as if in deep reflection, he uttered a groan of pain and continued: "I ought n' to a-done what I did. I married the old man's daughter, and she made me a good wife, but I left

her and tuck up with another 'oman. She grieved
over it until she died, so I am told. But there
was something worse than that. The old man's
oldest son came to talk with me about my leaving
his sister, and how grieved she was, and I got
mad and — I —, yes, I killed him." Here his
face became distorted, and, wringing his hands, he
said :

"Oh, I did wrong, sir ; I did wrong. He was
only an Injin, and a Coosa, but he was a good
man. He saved my life once when I was a-drown-
ing. I acted mean to kill him. If it was to do
over again I wouldn't do it. I wish I hadn't a-
done it. I wish the old man could forgive me
afore I die ; but that can't be — an Injin never
forgives."

He groaned again and was silent. There was
very little in what he said that had even a leaning
towards religion, (for the religious sentiment recog-
rizes God in all things, and he had not recognized
Him at all,) but it was so much nearer an approach
than he had ever before made, that Dr. Gordon
esteemed it a favorable time for leading his mind
that way, as far as he would consent to be led.
Indeed he indulged a little hope that, though the
wretched man had been thoroughly bred in heathen-
ism by his mother, yet possibly some germs oí
what he had heard from his father might now be
taking effect, and that he might even wish to have

a prayer offered for himself. For the purpose, therefore, of allowing him to express himself on this point, the Doctor said :

"My poor fellow ! I am sincerely sorry for you, and wish I could do something for your help. You will not forget, I presume, that there is another and a greater One whose forgiveness you need even more than the Indian's."

" Who is that?" Simpson hastily inquired. " Do you mean God Almighty ? I never did Him any harm, and he knows it."

" Never did Him any harm !" Dr. Gordon echoed in amazement. " Did you not just now confess your wrong to the Indian?"

"And what is that to Him ?" the other inquired almost fiercely. " He is no Injin."

" It is this much," replied Dr. Gordon, exceedingly grieved to have a dispute with a dying man, yet hoping that something might soften and set right the poor fellow's feeling, " this much, that the Lord is the heavenly Father of every person, of every color and condition, on the face of the earth, and like a father He regards every wrong done to one of His children as wrong done to Himself."

Simpson almost laughed with derision as he said, " O, go away, Doctor ! Don't try to scare a dying man with such a notion, when you yourself know, it can't be true "

Dr. Gordon could scarcely keep the tears from his eyes on hearing these almost blasphemous words from one in his condition. Of course he could say nothing more, after a request of the kind, coming with all the force of a command. He concluded the conference with saying:

"I leave you in the hands of the Lord, who has proclaimed himself 'slow to anger, abundant in mercy, and ready to forgive.'"

To this Simpson made no reply. He turned himself upon his side with a groan, and with what sounded like a half-uttered curse, but against whom, could not be determined, and begged some one to give him water. His friendly visitor saw that nothing more from him in the shape of words would be of any avail, and, indeed, nothing either in the shape of bodily comfort. The higher and the lower natures were both in a condition equally desperate.

All that any one could do was to save him from needless discomfort. A bed of soft elastic moss had already been provided. Now, a close tent of palmetto leaves was built around his bed to protect him against dew or possible rain in the night, and one of the company was detailed to stay with him as nurse, and with these preparations he was left to meet his fate. He lingered through the night, and until ten o'clock the next day, sullenly refusing to converse with any one. Then, with the oft-repeated experience of dying people who are, by some means unknown to the living, made conscious of approaching death, he called hastily for Tomkins, and said to him in piteous tones :

"Tomkins, don't let them Coosas sculp me. I know they'll do it, if you let 'em. I'd rather you would throw me into the river. Don't let 'em sculp and mangle me — don't, don't!"

These were his last words. He died like an Indian. The wild teachings of his mother had prevailed over those of his father, if any such had been given ; illustrating the well-known fact that the women of every family and community must lead in all matters pertaining to morality and religion, or nothing can be effected; nay, that when the mothers and sisters *mislead*, the corrective efforts by the other sex will be all made in vain.

The last request of the dying man was faithfully complied with. The body was first enveloped in its own clothing, so as to protect every part as perfectly as possible from the encroachment of fish and crabs; then it was encased in a rude substitute for a coffin, the best they could devise out of palmetto leaves and bark ; the whole was loaded with sand and shells, and lowered with appropriate ceremonies into the deepest water they could reach by means of a rudely constructed raft.

The duties attendant upon his death and burial afforded melancholy, but perhaps not unsuitable employment to that day of which the ardent David sung: "This is the day the Lord hath made; we will rejoice and be glad in it."* It was the Sabbath.

CHAPTER XXI.

SOMASSEE AND THE CANOES—PRODUCING FIRE WITHOUT MATCHES OR TINDER— WILD VEGE-TABLES—INDIAN MODE OF COOKING AN OPOSSUM —RETURN TO TAMPA—DR. GORDON'S ILLNESS.

HILE the company were enjoying their Monday morning's meal the sentinel gave the signal of alarm. Each man sprang to his musket and stood ready for duty; an armed Indian had appeared through a distant glade. The spy-glass, however, quieted all apprehension, and sent each man back to the more pleasant occupation which he had left. The Indian who approached was young Somassee. He had come according to the promise made by his father two days before, to report as to the possibility of obtaining canoes.

He said that several good ones, capable of containing three persons each, with their necessary luggage, could be had at a few hours distance in

*Psalm cxviii : 24.

the interior, and delivered, if desired, that same evening; that Chinnobee sent his "welcome-thanks" to the "medicine man," and reported his wound to be doing finely; also that he, Somassee, came, by his father's instruction, to say that he might accompany the party to the neighborhood of Tampa, on condition that he should not be mo-lested for the killing of Simpson.

Upon this last point, Dr. Gordon and the Sergeant in command consulted together. Somassee's presence on the voyage would, on many accounts, be highly desirable. As for the act of manslaughter, however irregular and criminal it would have been if committed by a white man in a white man's country, it was a very different thing, in a legal point of view, at the hands of an Indian, acting according to the usages of his people, and within the boundary recognized as theirs. Dr. Gordon recalled the fact, also, that in the infancy of civilization, justice, such as had been enacted in the case of Simpson, was *required by the Divine law* at the hand of the nearest kinsman of a murdered man. The greatest difficulty on Tomkins' part, was the military aspect of the case, for he said the rule is that "the uniform protects the soldier," and that, although *he* had not a word to say against the Indian's obeying the laws of his country, he was not sure but that his military superiors and his government might require the matter to

be taken up. It was, therefore, agreed that Somassee should go with them to the neighborhood
of Tampa, but should keep beyond the reach of
the military authorities for fear of the consequences :

"*I* will not touch him," said Tomkins, "until
so required by some one who has a right to command."

As for the canoes, it was thought that at least
three would be required, and that it would be best
to have them delivered at the earliest possible moment. With these instructions, with the promise
of freedom from molestation, and with all the
money necessary to effect the purchase, Somassee
departed on his errand.

Scarcely had he gone, however, before Dr. Gordon's mind, now relieved in a great measure from
a sense of responsibility concerning the safe return
of the men to their command, reverted with natural earnestness to the circumstances of his children, began to question whether he could not with
all propriety deliver the men to the command of
Tomkins on their return to Tampa, while he,
with Somassee to assist (and why not Wildcat
too ?) should take one of the canoes and push his
exploration farther down the coast. There was
only one difficulty in the way : ever since the arresting of their journey on Saturday, he had been
conscious o the coming on of a deep-seated and

serious illness, and ere the return of Somassee that evening with the boats, the symptoms had been so far developed as to convince him that duty, even to his missing children, required him to seek, as soon as possible, the attention of some one skilled in the medical art.

While preparing for their intended embarkation next morning, two very important deficiencies were discovered — one in the supply of food, and the other in their fire, or rather in the means of producing it. The rations were not actually exhausted, but they were so scant as to be insufficient for the two or three days that must elapse before they could reach Tampa. Tomkins, therefore, desired Wheeler and Wildcat, who had been so successful on a former occasion, to prepare for another fire-hunt that night, and also detailed Jones, who had been appointed fishing-master in the early part of the expedition, to select his companion and try his hand upon the finny tribes.

The latter promptly obeyed orders, and departed with Thompson, the Irishman, whom he proposed to initiate into the mysteries of Florida fishing. They had no boat, no net, no bait, and but one fishing-line between them, yet, in the course of several hours, they returned loaded, each with a string of fish as long and heavy as he could carry without dragging; and then asked permission to go out after brant and ducks, which they reported to be so plentiful in places that it was scarcely possible for a hat to fall, on the larger part of an aore, without covering some one of these birds.*

Wheeler and Wildcat were compelled, in their preparations for the night's hunt, to perform a feat which is by no means so easy as most people suppose, and that was to originate a fire on a damp a.y. Their last match had been used; all their tinder, too, was gone; and the rain which had extinguished their fire, and which continued to fall, had so thoroughly soaked everything exposed that, even if a fire were originated, it would be difficult to nurse it into a blaze. Woodsman though he was, and accustomed to all the crafts of a wild life, Wheeler knew that the task would be difficult. He, nevertheless, went manfully to work. First, he tried to ignite a dry cotton rag by using it as a wad over a small charge of powder, and shooting it upward from his gun; then by shooting it downward on the dry floor of the palmetto tent; then by enclosing it in the " pan " of his flint and steel musket, and packing it all round with a good priming of gun powder. Failing in all these, he had gone to a hollow tree, and obtained from the inside some dry, tindery wood, which he was en-

* The seaboard of Florida is so crowded with water-fowl in the winter-time, that this report of Jones was not much of an exaggeration.

gaged in trying to ignite by holding it at the muzzle of his gun and shooting against it a small charge of powder, when he saw Wildcat's face writhing with the signs of almost insuppressible laughter. Reminded, instantly, of the fact that Indians make it a religious duty to produce *new fire* every year, at the time of their green-corn dances, and that their young people are early trained to the art, he turned suddenly to his young friend, and said to him, with an appearance of great wrath,—

" You piece of Red-skin mischief? What are you laughing at?"

" I no laugh!" answered Wildcat, pretending to be as much alarmed as the other pretended to be angry.

" Come here, then, and start this fire," said Wheeler; " I know you have been taught how to do it."

" Got no fire-sticks," * Wildcat replied. " But Somassee got some. Wait till he come."

---

* By "fire-sticks" we are to understand two small pieces of wood, (one quite hard and the other moderately hard,) which Indians use in originating new fire. These are of several different forms, and are operated in different ways. The way most easily described is that in which the fire-block (a piece of walnut six inches long by two or three broad) has a slight *groove* hollowed in its surface, in which the other stick (a piece of seasoned hickory, sharpened at one end) is rubbed steadily back and forth until the friction produces *

"Do you know of no way to start a fire except by sticks?" asked Wheeler.

"Yes, I know," the other replied, "but I got no string."

"What kind of a string do you wish."

"Twine string, pretty good," Wildcat answered.

Wheeler felt in his pocket and produced several pieces of tarred twine, which as sailing master he had kept about him for the purpose of repairing the cordage of the barge. One of these Wildcat selected, and making its end fast to a peg, and giving it a turn around a small dry stick, he drew the cord moderately tight with one hand, while with the other he moved the stick rapidly back and forth. The friction soon caused both stick and string to smoke. Then a spark of fire appeared. This was enclosed as quickly as possible between two pieces of the dry decayed wood already provided, and waved between the hands in a long swinging motion through the air, until it was fanned into a flame.

spark. The other mode is by a fire-block with a little *hole* gouged in its centre, where a stick, the size of a man's finger or larger, is made to rub, either by a drill bow, or by being twirled between the palms of the hands, (which is the usual mode,) until the spark appears. The operation requires great skill, and there are few white persons who can succeed except after long and patient practice. These fire-sticks are usually carried suspended around the neck, or in the pouch, along with the tinder or lightwood.

All this part of the work had been done under the shelter of the tent; but that the fire should be of any avail it was necessary that it should be made in the open air, which was filled with fine drizzling rain. Yet the ingenuity of the two workers obviated even this difficulty. Wheeler stretched a blanket over the place of the intended fire, and Wildcat went to Magruder and said, —

"Where the fry-pan? Lend me."

Using this last bottom upward, as a temporary hearth, and keeping the blanket spread above until the incipient fire was strong enough to defy the falling drops, they fed their little blaze first with fine dry shavings, then with splinters a little larger, and partly with twigs and small branches, on the well-known rule that a *feeble fire will be fed with small wood,* while it will be killed with that which is large.

When Somassee returned with the canoes and was informed of the shortness of supplies, he said that he too would go out on the fire hunt that night, but in the meantime he would do something else; provide some vegetables. Asking Magruder, the cook, to accompany him with a basket and an axe, he returned before dark with three kinds of edible products. One of these was the cabbage palmetto, which though called cabbage is more in shape like a short club, a foot or more long, the size of a man's fist at one end, and of his wrist at

the other, being the tender terminal bud of the
tree palmetto. Another was the tanyah, a turnip-
looking root, growing abundantly in wet ground,
and highly esteemed as a table luxury. The
third was what none but an Indian could eat,
namely, the root of the Smilax (known by some as
the chainy briar, and by others as the bamboo, cf
which there are several varieties), somewhat like
an immense ground artichoke in shape, but not in
tenderness. When young and tender, it is boiled
and eaten as bread. When ripe it is pounded and
its starch separated from it by water, producing
the *red flour* of the Seminoles, as the coonta or
arrow-root produces their white flour.

These vegetables, added to the fish already obtained by Jones and Thompson, and to the ducks
and trout brought in afterwards, would have
superseded the necessity of the fire-hunt that night,
had not the minds of the hunters been set upon it,
as a matter of pleasure, as well as of profit. For
they went as proposed, and returned about ten
o'clock with a large buck, and two opossums.
The venison was committed to the culinary care
of Magruder, assisted by others; but the opossums
Somassee took into his own charge. After scalding off the hair, and cleansing, he introduced each
opossum into the cavity of a pumpkin, of which he
had brought several in the canoes, and burying
them under the embers of a large fire, allowed

them to remain there until pumpkin and 'possum were cooked together. It was a mode of preparing the flesh which the men seemed greatly to enjoy.

These labors extended far into the night, but being necessary preparation for their voyage, they were thus enabled to start all the earlier and more joyously the next morning.

The three canoes had a prosperous voyage. Late Thursday afternoon, November 11th, the company disembarked at Fort Brooke, after a prolonged absence of fifteen days, during which they had met with the loss of their barge, and of one of their men. The only remuneration Somassee would receive for his trouble was one of the canoes, to enable him to return to his father, and of which possession was given him upon the beach at some distance from the Fort, to avoid contact with the military authorities. Before leaving, he agreed upon a certain time and place in which Wildcat should meet him if he could obtain permission, and unite with him in another hunt for the young marooners.

Just as the company were disembarking, they saw far away over the waters, illumined by the declining sun, a dim speck approaching from the mouth of the bay. This was a boat, manned by two fishermen familiar with the coast, who had been dispatched by Major Burke, at his private expense, to obtain tidings of the barge's company, for whom he had been feeling increasingly anxious ever since the gale of the 31st. These men had gone as far as Charlotte Harbor, where they had received an account of the killing of Simpson, which had been exaggerated into a bloody fight between some United States troops and a party of Indians, with heavy loss on both sides. This story caused them to stop their cruise and to return home, keeping so far to sea as to be almost overwhelmed by the rough water.

By the time the company landed, Dr. Gordon was so feeble as to be unable to walk alone. He was supported to the officers' quarters by his friends, the Major, and the Surgeon of the post. His pale and haggard face gave such unmistakable evidence of the ravages of disease that the Surgeon insisted on taking him immediately in charge, and required him to go to bed.

"I do not see how I can possibly spare the time to be sick," said the sufferer.

"And I do not see how you can possibly avoid it," said the physician. "You are, no doubt, practitioner enough to know that diseases, like weeds, are more easily managed when they first appear than after they have gained strength. You have allowed yours too much the start already."

Before committing himself to the hands of the doctor, he called for his cousin and requested him to communicate with Mrs. Gordon, informing her of his present inability to write, but saying nothing of the accident befalling the young people, and advising her to remain in Charleston until she heard from him again. He also requested that a boat might be hired and dispatched, with a note to some reliable person at Key West, offering a large reward for the safe and speedy delivery of his children, and of the persons missing in his service. At the same time he took pen and paper, and in few words stated to Mrs. Gordon that he had just returned unwell from a cruise down the coast; that the Surgeon had forbidden his writing until the next weekly mail, at which time he hoped to communicate more fully; and that, for the present, he had requested her cousin, Major Burke, to write in his name all that he wished to say about her coming, and about himself.

With these instructions, and with the request also that a messenger might be dispatched to Bellevue, informing his servants of his return, and of his sickness, and calling for William, his body servant, to attend him as nurse, he invited the Surgeon to come in, and said to him, —

"Now, Doctor, I commit myself into your hands and the Lord's, asking f r as speedy a restoration to my work as your skill and his blessing may effect, well knowing that my case promises to put your skill to the test."

Within three hours he was wandering in the

delirium of a brain fever. His unrestrained utterances during this time gave evidence of two things, — the depth of that anguish by which he had been tried, and the secret of that remarkable tranquillity with which these sufferings had been borne.

The next morning his symptoms so far abated that he complained only of an intense headache, and Major Burke took advantage of this to write to Mrs. Gordon with at least verbal truth, and say that her husband seemed to be doing well. His letter, written over and over again until several sheets had been sacrificed in the endeavor, was in the following words, —

"TAMPA BAY, FLORIDA, Nov. 12, 1830.

" *My Dear Cousin:*

"Our mails are so few and far between, and your good husband is suffering so dreadfully under one of his unusually severe headaches, that, rather than have you made uneasy by not receiving a letter by the present mail, — especially as the preceding one was probably lost in a freshet,— I have consented to act as his amanuensis. Indeed, he has a touch of fever to-day — not enough for any one to perceive but our Surgeon, who, however, has seen fit to forbid his writing, lest it might aggravate the symptoms.

"I suspect that this sickness, if such it may be called, has been brought on partly by disquiet of mind about Sam, the carpenter, whom he had sent off with a half-breed Indian about ten days or a fortnight ago to a neighboring island, and of whom nothing has since been heard. Whether some accident has befallen them, or whether Sam has concluded to seek his freedom among the Seminole Indians, as many others of his color have done, we can only conjecture. The Doctor feels sure that something wrong has happened, for he says that Sam was very faithful and contented, and he fears that both he and the Indian may have been lost in the recent gale, as the boat in which they went off was not capable of standing very rough water. The Doctor felt so uneasy that he himself went down the coast to explore, and it is from this cruise that he has returned unwell.

"Your young folks are a charming set, especially my little cousin Mary, with whom (as young ladies are rather scarce at Tampa) I take the liberty of an occasional flirtation. Harold McIntosh, your nephew, is such a manly fellow, and Robert, your son, so intelligent, and little Frank, so full of his harmless fun, that they made themselves great favorites at the Fort, both with officers and men. I have not seen them, nor heard from them for some days, nor have they made me more than one real visit, Dr. Gordon's place being barely in sight, over the water, and too far off by land for a morning or evening call; but I hope to see them again in a few days, and have no doubt they will enjoy themselves with us. They were in the best of health when I last heard.

"Dr. Gordon requests me to suggest that, as the house is in a state so unfinished, in consequence of the protracted absence of Sam, you had better not come until he can announce that all is ready. I paid him a visit soon after his coming, and find that he keeps an excellent bachelor's hall. So you need feel no uneasiness about his being comfortably cared for. I'll answer for Judy's housekeeping qualities. or rather her cookery, for during my visit the housekeeper was my bright-faced little coz.

"The Doctor is having a delightful place fitted up for you, and I trust soon to see it graced by your own cheerful presence.

"Very truly and affectionately your cousin,

"WALTER BURKE."

'P. S.—The Doctor puts in a word more, to say, kisses to his dear little Anna and Tommie, and he hopes to send you a long letter by next mail.   W. B.

"Mrs. Anna H. Gordon, Charleston, S. C."

CHAPTER XXII.

ILLIAM arrived the same day, accord-
ing to orders, and on the same boat
came Judy. As soon as she heard of
her master's illness, she packed up a few
articles of her own, and such also of his as she
supposed would be useful, gave directions to her
obedient husband, Peter, what to do during her
absence, and when William came to the boat, he
found her already seated, and ready for departure.

" W'at you doin yuh, Judy?" he asked in remonstrance. But Judy answered not a word.

" You got no business yuh," he continued. Still
Judy was silent, retaining her place on one of the
thwarts, with her elbow on her knee, and her hand

251

half covering her face, and looking composedly down upon the several little packages beside her.

"He nebber sen' fuh you. Yo' name ain't in de paper at all," William persisted.

"But I gwine, dough," answered Judy, as composedly as a queen. Then with sudden energy she argued : " You tink I gwine let my mossa be sick 'mong dem stranger folks; no missis dey to nuss him ; no chillun; not eben Judy to wash he clothes, or mek he gruel. My name ent in de paper, for true, but I tell you w'at, William, wen people sick you men can't nuss 'em liken what us women. I gwine for sure, 'cept you pitch me out."

And go she did, and was so serviceable by her thoughtful and delicate attentions, that the Surgeon at last put her name too "in the paper," as she said, or at least told her to remain and help until her own master ordered her back to Bellevue.

This, however, did not take place for nearly a fortnight. Despite of all the Surgeon could do, the fever returned that night with increased violence and continued with little abatement far into the following week, when after a refreshing sleep, in which he had been watched over most carefully by the faithful Judy, he awoke with his mind perfectly clear, and from that moment began slowly to amend.

In the meantime, Wildcat, whose restlessness

had increased as Dr. Gordon's illness advanced,
applied to his patron and employer for permission
to return home, promising to be back before Dr.
Gordon should need his services for another trip,
and expressing the hope that ere his return he
might be able to obtain more satisfactory tidings
of his young friends. He left on the 14th, spent
one day with his mother, then joined Somassee at
a time and place agreed upon, and by the 27th returned to Tampa, reporting that he and his friend
had explored the coast landward, as Dr. Gordon
and the barge's company had explored it by water;
that, although he had not been able to see or hear
anything of the young marooners, he had brought
back something that might prove to be a sign of
them. This was a battered gourd, that had been
thickly coated with a mixture of beeswax and
rosin to make it water-tight, and adorned with a
tiny flag to attract attention, and contained a
writing that had been carefully sealed up within.
This gourd, with its contents, had been picked up
on the beach by a Mickasuky Indian, by whom it
had been broken open, and from whom it had been
purchased by Wildcat, at the cost of a few charges
of gunpowder.

Most eagerly did Dr. Gordon seize upon this
little paper and most powerfully restorative did
its contents prove. The Surgeon declared that it
was more effectual and health-giving than all the

medicines in his possession. It was nothing less than a note in the handwriting of his son Robert and though part of it was lost, and the remainder sadly obliterated by salt water, it gave almost all the information needed for hope and comfort. Its legible portions were as follows, —

"Saturday, Nov. 6, 1830
" * * * * * * * * * * *
Do not be distressed. * * island next the sea.
* * All of us are safe and well, and * * *
* * * * our boat was lost in the * * *
* * * * 31st * * * * * Sam * *
* * * arm and leg broke the night of the gale, but is now doing well. * * * next week begin on our canoe in which to return. * * ."

On the outside, the address was only legible in part, and afforded, after much deciphering, the following words, —

"To Dr. * * * don,
" Care of Major * * * *

" Whoever delivers * * * * * * liberally rewarded."

Oh what a relief these words were to the grief-worn father! True, no one could tell how greatly the words that were legible might have been altered from their apparent meaning by the intervening words which could not be read; but of several things there could be no doubt, — his children and Sam were alive and well six days after

the gale. It was almost as certain that they were
on some island, where they had lost their boat in
the gale, where they had been joined by Sam, who
had met with a serious, though not fatal, accident,
and where they intended to prepare a canoe and
attempt their return by water.

With this cheering intelligence he dispatched
Judy to Bellevue to make certain preparations for
him in anticipation of his speedily going off on
another cruise, and also sent word to Somassee,
who lingered in the neighborhood, requesting him
to be ready to join him in another exploring tour
the following week.

The day after Wildcat's return, Dr. Gordon made
his first appearance in the open air ; at which time,
taking a comfortable seat, he requested permission
to see the crew of the ill-fated barge. On their coming together, he expressed, in the presence of their
Commandant and others, his high appreciation of
their conduct as soldiers while acting in his service, and his thanks to them as men for the sympathy and respect they had uniformly shown him
during the expedition; and he concluded by delivering to Tomkins a little bag full of shining
dollars, which he begged might be distributed
among the men, reserving to Tomkins and Wheeler
a somewhat larger share in proportion to their enlarged responsibility.

This complimentary language, in the hearing

of their officers, enhanced by his act of liberality, soon won for him the hearts of all whom he addressed, and, through them, the good will of the soldiers in the Fort. After they had retired, he asked permission for Wheeler and Wildcat to accompany him in the yet unfinished work of exploring the coast, and on its being granted, he fixed a day in which they, with Somassee, should meet him at Bellevue, prepared for a tour of indefinite extent.

The following Monday morning, Wildcat announced a message from Somassee, that by the time of " high sun " next day, he would be at Bellevue, ready for service.

Dr. Gordon called for his physician and informed him of his desire to set out immediately upon his expected tour. The surgeon shook his head, saying, —

" Impossible, sir, impossible, after such an attack of brain fever, to go to work so soon."

His patient, however, conscious of a rapid return of health and strength, resolved that he would at once begin his *preparations*, although in deference to the opinion of his esteemed adviser he would delay his departure from Fort Brooke until next day. That delay came near being fatal.

A little coal of fire tightly compressed in a handful of raw cotton can be kept alive for hours; *

---

* Our Southern negroes sometimes carry in this way their fire for smoking in the cotton fields.

and if closely packed in dry cotton clothing, it will smoulder perhaps for days before burning its way through, and bursting into flames. The laundress in the officers' quarters of Fort Brooke was an inveterate smoker. While engaged in her work that day an unobserved coal had been jostled from her pipe and nicely covered between two pieces of highly inflammable clothing. The package, thus unconsciously prepared for future danger, was carried, and, notwithstanding a very suspicious smell, was carefully laid against a wooden wall in a closet almost adjoining Dr. Gordon's room.

Between that room and the one occupied by Major Burke, was a small apartment appropriated to Wildcat, who on the present occasion had invited Wheeler to spend the night with him, both having already obtained leave of absence. Away in the dead of night, Wildcat was awakened by a sense of suffocation and a smell of fire. He roused his companion, and they went immediately to the next room to apprise their Commandant. Major Burke had had experience enough in such scenes to know that the more perfectly composed and energetic the person in control can be, the better. Though just aroused from sleep, his directions were few, simple, and to the point. They were, to raise no alarm at present, in order to avoid needless confusion; to have certain persons come

R

to him, each with a bucket of water and some tumblers; * and for Wheeler and Wildcat to accompany him in a farther search for the place of the fire.

They went rapidly, though quietly, along the corridor, guided by the smell, until they saw a whitish smoke stealing through Dr. Gordon's doorway. They knocked lightly, but received no reply; then more loudly; then with a gentle call to the sleepers within. Receiving still no reply, the Major opened the door, and through the cloud of thin, though suffocating smoke, they saw Dr. Gordon upon his bed, and William, his servant, on a pallet, each sleeping a sleep that soon would have known no waking—the noxious vapors that always arise from a smouldering fire or from burning charcoal, having completely filled the room.

"Hold your breath, or at least breathe as little as possible the vapors of the room," said the Major to his companions. "We must go in and remove them."

William, whose face was fortunately near a crevice that allowed the coming in of fresh air, was aroused from his lethargy by the act of handling.

---

* In contending with fire, it is usually all-important to economize the water at command. For this purpose, at the beginning, *a tumbler* is very useful, as it projects the water, without waste, upon any particular spot selected. Fire-buckets are made tumbler-shaped.

He opened his eyes, saw the room full of smoke, and sprang to his feet, ready to assist, though feeling weak and confused. Dr. Gordon, however, did not recover consciousness until he had been some time in the open air.

Once in the room with a light, it was manifest that the smoke came through the wall, and that the place of the fire must be sought beyond. The next room, which they now wished to examine, was so densely filled with smoke that it was almost dangerous to enter. Major Burke and his attendants stood at the door, through which a great volume of the outer air rushed in the moment it was opened, and from which a quantity of the smoke surged back like a reflected billow, but no fire was to be seen.

"I can go in there now and find where the fire is," said Wheeler, after allowing some of the smoke to be exchanged for air.

He took a silk handkerchief, wet it in one of the buckets, which had by this time come, tied it closely around his mouth that his breath might be strained of the smoke in case of need, and was preparing to enter, when he took a long string from his pocket, fastened one end around his wrist, and gave the other to the Major to hold, saying,—

"It is possible the smoke may blind me; if so, I will feel my way out by this string."

He drew a full breath and pushed his way to

the opposite wall, which he felt all over with his hands, but discovering no unusual heat, returned to the door for another breath. On entering the second time, he made first for a window, the sash of which he raised, and remained long enough to breathe again, when he passed to the other wall, ran his hand rapidly over it, and returned to the door, saying, —

"I have found it at last. It is in that closet."

The door of the closet was locked, and the key was in the pocket of the laundress, who was asleep in a distant part of the building. The Major gave orders that it should be forced; before doing which, however, he paused and said, —

"We must open cautiously. The fire is smouldering now, but the moment air is admitted, it will burst into a blaze."

Wheeler carefully pried it open with an axe, and held it slightly ajar, saying as he did so, "I see the fire; now bring water."

But, as he uttered these words, a loaded shelf, whose supports had been burned away, fell with such force against the door as to throw it wide open, and instantly the whole closet, with its contents, was in a blaze. That was not the worst, but the fire, having already burned a passway through the wooden ceiling, and thus communi cating with the attic above, went roaring toward the roof.

There was no use in longer trying to avoid public alarm. The building was on fire, and the only possible hope of saving it was by the rapid and energetic union of all the forces at command. The roll of the drum and the alarm cries soon aroused the whole garrison.

The cry of Fire!—however modulated into music by the magic of distance—has always a horrid sound when near at hand It is then closely akin to the ever-horrid cry of Murder! which those who hear once can never forget. Either is sufficient to arouse from the deepest sleep all within its hearing.

The rooms, the galleries, the corridors of the building were soon alive with men, among whom were some women and children, many of them in their night clothes, and most of them in a state of interesting undress; while manly voices were to be heard quieting the fears of the over-timid, and stimulating the efforts of all to remove themselves and their effects to a place of safety.

It is in the highest degree encouraging to see what almost miracles can be effected by coolness, (*the queen of virtues* in time of danger,) and by well-directed efforts. There being no fire-engine at command, the men of the garrison were formed into line from the scene of fire to the nearest supply of water, and so arranged that a simple swing of the arms at regular intervals was sufficient to keep both lines of buckets in constant motion, to and from the fire. A few persons, most experienced in the art of fire-fighting, were stationed near the flames, and to them was left the control of the water conveyed by the united efforts of the rest. They were so successful that, in a very short time the enemy, that seemed at first like a maniac broke loose from his chains, laughing with joy at the liberty of unbounded destruction, was thoroughly subdued.

In the meantime, several acts of skill and courage were performed not unworthy of notice. In one of the rooms densely filled with smoke, a valuable package had been left. The owner, unwilling to lose it, yet unable without suffocation to *walk* through the smoke, crawled on his hands and knees, recovered the prize, and returned in safety, saying that the air most fit for respiration in a burning room is always *next the floor*. In another of the endangered rooms, two little children had been left by their nurse in her terror. A daring fellow rushed up the stairway, snatched the helpless little things from their bed, and was returning with one under each arm when he saw his retreat cut off by the progress of the flames. Going to a window, he threw out a feather bed, and called to some persons below to hold it stretched directly beneath him, when he dropped into it, first one child, then, after its removal, the other.

These persons called to him to save himself in the same manner, promising to hold the bed stiffly enough to break his fall. But he preferred a more independent mode. — Quickly tearing several sheets into strips of suitable strength, and knotting them together, he formed a rope, which he made fast to the children's crib, drawn near the window, and by this means slid in safety to the earth.

The next morning Dr. Gordon, with his servant, William, departed in one of the canoes for Bellevue, leaving the other for Wheeler and Wildcat, who were to follow at a later hour. On approaching his residence, he could discern by various indications that his servants, left to themselves during his protracted absence, had been neither idle nor faithless. There was visible from a distance a small lot enclosed by rails newly split and put up; also a quantity of new palings, rived from the heart of pine, and piled together in square pens to dry and straighten, and a large black smoke, attended by a loud and incessant crackling, announced from afar a lime-kiln of burning oyster-shells. The first was the work of William, the second of Peter, and the last, of both combined.

Dr. Gordon was rejoiced to see, lying at his landing, a masted boat. This had come in answer to an advertisement from him for the hire of such an one for a month. She was all that he could desire, being complete both as a row-boat and a sailer, having a false keel that could be instantly raised or lowered, and a mast that could be stepped or unstepped at will.

By "high sun," or noon, Somassee arrived, according to appointment, and toward the close of the day, Wheeler and Wildcat made their appearance. Ere they lay down to rest that night, everything was ready for departure in the morning.

CHAPTER XXIII.

SETTING OUT — JUDY'S FAREWELL — MANATEE BAY — TAKING PASSAGE — FRESH WATER SPRING IN THE OCEAN — NOVEL CORN-MILL — BUTTER SAUSAGES — WATER-PROOF MATCH-BOX — SEA-SICKNESS, AND HOW IT WAS MITIGATED — SUNDAY SERVICE — SAILORS AS A CLASS — PARTING COMPANY.

ARLY next morning the faithful Judy, with her "old man," Peter, stood by the waterside holding her master by the hand, while the masted boat, with its four oarsmen, all seated, with a light canoe attached to its stern by a cord of twisted leerskin, was ready to depart. The four oarsmen were Wheeler, Somassee, Wildcat, and William. Both the larger and the smaller craft were evidently

supplied for a cruise of several weeks. Judy's last words were, —

"Yes, mossa, ef my missis git yah fore you do, I'll hab ebery ting ready fuh um, and I won't tell um one wud 'bout de chillun. God bless my mossa! and my missis too, and dem chillun wuh (what's) gone!"

With a look of kindness and confidence, Dr. Gordon shook her hand, and Peter's, then passed into the boat, where he took his seat at the helm. The fastening was cast loose, the boat shoved off, the sails spread, the false keel dropped, and away they scudded over the bright waters of the Bay, with Somassee's canoe dancing merrily on the waves behind. It was five weeks, to the day, and almost to the hour, since the greater part of that same company sailed from that spot on the identical errand that called them now.

Blessed with fair wind and pleasant weather, they soon made Riley's island, where they landed, and Dr. Gordon went to see Pancheta, Riley's wife, for the double purpose of leaving with her some stores, and of giving her the best news he could about her missing husband.

Stopping for a time in Manatee Bay, and looking upon its crystal waters, enclosed by fine bluffs, surmounted by a noble growth of oak and pine that came down almost to the water's edge, Dr. Gordon, who had been too ill in mind, as well

as in body, to notice it on his passage three weeks
before, could not but think that, beautiful as
Tampa is, it finds its more than equal here.
Manatee! the home of the ponderous sea cow, (or,
as the Indians call it, the Big Beaver,) no one can
forget its tranquil beauty that looks upon it once.

Passing rapidly down the coast without stopping to explore, they soon reached Gasparilla Pass,
off which they spied a schooner sailing south,
which they signaled, and ascertaining that she was
bound coastwise to Charleston, Dr. Gordon engaged a passage for himself and crew, boats and
all, as far as Cape Sable, which he intended to
make the beginning of his present tour of exploration.

During this voyage, aboard ship, he penned
another letter to Mrs. Gordon, informing her that
in a recent note received from their son Robert,
who, with his cousin Harold, had gone on a marooning expedition, he was informed that they had
found Sam, the carpenter, etc., etc., and that he,
Dr. Gordon, was on his way there to bring them
all back. Accustomed as he had ever been to ex·
press himself with candor, and especially so to her,
it was exceedingly difficult so to frame his language as to tell the truth without arousing her
suspicions. He wrote his letter, however, and
left it in the captain's hands for mailing immediately on his arrival at the city.

The captain was quite an original character, of an inventive turn, and full of humor, causing the time of his guests to pass away very pleasantly. Dr. Gordon gained from him several new ideas, interesting in their way, and not destitute of importance.

"Off the coast of Florida," said he, "is a great curiosity, which I never pass without looking at with interest. It is a spring of fresh water in the ocean. How large it is I have never been able to determine, for it varies at different times, but it shows itself on the surface sometimes for the greater part of a mile. I suppose it is the outlet of one of those underground rivers for which Florida is famous. Fresh water, you know, seems to dislike mixing with the salt. You may see it any day upon the coast, floating a great distance side by side with the tide-water, as you can tell by their difference of color, and were you in a boat, lying between the two, you might dip up the fresh on one side and the salt on the other. Moreover, it is lighter than the salt, and in calm weather it will spread and float a great way on its surface. The spring is known to but few, even of those who are otherwise familiar with the coast but it was pointed out to me many years since and I have so often passed over it, and tasted it, that I can distinguish it now at a great distance

by its different color, and by its peculiar wave.*
Last year a curious little circumstance happened
in connection with it which may be worth telling.
It was after a severe and long-continued gale, that
I was hailed at that very spot by a vessel in distress.

"'What do you want?' I asked through my
speaking-trumpet.

"'Water to drink,' the other replied. 'We
lost our supply in the gale.'

"'Then drop your buckets alongside and drink
your fill,' I said.

"'Don't mock us,' the other replied; 'we are
perishing.'

"'I am not mocking,' I answered. 'Do as I
say, and you will have more water, and better,
than I can possibly give you.'

"I observed several buckets go pitching over
the vessel's side, and in a moment the men were
drinking greedily.

"'Thank you! thank you! This looks like a
miracle!' came from the other vessel.

* The above account is no fiction of the author's. It is the
substance of a statement actually made, in very nearly the
circumstances described, by the gentlemanly commander of
a Revenue Cutter, who was as well posted as any man living
in the geography of the Florida waters, and who stated many
other wonderful things about the devil-fish and the gigantic
prawn of Southern Florida, that are confirmed by other authorities. The author has regretted many times since that
he did not ask for and record the exact locality of this wonderful spring.

"But it was no miracle. It was only the knowledge of a singular fact in the geography of the sea in those parts that every sailor, it seems to me, ought to have had."

A novel device of the captain's for grinding corn attracted Dr. Gordon's attention soon after he came aboard. It consisted of a large iron pot, suspended by a rope from the yard arm, and having within it a cannon-ball of twenty or thirty pounds weight. Only a small quantity of corn was put in at a time, and the rolling around of the ball, caused by a rocking of the pot by hand, crushed the grains to powder. He gave as an excuse for this odd contrivance, the fact that it was his rule to carry on his voyages a sack each of corn meal and grits, but that having forgotten it when last in port, he had rigged up the pot and cannon-ball as the best substitute he could think of for a mill on shipboard. He said, too, that any degree of fineness could be obtained by this means, from the most impalpable powder to a bare cracking of the grain, only that it would be very irregularly done; and that he doubted not he could grind his wheat, or coffee, or spices by the same plan, in case of need. Pleased with the simplicity and effectiveness of the device, although it worked slowly, Dr. Gordon made a note of it, thinking that it might some day be practically useful.

Another peculiarity of the captain's was his

butter. It always came to table in sausage shape, and, strange to say, in sausage skins. He said that he had recently met with it in the West Indies, where it had been imported from England. put up in this way, and that it was the only butter there worth eating.

"Whether its sweetness is owing to its being thus put up, or to its original manufacture, or to both combined," said he, "I do not know. But I do know that this is nice, and I know, too, that pemmican, Bologna sausage, and other force-meats, keep all the better for being put up in skins. When this supply is out, I am going to try the experiment with my home-made."

It is but fair, however, to say that the captain obtained, as well as communicated, some new ideas during the voyage. He was pleased with Dr. Gordon's simple device for keeping his matches dry, by means of a strong vial tightly corked, which he carried in his pocket.

"Do you know," said he, "I have wished a thousand times that somebody would invent a *sailor's match-box*, so as to be proof against wet. And here it is in my own closet, though I never knew it till now."

Among the other novelties of the occasion must not be forgotten the experiences of Somassee and Wildcat. Versed as they were in all that pertained to wood-craft, they had never before been at sea, at least not in a sailing vessel, and were, therefore, peculiarly liable to what befalls most landsmen on their introduction to this new life

The vessel was now rolling in what was called "a chopped sea," which sometimes has an effect even on old sailors. It is a condition of the sea produced by a sudden change of wind raising a new set of waves across the course of the old, and chopping them into what a Georgia backwoodsman would call potato hills. The two redskins had at first enjoyed themselves vastly in an inspection of the rigging, the sails, and the action of the wind upon the canvas, but after an hour's tossing upon the rough water they began to look somewhat serious, then a little pale, and finally distressed. Indian-like, they struggled hard against the coming evil, first to ignore, then to endure, but it was all in vain; for, though an Indian may be trained to scorn pain and to laugh even at death,—and Somassee and Wildcat were well trained,—sea-sickness is quite another thing; it will neither be scorned nor laughed at. The two sufferers, after preserving their dignity as long as possible, were at last compelled to yield to their fate. Each looked inquiringly at the other; but seeing on the other's face only a reflection of his own discomfort, they hastily separated, ran to opposite sides of the vessel, leaned for sometime over the gunwales, and then came away, looking very forlorn. They said nothing, but the kind-hearted captain, reading their cases in their countenances, offered them the usual round of sailor remedies—brandy, red pepper, and salt-water. These having failed, Wheeler prevailed upon Somassee to lie with his back upon the deck and his feet raised high upon the mast, in which position he found relief.

Dr. Gordon tried, in Wildcat's case, but with less success, the experiment of looking steadily at a tumbler full of water, which he held in his hand. After a few hours the unpleasant motion of the ship subsided into a gently-prolonged swing, which proved more quickly and powerfully restorative than all the captain's remedies, or the other's devices.

The first day's sail had brought them nearly to the Cape. The second day was one of calms and of baffling winds. The progress was so slow that Dr. Gordon would have bid adieu to his pleasant host and taken to his boat, but for two considerations,—one was that the captain declared the weather to be very uncertain, and, in that latitude, very unsafe; the other was, that the day was the Sabbath, which Dr. Gordon preferred to spend, if possible, in worship. He, therefore, informed the captain that, though not by profession a clergyman, he was accustomed to conducting religious service, either with a book or without, and that, if it was agreeable to him and his crew, he would take pleasure in rendering such aid as he could in the services aboard.

Assent was most cordially given, the captain saying, that although he was not, at that time, in membership with any Christian church, he once had been, and had not forgotten how pleasant it used to be to try to serve God ; and that it was his invariable custom, when in the city of Charleston, to attend service in the Mariner's Church, conducted by the earnest and sailor-souled chaplain there. He also showed Dr. Gordon a copy of the Sailor's Prayer-Book, which he himself used sometimes, in case of a funeral at sea, or other emergency requiring a form of worship.

At half-past ten o'clock, the crew of the schooner, all neatly clad, together with the few passengers, assembled on the open deck, when Dr. Gordon, ably seconded by the captain, led their devotions, and made a short, "free and easy" address. The sailors seemed greatly to enjoy the services, as sailors generally do when they are feelingly conducted. Rough and wicked as they ordinarily appear to be, there is more of child-like simplicity among them as a class, than is to be found perhaps in any other class of our people, and, in proportion, as many strong hearts, big as a man's, yet tender as a child's, and as readily responsive to earnest religious appeals. They *appear* to be a cast-off

s

class, only because they *have been cast off* by the greater part of their fellow-men. After service, one of them, a roughly-clad fellow, with tarred hands and weather-beaten visage, came to Dr Gordon, made himself known as the runaway son of an English clergyman, gave the Doctor's extended hand a hearty grip, and with tears in his eyes, remarked, —

"We cannot say to-day, as we too often can, that *there is no Sabbath in four fathoms water.*"

Late in the afternoon, the schooner came abreast of Punta Fancha, known now as Cape Sable, where she was brought to anchor, a musket-shot from shore, in nine feet water, this being the nearest approach to land she could make. The captain seemed really sorry to part company, and, when the time of settlement came, refused to receive a cent, saying, —

"I have been more than paid in the profit of your company."

"But we have partaken of your stores, and—"

"Nobody but yourself, for the men ate of their own, and I am only sorry that you cannot stay longer."

"But, sir, you received my boats as freight, and agreed to—"

The captain interrupted him again, saying, "No matter what I agreed to before I knew you. Your boats have not hurt my ship. And now please say not another word about pay, for remember,'' and he laughed at his make-shift of a reason, " to-day is Sunday, and we must have no money deal-ings."

Dr. Gordon laughed too, and yielded the point. They shook hands and parted, with the hope that they might some day meet again.

CHAPTER XXIV.

CAPE SABLE — INDIAN HUNTERS — DISMAL COAST — PLEASANT-LOOKING ISLAND — WHAT DR. GORDON FOUND — WHAT WHEELER SAW — CONJECTURES — " LIVING LIKE PRINCES," — FIRE SIGNAL — MOC-CASSIN TRACKS — ALMOST FOUND — LONG TRAMP — STRANDED CANOE — WILDCAT ACTS OUT OF CHARACTER — VOYAGE RESUMED.

APE Sable consists in reality of three capes, all of which rise pleasantly, though not very high above water, and present the appearance, inland, of an immense old field, without bush, stump, or fence. Its sur-face is composed of a rich grey soil, largely inter-mixed with disintegrated shells, and is what used to be known by the name of " The Yemasee old field," but it is probably a small prairie, or natural

meadow, extending from the sea to the hammock land that lies behind it, stocked with live oaks, magnolias, enormous vines of tropical luxuriance, an occasional mahogany-tree and huava palm.

By advice of the captain, Dr. Gordon landed on the middle of one of these capes, for the sake of fresh water, to be had in a natural well there, which all visitors find distinctly marked by the only trees or bushes growing on the point—a tuft of white mangroves or button-tree. So far as respects fresh water, however, Somassee remarked that there need be no concern, for it underlies the whole coast of Florida, and can be had anywhere by scooping a little basin in the sand, a few inches above salt water—a fact which if known to previous hunters and other whites might have prevented much discomfort and perhaps loss of life.

Not far from the well they saw the smoke of an Indian lodge, and on sending Somassee and Wildcat to ascertain who the occupants were, they learned that they were a party of Indian hunters who had come from the neighborhood of Charlotte Harbor, left their boats concealed in a neighboring creek, and were now awaiting the arrival of comrades before going to the hunting grounds adjoining Biscayne Bay. They seemed to be very poor, and received with gratitude a few pounds of ship bread, and a small piece of meat sent them by Dr. Gordon. On being questioned as to the

missing company of young folks, they answered
that they had heard rumors of a boat full of young
people being carried off, but no more. Somassee
informed them that the father of the children had
come to look for them, and that he would pay a
.arge reward to any who should restore them to
nim. They replied that if any one might be re-
lied upon to find them, it would be the father, and
that if he had searched for them thus far in vain,
no one else need hope for success ; nevertheless
that they would try what they could do on their
way back from the hunting grounds.

Early next morning, the company left Cape
Sable, and for two days had most dismal work,
sailing and rowing amid thousands of little mangrove islands, that barely rise above the water and
choke the mouths of all creeks and rivers emptying from the everglades into the Gulf. The marsh
seemed to be without limit. The two boats pene-
trated it for miles, yet it had every appearance of
extending as many miles beyond. Indeed it was
one of those doubtful margins between land and
water, so equally divided between both that it
might puzzle any one to determine to which it belonged. There were visible no spots fit for the
habitation of a bear or a panther, much less of a
human being ; and the only creatures possessing life
seen by any of the company during that part of the
cruise, were alligators, turtles, and water birds.

Having, however, passed these dismal places, they came on the third day to a clear coast, with well-defined creeks and rivers, and decked with pleasant-looking islands. Here it was, that their search may be said to have really commenced; and here, where Somassee's canoe was first called into requisition; for while the large boat sailed, or rowed, as the case might be, around the seaward limits of the islands, landing and looking around at every convenient point, and firing volleys of guns to attract attention, the canoe went by the inside passage, and met them at the northern end of each. In passing around one of these, the larger boat was so long detained in waiting for the smaller, which was compelled to go half way past the next island before turning toward sea, that Dr. Gordon instructed Somassee, in a similar case, to keep on to the inlet beyond.

In process of time they arrived at a long and pleasant-looking island with a hard smooth beach, having at the southern extremity a river or inlet bordered on each side by a wide mangrove-marsh. On nearing its southern point Dr. Gordon requested Somassee and Wildcat to take, as usual, the inside passage, and to meet him at some place suitable for encampment on this island or the next.

"At next island," replied Somassee, exchanging significant looks with Wildcat.

"Well, let it be the next; only do not go beyond it unless compelled," said Dr. Gordon, and with this they parted.

The canoe entered the creek and soon disappeared, while the larger boat sailed slowly along, stopping here and there to allow some of the parties aboard to land and examine the interior.

Dr. Gordon had taken his turn and was walking leisurely along the beach, which was profusely covered with shells of every description, some being of exquisite beauty, when his eye was caught by the appearance of something white. He approached; it was a piece of linen, half buried in the sand beside a gigantic conch-shell, over the upturned lip of which it partly hung, moving in the breeze. He drew it out; it was a pocket-handkerchief, of small size, such as is used by children. He rinsed it in a little pool of water, in the hollow of the sands. There, in one corner, neatly marked,—he could discern the style of his wife's needlework,—were the initials of his own dear little son, F. G.

Clasping the precious relic to his bosom, and lifting his eyes upward, he could only ejaculate,— "Father, I thank thee!" when he reeled, and almost fell upon the shelly beach.

The boat had by this time passed ahead, and Wheeler, who was at the helm, and whose attention had been engrossed by something forward, was suddenly accosted by William, who said,—

"Stop! some 'ns de matter wi' massa! He most fall down, jes' now."

Wheeler immediately put the boat about and made for shore; and seeing Dr. Gordon earnestly looking at something in his hand, called out,—

"What have you found, Doctor?"

For a moment no answer was returned; only the white handkerchief in Dr. Gordon's hand fluttered in the breeze; then followed, in a hesitating, almost incoherent way the words—

"I—hope—we—have found them."

"I trust so, indeed!" returned Wheeler, moved by strong sympathy, as he examined the interesting little token.

"And if I am not mistaken," he continued, "there is something more for you at yonder point. When William called to me, I was just about to set the spy-glass upon it. I think it is a flying signal."

They re-embarked, and on attaining a few boat lengths from shore, the object alluded to by Wheeler was plainly visible through the spy-glass, a white signal flying from a pole, around which the greater part of it had been wrapped by the daily shifting of the breeze. They went, fast as oars and sails could carry them, to the northern end of the island, where a river-like inlet entered squarely from the sea. Half way up the bluff, and deeply planted in its sands, was a pole, and on it was fastened part of a linen sheet, on which Dr. Gordon recognized, after it was taken down, the joint initials of himself and wife. Near the flag-staff was a pile of wood, overlying a quantity of grass, leaves, twigs and other combustibles, for the evident purpose of making a quick and large fire-signal; and only a few steps from this pile was a spot covered with ashes and charred fragments, proving that a fire-signal had been attempted there before.

"Your young people must have seen some vessel passing," remarked Wheeler, surveying the signs. "Though by the weather-beaten look of this spot I should judge it was at least a month ago. Possibly they have been taken off."

"Then why this new pile of wood, and this flying signal?" argued Dr. Gordon.

"Only because in the hurry of leaving, they forgot to remove them," Wheeler answered.

"Come on, mossa! H'yuh's a nurrah sign!" shouted William from the bend beyond.

They hurried there and saw a basin scooped in the sand for fresh water, which on being tested, proved to be both good and abundant, and surrounded with a little palisade to protect it from the tide. Above the spring, in the dry sand at the foot of the bluff, was a worn path, plentifully marked with footprints, some of which were very recent, and none of them older than the last spring tide, which had covered the whole beach only ten or twelve days before.

"This proves that they did not leave the island at the time of the fire-signal," said Dr. Gordon.

"I give up the point," answered Wheeler. "Some of these tracks are certainly not a week old, if they are three days. But where are the young folks themselves?"

So conclusive was the evidence of their having been on this very spot, only a few days before, if not still in the neighborhood, that Dr. Gordon expected every moment to see one or the other of them running to meet him.

"Our guns! our guns!" he exclaimed with sudden energy, "let us give a volley to call their attention. Go, William, and bring them from the boat."

While William was gone on this errand, Dr. Gordon and Wheeler followed the foot-path. It kept along the sands for a little way, then led up the bluff to a magnificent live-oak that graced the level above. This tree was not tall, (live-oaks never are, seldom attaining the height of more than fifty feet,) but it was broad, and its long branches, covered with glossy green leaves, and draped with grey moss, which hung in streamers or festoons, eight, ten or fifteen feet long, overspread a circle of more than a hundred feet in diameter. Beneath the shady cover of this tree,

were plentiful signs of a very recent date—bones
of ham, and of fresh venison, partly gnawed by
the dog —deer tails and scraps of deer skin—
feathers of the wild turkey—fish bones, and
oyster and crab shells, with some of the flesh still
in a state of preservation, and so many other signs
of good living, that Wheeler, on seeing them,
smacked his lips, and said,—

"Doctor, I think you will find your young marooners decidedly fatter now than they were when
they left home. I long to join them in their good
cheer. They have been living here like princes."

In addition to these pleasant signs, were traces
of the tent, pitched under the oak — the holes left
by the centre pole and by the pins, fresh almost as
if made the day before—and there, also, were
three thick beds of moss, which had served for
mattresses, each with its nest-like place for the
body of the sleeper, still remaining, and dry as it
was before the tent was removed, proving that it
had been deserted since the last rain.

But where were the young people? And why
did they not respond to the signals? Either the
island was larger than most others on the coast,
and they had removed to some distant point, or
they had left it altogether.

One fact in the case perplexed, and, for a time,
disturbed Dr. Gordon. It was that the footprints
of *moccasined feet* were as abundant as the tracks

left by shoes. Now, who were these moccasin wearers? and why were they intermingling so freely with his children? True, the tracks all seemed to answer in size to the age of his own missing ones, and one of them especially to that of his little Frank. But Indians are proverbial for their small and handsomely shaped feet. Dr. Gordon could not resist the occasional incoming of some horrible thoughts, and they finally troubled him so much that he gave them utterance to Wheeler, who at once replied, —

"You count four young people in the missing company, do you not? Well, I count only four persons among all these tracks; and if the small foot in moccasins is not that of your little boy, I see no track of him at all. Rest assured, sir, their shoes began to give way, and they have supplied their place with moccasins. Remember, they have now been gone six weeks; and children's shoes wear out very fast—at least this used to be so when I was a child."

By this time William approached with the guns, and they fired volley after volley, then went to the flag-staff and raised the smoke-signal, by setting fire to the pile heaped there, and adding more green wood to it. Still there was no response; and as evening drew on, Dr. Gordon, recalling what had been said in the message by gourd, of their intending to make a canoe the next week, began to fear (or to hope, he hardly knew which), that they had left the island for home. Ere dark, however, Wheeler, who had been exercising his wild-woods skill in scrutinizing the tracks made in different directions, called Dr. Gordon to notice that the plainest and freshest of them all led to the water's edge, where they had evidently embarked, after passing and repassing many times between the tree and the river, as if taking many turns to carry off what they had.

"See here," said he, "is a moccasin track answering to your nephew's, and another that fits the foot of your little boy; and here, also, are shoe-prints, answering to the feet of your son and your daughter. And if this here is not the track left by a negro, I never saw one before, and a one-legged negro at that—at least *using* only one leg, for there is the sign of but one foot, and on each side are the holes left by his crutches. Doctor, your young folks left this place by water, not more than four days ago,—stop! let me count the tide-marks."

He examined them, then reported, "There are two tide-marks left since the first set of the tracks were made, and one since the other set. And as there is only one tide a day on this coast, this will make two days. To-day is Wednesday. They must have left yesterday before high water, or on Monday evening, after the tide."

O, how near this was to meeting them! Dr. Gordon felt almost disappointed, although he was pretty well assured that in leaving the island they had made direct for Tampa, and that on his return he should find them there. It was therefore with a strange mixture of satisfaction and disappointment that he lay awake that night, reflecting upon the altered state of affairs, and saying to himself, —

"Had we only kept on, in our own boats, instead of going by schooner to Cape Sable, we should have met them here. Yet I esteemed our meeting that schooner a fortunate circumstance, and engaged a passage aboard as the surest and the shortest way of gaining my end! How little we know what lies before us! How perfectly under the finger of Providence!

> "'Sure, there's a destiny that shapes our ends,
>   Rough-hew them as we may.'"

One result of his reflections during the night, was a decision expressed to Wheeler, as soon as they awaked, that he would remain at the island that day for the purpose of giving it a thorough search before leaving. Immediately after breakfast, therefore, while Wheeler shoved the boat from shore, anchored her in the stream, and remained aboard as guard, Dr. Gordon, with William, went to explore the island. The sea-side and its immediate neighborhood having been already examined, and there being every reason to

believe that the margin toward the main had been
observed with equal fidelity by Somassee and
Wildcat, he resolved to strike across as near as he
could through its centre, then to return by its
eastern margin.

This plan, which was certainly good, was not
so easy of accomplishment, for the inland growth
was very dense, and, moreover, it was tangled with
vines, myrtles, dwarf palmettos and other shrubs,
which so impeded their march that they scarcely
made more than two miles an hour. Having
toiled onward, through brake and brier, until they
caught a glimpse of the river and marsh to the
south, they turned toward the main and tried to
follow the eastern shore of the island. This was,
however, next to impossible, from the great number of baygalls, or miry bottoms, setting in from
the marsh beyond ; so, after going little more than
a mile, they struck a course again for the beach,
and reached the boat exceedingly weary and hungry.

After rest and refreshment, they set off a second
time, and went several miles around the northern
and north-eastern edge, but finding at last the
same kind of growth which had impeded their
course in the forenoon, and feeling confident that
his children would not select so undesirable a location for their abode, he once more returned to
the beach, satisfied now that they had left the island and embarked for home Every hour ae

half hour through the day one or the other had fired a gun, in hopes to reach the ears of the young people, if still upon the island; and this was continued, although the wind was blowing so freshly from the east as to deaden all sounds which crossed its course.

Nothing remained, now, but to leave the island, and rejoin the canoe, which had been separated from them for more than a day. Before embarking, however, Dr. Gordon went to the flag-staff and fastened to it by wooden pegs a copy of an advertisement, of which he had had a number prepared, in a fair round hand, by a good scribe at Tampa, and had posted one at every favorable place upon the coast, from Cape Sable to this point.

About an hour and a half by sun they left the island, and passed up the coast, examining as they went, until near dark, when they met Somassee and Wildcat awaiting them at the next inlet. The voyagers by canoe had seen nothing of the missing company, nor even any signs of them along the way: their only approach to this being the discovery in the marsh, upon a heap of dead mangroves, of a stranded canoe, which Dr. Gordon strongly suspected to be Riley's. The joy of Wildcat, in this almost discovery of his young friends, was unbounded; and he gave to it an utterance so unrestrained and un-Indian-like, that Somassee looked on with surprise, and said to him in intended rebuke, that any one, to hear him speak, might almost take him for a " pale face."

The evidence of the young people's embarkation and probable return to Tampa was so strong, that all retired to rest that night in fine spirits. Next morning, bright and early, they resumed their voyage, and to some extent their explorations : but though they landed at various points and examined the coast, they did not spend much time in needless delays, being all conscious of a strong attraction toward Tampa, in the hope of meeting there the objects of their long and laborious search.

CHAPTER XXV.

CHEERY RETURN— JUDY'S WELCOME— SAD DISAP-
POINTMENT— FORT BROOKE — BAD NEWS— UN-
EXPECTED JOURNEY—EARLY STEAMBOATS ON
THE ST. JOHN'S RIVER— TRAVELLERS' RULES AND
TRAVELLERS' FARE IN A WILD COUNTRY— SIGNS
OF A DISTANT STEAMBOAT—NEGRO SONGS— GET-
TING ABOARD— LETTERS AND PLANS— MRS. GOR-
DON— MRS. M^CINTOSH— ABREAST OF BELLEVUE —
THE PILOT-BOAT— OLD TAHGA — PREPARE FOR
ANOTHER TOUR.

UR story has already spread over much ground, and there remains so much more to be told, that we are compelled to pass rapidly over the incidents of the next few weeks, and will condense into a few

T

pages, the history of as much time as has been occupied with all the previous narrative.

After leaving the island, where the signs of the
young people were so abundant and fresh, the two
boats moved rapidly and cheerily toward Tampa,
peeping into the inlets, and peering over the sand-
capped bluffs wherever convenient; but scarcely
devoting to any part what may be called a fair
examination, and at the same time enlivening their
passage with jest and story and song.

So firmly persuaded were they all of the young
people's return home, that soon after entering the
Bay, and while Bellevue was barely within sight,
Dr. Gordon drew out the spy-glass to a nicely
adjusted focus, fixed it steadily upon his house and
premises, hoping to have his eyes gladdened with
the familiar form of some one of those who had
been so long lost and now probably restored. Unable, however, to discover any indication of their
presence, he passed the glass to Wheeler, who, after examining, transferred it to Wildcat and Somassee. All looked eagerly, but in vain. The only
person they saw, even when near the landing, was
Judy, who, faithful soul, was hurrying down the
bluff, waving her hands in joyful welcome.

"Huddie, mossa! huddie! I so glad to see you!"
she said.

"Thank you, and how-d'ye back again," returned her master, then added in anxious tones, "I
hope the young people are with you and all well."

"Eh! \n! my mossa!" she replied, the tears starting into her eyes, "How you talk! No chillun yuh!"

The shock created by these words was visible, not only on Dr. Gordon, but in the whole company. Wheeler fixed his eyes on the agitated father, and seeing him turn pale and tremble from head to foot, offered him at once his water canteen, saying in a very confident tone as he did so, —

"They must have passed on to Fort Brooke. Come, let us go there at once."

"Maybe we pass em on de way," suggested William. "We been trabbel mighty fast comin' back."

Dr. Gordon yielded, as best he could, to these words of hope, but they furnished little consolation; for the returning boat, in going to Fort Brooke from the Gulf, must of necessity have passed Bellevue, and would doubtless have stopped there to report; and as for having passed them on the way, that was possible, but the hope of it was very forlorn. With spirits greatly depressed, and with a few sad words to Judy, explaining the case, and instructing her what to do if the young folks should still make their appearance, the suggestion of Wheeler was adopted, the sails were once more spread, and the boats passed on.

The trial of the chief actor in these scenes was not yet at its end. On reaching the Fort, a letter

from Charleston was received, announcing that a
rumor of the accident which had befallen the
young people had reached the city—that every
effort had been made to keep it from Mrs. Gordon,
but in vain—that the effect upon her already
weakened nervous system had been such as to
bring her to death's door, and that, although the
physician hoped for better things, it was his opinion that if Dr. Gordon wished to see her alive, he
must return without delay.

Many persons might suppose that this new grief
would have crushed the afflicted man to the earth ;
but it is usually true of manly spirits that new
trials bring out new energies, and, instead of depressing, cause them to act with redoubled vigor.
It was mid-day of Monday, December 13th, when
Dr. Gordon received this intelligence, and by six
o'clock the next morning he was bestriding a stout
Indian pony, with Somassee, similarly mounted,
as guide and companion through the Seminole
territory, on a journey to the eastern side of the
peninsula, where he hoped to obtain passage to
Charleston.

His last words to Major Burke, uttered with
almost tearful earnestness in the act of setting out,
were, "Don't give them up, cousin! Don't let
the search even *slacken*, because I am not here to
push it. They are almost certainly on the way
here, or have been stopped by some misadventure.

And may the Lord's blessing, and the blessings of those ready to perish, be with you!"

The route pursued by the two travellers was the same as that so sadly marked a few years later by the march and massacre of a body of United States soldiers, under command of the gallant Major Dade; and they hoped to reach some place on the river St. John's where the Doctor might take passage aboard one or other of the few little steamboats beginning at that time to ply between the settlements on that noble river and the seaboard cities of South Carolina and Georgia. It was not true, then, as now, however, that the arrival and departure of boats at the different landings could be calculated to the hour; they plied there for produce rather than for passengers, and being small in size, and furnished with feeble machinery, were compelled to be very submissive to all changes of the wind and weather. The expectation of finding a boat upon the river, or even at the the seaport, St. Augustine, after his long overland journey, was very unreliable.

As it was necessary to economize in the highest degree the travelling powers of both men and beasts, Dr. Gordon commenced by making the first day's journey quite short, the second longer, and the third longer still. Each day's journey was begun in a slow walk, gradually increased to the highest speed which could be continued, with a

few resting spells throughout the day. The night's
lodging and accommodation were generally of a
very simple and unexpensive kind; the ponies
were hobbled and turned loose to graze, after
having been fed upon a few handfuls of corn
brought for the purpose, and the supper of the
travellers consisted of a few grains from the same
bag, parched and eaten with a little sugar or salt.
Somassee kept a watchful eye upon the ponies
throughout the first half of the night, never per-
mitting them to wander far, then bringing them
to camp and haltering them, that they might obtain their needful sleep. This sleep, of about two
hours before day, being more needful to a horse
than that of all the rest of the night besides, and
being all that is absolutely needed for his refreshment, they were careful never to disturb.

The face of the country between Tampa and
the St. John's river is a perfect level; the road
(or as Somassee called it, the trail), was generally
firm and smooth, and the travellers made such
good use of their time, that by Saturday night they
succeeded in reaching the northern bend of the
river, and there stopped with a planter in sight
of the then infant town of Jacksonville, appearing miles away upon the other bank. Here Dr.
Gordon resolved to pause for a day and spend the
Sabbath, being influenced to this not only by the
higher motive of yielding obedience to a plain

teaching of the Bible, but also from the lower
motive of giving rest to wearied muscles, and thus
being prepared for whatever labors may yet be
necessary. To his great joy, he learned that by
Monday, mid-day, the *Magnolia*, a pleasant little
steamboat plying between the plantations here and
the city of Charleston, might be expected to pass
on her northward trip.

At the predicted time, a little volume of black
smoke, far up the lake-like river, began to roll
over the gigantic cypresses and rich-looking magnolias, announcing that the expected steamboat
would soon be in sight. This was followed in the
course of time by a noisy clack! clack! of machinery, and by a roar, as of water disturbed; for
the operations by steam of that day were far less
quiet than they are now.

The gentlemanly planter, at whose house Dr.
Gordon had spent his day of delightful rest, and
who had placed at his disposal a handsome plantation boat, manned by four lusty negroes, was so
loth, when the time came, to part with his guest,
that he made some excuse for accompanying him
to the steamboat.

No sooner were they fairly under way than a
significant " Ah-oo! " was heard from one of the
oarsmen, who, without further preliminary or permission, started a low, plaintive melody, in which
the others united, swelling it louder and louder

until it might have been heard to the distance of a mile. Not much could be said in praise of either the poetry or music, but the voices were rich and well toned, and the performers seemed greatly to enjoy their own performance. Negroes are proverbially fond of music, and never are they more inclined to indulge in it than when upon the water. Their songs, always simple in language and utterance, are then marked by a peculiar expression of sound which cannot be better described than by calling it *water-music.* A boat-song can always be recognized, and it is seldom, if ever, heard upon land. Negroes are capital time-keepers, and the effect of their songs while tugging at the oar is to impart such regularity and force to the stroke, that it is usually good economy to encourage their singing. The boat glided swiftly over the glassy surface. There was ever a hissing ripple at the bows, and a tiny jet, raised by the cutwater, gracefully projecting a few inches beyond.

On nearing the steamboat, Somassee, who was in company, received his last instructions, together with a note to the commandant at Fort Brooke; the planter and his guest bade each other adieu with mutual regret; the teeth of the negroes shone with pleasure at the sight of sundry little silver coins chinking in their hands; the steamboat glided noiselessly up, propelled by its own momentum for the last quarter of a mile, the revolution of the paddle-wheels having been arrested on a signal from the planter ; a rope ladder was lowered from its side, up which the new passenger ascended to the deck, followed by his baggage ; the tinkle of a little bell, touched by the captain, set in motion the paddle-wheels, which renewed their deep digging into the water, and the obedient boat was once more ploughing her foamy way toward Jacksonville, the ocean, and Charleston.

At that day it was customary for the weak steam craft engaged in our coast trade, to avoid the dangers of the ocean by seeking the smooth water lying between the main and the almost continuous chain of islands extending along the Atlantic shore from Florida to Maryland. On this occasion, however, the weather was so calm, and the ocean so smooth, that the adventurous captain pushed boldly to sea, instead of following the crooked creeks and the narrow cuts of the inside passage, and being thus delayed only by the necessary stopping at the several sea-ports, St. Mary's, Darien, and Savannah, he was enabled to make the trip in the almost unparalleled space of two and a half days.

Early in the voyage, Dr. Gordon penned a letter to his sister in Montgomery, Alabama, — Mrs. McIntosh, mother of his nephew Harold, who had been a partaker in the misfortune of his children, — announcing as gently and hopefully as possible the sore troubles of the past few weeks, and begging her to put her affairs in order for leaving home without delay, after his next letter, and joining him in Charleston, or at Tampa, as might then be specified. This letter he mailed in Savannah, promising to write again by first opportunity after being able to learn what was desirable in the case.

On reaching Charleston, he was greatly relieved to learn that Mrs. Gordon was not only alive, but much more calm and resigned, although still almost crazed with grief at the possible loss of her children. His last letter, received during her illness, and at a moment when she was hopelessly sinking under her sorrows, had communicated intelligence so much more definite and cheering, that she began instantly to rally, and was now, the physician declared, in a fair way to recover.

Her large, lustrous eyes flashed with joy on the entrance of her husband, and before a word was uttered she read in his calm countenance the general state of the case.

"Have you found them?" she asked, with a wild, yet subdued energy, the moment she was able to speak.

"Not exactly, but almost," he replied, smiling. "We were so near as to see their fresh tracks and other signs, and to this moment I cannot understand how we missed each other."

He then narrated, in cheerful tone, the scene

upon the island, the discovery of Frank's handkerchief, the flying signal, bearing her own mark,
the traces of the tent under the oak, the bones and
shells, and other evidences of good living, and the
tracks leading to the water, where they had evidently embarked. He concluded by saying, —

"I am persuaded they left the island on their
return to Tampa, and I cannot account for our not
overtaking them on the way, or not finding them
at Bellevue, except by supposing that, in seeking
the inside passage back, they had lost their way in
some of the many creeks and inlets that entangle
the coast. They were evidently safe and well
two days, possibly one day, before my visit to the
island."

Mrs. Gordon was a lady of great gentleness and
sweetness of manner, yet, when roused, capable of
as much energy and resoluteness as was suitable
to her sex. And she *was roused now*. Reduced
as she had been by disease and distress, unable
even yet to sit alone, she expressed her resolution
to accompany her husband on the first vessel that
offered passage to Tampa, and thence, if necessary,
to go with him on another exploring tour down
the coast. This wild, and almost maniacal, resolve
on her part, caused Dr. Gordon great perplexity.
He could see in it nothing but embarrassment to
his own more effective movements, but well knowing the uselessness of attempting to reason with

a mother half crazed with grief, he resolved to yield, as far as possible, to her desire, and to make at once arrangements for carrying it out.

He then wrote to his sister, Mrs. McIntosh, requesting her to join him at her earliest convenience at Tampa, prepared for an indefinite stay, and putting at her disposal the means for hiring, or, if necessary, for purchasing a small sailing-vessel at Mobile, which she might command for bringing her direct to Tampa, and which might afterward be used for any other purpose.

A few days after this there appeared in the city papers an advertisement of a vessel prepared to sail in a short time for New Orleans, with the expectation of stopping at several points upon the Gulf coast, and among them at Tampa. This determined him to execute his plan at once, for Mrs. Gordon's health had rapidly improved since his return, and he could not ask for a more hopeful means of farther improvement in her weak state than the tranquillizing influence of a pleasant sea voyage. He, therefore, engaged a passage for her and himself, and arranged that their two younger chillren should be left in the care of a relative. A third letter to Mrs. McIntosh announced his expectation of speedy departure, and gave her the names of several parties in Mobile to whom he had written to look out for her a suitable and trustworthy person as sailing-master.

The day before Dr. Gordon embarked he was pained to receive a letter from his cousin, Major Burke, informing him that up to the date of writing no tidings had been obtained from the missing company of juveniles. He said nothing of this to Mrs. Gordon, hoping to hear better things on his arrival at Tampa, and relying greatly upon her improvement in health during the voyage to enable her to sustain the disappointment if the young people should not by that time have arrived; but the intelligence had an irresistibly depressing effect upon his own feelings. "What could have become of them after leaving the island?" was a question constantly recurring, and never satisfactorily answered. It was, therefore, with unfeigned delight that he hailed the hour of his departure, and that he watched the steady progress of the vessel as she ploughed her prosperous way from the beautiful harbor he left, to the still more beau·tiful one he sought.

On coming abreast of Bellevue, where the vessel lay to, before passing on to the town and the fort, Dr. Gordon asked to be taken ashore. For prudential reasons he chose to go alone. Besides apprising the servants of Mrs. Gordon's arrival, he wished to learn whether the young people had returned, and fearing the effect upon his wife of the dreaded disappointment, he preferred to be able, in case of need, to convey her directly to the fort, where she would have the cheering presence of her cousin, and the medical aid of the surgeon who had so skilfully treated his own case.

Ere the yawl had pulled over half the distance, Judy, Peter, and William were at the landing ready to welcome him, and he knew by the absence of other figures from the group that he must prepare himself for evil tidings. On asking Judy if anything had been heard from the young people, her reply was, —

"Not one wud, my dear mossa! Not one wud, sept w'at you bring yo'self, long time ago."

With heavy heart he returned to the vessel, picturing to himself the scene of anguish he was destined to behold, and taxing his medical knowledge for the means necessary to relief. To his surprise, no less than to his joy, he discovered that Mrs. Gordon bore the disappointment with great equanimity; a few natural tears attested her sorrow, but she soon began to act the unexpected part of comforter to himself. Dr. Gordon was first astonished, then alarmed; he feared that his wife was exhibiting the horrid composure of insanity. Some days afterward, however, observing no other indications of an unsettled mind, and inquiring whether there had been anything to prepare her for this disappointment, she replied, with a sweet, submissive smile, —

"Yes; all through the voyage I made it a re-

ligious duty, day after day, to try and say with
sincerity, 'Not my will, but thine, O Lord, be
done!' I think, too, that you yourself helped me
in a way that you did not intend or suspect. Your
occasional seasons of sadness, and your carefully
worded language while endeavoring to speak hopefully, all tended to persuade me that something
weighed heavily upon your own heart. I, therefore, made up my mind, as otherwise I probably
should not, to prepare, if possible, for the worst.
And now, my dear husband, I am ready to join
you in thanking God that, although called to
grieve over the *absence* of our children, we have
no right yet to grieve over their *loss.*"

This language instantly relieved Dr. Gordon
of all fears as to his wife's saneness, and awakened
in him a higher respect for her than ever before.
It proved that she was a woman who could be as
heroic in suffering as a man was bound to be in
action.

When the vessel resumed her voyage from Bellevue, it came to anchor first at the fort, then at
the town. Dr. Gordon was anxious to obtain from
his cousin all the intelligence of his children received during his absence, and to determine as
quickly as possible what more could be attempted
on their behalf. To his disquiet, and indeed his
distress, he learned that none had been obtained,
not a word, nor even a sign, since his own tour.

It seemed to him as if the sensible remark of the
Indian hunter at Cape Sable possessed an almost
prophetic significance: " If the father of the missing children has looked for them thus far in vain,
no one else need try."

His fears that a renewed distress would soon
prey upon the yet feeble health of his wife was
just beginning to be realized, when a small but
graceful little vessel moved swiftly in from the
distant bar. It was a pilot boat. Besides two
white men aboard, who were evidently sailors,
there was a lady sitting on the scanty after deck,
with a small black servant beside her, while an
elderly Indian leaned against the mast, and seemed
to exchange words with her. A glance through
the spy-glass informed Dr. Gordon that the lady
was his expected sister, Mrs. McIntosh ; he, therefore, waved a signal with his handkerchief, and
pointed to a temporary wharf erected by him at a
place convenient for landing.

The joy of meeting a dearly beloved sister was,
however, miserably dashed with the dread of
making to her that unsatisfactory report of the
missing ones, which was all that he had to give.
Her first inquiry, after salutation, was on that
point, of course, and he replied by telling her the
truth, though in as hopeful a light as he could.
She bore the disappointment with all the quietness
that might be expected of a woman strong both in

mind and heart, and ere they reached the house she was ready to unite with him in trying to cheer the drooping spirit of her sister-in-law.

" Who are those you have aboard ?" asked he, soon after the first inquiries on both sides had been disposed of. " I see two white men and an Indian."

" One of the white men is the owner of the boat, a Scotchman, by name of Dunbar," she replied; " the other is a hired man, who wishes to stop at Tampa. The Indian is an old neighbor of ours, and a firm friend of Harold's."

" What ! old Torgah ? " asked Dr. Gordon.

" Yes," she replied; " but how do you know anything of him?"

" Through Harold himself, who took me to see him the last time I made you a visit," Dr. Gordon said; " and besides, Harold has so often mentioned his name since his stay with me, that it has become quite a household word. I judge from what he says that old Torgah must be a shrewd hunter, as well as faithful friend."

" There was no keeping him back when he heard of Harold's misfortune," added Mrs. McIntosh. " He begged only to be brought to Tampa, and to be told where the young folks were last seen, saying that he had friends among the Uchees and Yemassees of these parts, who would help him, and that he himself used to be familiar with the coast."

U

"I am glad you brought him," said Dr. Gordon, "and have no doubt he will be useful."

"He was dreadfully sea-sick on the voyage," Mrs. McIntosh continued, "and says he will never put his foot on a vessel's deck again; but that if you will only tell him which way to go he will set off to-morrow."

Torgah was immediately relieved from his weariness of the vessel by being called ashore and assigned quarters in an outer room of the premises, with the promise that he should soon have the opportunity he desired; and word was sent to Somassee to come as soon as possible in one of the canoes, prepared to go with his newly arrived countryman, an Alabama Indian, on another exploring tour.

There was not the delay of a day, or of an hour, on any one's part in the needful preparations. Even Mrs. Gordon, who had previously been so feeble, but whose health and spirits seemed to revive with the coming of her sister-in-law, and with the prospect of an immediate effort, declared that she was able and ready to leave the very next day. It was Wednesday, February 2d, when these preparations were commenced, and so vigorously were they pushed forward in the work necessary aboard, as well as ashore, that by Friday, Feb 4th, all was ready for departure.

CHAPTER XXVI.

UT who, at that day, ever heard of a
vessel leaving port on Friday? No, no;
Pilot Dunbar was too much of a sailor,
(to say nothing of his being a Scotchman, too,) to think of such a thing. It was far
more sailor-like to risk the displeasure of *God* by
weighing anchor on Sunday, than to risk *ill-luck*
by starting on Friday; for the sailor-rule in common use was, " The better the day, the better the
deed."

The sentiments of the cabin, however, differed
from those of the forecastle; and it so turned out
that, as Pilot Dunbar would not leave port on
Friday, and Saturday was too wet and stormy to
permit the going out of an invalid passenger, and

as Dr. Gordon held the Sabbath in too hi_gh esteem to desecrate it without necessity, they did not leave port until Monday.

The crew consisted of Pilot Dunbar, sailing-master, and Dr. Gordon, his assistant. Peter, who had learned from his expert wife, Judy, many of the arts of culinary life, and who could make an excellent pot of coffee, and a very eatable biscuit, was installed as cook, though, being somewhat of a sailor, part of his time was spent in handling the ropes. Torgah and Somassee, who had abjured the deck, and who occupied the canoe fastened astern by a long, light hawser, were not a part of the crew — they were *outside passengers,* ready to aid in any service requiring the use of the paddle.

A light breeze curled the surface of the bay, and the little vessel, on being loosed from her moorings, stretched her wings, and seemed to career joyously over the water, like a thing of life released from weary confinement.

The first pause they made was at Riley's Island, where Dr. Gordon went ashore to see Pancheta, and to inquire if she had received any intelligence of her husband. Pancheta was quite cordial, and, for an Indian woman, was communicative on every subject except that in which he felt the deepest interest; but on the subject of her husband she was mysteriously reserved. Dr. Gordon gathered

from her various hints, dropped as if they were
contraband, that she expected her husband back
during the light of the next moon, and that it was
possible he might return in company with the
young people; but where he was detained, and
why, and at what place the young people were to
be found, were points on which all his power of
questioning could gain nothing. Perhaps she herself did not know; and with this hopeful, but unsatisfactory information, he returned to the pilot
boat. The thought did not occur to him until
after he had left the island that the cause of her
reserve might be something of a national character, and that Torgah and Somassee would, in that
event, probably be more successful than himself.

That evening they came to anchor in Manatee
Bay, where the ladies enjoyed the exceeding soft-
ness of the light upon the woodland, and the placid beauty of the water. Next morning they
sailed a few miles up the river, that no place
might be left unexplored where it was possible for
the young people to have been detained. Somassee and Torgah, also, paddled ashore at every
point where there was the sign of habitation, for
the purpose of making inquiry.

Thus they continued down the coast, entering
every inlet and creek, examining carefully every
island and wooded key, inquiring of every person
whom Torgah and Somassee could find, and occa-

sionally firing a little cannon which Dr. Gordon
had put aboard as a means of calling attention at
a distance, until finally Torgah came with a request that he might be allowed to go a few hours'
journey into the interior, promising to return early
the next day. He said that an old wise man,
named Mahinlo, an old-time friend of his, lived
in those parts, and he wished to consult him; that
Mahinlo, in early life, had been a famous warrior,
but was now a "chief and brave of the Great
Spirit;" * that he knew more, and could tell more
of what was going on in the world than all the
other red men put together, and that if any person in the nation knew anything of the young
people, that person was Mahinlo. He proposed,
therefore, to make him a visit, with a suitable present, as was customary, and to gain from him whatever information was to be had. This proposition
so exactly suited the desires of Dr. Gordon, that
although he was now within a few hours' sail of
the island where he had seen the last traces of his
children, and he longed to reach the spot and look
again, he consented to the absence of the canoe
with the two red men for the night, appointing to
meet them in the morning at the next island.

Late in the evening, when the light of day was
fading into deep dusk, and allowing only a faint
view of distant objects, the little vessel entered a

* A religious teacher.

river-like inlet, and came to anchor in a broad
sheet of two fathoms water, open indeed to the
sea, but calm and placid as Tampa or Manatee.
Dimly visible, at a point next the sea, but made
quite distinct by the aid of the spy-glass, was the
flying signal, which, though wrapped mostly around
the staff, had still a portion floating in the breeze.
This he pointed out to Mrs. Gordon and his sister, who looked with tearful interest upon what
brought them more sensibly near the objects of
their anxiety than ever they had been before.

"Yonder," said he, " under that grand old tree,
they pitched their tent. And yonder, where you
may see the drift collected against some short
stakes driven into the sand, was their spring of
water, all surrounded with their tracks. And
there, upon the beach, marked by a fallen tree-top,
was the place where they embarked, and where
they left the last signs that we could discover. It
is possible that some of the footprints may still be
seen."

The sight, dim though it was, of the places last
trodden by their children, brought mingled joy
and sorrow to the hearts of the mother, and Dr.
Gordon's own voice trembled with emotion as he
added, —

"Yes, if Providence permit, we will go ashore
at our first possible moment in the morning, and
I will examine every spot on the island, not ex-

plored before, that can furnish any clue to their mysterious disappearance. In the meantime, if you will prepare your ears against the shock, I will give our usual signal by cannon."

As he said this, he looked at Dunbar, who had been steadfastly watching the heavens, and whose face had assumed an expression of deep anxiety.

"What do you see in that bright moon to make you look at it so earnestly?" Dr. Gordon asked of him.

"Trouble," answered the sailor, "if I am a judge of weather. Just look at that scud! It has gathered within the last two minutes. Did you ever see anything run so fast?"

The moon was at the half full and directly overhead. Across her brilliant face a light, vapory cloud, that increased every moment in density, was rushing with such velocity as to make one think of sea-birds hastening in terror from the water to a refuge on the land.

"It looks verily as if we are to have a squall, or something worse," said Dr. Gordon, "and sorry I am that you have no better help for managing your pretty little Sea-bird than Pete and myself. But what we can do you must not hesitate to call for."

"The Sea-bird needs little help. She can almost manage herself," replied the enthusiastic old tar, looking with pride and affection upon his trimly built craft. "But it will do no harm to tighten up a little."

"So do," said Dr. Gordon, "and while you are engaged in that I will go and give my signal."

The gathering darkness was quickly illumined by a red glare, and the timbers of the vessel quivered with a thundering discharge. A minute afterward the discharge was repeated, and then Dr. Gordon returned to aid Dunbar and Peter in trimming the vessel to meet the coming gale.

"We have no time to lose," said the sailor anxiously. "The ladies will find it safer below. The squall will be upon us in two minutes."

While Mrs. McIntosh aided her sister down the narrow companion-way, the Doctor and the others worked vigorously in making all snug. They had barely completed their task, and the vessel was slowly swinging round with the tide, when the distant moan of the sea, which had rapidly changed into a roar, began to sound like the increasing rumble of thunder, and at the same time a fierce and sudden blast of wind came with such force upon the broadside of the vessel as almost to lay her upon her beam ends. She rose, however, as gracefully as she had bowed, set her face sharp to the wind, and gave a straining pull upon her cable.

"All safe now, unless she drags," said Dunbar. "We have good water and a good bottom."

" Also a good vessel and good pilot," added Dr
Gordon, with a laugh.

" A good vessel, aye, aye ! " Dunbar responded,
" and if a good pilot, he would take the liberty to
say that the best place for you, too, is where the
ladies have gone. It will soon be too rough for
anybody on deck, except an old salt like me."

Dr. Gordon was in the act of going below when
he turned suddenly toward Dunbar, grasped him
almost spasmodically by the shoulder, and with
much earnestness asked, —

" Did you hear that?"

" I heard something like a cannon, but whether
from land or sea I could not say," he replied ;
" nor was I certain whether it was the sound of a
cannon, or of the surf bursting over the bar."

" Peter, did you hear it?" he then inquired of
his servant.

" Yes, mossa, 1 yerry good," Peter answered
" Cannon from land, sir."

" Then it is from my children," he said, with
strong emotion, "though they have had barely time
to load and fire since they heard my signal. At
least," he continued, moderating in his excitement
by a second thought, " that gun from shore *seems*
to have been a reply to mine from sea."

With the great addition to his hopes, furnished
by the supposed reply to his signal, Dr. Gordon
passed into the little cabin, reporting to the two

mothers the fact of the answer by cannon, and
making their hearts as glad as his own. They discussed fully and at length the probabilities of the
case, and concluded by convincing themselves that
their long and trying season of suspense was about
to have a joyful termination.

Ere they were half way through their discussion,
however, they were made aware that a storm of
unusual violence, as well as suddenness, was upon
them. Their little craft rose and fell, and leaped
and plunged, and seemed tortured almost to mad-
ness by its confinement by cable amid the rush and
tumble of the waters. Rain was soon added to
the wind. It came in great drops, not falling, but
shooting horizontally, like shot projected from a
gun.

Every now and then Dr. Gordon would ascend
the short and narrow stairway leading to the deck,
carefully open the door, and peep out to watch the
progress of the storm, then return and report the
result of his observations. In course of time, the
billows, which had become mixed with mire and
dirt by passing over the shoals, attained such mag-
nitude as to burst repeatedly over the deck, and
to enter every exposed place, compelling him to
desist from his observations, and not only to keep
the door closed, but even to caulk its crevices. In
this state of confinement, several hours passed away,
when a startling crash caused Dr. Gordon to exclaim,—

" There goes our mast ! "

And not long afterward a still more ominous sound was heard — a harsh grating at the stern. The little vessel had been forced from her moorings by the heavy dash of the waves, had dragged her anchor, and been drifted, stern foremost, against a ledge of that kind of rock * which underlies the greater part of peninsular Florida.

The sound of the grating stern, and afterward of the grating keel, as the boat was gradually forced around and thrown broadside upon the rock was dreadful. The ladies looked to Dr. Gordon for comfort, but for a long time they could not catch his eye; he looked persistently down, and his face was full of anxiety. They were, however, brave women — their faces were blanched, but they uttered no words of fear. They braced themselves to meet their fate, whatever it might be, with becoming composure. Yet, oh! how hard was it to think of perishing almost within hail of those dear ones whom they had come so far to rescue!

At the suggestion of his sister, Dr. Gordon opened his Bible, and, by the dim light of the cabin lamp, read the 130th Psalm, beginning, " Out of

---

* This rock, if such it may be called, since it is so soft as to be easily cut with an axe or saw, is composed of shells, in every stage of disintegretion, imbedded in a mortar made of its own detritus, mixed with sand, and is capable of great induration after exposure to the air.

the depths have I cried unto Thee, O Lord!"
Then they knelt down, as well as they could, and
he led them in an earnest, submissive prayer for
themselves and for the loved ones constituting
their more immediate world; after which they
took courage and spoke together more freely of
their condition and prospects.

"We can do nothing but wait, and prepare ourselves for whatever may betide," said he. "We
are perfectly in the Lord's hands, to do with us as
He will; not more so now than we have ever been,
only we *feel it more.*"

He paused, then suddenly added, "But I wonder that we have heard nothing all this time from
Dunbar and Peter. They might easily have hailed
us through the partition. I will call to them."

He went to the temporary wall of plank erected
to afford privacy to the cabin, gave some vigorous
knocks, and called aloud, but no answer came in
return.

"Can they be on deck?" he asked. "I will
look."

The little vessel was now leaning so much to
leeward that the waves striking against the keel
and the exposed bottom were broken, and did not
threaten the companionway as before. Dr. Gordon carefully opened the little door and peeped
out. The wind howled horribly, and all around
was pitchy dark, except the phosphorescence of the

water, which shone in spots, as if torches were
lighted there. He peered narrowly along the sloping deck. Nobody was visible. He shouted at
the top of his voice, "Dunbar! Peter!" but
there was no reply. The horrible truth forced
itself upon him, that they had been washed over-
board and lost.

With this painful conviction came also the
thought of danger by lack of their services. Who
was to close the hatchway to the forecastle? Was
it closed? If open, was not the vessel in imminent danger of filling? It was necessary instantly,
and at all risks, to see that it was closed. Possibly, too, by going there he might learn what had
befallen the men.

He returned to the cabin, took from a drawer
a small halyard,* ten or twelve yards long; fastened one end of it to his waist, and the other end
to a strong hook near the door, keeping the intervening length coiled in his hand, ready to be let
out at will ; then called his sister to take her place
at the doorway, ready to render assistance in case
of need. With these helps to his safety, he clambered cautiously along the sloping deck, supporting himself by every available means, until he arrived at the intended point. The hatch was not

---

* Halyards (literally haulyards, though sometimes spelled
aalliards) are ropes by which yards, sails, or signals are
hoisted.

closed. It seemed as if left with the expectation of immediate return, and fortunately it was so guarded that the billows which dashed along the deck were diverted from entering. Here Dr. Gordon stooped and called aloud. All was silent. He entered, lighted a match, and looked around. A little puddle of water was collected at one side. Dunbar's coat was hanging on a nail, and Peter's hat lay on his berth; but the owners of them were not there.

Dr. Gordon made the hatch as secure as possible, and worked his way back to the cabin door without accident, but with great sinking of heart. Besides the shock naturally felt in view of sudden death near at hand, arose the reflections: How are we to pass from the wreck to the shore? and how from that to Tampa? Instead of being able to help our children, in the event of their being found, we ourselves shall be in need of help.

On his return to the cabin, his first duty was to reply to the inquiries made of him concerning the men and the state of the vessel. He attempted no concealment, acknowledging the whole truth, that their little vessel was stranded; that the two men were no doubt lost, and that there were no means at hand for delivering themselves from their present situation.

When a man has done all that he can, and failed, he is apt to sink into gloomy apathy. With woman it is different; man's time of despair is her season of hope. She will find a bright side where a man sees nothing but darkness. The sexes were made for each other.

"Do you not expect the canoe in the morning with Torgah and Somassee?" asked Mrs. McIntosh, on seeing her brother's despondency.

"I do," he replied, "and we may therefore hope for deliverance, if our craft can stand till then this beating of the surf, and this grinding upon the rock."

"But the violence of the gale is over, is it not?" asked Mrs. Gordon. "I think the roar of the winds is not so great, nor the beating of the waves."

"You are right," said Dr. Gordon. "We will, therefore, hope for the best, and not trouble ourselves unnecessarily with what we cannot help."

With this philosophic resolve, in many cases more easily made than kept, they immediately commenced a cheerful conversation; then drawing the door close, and caulking the crevices as before, each sought such repose as was possible. More than once during the night Dr. Gordon opened carefully the little door to look out upon the storm, when finding it greatly abated, he at last gave himself up to the refreshment of sleep.

The light of day comes slowly when the gates of the east are banked with clouds, and more es-

pecially to those who have carefully closed every
crevice through which it can enter. Weary with
care and watchfulness, the shipwrecked company,
released from anxiety, sank into a sleep which
held them until long after the sun had broken
through the now dispersing clouds. They were
awakened by hearing a gentle thump against the
vessel's deck, as of some one trying to get in. Mrs.
McIntosh was about to say, "Brother, awake!
the canoe has come!" when she heard a soft halloo
that thrilled her very soul. The tone was in some
respects strange, yet it sounded familiar as the
beating of her own heart. There was no mis-
taking the voice that asked, hoarse with emotion,
" Is any one within?"

Mrs. McIntosh answered, " Yes, but who is
there?"

The person without said something which could
not be distinctly heard, but which sounded faintly
like the name of her own son; then another voice
took up the answer and said, —

" Harold—Harold and Robert."

For a moment Mrs. McIntosh made no reply,
nor did Dr. Gordon, who now stood by her side,
with his hands clasped, and his lips moving in
momentary prayer. As for Mrs. Gordon, she had
attempted to rush forward, but had sunk to the
floor insensible. Recovering his self-possession,
Dr. Gordon motioned his sister to attend to his

prostrate wife, while he went to the barred door, undid its fastenings, and let in the new comers.

Oh! the joy, the joy pervading the dark room of that stranded and almost broken vessel! Mrs. McIntosh received into her arms a son, almost a man, a noble expansion of the boy who left her less than a year before; and Dr. and Mrs. Gordon were rejoicing in the embraces of one whom they had almost despaired of seeing again, but in whom they could now rejoice as both son and deliverer.

CHAPTER XXVII.

*BREAKFAST UNDER AN ORANGE-TREE — MAROON-
ERS' HOME — THE MAROONERS THEMSELVES —
PREPARING TO RECOVER THE LOST BOAT — DUCKS,
FISH, ETC. — LOOK FOR BOAT — THE STRANDED
VESSEL — MYSTERIOUS SIGN — CAN WE LAUNCH
HER? AND HOW? — MECHANICAL RULE.*

N the morning of the second day after
the deliverance recorded in the preced-
ing chapter, a happy group assembled
round the breakfast-table of the Young
Marooners. It was under the fragrant canopy
of a large orange-tree,* of which there were many
growing wild upon the island, and even at this
late date were loaded with luscious-looking fruit.
Its pure white blossoms, interspersed with the tiny
green bulbs of the coming crop, and the golden

---

* *The bitter-sweet* — so called because its juicy cells, though
almost rivalling in sweetness the oranges of Sicily, are enveloped in a membrane and rind of great bitterness. Whether
indigenous to the soil of peninsular Florida, or introduced by
some preceding generation, it now grows as freely in the forests as the wild plum and the crab-apple do with us. And a
most beautiful tree it is, in every stage of its growth, and
at every season of the year

globes already ripe, were peeping out timidly from
amid the glossy leaves, and filling the air with
their delicious odors.   Few trees, outside the paradise of Adam and Eve, can surpass it in the
beauty of fruit, flower, and foliage, and, we may
add, in the rich delicacy of its fragrance.

Under the branches of this tree, Dr. Gordon,
Mrs. Gordon, and Mrs. McIntosh were seated as
guests around a dining-table of mahogany, the
history of which, and of the handsome chairs
accompanying it, had been given them the day
before, but cannot now be repeated.   Mary occupied the place of hostess, and Robert that of host,
while little Frank crowded in between father and
mother, and Harold sat lovingly beside his mother.
Sam, acting as waiter, stood behind the chair of
his young mistress, where he could most easily
survey the whole company, and be ready to attend
to any calls upon his service.

They were at the edge of a small prairie, or
natural savanna, a few acres in extent, having
near them, in full view, an old Indian hut, which,
though neatly built at first, was rapidly going to
decay.   Partly overhanging this hut were several
very old peach-trees, and, at the margin of the
forest farther on, was a thicket of wild plums.
Not many steps distant from the company, in
another direction, was the Marooners' tent.   It
was the same tent that had been brought away
from Bellevue in the runaway boat, but it had

undergone such alterations as to be scarcely recog-
nizable, having been increased by the addition to
its two original apartments, of several sheds or
wings, one of which was Sam's room, crowded
with tools, and sometimes used as a workshop, and
another, furnished with a stove and pipe, was
the family kitchen. This tent, securely pitched,
and well protected against wet by a double fly at
the top and a good drain at the bottom, was at the
same time defended against hostile attacks by a
strong palisade of stakes driven in the ground in
double or triple rows all around. Almost adjoining the palisade was a small covered inclosure,
divided into two parts, one of which was the home
of a she-goat, with a half-grown kid, and of a
beautiful white fawn, and the other was occupied
by a pair of young bear cubs, that were as tame
as either fawn or kid, and, like them, passed in
and out of their dwelling at pleasure. A little
farther off was a poultry-pen, containing wild turkeys, wild ducks, and brant, all more or less
maimed in their wings by shot, and now in the
process of fattening or of taming.

The table thus spread under the orange-tree,
and surrounded by the afore-mentioned company,
was plentifully supplied with venison, fish, oysters, ship-bread, butter and cheese, and (what was
a treat to the juveniles after their long privation)
a dish of delightful hominy, made from grits

brought from the pilot-boat. In these culinary preparations, Mary, aided by Sam, was the agent, although Mrs. McIntosh insisted upon helping her, and did prevail so far as to have the *drinkables* given up to her care, in consequence of which she prepared an abundant supply of excellent and refreshing coffee.

Of the juveniles, Frank Gordon, the youngest, was a merry little fellow, just turned eight years of age. His chief occupation, besides play, during their long sojourn upon the island, had been to keep his sister company, to assist in her various home duties, and to accompany his brother or cousin in their frequent hunts for deer and turkeys; but that in which he most prided himself was in being the nominal master of the little bears, who sometimes, in a wrestling match, proved that they could master him. Mary, his sister, was a bright-faced, curly-headed, rosy-cheeked girl of eleven years, and had addressed her nimble though inexperienced fingers to the duties of housemaid, housekeeper, cook, mother to Frank, and servant-of-all-work, though in this last office she was aided, as far as possible, by all the others. Robert, their brother, between fourteen and fifteen years of age, was a well-educated boy, of fine intellect and varied attainments, but in bodily development by no means robust. Harold McIntosh, their cousin, barely fifteen, was a strongly built youth, and, in many respects, the opposite of Robert, possessed

of a fine natural mind, but having had his education greatly neglected, although he had been trained
to all manly exercises, and was thereby the better
fitted for his present life in the woods. As for
clothing, Robert and Mary were dressed in the
usual garb of civilized life, but in garments that
their parents had never before seen, of which
they gave the explanation in connection with the
history of the mahogany table and chairs; while
Harold and Frank were clad from head to foot in
garments of dressed deerskin, which had been prepared and made by their own hands from the
game killed since coming to the island.

The parents looked with delight and surprise
upon their ruddy-faced children and the comforts
of their woodland home, and many a silent thanks-
giving ascended to the Father of all good for the
kindness shown them.

"I can understand now," said Mrs. Gordon to
Robert, in a tone of playful reproach, as they sat
around the breakfast-table that morning, "I can
understand now why you all made no greater
efforts to return home. Your island is so pleasant that I should have no great objection to being
detained here a few weeks myself."

"I confess, mother," replied Robert, "that we
did not do much work for more than a month
after coming here; but this was not from a desire
to stay. Indeed, Mary and Frank had many a
hearty cry before they became reconciled to their

banishment. You must remember that after we lost our boat, we had no means of getting away. We had no tools to work with, except fire, and our axes and hatchet, and we could not help hoping, and believing too, that father would set the whole country to work to find us, and also come himself to take us off."

"All which was done," said his father; "and had I not seen for myself, this tangled forest in which you have taken up your abode, it would be to me a mystery still, how you could have remained here so long undiscovered. Even now I can understand it only by supposing that the Indians are kept away, as you say Riley suggests, by a most violent superstition, and that the reefs and shoals which guard the coast at this point prevent all ordinary access to it from sea."

"Yes, uncle," Harold added; "and had it not been for our fortunate discovery, on Christmas day, of that pirate wreck in the marsh, from which we obtained our tools and most of our supplies, we should not have finished our boats yet. We must not only have worked very slowly and roughly for the want of tools, but so much of our time would have been occupied with hunting and fishing for something to eat, that we should not have been able, probably, to give much of it to work."

"I must visit that pirate wreck, as you call it, at the earliest opportunity," said Dr. Gordon. "But our first duty now, since the burial of poor

Peter and Dunbar on yesterday, is to provide the means for our return to Tampa. Robert, did you not say that our lost boat, my pleasure-boat that was, has been discovered?"

"Yes, father," he replied. "Not two hours before your cannon was fired the night of the gale, Harold obtained a view of her lying in the marsh."

Dr. Gordon then looked to Harold, who continued:

"She lies, or rather she then lay, in the soft mud of the marsh, about a hundred yards from the river. Sam was with me, and we rowed to several points, trying to get nearer, but in vain. I am almost sure it is our Bellevue boat, for she has the same build and the same stripes."

"Mary, dear," said Gordon, turning to his thrifty little hostess, " I wish to take Robert and Harold with me to see after my boat. We shall probably be gone all day, for if we do not succeed with the boat, we must go to our stranded vessel, and see what can be done to float her. Now, people cannot work with much comfort unless they have something to eat, so I beg that you will put up a good substantial lunch for us of such materials as you have at hand, without further cooking."

Mary at once left the table, went to her pantry, and soon returned with a well-filled basket. In the meantime, her father spoke to Robert and Harold, saying:

"We will go as soon as you can prepare the boat. But let me ask another question: What is the character of the marsh where the boat lies?"

"Very soft," Harold answered.

"So I understood," his uncle said; "but is the mud open, or is it covered with mangroves?"

"Partly open and partly covered. We could see openings through it all the way to the boat," replied Harold.

"Then," continued his uncle, "we may need several broad light planks to walk upon."

"Why, uncle," said Harold, in surprise, "all the plank at our command would not carry us a quarter of the way."

"If the marsh is properly open," returned his uncle, with a smile, "I could make two planks, or certainly three, carry me all the way. I would alternately stand upon each, and push the other ahead."

Harold smiled with pleasure at the simple device, and responded:

"If it is only a pair of *mud-shoes*, you want, like the Laplander's snow-shoes, I think we can supply you."

And off he and Robert went, each with his gun and a pair of oars upon his shoulder, and carrying other parts of the boat's rigging between them.

"Father, may I not go, too?" plead little Frank. "I am never in anybody's way, and I can help sometimes."

"That is the very reason I had for intending to leave you at home," his father answered, amused at the good opinion Frank had expressed of himself. "But if there is no need for you at home, you are welcome to go with us. What says mamma? What says auntie? What says sister?"

All answered promptly in consent, and the moment the question was decided, Frank jumped up and clapped his hands, saying:

"Well, there is something else I know you will want, and I will get it, for my share."

He ran to the tent, brought out a jug and a dipper, and was on his way to the spring, when his father said:

"You are a thoughtful little boy, Frank. We shall need water as much as lunch. But that jug will be too heavy for you to carry, when full of water. Give it to Sam, and do you come here."

Frank did as he was directed, and his father asked:

"Can you climb a tree?"

Frank answered: "The boys at home used to call me squirrel."

"But can you chimb an *orange*-tree?" his father asked again, alluding to the terrible thorns, (oftentimes forked or branching into several points,) by which access to the golden fruit is guarded.

"Yes, sir," Frank replied; "I have climbed them many a time, and been stuck, too. But we do not climb the orange-trees now."

"Indeed!" said his father; "then how do you get the fruit?"

"This way," he replied, drawing out from a neighboring bush a long, light pole, on the small end of which was firmly tied a small wooden hook; "this will get as many as we want."

He then asked his sister for a little bag, and taking up the pole, he said:

"The best oranges are yonder in the woods; but you must go with me."

"What, are you afraid?" his father asked.

"No, sir, I am not," he replied; "but brother Robert is, and so is cousin Harold."

Dr. Gordon looked for explanation to Mary, who had by this time returned, and she answered:

"The first night after we came to the prairie, a panther ran off with one of Nannie's kids, and from that time till now brother Robert and cousin Harold always carry their guns, and have charged Frank never to go into the woods alone."

"Very wisely charged," said her father, looking grave. "Then we must not take all the guns away from the tent. I will load mine and leave it with Sam."

"You need not do that, father, if you care to carry it," replied Mary, "for Sam has his own gun loaded, and I have mine, too, and we can all shoot, all except little Frank."

Dr. Gordon went with Frank to the tree having

ιne better oranges, loaded the little bag, which he
gave him to carry in place of the water; then
shouldering his gun, and taking a hatchet, he
went with him and Sam to the landing, where
Robert and Harold were already awaiting their
approach.

The boat-landing was a neat little cove, setting
in from the river on the eastern margin of the
island, and so completely surrounded by sea-myrtles and other shrubs as to be invisible to persons
passing by water.

The voyagers were soon afloat, Dr. Gordon at
the helm, and Robert and Harold at the oars, and
then the light and well-trimmed canoe shot rapidly
along the crooked river on her northward way.
Great flocks of wild ducks, various in size and
plumage, and of brant, (better known as the ordinary wild goose, gray in color, but having a
white ring around the throat,) crowded the surface of the river and also the muddy shore, where
they assembled in countless numbers to plume their
feathers and to exchange with each other a social
quack! quack! At the sharp angles of the rivei,
beyond the projecting points of which these birds
tried to conceal themselves, and where the ordinary
number was greatly increased by those which had
been previously scared up by the boat, they arose
in such clouds, and came so near overhead in their
circling flight, that Dr. Gordon and Robert were

tempted twice to give them the contents of their gun-barrels, and had the pleasure of seeing a shower of the different kinds come pouring obliquely from the living clouds above, and dotting the placid surface of the water below. Harold's piece was a rifle, and therefore unfit for such work, yet with his single ball, sent through the mingled strata overhead, he brought down two birds, one of which fell with broken wing, and one with severed neck. These several discharges furnished so liberal a supply of wild fowl, and the killing of more was so manifest a waste of life, that Dr. Gordon commanded a truce.

Nor was little Frank without enjoyment, though he wielded no gun. Besides an eager sympathy in the excitement of the sport, his chief amusement consisted in watching the fish. In passing near the mud-flats, where the shrimp, prawn, and mullet congregate to feed upon the rich slime of the river, it was a never-ceasing source of pleasure to him to observe the nimble leaping of these little creatures, that in their careless gambols threw themselves even into the boat itself.

"That's mine! and that! and that!" he exclaimed, in passing a certain shoal where several of the larger mullet leaped over the gunwale in such rapid succession that he could scarcely count them, tempting him to boast that he would soon have as many fish as his father and brother had birds. In the middle of the current, enormous sturgeons, as long as a man, would dart their full length from the water, and fall back with a heavy splash that could be heard a quarter of a mile; while a long line of porpoises, sometimes in platoons, sometimes in irregular file, would put their great snouts out of water, give a loud and prolonged Puff-f-f! then gracefully dive back again, showing, as they turned, their immense shiny backs, broad and round as the fattest of hogs.*

On arriving at the point recognized by Harold as that from which he had so plainly seen the lost boat three days before, they looked everywhere for her in vain. They rowed to other points, and even ascended the marsh, walking on the soft mud by means of the boards, then elevating themselves still more by standing upon their oars lodged on the mangroves.

"No doubt lifted and carried off by the last gale," Harold mournfully suggested. "What a pity to lose her!"

"Perhaps not lost," his uncle replied. "If moved only by the gale, she must lie not far off, and in the direction of wind and tide."

---

* The word porpoise means hog-fish, (from the French *pore-poisson*,) and the animal is known by some as "sea-hog," from the shape and size of its fat back, and its habit of rooting for eels and sea-worms, in the same manner as hogs root for their food.

"Shall we continue our search?" asked Robert.

"Not for three days," replied his father; "we shall then have a spring tide, and be able to row over a large part of the marsh, and possibly even to capture and bring her back."

They now went, without delay, to inspect the stranded vessel, and found her high and dry upon her side, full twenty feet from low-water mark, though not much above it. The bed in which she lay seemed to be mud, but probing with an iron ramrod revealed a stratum of shell-rock a few inches below. A drift of dead mangroves, mingled with other marsh growth, covered her hull, and gave her, at a distance, the appearance of a great pile of sea-weed. With the exception of her broken mast, and a partial fracture of her rudder and keel, she was perfectly sound.

On examining the cabin and forecastle, everything was found to lie just as it had been left two days before, and there was no sign of interference except in the pantry, which had evidently been entered and relieved of a ham of dried venison and a small bag of ship-bread. The loss was a trifle, but the fact was very distressing. The vessel had been *visited.* By *whom* it was important to know; for the party would, no doubt, repeat the visit, possibly with hostile intent, and in force sufficient to annoy, if not to overwhelm. For a few minutes Dr. Gordon and his boys pondered

the matter with feelings akin to what is so powerfully depicted by De Foe when he represents
Robinson Crusoe as discovering the human footprints in the sand of the seashore. Many were
the conjectures advanced in explanation of the
mystery, and rejected as unsatisfactory, until Harold, who for some reason had gone out to the canoe,
was heard to exclaim :

"Come here, uncle! Come here, Robert! I
can explain it now."

They went in answer to his call, and saw him
looking eagerly at some marks made with red
ochre upon the slope of the deck, just over the
companionway. These marks composed a most
uncouth figure, with six points standing out from
an oval body, which Dr. Gordon and Robert
would have studied long without being able to
decipher, but which Harold explained, joyfully :

"That is old Torgah's mark. It is intended
for the figure of a *ground-mole*. He told me that
Torgah was his *home* name, but that he was known
in the nation by the Muscogee name of Tuck-assee-
Emathla, which means ground-mole warrior,
because he had once killed his enemy by *undermining*, like a mole, and that now, wheresoever
the figure of a *tuck-assee* is seen, it is known to
mean himself, and that when it is marked upon
anything it wil protect it, so far as his name has
any influence."

W

"So he has been here! and, no doubt, Somassee too," said Dr. Gordon. "The venison ham they took was their own. They have shown their fidelity by coming according to promise, and by leaving a protecting mark upon what they supposed I should wish to be saved. I would scarcely have expected this from red-skins."

"Torgah will do anything for me or for mine," rejoined Harold enthusiastically. "I will trust my life in his hands."

"You think well of your old friend," said his uncle, with a smile. "I trust the future will sustain your good opinion."

Satisfied now that all was right, Dr. Gordon proceeded to examine the vessel with a view to getting her afloat. Accustomed to mechanical operations, and never better satisfied than when having some problem of the kind to solve, he was, however, sorely puzzled with the question now before him. He looked long and carefully at vessel, ground, and water, and became perfectly absorbed in thought, while Robert and Harold continued silent spectators, or conversed with each other in whispers. At last little Frank broke silence by asking:

"Father, do you think you can get her off?"

"O yes, with time and work enough," he replied.

"I am glad to hear you say so," said Harold, "but for my part, I do not see how the work of getting her off is even to be *begun*."

"I can tell you of several ways," replied his uncle, "but the question with me is, whether the getting of her off will be worth the time and labor of doing it?"

"She is very heavy, and we are very weak," continued Harold, "and I shall be much obliged to you, uncle, if you will give me some ideas on the subject. I am perfectly lost when thinking of it."

"I will give you your choice of three modes, and see which of them you like best," his uncle replied. "The first is to act upon the principle involved in the name of your old friend, *Tuck-assee*, the Underminer: we can dig a canal long and deep enough to float her off at high tide."

"I understand that, and like it, too," said Harold, "but how are we to keep this heavy thing from sinking upon us when we have under-mined her?"

"By props, to be removed at the right time," answered Dr. Gordon. "A second mode is to lift her upon a system of skids or ways strong enough to support her weight, and let her slide down their greased surface, as in ordinary launch-ing, except that our vessel must go sideway."

"I understand that, too," Harold repeated, with a smile of pleasure.

"A third mode," continued his uncle, "is that used in house-moving. We must lift her suffi-ciently to set her on a level, or partially inclined way of strong timber, along which we must move her by means of rollers."

"Yes, uncle, that is plain enough, too,—all but one thing," Harold interposed; "but how are we four (counting in Sam) to lift this heavy vessel imbedded in the mud?"

"Have we not a foundation of rock?" asked his uncle in reply.

Harold nodded assent.

"Have we not plenty of timber on the island long enough and strong enough for all the levers that can be wanted?"

Harold nodded again.

"With sufficient leverage, and with a foundation on which to work, we four can raise any assignable weight," his uncle continued, "only the greater the disproportion between power and weight, the longer the time that will be occupied. Archimedes is reported to have said, 'Give me a lever long enough, and I can move the world.'"

Harold mused awhile without reply, and Dr. Gordon continued:

"If you are in difficulty about managing the very large and heavy levers necessary in this work, I will show you how to do that when the time for working has come. All that I can give you now is the principle."

"For which I am very much obliged to you," replied Harold, with a look of gratitude. "You have made me feel ten times stronger already."

Having completed the necessary surveys, and taken from the vessel such stores as were needed at the tent, and especially such things as might be endangered by being left, they prepared to return. On their way, Dr. Gordon said to Harold:

"I have given you some ideas, which seem to have interested you, on the subject of lifting and moving heavy weights. I will now give you a rule about machinery in general, which may help you, as it has oftentimes helped me. You may feel assured that *anything can be accomplished by machinery which requires only the action of* A GIVEN POWER, IN A GIVEN DIRECTION, FOR A GIVEN TIME.

"Take, as a sample, our question of to-day. We know that we can launch our vessel, because this requires only the action of a power sufficient to lift her from her bed, and then a power sufficient to shove or pull her to the water. And though our personal strength is small, we know that we can increase it indefinitely by the use of mechanical leverage within reach.

"But when a machine requires thought or judgment, or when it requires unlimited time, (as in all 'perpetual motion' machines,) we at once pronounce it impossible."

The company reached the tent by the middle of the afternoon, wearied, yet hopeful.

CHAPTER XXVIII.

VISIT TO THE PIRATE WRECK — NIGHT WORK.

CONTEMPORANEOUS with these adventures, there lived in the wild woods of Texas a hunter and warrior whose name* was in every mouth, from Maine to Mexico, but of whom the only distinct vestige now remaining in the public mind is the widespread adage, "*Be sure you are right, then* GO AHEAD."

This had become, at first in jest, afterward in earnest, a favorite maxim with Dr. Gordon. On returning from the tour which had occupied them most of the day, he had said to the boys, —

"What we do for launching the pilot boat within a month must be done quickly. On Tuesday will probably be the highest tide of the season, being the spring tide of the vernal equinox. But in order to launch her, we must cut away that bed of shell-rock on which she lies, and to cut that away we must have mattocks, or their equiva-

* David Crockett.

lent. Have you anything of the kind among your tools?"

"Nothing," Robert replied; "nor do I recollect seeing anything answering to it among the tools of the pirate wreck."

"As the rock is very soft, possibly some broad chisels driven deeply might effect our purpose," Dr. Gordon added. "We might also accomplish a good deal by a few deeply laid blasts of gunpowder, but I prefer not to employ that for fear of attracting the attention of the wild people on the mainland."

"We have cannon powder enough at the tent, or rather near it, hidden away in some hollow trees," Harold observed; "and as for chisels, I recollect seeing several very broad ones in the tool-chest of the pirate."

"You have alluded so often to that wreck, and spoken so confidently of its piratical character, that I must certainly visit her and judge for myself," said Dr. Gordon. "Perhaps, too, we may find there all the tools, or substitutes for them, that we may need. How far is she from your landing?"

"About a mile," the boys replied, "and very easy of approach at quarter tide, which we will have late this afternoon."

"Exactly suiting our time," rejoined Dr. Gordon, "and I propose to go so soon as we can feel sufficiently rested after our return."

During the half hour that they spent at the tent, Dr. Gordon called up Sam and inquired what tools he recollected seeing at the wreck suited to his purpose, to which Sam replied, —

"I nebber see no mattock, mossa. Mebbe some day, doe. But I see plenty o' big chisel."

Leaving Frank at home now, and taking Sam in his place, the company set off on this new errand. The long slow tide of the Gulf was just turning from ebb to flood as they left the landing, and when they reached the mouth of the creek where the wreck lay, the little tide-wave, which always preceded the rise, had just entered it. Broad and clear as the mouth of the creek was, all objects a little beyond were concealed from the view of persons passing, by a rankly grown hammock of myrtle and cedar. The wrecked vessel lay, bottom upward, directly across the bed of the drain, and a heavy raft of seaweeds and other growth covered completely the side on which they approached her. Unfavorably situated as she was for making an impression, no one could scan her proportions without being struck with her beauty as a model of strength and speed.

The mass of weeds drifted against the stern greatly facilitated their ascent to the upturned bottom, upon which they passed next the keel to a scuttle cut amidships by the boys, on a former occasion, and affording easy access to the dark interior. Robert and Harold, whose frequent visits had familiarized them with everything there, were preparing to descend at once into the scuttle, but quickly drew back in disgust, — an intolerable odor of decaying matter, animal and vegetable, was finding vent at the hole and threatening to prevent all further progress.

"This is worse than it has ever been before," said Harold, turning a little pale.

"There was none of it at our last visit, though that was only last week," added Robert, with a disappointed look.

"You seem to forget, boys, that in the meantime there has been a severe gale, which no doubt has wet the substances within," said Dr. Gordon. "There certainly is a horrid odor, but what concerns me most is whether it may not be noxious as well as nauseous. We must test it before we descend."

Harold laughed. "I can never forget that old well at Bellevue," said he, "where I dropped my knife, and would certainly have been suffocated in going after it had not Robert first tested the air by a lighted splinter."

"As we will test this now, except that we will use a candle instead," returned his uncle, with a smile.

A light rod was soon constructed of several switches, selected from the raft, and tied together;

a candle, brought for the purpose of exploring, was fastened securely to the lower end, then lighted and lowered slowly into the vessel's hold. Instead of being extinguished, however, as it would have been had the hold been filled with deadly vapor, it burned as brightly as ever, on seeing which, Dr. Gordon said :

" We need not fear suffocation, for air that will support combustion will also support life. Could we now guard against *infection*, which is sometimes caused by such vapors, we might feel perfectly safe, though our olfactories should suffer. But I think we may risk it. Boys, get your noses ready ! "

With this command, as much in earnest as in jest, though given with a laugh, Dr. Gordon covered his own nose with a handkerchief, which he first damped, remarking, —

" Silk is an excellent strainer for the breath. A dry handkerchief kept closely round the nostrils is a great protection against dust, and a damp one is as great a protection against smoke and malaria."

A small rope ladder had been attached to the scuttle in a previous visit. In descending that, and approaching the inverted deck, all were conscious of a current of air passing upward, which they were tempted to breathe, and which they found, to their joy, almost as pure as the air outside.

"This puts us at our ease," said Dr. Gordon. "We may breathe now, and talk and work too, without feeling ourselves all the time under pressure. The bad air, in whatever sense it may be bad, is in the hold above us, and finds its vent through the scuttle."

They went into the tool-room, and discovered there, not only the chisels described, and other things belonging to carpenter's and shipwright's work, but many things pertaining to a smithery, though none of them bore the marks of having been used. There were hammers large and small, and tongs of several kinds, an anvil, a pair of double bellows for keeping up a continuous blast, and steel and iron in bars, and even a small pile of charcoal. No mattock was to be seen, nor hoe, nor spade, (these travellers upon the water seemed to have had no thought of ever being on land,) but Dr. Gordon selected one or two iron rods, which he judged might, by a little bending and flattening, be made to accomplish his purpose, and in order to insure the necessary forging, he resolved to carry back the anvil, the bellows, and other things needful.

From the tool-room they went to the gunner's room, then to the forecastle, by an opening that had been cut through the thick partition, then back to the after-cabin and officers' room. In every department the evidences of a warlike character were so manifest, that the only question to be decided was whether the vessel was lawfully or unlawfully in arms.

"She may have been a *privateer*," suggested Dr. Gordon, "or an armed vessel in search of pirates; though I confess the burden of proof goes to show that her character was piratical. If so, her murderous crew have met with a just, though awful retribution. Did I not hear you say, boys, that there was a strong, iron box somewhere about which you had not examined?'

"It is in a closet in the after-cabin," replied Harold. "We have not opened it, partly for two reasons: we did not know how, and we were somewhat in doubt whether we ought to open it if we could."

"Very good reasons," his uncle said, "but over-borne, I think, by the fact that by opening it we may obtain some more certain clue to the ownership and character of the vessel. Lead me to it."

They went, all together. The box, though not very large, was heavy, as if made of thick, solid metal, or filled with something possessed of great weight. In the capsizing of the vessel it had been thrown with its door downward, so there was reason to expect that the confined air, having no escape, would have kept the papers and other valuables within in a state of tolerable preservation.

By their united strength the box was heaved

over, and its door exposed conveniently to work. A strong, sharp cold chisel, highly tempered, for cutting iron, was brought, together with a black-smith's hammer, by means of which two holes were cut in the iron door large enough to admit the end of a bar of steel, to be used as a lever, and by which the door was soon pried from its place.

Upon the shelves within, and in the several compartments into which the interior was divided, were many small packages, some of which were quite heavy, and carefully wrapped, tied, and la-belled in Spanish, both within and without. There was a large box filled with Mexican dollars, and a small box heavy with gold coin, of several differ-ent nations. These boxes seemed to be the treas-ury, all the other packages bearing the marks of private property.

The first of the labelled packages, opened by special request of the boys, was quite small, but very neatly put up. Upon a paper outside, it bore the partly obliterated name "*Ros*." The names recorded within were Manuel De Rosa, Elena, his wife, and Maria and Gualterio, their children, all hailing from Vera Cruz, Mexico. The contents were highly valuable, consisting of diamonds, opals, and rubies, of such purity and workmanship that they would be valued by a jeweller at a small fortune.

"This package," said Dr. Gordon, "must be carefully preserved for the rightful heirs, if it has not been forfeited by the misdeeds of the last possessor. It may gain us a clue to the others, and to the true character and history of the unfortunate vessel."

Other packages, which were opened, then carefully bound again, contained every variety of valuables in small compass — gold chains, rings, bracelets, jewels, and even a few costly watches. One of them was labelled Mateo Molina, Nicaragua; another Guillermo Ximenez, Matagorda; another simply, Juanico; a fourth, Faquita, (Fanny,) New York; one bore the fancy name of Silbador, (whistler;) and another still was marked on the outside, Antonillo Anade, (Tony Duck,) on an inner envelope Anadino, (little duck,) and on a paper still further inside, Anadoncillo, (big young duck.)

"Mr. Duck seems to have had an unusual number of pet names," said Dr. Gordon, "but not one of them, probably, his true one."

"I think he must have been a funny little duck-legged man, and a great favorite with the person who prepared these labels," added Robert.

Harold looked and listened very gravely. The ludicrous associations with the last name which made his uncle and cousin laugh, scarcely caused his lips to curl with a smile.

"Tony Duck!" said he, musing. "I think we have something of his already. Do you not re-collect, Robert, the short-legged skeleton in blue jacket and trousers, that frightened us so badly in the forecastle, by being moved through the water by a fish?"

"Indeed I do," Robert answered; "and I recol-lect, too, we were much interested in some old and well-worn letters in a female hand, containing the name of Antonio; and lying side by side in the pocket-book were three faded miniatures on ivory, two of a venerable couple, that we took to be father and mother, and one of a beautiful girl that we judged to be this young man's sister, be-cause she was evidently the daughter of the old people."

"Did you preserve those letters and likenesses?" Dr. Gordon asked.

"O yes, father," Robert replied, "we destroyed nothing that could possibly be of use."

"And we even saved a lock of hair from each skeleton that we could reach," added Harold.

"They will be important links in the chain of inquiries to be made," said Dr. Gordon. "And now, boys, let us get ready to return."

They put aboard the tools and the smaller pack-ages from the iron chest, together with the little box of gold, — that containing the silver being too heavy for them to move at present, or to carry upon their heavily freighted canoe.

So much was to be done, and so short tne time in which to do it, that Dr. Gordon and the boys gave themselves no rest on their return from the pirate wreck, until the bellows and anvil had been put in position, and two of the rods of iron forged into the shape of mattock and handle. In the midst of the work, Robert remarked, —

" A mattock and an adze are so much alike that I wonder whether one might not be made to serve for the other."

" Certainly it might," his father replied, " but have you any adzes ?"

" Yes, father, two of them, that we used in digging out our boats. They are stowed away in a hollow tree near our place of work. I am sorry we never thought of them till this moment. But ' out of sight, out of mind,' you know. Shall I get them ? I can have them here in ten minutes."

" They will be rather light for digging in that rock," returned his father, " but no doubt quite as efficient as the clumsy substitutes I am now trying to forge. By all means bring them."

It was now long after dark, but so earnest were they to be ready for work in the marsh early in the morning that the two boys lighted a torch of rich pine and went to a cypress swamp, a quarter of a mile distant, and returned with an arm-load each of the tools left there in concealment. The adzes promised, on examination, to be all that could be expected, and with this assurance the now weary laborers ceased their work and yielded themselves to the delights of rest.

The sun was scarcely half an hour high the next morning before the company, consisting of Dr. Gordon, Robert, Harold, and Sam, in two canoes, were on their way to the stranded vessel. They found her just as she had been left the day before, without any indication of having been visited. Torgah's rough figure of the ground-mole remained as it was, and so did the mark appended to it by Harold, who said that Torgah would recognize it as his, being the figure of a squirrel in sitting posture, with something in its paws, and its tail curled over its back.

While the tide was down they worked at the lower part of the bank, cutting it into broad and deep channels to admit the timbers, on which, as on a railroad, the vessel was to pass down on rollers. By using all diligence, these channels were excavated, and the lower edge of the bank cut so as not to interfere with the passage down; and in the afternoon they went to the nearest wooded part of the island to obtain the necessary timbers. These pieces were so numerous and so unwieldly that no more could be done that day than to prepare them for being rolled into the water, where they were to be made int a raft, and pulled or poled to their destined place.

Late that evening the laborers returned home, weary with more than usual toil, and rejoicing in the prospective rest of the next day, which was the Christian Sabbath. Dr. Gordon called his family together, according to custom, and after a few verses, slowly and solemnly read from the Good Book, and a short hymn of praise, they united in a prayer, in which all acknowledged their obligations to the kind Providence which, in the course of the week now closing, had delivered a portion of them from death, restored them all so happily to each other, and promised to bless them in time to come. These allusions were so touching that Dr. Gordon's voice trembled as he gave them utterance, and all arose from their knees with a grateful consciousness of having been drawn nearer than ever to the great Being of beings.

CHAPTER XXIX.

BEAUTIFUL DAWN— LAWYER'S REMARK— HOW DO
WE KNOW THERE IS A GOD?

HE Sabbath dawned with rare beauty. First a gray belt of pure, soft light, following close upon the light of the departed moon, streaked the lower margin of the sky, extending rapidly north and south, and spreading higher, brighter, and more beautiful. Then followed a rosy tinge, contrasting sweetly with the pure gray, like the hue of health upon a fair young cheek. Finally came the rich, golden light that immediately precedes the burst of glorious day.

" Often as I have looked upon scenes like this," said Mrs. McIntosh to her sister, " I never can witness this sudden burst of light without feeling my pulse quicken, and my heart throb."

" And I never can witness this gradual, yet rapid growth of day, from dawn to dazzling light, without thinking of that beautiful Bible image, ' The path of the just is as the shining light, that shineth more and more unto the perfect day.'"— Prov. iv. 18.

But the eye was not the only organ of sense re-galed that morning. As the light thus rose, and spread, and brightened, the woods became vocal with innumerable songsters. The brown-winged thrush, known generally as the *thrasher*, and by some as the French mocking-bird,* leaped from the spray where it had spent the night, selected a spot better suited for song, and then gave utter-ance to that delicious liquid music by which it worships its Creator, first of the birds in the open-ing dawn, and last of them in the dusk. In a few minutes it was followed by the red bird, or crimson finch, repeating its few, but never weary-ing notes. Then came the mocking-bird, or gray thrush, imitating every other bird of the forest and of the sea-shore, and by its grace of utterance making those notes pleasant which originally were discordant ; and with it came the wrens, and other sweet-voiced birds, uniting in the soft chorus that rose from the grand orchestra of nature.

It was not to the eyes and ears of all the deni-zens of the tent, however, that these scenes and sounds brought pleasure. Dr. Gordon and the

---

* It imitates other birds very sweetly, and in some of its notes excels even the gray mocking-bird that is so generally admired.

boys were locked in slumber till long after the sun
had risen. The ladies, who had left the tent so
quietly as not to disturb the tired sleepers, enjoyed
exceedingly the sweetness of this rural Sabbath
morning, and sitting down with Mary and Frank,
read devoutly together the Psalm which says:
" The heavens declare the glory of God, and the
firmament sheweth His handiwork," and as they
read they looked lovingly " through Nature up to
Nature's God."

When the family assembled at morning worship,
Dr. Gordon read the same Psalm, the nineteenth,
noticing such changes in the meaning as were authorized by the marginal* readings, and then,
alluding to what he had been informed by his wife
of the pleasant recognition of God in his works,
he said, —

" I was present once when an intelligent officer
in the church, who was a lawyer by profession,
suggested to his pastor the propriety of preaching
on the evidences of the Divine existence

" ' You surprise me,' said his pastor. ' Do you
suppose a discourse on that subject to be called

---

* These notes, or readings, found in all Reference Bibles,
were placed there by the authorized translators as of equal
authority with the ordinary text. It is common with stu-
dents of the Scripture to read both, and it is not unusual
for them to adopt the marginal reading in preference to the
text

for ?   Are there any Atheists among us? cr even persons who doubt that there is a God?'

"The lawyer smiled. 'My dear sir, said he, 'my profession calls me to an intimate acquaintance with the worst part of the public mind, as yours calls you to an acquaintance with the better. It is my deliberate conviction that at least one in every three or four of the people have no real belief in the existence either of a God, or of an immortal soul.'

"The pastor was shocked, and so, I confess, was I, for the lawyer was a man of eminence, and was not apt to speak unadvisedly. I have thought many times since that it would be well for most people to review occasionally the foundations of their faith, and even to ask themselves, How do I know there is a God, a soul, a hereafter ?"

Without saying a word in reply to these points of inquiry, Dr. Gordon left the subject, fully persuaded that it would be brought up at some future time. In this expectation he was not mistaken, for, in the course of the day, Robert and Harold, who had been observed in more than one earnest conversation during the intervals of their informal worship, came to him and said, —

"We no more doubt there is a God than we doubt there is a world, and that we are living in it.   But how could we prove this to a person who does not believe it, and is not willing to believe?"

"You cannot do it," he promptly replied ; "*no man* can do it. 'The blindest of all people are those who are unwilling to see. The Great Teacher has said of such that 'if one came to them from the dead, yet would they not believe.' And it is probable that, even when the God of Israel revealed himself in the thunderings and lightnings of Sinai, and spoke to the people by an audible voice, there were some present who questioned whether all this display was not the product of jugglery and art. You know that when our Lord and Saviour Jesus Christ performed those wonderful works, which compelled one man to say, 'We know that thou art a teacher come from God, because no man can do these miracles that thou doest except God be with him ;' others, who could not deny his superhuman powers, but who were not so ingenuous, endeavored to satisfy themselves and each other by saying, ' He doth not cast out devils, but by Beelzebub, the prince of the devils.' I, therefore, say that you cannot convince a person that there is a God until you *gain his sincere consent* to believe on being furnished with the evidence."

"But suppose, uncle," said Harold, "that you meet one who says, ' I do not *doubt*, only I do not *believe*, as I wish. That there is a world around me I know, because I see it, and that there are persons around me I know, because I see, and

hear, and have dealings with them; but God I
have never seen, nor heard, nor dealt with, and
therefore I cannot believe in him as I wish;'
what would you say to him?"

"That his case was like that of most other people," his uncle replied. "Comparatively few believe in the existence of a God, further than not
to call it into question. They simply take it for
granted, without really believing it. We believe
those things only which influence us so far that we
may be said to *live by* them, or in view of them, as
truth. For example, we believe or *live by the
truth* that two and two make four, and no one can
persuade us to *live by* the assertion that they make
five. So a real belief in the existence of a God is
such a practical conviction of its truth that we
live by it. Now, your question is, How shall a
person believe that there is a God, just as he be-
lieves that there is a world, and that there are
persons around him? and my answer is, that he
must first gain his own consent to *live by* the truth
in the one case, as he does in the other.

"Well, now, suppose he has gained his own consent, fully, freely, and that he is on the look out
for evidence; you ask what evidence can be given
him. I answer—" Dr. Gordon paused, looked
around for an illustration, then seeing a book in
Harold's hand — a copy of the New Testament,
which he had been reading — he went on to say,—

"How came you, Harold, with that book?"

"It is my own, sir; I brought it from home," he replied.

"But how came it into your possession?"

"My mother bought it for me in Montgomery."

"But how came the merchant there with it?"

"I suppose he bought it from somebody else."

"But how came that somebody else with it?"

"He bought it, probably, from the person that made it."

"But why do you suppose any one made it?"

"Because it is a book, and it could not make itself."

"But why not suppose that it came by chance?"

"I cannot suppose that," replied Harold, "because chance could not possibly put together so many things as are necessary to make a book — the paper, the printing, the binding; and more than that, there are many other books exactly like this, and if chance could by any possibility make one, it could not be expected to make more. It *must* have had a maker. Indeed, every book must have had a maker; and as I come to think of it, every page in every book must have had a maker, —yes, and every word, every letter, every part of the paper, printing, and putting together."

"Very well," said his uncle. "Now look at that *oak-tree*. It has upon it more leaves than there are pages in your book. Every leaf is com-

posed of a mid-rib and side-ribs, and fibres crossing from one side to the other, like beautiful lace-
work, and the spaces between are filled with green
matter, glossy on one side to shed rain, and on the
other side occupied with numberless pores to admit air and moisture. These pores are most in-
geniously contrived, being in shape somewhat like
a long letter O, sharp at both ends, and made of
such material, in such way that in dry weather
they open wide to catch all the moisture possible,
and in wet weather they contract so that no moisture can enter. These ingenious little pores are
more numerous in each leaf than the letters are on
each page of your book. Besides these wonder-
fully constructed leaves, there are flowers and
fruits to be reckoned in our account, each as wonderful in its way as the leaf. Then there are the
roots, by tens of thousands, little hair-like things,
each with its tiny mouth wide open at the end for
sucking up water from the earth. And there is
the wood itself, a wonderful structure, made up of
tubes bundled together, each with its apparatus of
valves and pumps for forcing the water twenty,
thirty, fifty feet high, to the topmost branch. Su-
peradded to all these, and more wonderful still, is
its power of elaborating seeds, in each of which is
wrapped up, in small compass, a young tree of its
own kind, and then of dropping that seed at the
time of the year suited for its growing up and becoming a tree like itself.

"Now compare the tree with the book. Which has the greater number of parts put together?"

"The tree," answered Harold, "for the book is made up of paper, print, and binding, while the tree is made up of leaf, stem, fruit, wood, bark, roots, and each of these made up of many parts in itself. The tree has, beyond comparison, the greater number of parts."

"What is the probability that chance put their various parts together to make a tree?"

"It is not probable at all," he replied. "It is *just nakedly impossible.*"

"Well," said his uncle, "you have in this illustration one of the arguments from nature for believing that there is a God. For to say it is impossible for the tree to have come by chance, is equivalent to saying that it must have had a Maker. And what is thus true of this tree must be, in like manner, true of *every* tree, and shrub, and vine, and blade of grass, and, much more, of every bird and beast, reptile and fish, worm and insect. *This Maker of all things we call God.*"

At this point, Robert put in an inquiry,—

"How would you reply to one who should contend that the trees we see now are only so many parts of a series, without beginning or end; that they have *always* been growing and propagating their kind?"

"I would reply to him," said his father, "that

his theory only removed the difficulty a few steps
further back, for every numerical series must have
a beginning, and, moreover, it is not only of the
first tree of each series that our argument holds
good, but of every tree in itself. Each bears its
own testimony. More than this, if the science of
geology teaches anything with certainty, it teaches
that the time was when trees did not grow upon
the earth,—the soil and temperature of our planet's
surface did not admit of their growth. They came
after certain other changes; therefore *they had a
beginning*, and therefore they must have had a
Creator."

"I am satisfied," said Robert, "for, so far as I
can see, one of three things must be true: that
this tree came into existence by chance; or that it
always existed in kind; or that it had a Creator.
But it *did not* always exist; it *could not* have come
by chance; therefore it must have been created."

A new form of the thought here occurred to Dr.
Gordon, and he said,—

"To calculate the probability or improbability of
so simple a thing as a book being produced by
chance, let us suppose that all the paper, and type,
ink, and other materials necessary for printing and
binding are provided; and, if you will, all the frames
and cases and levers and rollers used in printing,
besides. Let us suppose, too, that in producing
a book, there is necessary a certain degree of blind

power, say a one-horse power, and that this is
provided in the shape of a neat little waterfall.
Let us see now how many parts will be necessary
to make our book. In an ordinary New Testament, there are, — counting the headings of chap-
ters, numbering of verses, punctuation marks, etc., —
at least half a million of letters, figures, and other
marks, each requiring a type. We will put all
these types, with the necessary paper, ink, leather,
thread, pasteboard, rollers, printing frames, etc.,
into a bag, jumbled together, and carry them to
that neat little waterfall of one-horse power, and
there empty them all in. How long will we probably have to wait before we may reasonably expect to see an elegant little copy of the New Testament, like that Harold has, come out of the
water?"

Robert laughed, and Harold clapped his hands
with delight.

"We should wait forever!" they answered, "and
not see it then."

"The same may be said, only with incompara-
bly more emphasis," Dr. Gordon added, "of every
one of the millions upon millions, and the billions
upon billions of trees, and shrubs, and animals on
earth."

"How absolutely certain it is that there must
be a God!" said Harold; then added in a soft,
sad tone, "I wish I knew more of him."

"There are three ways of becoming acquainted with him," responded his uncle. "One is by studying him in his *Works*, as we have just been attempting in that tree. Another, far more direct and satisfactory, is to study him in his *Word*. And a third, still more satisfactory, indeed the only way to make the other modes effectual, is by *Intercourse* with him. In all these modes of study we need no other earthly aid than a willing heart."

CHAPTER XXX.

HE work proposed for Monday was such
as Dr. Gordon foresaw would require
the exercise of all their powers, assisted
by whatever mechanical contrivances
could be commanded. At a very early hour, therefore, he called together his working force, and went
first to the pirate wreck, from which he brought
away a number of pulleys and several coils of rope,
large and small, which he had observed on a former visit, together with some strong canvas bags,
and as many cannon-balls as the two boats could
conveniently carry with the previous freight, in-
cluding now the box of Mexican dollars. The
boys were curious to know what he proposed to do
with the cannon-balls, but this he refused to tell
them, saying —

" You will learn in due time, and find that they

will add greatly to our power, exactly at the moment when we most feel its need. In the meantime, however, I will take occasion to say that in moving very heavy weights, like the one we now propose, no better roller can be devised than cannon-balls moving in a solid iron groove. Large brick houses, chimneys and all, are sometimes moved in this way. But as we have no iron grooves for the pathway of our balls, and as the weight of our vessel would be apt to bury them in a pathway of wood, we must content ourselves with wooden rollers instead."

From the pirate wreck they returned to the tent to breakfast, and leaving there the box of silver, resumed afterward their course to the pilot boat, where they discharged their freight of cannon-balls, and went with their ropes and pulleys to the place where the timbers lay ready for transportation. The work of removing them occupied hours, and many and ingenious were the methods devised for getting the cumbrous masses to the water. No doubt persons of a mechanical turn would be interested to know what these methods were; but all persons have not this taste, and in deference to them there will be only one of the devices described, and that on account of its novelty.

Most of the logs had been removed by rollers, laid on the bare ground. In some cases where the soil was soft and sandy, or otherwise obstructive,

the difficulty was remedied by the laying down of
a pair of straight parallel poles, as a railway upon
which the rollers moved as fast as the pullers and
pushers could expect. One of the logs, however,
was of more than usual weight, and its passage
was obstructed not only by a soft soil requiring
the use of the railway, but by a rise in the ground:
and so difficult was the task of making it travel,
that Dr. Gordon was on the point of giving it up
and of cutting another in its stead. At this moment a bright idea occurred to him. The selected
pathway led between two trees with long pendant
branches, covered with grapevines. Pointing to
them he said.

"I will make these trees and vines help carry
this log over the rising ground."

The boys looked on with curiosity, and rendered
all needful assistance without being able to conceive how it was that trees and vines could be har-
nessed to a load; but they were soon delighted
with the result. Several grapevines were cut and
attached firmly to one end of the log, when the
other ends were drawn forward and fastened to
long, elastic branches of the trees, which had been
strained backward as far as their united strength
could draw them.

"Each one of these limbs," said Dr. Gordon,
"is pulling with a three or four-man power. I
think by the time we have put three or four of

Y

them to work, there will be little need for our assistance, until their force is spent.

"Live and larn! as old Tom Starboard used to say," exclaimed Harold. "But I confess that a standing tree is one of the last things I should have thought of using as a draught-horse!"

"The device is not mine," said his uncle. "I read of it as a method practised by some of the South American Indians. Indeed, I know a hunter who is in the habit of lifting a heavy deer to his horse's crupper by the help of a bent limb."

On being delivered at the waterside, these logs were bound together into a raft, and, by the united action of the rising tide, a slight breeze, and the strong pull of two pairs of oars, came soon to their destination. Then, each was put as near as possible in place and fastened, to await a farther moving up with the rising tide. After which, Dr. Gordon set all hands to work emptying the vessel of its ballast and other movable weights, and preparing to lift her from her bed in the mud.

His plan for effecting this, with the small force at his disposal, was as follows: First of all he fitted a strong bolster of wood under the bow to receive the strain of the levers, and wedged it close up with smaller pieces, so as to diffuse the pressure over a large surface. Under this bolster, which was purposely laid on the surface of the mud, he inserted the flattened ends of three strong levers, each about twenty-five feet long, with its other end lifted about fifteen feet into the air. Under these levers, close to their lower ends, and resting on the rock, was a solid log of wood for a fulcrum. The elevated ends of the levers were connected by a stout bar of wood lashed to them, and on this bar were fixed three pulleys, each with a rope passed through it, ready for use.

"Now, boys," said Dr. Gordon, "I will show you the use of the cannon-balls, and if my calculation is correct, you will see the bow of the boat begin to rise from the mud before we have used them all."

With these words, he took one of the canvas bags, loaded it with about two hundred pounds' weight of balls, and drew it up by the pulley to the end of the central lever.

"There goes a weight," said he, "which, with the leverage, ought to lift from two to three thousand pounds at the lower end."

In loading and drawing up a second bag in like manner, to one of the outside levers, the boys heard a sound under the vessel as of "sucking" in the mud.

"She is rising! she is rising!" shouted Harold.

But she did not rise until the third bag was loaded and drawn up, when with a loud "sucking" noise under the vessel, the elevated ends of the levers sank gracefully down, and bolster and vessel were lifted the greater part of a foot.

As this took place, the boys gave a loud "Hurra!" and Dr. Gordon said, —

"A few more such lifts, first at one end, then at the other, will raise her high enough to admit the rollers underneath, and then heigho! for a travel to the water."

"And now what?" asked Robert.

"First, to make that secure which we have gained," he replied, and with that he blocked up the bolster and wedged it fast, to keep it from sinking.

The stern was then treated in like manner as the bow had been, and they were preparing to elevate the bows still more, when the increasing tide compelled them to desist. This rise of the water, although arresting the work of raising the vessel, was an important help in bringing the heavy timbers to their places, where they were made fast, in readiness for the next day's use.

"Well, boys," said Dr. Gordon, "as we are driven from our work here, let us take advantage of the high water to look for our lost boat."

They re-embarked, and going up the so-called river, which was only a small arm of the sea enclosing their island, they pushed their canoes into every little opening of the marsh, where the increasing tide promised water enough for the search. The declining sun shone full in the direction they looked and strongly illuminated every object in the marsh, but their search was in vain. The boat was certainly not there, possibly carried back to sea with the receding tide of the gale, or, what was more probable, driven toward the mainland, and fallen into the hands of some of the dwellers on the coast.

All were saddened at the loss, and their spirits seemed so much depressed that Dr. Gordon roused himself to present some theme that would divert their minds. As the boys had expressed so much pleasure in the working of the loaded levers, he took this occasion to interest them in another talk on the subject of mechanical powers, and of machinery in the general.

"In bringing our logs to the water," said he, "we used sometimes the simple lever, and sometimes the pulley, but there is another mode of operating which partially combines the principles of both powers, without using the instrument peculiar to either; it is called *parbuckling.* This is generally practised by sailors and stevedores in raising or lowering casks and other heavy round bodies on an inclined plane; and there are two forms of it. One is practised by passing one or more cords *once round* the barrel, log, or other object to be moved, making one end fast in the line of motion, and pulling at the end that is free. The other is by making one end of the rope fast to the object itself, then wrapping it several times round and pulling at the loose end. In both these cases the power is greatly increased.

"And speaking of rolling, sometimes an object not naturally round can be made to roll by fastening to its irregular sides whatever may be necessary to give it roundness; and for a reason somewhat akin to this, a barrel *full* of liquid, or of anything else movable, is more easily rolled than one that is only half full."

Having discussed these points sufficiently to get them fully in mind, he went on to say:—

"The other day I gave you a useful rule for determining what operations can be effected by machinery. I will now give you one to guard against needless discouragement in the working of a balky machine. It is this,—that *what a machine has been made to do once, it may be made to do* TWICE, THREE TIMES, ALWAYS, AND WITH CERTAINTY, *until worn out,*—*provided always, however, that the circumstances under which it works are the same;* for a machine driven by a blind power has no choice; it must yield to the forces impressed upon it."

With this instructive conversation they made their way homeward, while the sun departed, and the shades of evening gathered round them. Forgetting by this time the loss of the boat, and remembering only the successful work of the day, they reached home in fine spirits, and cheered the hearts of the others with the prospect of launching their little vessel the next day.

"The sleep of the laboring man is sweet." *
Next to love, it is probably the most perfect
blessing enjoyed by the majority of mankind, and
when love and sleep can be enjoyed together, as
in the case of mother and babe, before losing consciousness, or as in a company such as retired early
that night to their couches in the marooners' tent,
earth has little more to add. There was a poet
living at that very time who seemed to appreciate
the blessing. Said he, —

> "Night is the time for rest.
>   How sweet when labors close
>   To gather round the aching breast
>   The curtains of repose!
> Stretch the tired limbs, and rest the head
> Upon one's own delightful bed." †

And "early to bed" is the secret of "early to
rise." This is as true of people as of their poultry.
The student, who, to avoid interruptions, is compelled to burn the midnight lamp, must usually
forego the privileges of early day; and so must the
midnight moth of pleasure that flutters around the
candle of dissipation. Let every laborer thank
God for this great blessing, conferred more freely
upon the sweaty brow than upon the crowned head

At the time of day usually known as cock-crow-
ing, but in this case marked only by certain quacks¹

* Eccles., v. 12.
† James Montgomery

and twits! from the poultry-house, and by the voice of early birds, the weary laborers of the day before sprang lightly from their couches, hastened through their simple toilet, and met together at breakfast.

A quarter of an hour afterward, the thump of oars and the splash of water sounded from the river and gradually died away in the distance. The launchers were returning to their work. They passed cheerily up the river, discussing the various means of accomplishing their work, wishing they had a stronger force, and wondering why Torgah and Somassee had not come, ere this, to their assistance.

On doubling a point of marsh near their place of labor, Sam's sudden "Eh! eh!" called their attention forward, where they were all surprised to see, not half a mile distant, the Bellevue boat hurrying toward sea under the sturdy strokes of four Indian paddlers, who were exerting all their strength to get away, while the head of a fifth lay reclining upon the stern, as if belonging to a dead man, or to one unable to help himself.

"Hallo there!" shouted Robert, at the top of his voice.

"Hat-is-chay!" (Stop!) "That is our boat!" added Harold in his excitement, mixing up Indian and English.

The calls, however, were not regarded, possibly not heard, for three furlongs is further than most voices can reach, even over water. At Dr. Gordon's suggestion, they united in a prolonged nalloo, each giving greater impetus to his voice by curving the hands around the mouth as a sort of speaking-trumpet. Still there was no response; and the only indication of being heard was a slight inclination of the head by one of the Indians, as if for the purpose of observation.

"They pretend not to hear us," said Harold; "but a gun they cannot fail to hear. Suppose, uncle, we give them one. They will know by this that we are in earnest, and armed too."

"Sam's musket will give the loudest report," replied Dr. Gordon, adopting the suggestion. "Shoot it into the air, Sam."

The piece, heavily loaded, shook the air like small thunder. Still the boat held on its way, and the paddles moved perceptibly faster and dug more deeply into the rippling water. All this time the two canoes had been urging their way forward, scarcely having lost a stroke of the oars, yet scarcely having made any perceptible gain in the chase. They were now abreast of the stranded vessel.

"Harold," said Dr. Gordon, "drop your anchor in this shallow water, and come aboard here, you and Sam, with your guns and oars. Let us see whether our four oars cannot outstrip their four paddles."

The exchange of place was made almost without stopping, and all hands then bent themselves to the oars with such vigor and precision that the light canoe darted through the water in successive leaps.

"We shall soon overhaul them at this rate," said Dr. Gordon, tying his white handkerchief to a ramrod as a flag of truce. "And I hope as soon as they see that we come with peaceable intent, and that they cannot get away from us, they will slacken speed, and come to a parley."

The distance between pursuers and pursued diminished rapidly, and the flag gave frequent and significant tokens of peace, but the chased boat showed no sign of slackening speed, or of exchanging words. Dr. Gordon was doubtful what to do, for they were coming now within fair rifle range, and it must soon be determined whether they were to fight or keep the peace. Summoning to use the few words of Indian language that could be commanded, either by himself or by Harold, and at the same time waving his flag of peace, he called aloud in the Muscogee dialect,—

"Eesta-chattee ! Hat-is-chay !" (Indian ! stop !)

Then, as one of them turned his head to look, Dr. Gordon held out his hand, waving the white flag and saying, "Tuck-a-noy ! tuck-a-noy !" (Money ! money !) then changing to the Cherokee language, he hallooed, "Tay-luh ! tah-lo-ne-ca !" (Money ! gold money !)

It was, however, all in vain. The boat held on her way, right toward the surf, that broke over a low sand-flat, as if resolved to plunge into it rather than be captured. He had just said, " I fear we shall not be able to recover her without a fight, and I would not bring that on for ten boats," when one of the Indians turned suddenly round and levelled his rifle.

A small jet of smoke shot several yards forward; then there was a slight splash in the water, followed by a light "tap," as the ball buried itself deep in the bow of the canoe.

" A pretty decided hint," said Dr. Gordon.

"The villain!" exclaimed Harold, angered beyond control by this act of wanton hostility; then, snatching up his rifle, he was about to give the boat a ball in return, when the quiet voice of his uncle was heard saying, —

" Do not shoot at the *boat*, Harold. Send your ball to ricochet on the water beyond her. That will show that we could hurt them if we would, but that our intentions are peaceable. Perhaps they will stop."

Away went the ball, tipping here and there upon the now roughening surface, and throwing up a little shower of spray wherever it struck. The Indians seeing the ball pass far beyond them in its dangerous play, were evidently disturbed, for they turned their heads back to see if more

balls were about to come; still they pushed on.
Dr. Gordon then said to Harold, —

"Take the *musket*, and give them a larger ball
in the same way, only further ahead," and as it
went the flag waved, and Dr. Gordon shouted his
mixed dialects, "Hatischay! tuckanoy! tay-luh!"
etc.; but the only response he received, as the
boat neared the breakers, was the levelling of another rifle, which, however, was not discharged, but
accompanied by an imperative exclamation in Indian that sounded as if it were the Creek word
"Hy-ee-bus-chay!" (Be off! or, Go away!)

The water rolling over the shoals from sea was
by this time too rough for the canoe, and it was
manifest that she could not safety go much further.
Dr. Gordon then said,—

"I am now convinced that we cannot peaceably
recover our boat. Let us therefore return. We
have shown these marauders that we *can* fight if
we choose, and that we are not afraid of them.
No doubt their object in making for this rough
water, where their boat can live and our's cannot,
is to get rid of us. We will, therefore, use it as
our excuse for giving up the chase."

Harold's countenance indicated great disappointment, and so, in a degree, did Robert's. Their
blood was up; but they yielded without a word
of remonstrance. They only looked longingly at
the beautiful boat that was now almost ready to

pñunge into the surf at a place where there was a partial opening, and Harold was heard to mutter something between his clenched teeth that did not sound very complimentary to the persons ahead. They turned, and in the act of doing so, saw the Indians drop their paddles, put their hands to their mouths, and work their fingers very fast against their lips. A second afterward there came rattling over the waters a shrill, broken sound ; it was the Indians' yell of triumph.

The chase had occupied them the greater part of an hour, during which their thoughts had been so much engrossed with what was before them that they had not stopped to inquire what mischief might have been enacted at the pilot boat. Directing their thoughts now to that point, the oar-strokes were so quickened with anxiety that the distance was soon overpassed. Hastily mooring the canoe, they sprang ashore, and were about to hurry around, when Dr. Gordon warned them to be cautious.

"Hostile visitors have been here," he said, "and there is no conjecturing what traps they may have laid for us."

A guarded inspection of the vessel and its surroundings, however, revealed no changes, except the disfiguration of Torgah's *tuckassee,* as if in contempt, and the falling of one of the long, heavy levers, which seemed to have inflicted a terrible wound on some one, since the mud just beside it was marked with fresh blood, imperfectly covered with a few handfuls of trodden weeds. Several coils of the smaller rope were also missing, and so was Sam's hatchet, which had been left sticking in one of the timbers. If their object was plunder, they were grievously disappointed, and Robert expressed the hope that the ill-luck befalling the one whose blood they saw, would deter them from any future visits to the Enchanted Island.

Not many minutes now elapsed before they were at work again upon their launch. The bow and stern were alternately lifted and blocked. Three strong railways of parallel logs were laid in the channels cut for them in the rock. On each of these railways was laid a system of rollers, kept in place by strings that would easily break. And between these rollers and the vessel some stout timbers were inserted, upon which the vessel was eased down from the blocks, and these propped to wait till all was ready.

By the middle of the afternoon, Dr. Gordon, judging that the tide had risen sufficiently for their purpose, stationed Robert and Harold at the two props which held back the vessel. Each had an axe in hand, thrown back, and ready for striking.

" Are you ready ?"

" Aye, aye."

" Then let go !"

And as the word "go" was uttered, each axe
fell with a heavy blow upon the prop, knocking
it away. The vessel began to move. The underlying timbers gave a groan as the heavy burden
they bore crushed them against the rock, and the
pilot boat moved with increasing speed, and plunged,
keel foremost, into the water, where she lay partly
upon her beam ends. A hawser attached to one
of the canoes, and pulled by the stout oars of Harold and Sam, brought the stern out into deeper
water, and proved that she was fully afloat.

"Now for ballast!" said Dr. Gordon.

They made a temporary gangway of the logs
at hand, shouldered or lifted between them the
rough "pigs" of iron, each of fifty or one hundred pounds' weight, laid them near the keel,
when their weight soon caused the boat to right
herself.

"It may not be safe to leave her at this place
all night," said Dr. Gordon. "I fear another visit
from our dark-skinned friends. We must tow her
to the island, where she will probably be protected
by their superstitious fears, and we had better put
aboard of her all we wish to save from depreda-
tion."

They gathered up the anchor and cable, the little cannon, which had been buried in the mud, the
broken mast and spars, in fact, everything within
reach pertaining to the vessel, and had the pleas-

ure of seeing her follow the pull of tne two canoes as kindly as a tame buffalo follows the cord
passed through its nose. They cast anchor near
shore in deep water, at a place which, from the
excellent sport it afforded, had been named by the
boys Fish Point.

CHAPTER XXXI.

*CONSULTATION — PREPARE TO MOVE — SOMEBODY
IN THE MARSH — WHO CAN IT BE ? — THE TESTS.*

N the way home from their now floating
vessel, Dr. Gordon and the boys had
time to think and talk over the exciting
circumstances of the morning, and there
arose, in consequence, several serious inquiries .
Would it be proper or safe to leave the dear ones
at the tent exposed to possible hostilities from the
Indians, while their defenders were working, as
they had been, miles away ? Ought they not to
be removed at once, with all needful effects, to
some point on the bluff, where all would be in
constant communication ? If so, to what point,
commanding the necessary conveniences, particularly of water ? And last, though not least, should

anything be said to them of the partial collision
with the Indians that morning?

The decision on these points was very prompt:
The family ought not to be left in their previous
unprotected condition; they should be removed
at once to the bluff, and Harold and Robert decided that, although the water at the spring near
the live oak, where they first pitched their tent,
was the best on the beach, yet that to be had at
Fish Point could be endured for the few days of
their probable future stay. As to the last question, Whether the ladies should be informed of
the circumstances of the morning, Dr. Gordon
said, —

"By all means. I do not believe in the propriety of regarding all women and children as
cowards. Some of them are, as is true of some men,
and should, therefore, be treated as such; but no
one who knows the mother and aunt of you boys
will do them the injustice of putting them in that
category; no, nor Mary either, nor even little
Frank. Gentle and loving as they are, they can
probably face death as composedly as any of us;
and I believe, too, that were they called to so unsuitable an employment, they would help us in an
Indian fight, by loading our guns for us, or by
anything else they could do, as effectively as any
other persons in their circumstances. My judgment is that we tell them the whole story. More-

over, by so doing, we shall have this great advantage, that in deciding the other questions, which concern their immediate interests, and in which they have a right to be heard in their own behalf, we shall be able to unite their judgment with our own."

When the boats came within earshot of home, Dr. Gordon called upon Sam for one of his mellow boat songs, in the chorus of which they all united, although it was marked by no excellence except its mild, water-like music; and as they neared the landing, the cheerful halloo of the boys was answered by the merry shout of little Frank, who came running to meet them, and to carry his father's gun and its accoutrements.

After quietly resting, and enjoying each other's company for a time, Dr. Gordon said to his wife and sister,—

"I have often heard the nautical proverb, 'A stern chase is a long chase,' but I never knew by experience what it was until to-day."

He then described the incidents of the morning, to which all listened with profound, and, in some degree, painful, attention.

"And now," said he, "arises the question, What are we to do? We must go on with our work, which it is not possible to bring to the tent, and we have been discussing the propriety of removing our tent to the work. What do you think

of it? I do not ask you to answer without reflection. We shall soon have our usual evening
worship, and I think that all-important questions
concerning household interests are more safely decided under the influence of household prayer."

The judgment, when called for, was decided
and unanimous, that now the vessel was actually
launched and anchored on the island side of the
river, it was far preferable, irrespective of danger
from Indians, that the family be within a minute's
reach of each other, rather than the laborers should
be compelled to make their six miles' circuit by
water twice every day.

"Remember," said Dr. Gordon, "the work of
removal and of fitting up with comfort will probably occupy at least two days, even if we should
construct a raft large enough to carry all our movables at once."

"But why carry so much, and why do much
fitting up?" argued Mrs. Gordon. "We shall
probably be here but a few days more."

"Yes," Mrs. McIntosh interjected, "and during
that time why can we not make the pilot boat our
home, as we did in coming?"

"Ah!" exclaimed Dr. Gordon, "how good it
is to have sensible women for advisers in a time
of need! They are so much quicker-witted than
we of the stronger sex, that while we are slowly
working out our conclusions by hard thinking,

they *jump* directly to theirs. Yes," he appended, after a moment's thought, "and they generally jump right."

It was the understanding of all, as they retired to rest that night, that the morrow should be devoted to removal. And the programme, so far as it could be hastily made out, was that the two canoes should each make two trips, carrying such things as they could accommodate, while the more bulky articles, such as the table, sofa, and chairs, which they preferred to carry home, together with the goats, fawn, cubs, and other pets, should be made secure on a large raft, to be floated up the east river with the flood tide, in time for the canoes in their second trip to pull it around the bend, so that it could float down the north river on the ebb. The management of the raft was committed to Sam, who was experienced in such matters, and who volunteered to undertake it alone, saying, in prospect of possible interference from the Indians, —

" I no feerd. Injin nebber trouble nigger."

This was the programme, and it seemed to be both practicable and prudent, especially with the proviso that Harold should take the two dogs and go first to Fish Point, after early breakfast, to see if all was safe, and that until his return and favorable report, there should be no removal. It was

their experience, however, as sung by a facetious
bard, and often repeated since his day, that

> " The best laid plans of mice and men
>   Aft gang aglee "

The making and loading of the raft, and the
taking down, packing up, and transfer of articles
to the landing, a quarter of a mile away, went on
famously; but Harold, who set out after early
breakfast, with rifle in hand and spy-glass in his
bosom, did not return until Dr. Gordon became so
uneasy that he and Robert were in the act of going
to look after him. When at last he came in, with
quite a joyous look, he said he wished one of the
canoes to enable him to cross the river.

" What do you mean?" inquired his uncle with
surprise.

" I will tell you," he answered, "and then you
may judge for yourself. When I reached Fish
Point, I did not go directly to the bluff, but hid
myself in a clump of myrtles to reconnoitre. The
pilot boat was swinging quietly at anchor, just as
we had left her, and there had been no interference
with her of any sort; as I ran my eye along the
opposite shore, nearly half a mile away, I saw
what I took to be the head of an Indian peeping
through the mangroves. I immediately drew out
the spy-glass and examined more closely. There
was no doubt of the fact—the head was there; I

could see the eyes and mouth with perfect distinctness, and could distinguish the various turnings
of the face. I kept concealed for full two hours,
moving from one point of observation to another,
and examining most carefully with the glass, to
see if any one else was there. Convinced, at last,
that the person was alone, and that he would
remain where he was, without some movement on
my part, I walked boldly out from the bushes, as
if I had just arrived to look after the vessel, and
had no suspicion of any one being on the other
shore. The moment I appeared, the person, whoever he was, squatted, so as to be entirely concealed. This, of course, was sign enough that he
took me for an enemy.

"I walked about the bluff and beach for half
an hour, watching him, without appearing to do
so, and going occasionally into the bushes, where
I could use my spy-glass without being seen, but
he made no movement to come out and show himself. All this time the two dogs were absent. I
never knew Mum to do so before, but I suppose
he must have been led off by Fidelle on the trail
of something good to eat, for when they came up
they looked very full, and also much pleased, as
if they had been enjoying themselves. It was not
two minutes after they came up and began to fawn
upon me, before I saw the screen of mangroves on
the other side of the river thrown down and some-

body step out upon the shelly beach and wave his
hand to me. In return, I took off my cap and
waved it to him. He then pointed to the water,
beckoned me to come over, and made motions like
a person paddling a canoe. To this I shook my
head and beckoned him to come to me, making the
same motions of paddling. He also shook his
head, and stood for some time, as if not knowing
what to do. He next pointed to the dogs, putting his hands down low to show what he meant,
after which he took up something, which he threw
on the water, and made the motions of a water-
dog, like Fidelle swimming after it and bringing
it out; then pointing again, he imitated Mum or
the slow track of a deer. By this time I began to
suspect that the person must be either Riley or
Wildcat, for I could see that he was a half-breed,
and these are the only Indians I know of who
could describe our dogs. Just then another device occurred to me. Riley and Wildcat both
know my mark of the squirrel. So I took off my
hunting-shirt, and whatever else was necessary,
and made them into a large figure, such as he could
recognize, of a squirrel eating a nut, and no sooner
had I done so than he clapped his hands with joy,
threw himself on all fours, and moved stealthily,
like a *cat* creeping upon its prey, then made a sudden leap and grasped something, which he pretended at one time to hold in his mouth, and at

another time to pat and play with it. This said
c▲r as plainly as actions could, and I was so well
satisfied that I motioned to him that I would
get a boat and come for him. Now, shall I do it?"

"By all means," replied his uncle; "but you
must not go alone. Either Robert or I must go
with you, and"—

"Not you, father, not you," said. Robert hastily. "Please let me go."

"And why you?" asked his father with a
laugh. "Because you know better than I how
to manage?"

"No, sir, oh! no," he replied, "but because —
because—you are—you are more needful to the
family than I am."

Dr. Gordon looked kindly upon his son, and
said, —

"Go, but be sure you keep a sharp lookout on
the way, and that you keep near this side the
river until you meet me at Fish Point."

Off hurried the boys on their joyful errand,
taking with them in the boat, by Dr. Gordon's direction, several charges of powder, ball, and canister-shot for the little cannon aboard ship, while he
loaded up the small cannon at the tent, and said
to his wife and sister, —

"If you need our return sooner than we otherwise come, fire off this cannon, or let Sam do it
for you, and I and the boys will join you at the

earliest possible m**ɔ**ment. I go to Fish Point to
observe for myself the state of the case, and to be
sure that the boys are not decoyed into any Indian
snare."

The distance to the Point was six miles by **wa**-
ter, and barely two miles by the path blazed out
overland, yet the boat hove in sight by the time
Dr. Gordon arrived. His closest scrutiny with
the eye, for he had given the spy-glass to the
boys, did not enable him to discern any one on
the other shore, but no sooner did the boat with the
boys make its appearance, than the thick screen of
mangrove branches was thrown down, revealing a
person in Indian costume standing upon what appeared to be a seat or bed made of the surrounding herbage. An examination with the spy-glass
left scarcely the possibility of doubt that the person there was the faithful Indian boy, yet **Dr**
Gordon said to his son and nephew, —

"Before you pass to the other side, there are
two things I wish to do : First, to plant this cannon so as to cover your passage back and forth, in
case that boy may have been *compelled* to act as
a decoy ; and the second is, to prove whether that
is Wildcat. Get each of you a stick about six
feet long, and come with me."

He led them to the top of the low, but almost
perpendicular bluff, made them each take a hand
of his, and move along slowly, using **their sticks**

as if groping in the dark, in doing which they saw
the person across the river imitating them. When
they came to the edge of the bluff, and were beginning to turn, they saw this person pretend suddenly to pitch forward, and to grasp hold of some
one who was pulling him back.

"That is enough," said Dr. Gordon ; "nobody
but Wildcat could have acted out that sign. Go,
without hesitation, and bring him here, if he will
come; and if he is at all troubled with that superstition about the Island, tell him from me, as
a 'medicine man,' that the white blood in his
veins frees him from all enchantment."

The boys waved their caps with a cheer, then
sprang into the canoe, and made the water boil
under her bows as she skimmed her way across.
Their excited motions were plainly visible as they
neared the other side, when their young friend
rushed knee-deep into the water to meet them,
and where, after a short parley, he entered the
boat with them and took the helm, steering right
for the point on which Dr. Gordon stood.

Not many minutes now elapsed before Wildcat,
whose animated face sobered to decided seriousness as he approached the once-dreaded island,
leaped ashore and grasped the hand of his friend
and patron, and looked with joy into his face.

"Glad to see you again, Wildcat," said Dr.
Gordon, "but how came you all alone on that
dreadful marsh ?"

"Can't tell much now," he replied; "too much starve. Drink little bit; eat little bit; then tell."

"I have just what you want," said Dr. Gordon, first handing him a canteen of water, then taking from his pocket several cakes of ship-bread, which he gave him, saying with a laugh, as he did so, "Here, boys, is another illustration of my old Spanish proverb, 'Prayer and provender hinder no man's journey.'"

Wildcat dispatched the biscuits and the contents of the canteen as if he were almost famished, remarking, by way of apology, that he had eaten and drank nothing all day, all night, and part of the day before.

They then embarked, and on the way home he gave the following account, which, for the reader's sake, is recorded in tolerable English, and is also enlarged by the addition of particulars which they afterward obtained from him and others

CHAPTER XXXII.

MAHINLO—YAHA-LUSTY—THE WHITE MAN'S CHARM —SLEEPING IN A TREE.

HEN that big wind came during the last moon," said Wildcat, "Major Burke was troubled. We had not heard a word about you," (addressing Dr. Gordon,) "from the time you left. I told him I would go and look for you, and he was so glad he offered me anything I would ask. I said I only wanted my gun and a handful of small silver money. I went first to my mother, gave her part of the money, and obtained her permission to go. As soon as she knew my object, she told me that Mahinlo, the old prophet, who had once been my teacher, and who was her friend, and would do anything for her or for me, had removed from Alachua, and was now living in the Caloosa settlement, near Great Spirit Island, where he often went to visit the grave of his father. After leaving my mother I went straight to him. He was glad to see me, and wanted me to stay in one of

896

his lodges and learn under him again; but I answered that I could not stay then, and told him
the reason; then I gave him almost all the money
that was left, and asked him to tell me what the
Great Spirit had let him know about you all. He
answered that you were all together on Great
Spirit Island; that you were alive and well, but
that you were in danger without knowing it, and
that I could be of service to you by waiting until
he gave me word.

"Near him lives a wild chief named Yaha-
Lusty, which means Black Wolf. This man can
muster about twenty warriors. He is a Caloosa,
the last of his tribe, and claims all this part of
the coast in the name of his fathers. His warriors are made up of negroes and runaways from
other tribes. They are very bad people. They
dare not disobey Mahinlo, because he is a great
prophet, and they are afraid of him. But they
steal from everybody else, and will hardly obey
even the Top-chief himself, whom we call Micco-
Nopee.* It is Yaha-Lusty, as much as any one
else, who is breeding all this trouble between the
white and red men, for he hates the pale-faces, and
would have waylaid and killed you all before this
time, had he not been scared off by something
Mahinlo said, and he wants now, more than ever,
to kill and scalp you every one.

* This word is made up of *Micco*, chief, and *Anuppa*, topmost.

"Mahinlo told me that he himself was on the island, on a visit to the grave of his father, at the time you, Robert and Harold, first came. He lay hidden in the bushes on the bluff right above your tent, where he could hear almost every word you said, (for he understands your language well,) and where he heard you all, that evening and the next morning, when you knelt down and said, 'Our Father which art in Heaven.' It was that prayer more than anything else, which made him your friend; for when he was a boy, he had spent a year or more in the family of a good man who used to repeat that prayer with his family twice every day. It was a long time since Mahinlo had heard it from any lips except his own, and it sounded very sweet. He has been here many a time since, when you knew nothing of it, though he says that once you came near shooting him,— that was when you killed a black squirrel in an oak-tree, to which your dogs had chased him."

"It was at this very bluff," interrupted Harold, with a merry laugh, "the morning after we first landed. I thought our dogs acted very strangely, but I had no suspicion of there being a red man in the tree at that time."

"When Mahinlo learned that I could repeat that prayer," continued Wildcat, "he said that it made me safe from all enchantment; that he himself repeated it every day of his life, and he regarded it as the strongest charm against evil that any man can have.

" Yaha-Lusty is dreadfully afraid of this island, and he and his men have, consequently, kept so far off from it that, until the night of the last big wind, when they heard the cannons fire, they had no suspicion of any persons being here. Ever since then he has been anxious to come, to look for plunder, but Mahinlo has kept him away by telling him that if he wishes to return alive, he must first learn perfectly the white man's charm, which he must repeat twice every day for a week before his visit, and once every hour while on the island.

" From that day to this, Yaha-Lusty and his chief men have been trying to learn that charm; but they have not learned it yet, and Mahinlo thinks they never will.

" Day before yesterday he brought the prophet a big fat deer, as a present, and wanted to know whether he and his men had not learned enough of the charm to protect them in going close around the island to reconnoitre, promising that, as they went, the charm, so far as they knew it, should be repeated all the time.

" Mahinlo answered that they might go and try, but that unless they could say every word perfectly, he would not answer for consequences; and more than that, he assured them that if they interfered with anything belonging to the island, and especially if a single drop of blood should be spilt during the trip, they might expect something terrible.

"Yaha-Lusty and his men were so eager for the trip that they set out that same evening. The next day, when the sun was about half up the sky, they returned in great trouble, and at the same time very angry. Yaha-Lusty's favorite warrior had been killed. From the account he gave Mahinlo, we suppose that they passed down the east river and came back by the coast. Soon after sunrise next morning they saw your stranded pilot boat, and the works about her, and went ashore to examine. Judging from the size and weight of the timbers brought together, and especially from the strength shown in raising the vessel, they supposed that there must have been at least twenty men at work, and not knowing how soon these men might return and catch them there, they stayed only a little while. Yaha-Lusty declared to Mahinlo that he did not touch anything belonging to the vessel, and that when he went into the cabin to see what it contained, he gave especial instructions to the men to let everything alone, on the peril of their lives; but, he said, that Paw-me-tubbee, his Choctaw warrior, was so great a thief he could not resist the temptation to steal a hatchet and some rope, and that when he, Yaha-Lusty, came out from the vessel, he heard a cry, and saw Paw-me-tubbe lying on the mud with his head mashed by the fall of a heavy timber.

" This accident put them into a great fright, and made them believe in Mahinlo more than ever. They took up their dead warrior, put him in the boat, and paddled away, every man saying over the charm to himself so loud and so fast that they did not know of your being near until they heard the sound of your guns.

" After Yaha-Lusty had left, Mahinlo called me to him, and told me that the time had come now for me to help you. He took me into his dark room, where he talks with the Great Spirit, and where he keeps his charms and medicines. He rubbed my eyes, my ears, my nose, my mouth, my head and breast with sassafras-oil mixed with calamus, and said, —

" ' Go! no enchantment now against you. Be a son and a brother to your friends on the Island. Tell them there is danger—to leave as soon as they can, and never to trust themselves off the Island within gun-shot of any hiding place.'

" Then he gave me a nice little canoe, and put in it some parched corn and dried venison, and said, ' Go! go now. Your friends are yonder,' pointing this way 'Don't let Yaha-Lusty or his men see you. And don't neglect the charm.'

" It was half-way between high sun and low sun
2 A

when I left. I came along softly and slowly,
thinking over all that Mahinlo had said to me,
and was passing close to the woods of the island
above this, when I heard not far off the bleat of
deer. I landed, tied my canoe, and went into the
woods, expecting every moment to see them, for I
could hear their tramp, and even the rustling of
the leaves as they passed. Soon I began to suspect this was a trick, and hurried back to my boat.
But I was too late. Some one, no doubt, of Yaha-
Lusty's men had robbed me.

" Night was now fast coming on, and being
afraid somebody might steal my gun too, I found
a bushy tree with level branches and climbed into
it, tying my gun to a branch overhead, and fastening myself so that I should not fall off.

"Before daylight I left my resting-place and
came to the south end of the island. Here I
climbed a tree and looked over to your side. It
was very far away. I could barely see your little
vessel at anchor near shore, but I knew that you
all could not be very far off from it, and that if I
could only get within hail or within sight, we
should soon be together. The marsh, you know, is
very wide. If it had been all mangrove, I should
never have been able to get through; but a part
of it was covered with a hard, rough grass, and
there was a long ridge of sand and shell that
helped me much, so that I made my way at last

tt the river, and took my seat on a bundle of dead
weeds behind a bush, where I could see and not be
seen.

"There I sat a long time, wondering whether
something bad had not happened to keep you from
the vessel that I knew, by what Yaha-Lusty had
said, you must have been working upon very
busily for some days. At last I saw somebody
dressed like an Indian, with his rifle on his shoulder, come out from the bushes, and walk about the
bluff, looking at the vessel. The sight of those
deerskin clothes made my heart sick, for I was
afraid some of Yaha-Lusty's men had come over
and done you a harm. So I kept myself closely
hid. But when Mum and Fidelle came out of the
woods and began to play about you, Harold, I
knew that the person was no other than yourself."

"I had been watching you long before," said Harold. "I saw you when you broke some mangrove
twigs and fastened them before you as a screen."

Wildcat looked admiringly at his friend, and
said with a quiet laugh, —

"You make good Ingin, some day; you beat
me hide."

"I have one more question to ask," said Dr.
Gordon. "What is the matter with Torgah and
Somassee that they have not come? Or do you
know anything about them?"

Wildcat looked grave, and paused a moment

before he replied. "Torgah and Somassee well, want to come. Can't come yet. Riley too."

Dr. Gordon recollected Pancheta's cautious communication. He perceived that there was some secret influence at work, which Wildcat as an Indian was not at liberty to reveal. He asked no more.

CHAPTER XXXIII.

WILDCAT AT THE PRAIRIE — RECONNOITRING AND DEER-VOYAGE — JOSHUA THRIGPEN — FRANK AND THE ALLIGATOR — TELEGRAPHING — SAM HAS NO USE FOR INDIANS.

ILDCAT'S narrative revealed such hostility of feeling and of purpose upon the mainland, that notwithstanding the friendliness of Mahinlo and others, it was manifestly the duty of our islanders to return as early as they could to Tampa, and also to keep as near together as possible for protection during the remainder of their sojourn.

The voyage back was made without misadventure and almost without incident. On their arrival at the landing, Mary and Frank both hastened to meet them and to give a cordial greeting to their Indian friend. Mrs. Gordon and Mrs. McIntosh knew him only by report, yet his attachment to their young folks had been so devoted as to awaken in them the deepest interest. Wildcat soon found himself at home, and he took pleasure in showing it as far as was consistent with propriety. The mental habits of most Indians, in some respects, resemble the local instincts of a cat; they can never feel entirely at ease in a new place, until they have a reliable knowledge of it and of its surroundings. Wildcat was not long at the tent, before he became restless, and made some excuse for going out with Robert and Harold to survey the premises. The cubs, the fawn, the wild fowl in the poultry pen, were all, in turn, the objects of his interest. From them he was conducted to the edge of a bay gall,* where was a spring of delightful water flowing from the base of a hollow tree. The little prairie, too, delighted him; but when on its border he came in sight of a ruinous hut, enclosing a grave neatly protected by a pen-like covering of poles, he became deeply awed. For a time surveying it from a distance, he slowly approached, and looking through the half-closed doorway upon the interior, where everything had been respected by the present dwellers on the island, he said, —

"Old prophet's home. You no trouble it. Mahinlo glad. He watch you close."

"Trouble it? Oh! no," said Harold, "we have been better taught than to disturb a dead man's *home*, as you call it."

* A miry bottom.

"No, indeed," added Robert; "my father has always taught us to talk softly around a grave, and to act there somewhat as we do upon entering a church."

"Mahinlo see you sometimes when you no see him," said Wildcat. "You make him glad. He love you."

The sun had passed the meridian, and begun to slope toward the west ere the boat had returned. By the time all were rested and had dined, it was too late to attempt that day to change their place of abode. They therefore brought back to the tent all things needful for comfort that night, and then proceeded to load the raft in readiness for an early move in the morning. Sam, whose duties on his master's plantation as captain of the flat-boat during rice-harvest, had made him quite expert in the business, added now the assurance that he would not need the assistance of the boats at the bend where the tides met, since he could float up to it on the flood tide, then pole around and wait for the ebb to carry him to Fish Point. He still insisted, too, that so far as danger from Indians was concerned, it would be safer for him to go alone, and this was vigorously supported by Wildcat, who held that whatever might be the hostility of Yaha-Lusty or his men toward the whites, there was none toward the blacks.

"If these are the facts in the case," said Dr

Gordon, addressing his boys, "I am in favor of an important change in our plan of transportation; that while the raft makes the trip by the river, as it must, we make it by sea. This will be acting according to the advice of Mahinlo sent us this morning."

The necessary work being all completed an hour by sun, Harold asked permission for himself and Wildcat to go to Fish Point on a tour of observation. Their guns were taken as a matter of course, and so was Mum; and this led them into a temptation which a hunter finds it very difficult to withstand. A herd of large, beautiful deer, roused unawares by them, sprang up, and with broad, flaunting tails, loped lazily along within easy reach of their rifles. The leader was a stately buck, and their pieces were instantly levelled upon him, when the shot was arrested by the ready prudence of Harold.

"Stop, Wildcat!" said he, "we are too near the bluff. We must reconnoitre first."

Wildcat's rifle dropped slowly from its aim, and he looked sadly disappointed, although a moment after he said, —

"You right! you right! musn't shoot yet."

They went directly to the Point, which they approached with caution, peeping right and left through the bushes, and examining with the spyglass the opposite shore and the distant reaches of the river. Nothing wrong or even suspicious was discoverable. They then turned their faces homeward, when scarcely had they passed out of sight of the Point, ere their recent act of self-denial was rewarded.

Mum was an admirably trained "still hunter." His stealthy tread, his pointed nose, his pricked-up ears, his short tail erect, gave signs of game near at hand. The boys followed close behind him with their guns ready. There was a tramp, then a rush not twenty yards away, and the same herd they had seen on coming, passed them again. The crack of both rifles was heard almost simultaneously, and the buck on which they had directed their pieces leaped high into the air, and fell dead with two bullet holes in his shoulder.

"Too big and fat for us to carry," said Harold, as he rolled the body on one side to feel its weight.

"Can hang it up," suggested Wildcat, looking around for a sapling.

It was as much as they could do, with their united strength, to draw the body to a slender tree, which one of them climbed and bent down. But the weight was more than the tree would carry back.

"Cut deer in two and hang on two tree," again suggested Wildcat.

One of these trees, however, was so low that Harold added another device to protect his game from wolves. He inflated the deer's bladder, and hung it to dangle from an adjoining limb, remarking as he did so, —

" I have heard old Torgah say that no wolf will come near a thing like this."

They reached the tent about dark, quite content to rest themselves after their tramp, and giving a satisfactory account of what they had seen and done.

In the family worship that evening — the first of the kind probably the young Indian had ever attended — it was noticed that Wildcat listened with profound attention, and that when they united audibly in the Lord's Prayer, his voice was heard repeating in musical, though broken English, the words of which Mahinlo had spoken so reverently as "the white man's charm."

At break of day next morning, all were on foot, even Mrs. Gordon, preparing for the remove; and the sun was not very high before the voyagers set out, the canoes going south and the raft going north. As the distance between them increased, and they began to lose sight of each other, Sam waved his adieus with his hat, and then raised a boat-song, not reflecting that a safer plan to escape notice from the Indians would have been to float along in silence. The canoes, carrying respectively Dr. and Mrs. Gordon, Robert and Mary in one, and Mrs. McIntosh, Harold, Frank, and Wildcat in the other, together with their trunks, blankets, provisions, cooking utensils, etc., passed down the river under the impulse both of sails and oars. The canoes having no keels with which to resist lee-way, were not helped in their progress by the sails, nevertheless the wind, which was from the east, and consequently off shore, insured them smooth water at sea.

In passing down the river, Harold pointed out to his mother and Wildcat the place of the pirate wreck, now barely visible behind its cumbrous wall of sea-weeds, far up the little creek ; and a mile or two lower down, he showed her the place where he and the others had had a desperate encounter with a bear that they had robbed of her whelps.

At the southern end of the island their attention was attracted by a number of gulls and other sea-birds gathered around some object high upon the beach. The boats went ashore, and Dr. Gordon and the boys were horrified to find there the body of a dead man. It was so thoroughly picked and mutilated that on the first approach they were at a loss to determine whether it had belonged to a white man, Indian, or negro. A little closer inspection enabled them to determine from the hair that it was that of a white man, and from the clothing that he was probably a fisher-man or a wrecker. On examining the pockets, they found several letters addressed to parties at Key

West, purporting to be in the care of Joshua Thrigpen. One of these was in the familiar hand-writ-
ing of Major Burke, of Fort Brooke, addressed to
the commandant at Key West. Not being marked
"Official," Dr. Gordon took the liberty of opening
this last, confident that it concerned himself more
than any one else. And so it proved; for it was
a letter written at his request during his sickness
in November, endeavoring to enlist the interest of
certain persons at Key West in looking for his children, and offering a large reward for their recovery.

"Poor fellow!" said Dr. Gordon, surveying
the mangled remains, "he succeeded in reaching
the place of which he was so anxious to know, and
here he has perished."

But what could have so delayed him? for the
body furnished circumstantial evidence that he
had not been dead more than a week, yet it was
nearly four months since he left Tampa. This
question they could not solve, so gathering as well
as they could all that pertained to him, and secur-
ing all that was worth preserving of the contents
of his pockets, they dug a grave and buried him
there, with an inscription in the following words,
deeply pencilled on an adjoining tree,—

"Joshua Thrigpen. Found dead, March 2d,
1831 Buried six feet north.
                    "Charles Gordon, M. D.,
                              "Tampa Bay, Fla."

This work detained them an hour or more, during which time Mary and Frank had a delightful run upon the hard beach, which was plentifully sprinkled with shells and sea-weeds of various kinds, and many of exquisite beauty. Among the curiosities brought by them to the boat, was something which Frank took to be the enormous rattle of a rattlesnake, which it strongly resembled in structure, although it was as long as his arm. At first he was afraid to handle it, but Mary showed him that it was the egg of a conch, made of many flat cells, united by a ligature in the middle, and each containing a number of little tiny conchs.

A mile or two further up the beach, the shells were larger and more abundant. Dr. Gordon there pointed out the place where he had discovered Frank's handkerchief partly buried in the sand, and asked him and Mary when and how he happened to lose it. Frank had no recollection of it whatever; but Harold answered, —

"The only time when it could have happened was soon after we came here. Don't you recollect, Frank, that you and Mary came out to this place with me to gather shells?"

"Yes," he replied, "I remember it well enough. But father did not ask about that at all. He asked when I lost my handkerchief, and I did not lose it then."

"The handkerchief could not have brought itself," argued Harold. " Don't you think, Frank, you must have brought and left it the only time you came here ?"

" But I did not leave it," persisted Frank, " for I carried it back full of shells, and you helped me yourself to carry it, because it was so heavy."

Harold's recollection of the matter now coincided with Frank's, and he was beginning to feel somewhat perplexed to account for the apparent mystery, when Frank clapped his hands saying, " I know ! I know !" then as suddenly stopped.

"What do you know, Frank ?" he asked. But Frank put on a sullen look and refused to tell. Harold perceived that something unusual was in Frank's mind, connected with the handkerchief, and in a spirit of mischief he urged him to tell it. But Frank persisted in his silence until his mother said :

" I do not wish you to tell us, Frank, unless you choose. Only I hope it was nothing bad that makes you unwilling."

" No, ma'am," he answered very promptly ; then went on in a hesitating manner to say, " only it was n't—, it was n't—, it was n't exactly —, only I have not told anybody about it yet, and it makes me feel bad to think about it."

" Indeed," said she, " that makes me wish to know what it is."

" Well," he replied, " an alligator almost caught me that day. And it makes me feel uncom-

fortable to think how he would have chewed
me up!"

"Why, my son! when was this?" his mother
asked in alarm.

"Oh! a long time ago," he answered; "it was
after sister Mary sent off her little schooner *Hope*,
to tell you all where we were. I thought I would
send off a vessel too. I took the hatchet and cut
me a flat piece of wood, a bigger one than sister's,
because I wanted it to sail further, and I sharpened one end of it and put a rudder at the other
end, as I had seen cousin Harold do; and then I
made a mast and put on my handkerchief for a
sail, and took it down to the river. It went very
well for awhile, until it lodged against what I
thought was an ugly black log of wood, lying close
in the water-side. But when I pushed it with a
stick to make it go, the log moved, and slapped
around at me so hard that the water splashed all
over my face and blinded me; and when I looked
again, I saw a great big alligator as long as a fence-
rail, swimming away, and my handkerchief hitched
to one of the scales of his back. This is the way my
handkerchief came here; the alligator brought it."

Mrs. Gordon turned red and pale by turns, as
her little boy gave this graphic account of his narrow escape.

"Where did this happen?" she inquired.

"Near the spring where we first lived," he answered.

Mary caught her mother's eye fixed upon her with a look of inquiry which seemed to say, How came you to let your brother get into such danger? She felt very badly, and did not know how to excuse her seeming neglect, until Frank added,—

"It was one day when cousin Harold was lame, and when you all were so busy curing the venison that brother Robert and I killed."

"Why, Frank!" exclaimed Mary, "you say it happened a long time ago, and yet you never told us a word of it until now! What kept you from telling?"

"I was afraid you would not let me go to the river again," replied Frank.

Dr. Gordon, who had been a silent, but interested listener, now remarked,— "Well, Frank, I hope this will be a lesson to you as long as you live, how you go near water in which there are alligators."

Without further incident they reached the northern end of the island, and as they turned the point to come in from sea, they discovered the pilot boat riding safely at anchor; and far up the river, barely discernible with the spy-glass, they could see the raft moored at the bend of the marsh awaiting the ebb-tide, and Sam sitting on one of the chairs. While Robert was using the glass, he started with surprise, and said,—

"Father! Cousin Harold! the Indians have been after Sam."

His father seized the offered glass, and after poising it steadily upon the distant point, passed it to Harold, saying, — "I see Sam aboard, and everything seemingly in quiet. But just beyond the raft you may discover several paddles in motion as if they belong to a large boat trying to keep hidden from us by hugging the shore." Harold looked and passed the glass to Wildcat.

Both made a hasty examination and came to the conclusion that whatever might have been said or done by their distant visitors, they were now leaving Sam in peace. But as Wildcat looked, he added, —

"That Yaha-Lusty in Bellevue boat!"

"I am glad he has let my things on the raft alone," said Dr. Gordon.

"He 'fraid to trouble 'em; fraid of Mahinlo," Wildcat affirmed.

"Shall we not go and see if Sam needs anything?" Harold asked.

"Not unless he gives some signal," his father returned. "He can see us as well as we can see him, and if he is in need you may be sure he will let us know it."

When they reached the vessel, Dr. Gordon raised an oar, on which he had tied a white handkerchief; and within two minutes, Sam's pole went up bearing also something white, but having his black hat on top. Wildcat looked on inquisitively. Robert exclaimed, —

"The white means, All right! We say so to Sam by *our* white. He says the same to us by his. But he puts on something black, and that means Danger. The two colors mean, Danger, but All Right! See, now, father makes his oar bow to Sam, which Sam will understand to ask, Do you need anything? and if Sam needs, he will say Yes, by making his pole bow too. But see, the top of his pole waves from side to side, like a person shaking his head; that means No."

"Sam seems to be well drilled," observed Harold.

"It was a part of his training as captain of my rice-boats," his uncle answered.

All hands now went to work to prepare their future abode. Dr. Gordon had intended to pitch and occupy the tent on land, but a more mature reflection decided him to place the non-combatants at once in the more secure, though less comfortable shelter of the vessel. There they disembarked from the canoes, the freight was discharged, and the ladies set about making things comfortable, while Dr. Gordon and the boys provided wood and water, set up the stove for use, and did whatever else was necessary, yet not suitable, for delicate hands.

Late in the afternoon the vessel swung round with her stern seaward. The ebb-tide had commenced, but before the downward current had extended to the raft, Sam had pushed from shore and was awaiting it. As he came floating into the broad water, the boys manned one of the canoes and went to meet him. Hardly had they come within talking distance before they heard his sonorous voice singing out, —

"Injin been yuh!"

The distance was too great to admit of reply by words, and they, therefore, welcomed him by a loud halloo and a wave of their caps.

"I tell you so," he shouted, on a somewhat nearer approach, "I tell you Injin never trouble nigger. Ee tek de little cannon, dough, and de powder and de shot. Ee say you 'ent got no business wi' so much cannon; ee want some eeself."

This partial robbery was a new feature in the case. It was an advance toward hostility which Wildcat's words had not prepared them to expect. What did it mean? When Sam came aboard and rendered a full and deliberate report to his master, he informed them that while he was moored at the bend, he saw, far up the river, a large boat manned by half a dozen Indians stealing cautiously along the opposite shore. It was the same party they had chased to sea, and they were in the same boat. After peeping around the point and ascertaining there was no danger, they came over the river, asked him who he was, where he came from, what he was doing there, and what he had aboard. He told them, in reply, that he belonged to Dr. Gordon, that he and his master's company had been driven there by a gale and were trying to get away, and that he had on board such and such things, which they could plainly see. They asked why the canoes had gone by sea, when the passage by river was so much shorter and more pleasant. To which he replied, that the ladies were tired of the smell of the marsh, and wanted to see the beach. They then inquired how many and who were in the company, and what they proposed to do. These questions he pretended not to understand, and replied : " Yes, he knew it was a ' mighty dangersome place,' full of ghosts and bad spirits, and that Dr. Gordon and his company were trying hard to get away for fear they should be destroyed, as everybody else had been who had gone there. They then proposed to deliver him from his danger at once by receiving him into their tribe, and making him free, and giving him an Indian wife, or three or four wives if he preferred, who should all work for him and make him a rich man. Sam said that at first he did not know how to answer them, for they seemed determined to take him anyhow ; but he told them at last that he did not need anybody to work for him, that he had a good house at home, and plenty of victuals and clothes ; that he did not want any more wives, for he had one already, and she was more than he could manage, and that as for being free, he had a good master, and was just as free as any black man could be that had a wife at all. He said that when he had given them this answer, they looked at one another and said, " Ugh ! ugh !" and then went away, appearing to be much put out, and carried away the cannon and all that belonged to it.

" And how do you like your new acquaintances?" asked Robert, who observed that several times Sam's face had given indication of strong disgust.

" I ent get no use fuh um," he replied with emphasis.

" But they treated you very respectfully," persisted Robert.

Sam looked his dissent, and simply replied, — " Injin too sassy."

It was some time before the fact was revealed that one of Yaha-Lusty's men, in expressing his disappointment at Sam's refusal, had quoted the common Indian saying : "White man f.rst ; Injin next ; den dog, and after dog, nigger."

CHAPTER XXXIV.

D O you expect an attack to-night?" asked Harold, as something was said of post-ing sentinels on deck.

"I never expect evil," his uncle re-plied, "though I try always to prepare for it."

"But, father," argued Robert, who was usually ready to inaugurate a discussion, "does not this posting of sentinels imply that evil is expected?"

"Not necessarily," his father answered: "on the contrary, it rather implies an expectation of warding it off in case it should appear. When I was a boy, my father gave me an excellent rule, which I am glad to say I have remembered and acted upon almost every day since. It was this. '*Never anticipate evil. Foresee it, and prepare*

421

against it,' always, if you can; but never hurry
trouble on yourself. More than likely it will not
come at all, except by anticipation, and even if it
should, your suffering beforehand will not make it
lighter. In every experience in life, there is good
as well as evil, and, if we are allowed to have a
choice, it is certainly the part of wisdom to anticipate the good. '*Never eat ashes,*' said he, '*if you
can feed on honey.*'"

Harold laughed. "But, uncle," he asked, "what
good can you anticipate from the coming of Indians
to-night?"

"This good," his uncle replied, "that if they
come, and are repelled, they will be apt hereafter
to let us alone."

The sentinels were assigned to their duties; the
deck of the little vessel was put in the best possible condition for defence, and each one of the
"warriors" aboard took his turn in the nightly
watch, but no Indians came, and no disturbance
was experienced beyond the blowing of a porpoise
or the splash of a sportive sturgeon.

The next morning they were all early on foot,
but not quite so early as usual at their work. A
family can seldom make a sudden change of abode
without experiencing unforeseen delays in getting
the necessaries of life into proper working trim.
The venison brought in by the boys, the evening
before, had not been fully prepared for use;

several of the stores had to be looked up, and the wood cut by Sam for the ship stove, did not fit. To add to these delays, Frank's nose set into violent bleeding. His mother exhausted upon him all her usual devices of applying something cold to the back of the neck, and of making him snuff cold water up the bleeding nostril. Wildcat looked with curiosity upon these several attempts, and seeing them fail said, half jocosely, half in earnest, —

"Give him me. I cure him."

Having received permission, he asked Frank, —
"Which side bleed?"

Frank showed him the left nostril, and Wildcat, taking him by the left hand, made him hold it up high over his head, instructing him to stand at the same time upon the right foot, and to lean his head accordingly. For a time the bleeding seemed to stop, but beginning again as violently as ever, Wildcat asked Mrs. Gordon for a towel, and going toward the fore-hatch said to Frank, —

"Come down here, I cure you here."

On getting below deck and beyond sight, he made Frank strip off his clothes, then threw a sudden dash of cold water upon the lower part of his body, saying in a spirit of fun as he did so, —

"Musn't holla! Me will holla for you."

Then as Frank jerked in his breath preparatory to an exclamation, Wildcat uttered a loud "Ugh!" as if shuddering with cold. A second dash of cold water was followed by two of these grunts, and a third by three, when Wildcat pronounced the cure complete. And so it was; for cold water has not only a powerfully styptic effect when applied to a bleeding *wound*, but it is almost as efficacious on a bleeding nostril when applied by sudden shock to the lower part of the body.

Frank quickly dressed himself, and the two returned with great glee to the company, Wildcat leading him by the hand to Dr. Gordon, and saying with mock boast, —

"1 great medicine man. Esta-chattee beat Buckra." *

Dr. Gordon smiled, and said to his gay young ward, —

"I think I shall have to take you into partnership, and after awhile send you back home as *Doctor* Wildcat."

Frank's call upon Doctor Wildcat's services did not end, however, with the stopping of the nose bleed. There were two dishes for breakfast that morning of which he was excessively fond, venison steaks and fried oysters, and he manœuvred with

---

* *Indian beat white man.* The term *buckra*, which is said to have been brought from the Calabar coast, and to have been used originally to mean "white demon," is in general use among the negroes on our Atlantic and Gulf coast, also in the West Indies, and to some extent among the Florida Indians, to mean white folks, in distinction from black or red people.

such skill as to obtain more than his share of both.
The consequence was that a few minutes after
breakfast he was attacked with an incontrollable
fit of hiccups. In vain he tried the usual mode
of cure by drinking nine swallows of water without taking breath; in vain, too, he tried Harold's
plan of *holding his breath twice as long as he could*,
(which being interpreted practically meant holding
his breath as long as he could, twice;) in vain did
his brother and cousin try to scare off the fit by
sudden surprises; it was not to be relieved by
ordinary means. Wildcat looked on as a quiet
observer of these modes, and at last said, —

"Injin doctor can cure that, too."

Upon taking the case in hand, he made Frank
press the point of his third finger against that of
his thumb, and hold them together for several
minutes; but as the remedy proved ineffectual, he
tied a string tightly around the wrist, saying, —

"He cure now!"

Whether owing to efficacy in the means used,
or, as may have been possible, to Frank's diver-
sion of mind, the result was that Dr. Wildcat
advanced another step toward earning his di-
ploma.

Meanwhile the work of refitting the little vessel
had been going on. Dr. Gordon at first thought
that a splicing of the broken mast would suffice
for present necessities, but he was soon convinced

that time would be saved by replacing it at once with a new one. Leaving Robert to aid Sam in removing the old stump, he took Harold and Wildcat, and, by special request, little Frank, and went ashore to look for a suitable tree. Any one might have supposed, in looking at the well-grown forest, in which there seemed to be every variety of timber, that the selection need not have detained them five minutes.

But when the necessary conditions came to be exacted, that it should be of certain length, certain diameter, certain taper, straight, tough, free from large knots, and near the waterside, the search was far more prolonged than would have been expected.

Discovery at last rewarded their search, and a beautiful tree they obtained — a young ash, straight as an arrow, and almost without a knot. It was soon felled, stripped of its bark, and ready for transportation. In endeavoring to adjust the tackling previous to its being put into posture, it was discovered that certain parts of the cordage had been so greatly injured by the rough handling of the gale as to require renewal, and that there was no prospect of obtaining what was needed except by another visit to the pirate wreck. Here they all recollected having seen a quantity of the very article called for, indeed a portion of it had been brought away at their last visit, and had been stolen by Yaha-Lusty's men. And now since a

visit to the wreck was determined upon, the question arose, Who was to go? Each offered his services, and gave some reason appropriate to his own
case, but Dr. Gordon put his veto on all applica-
tions except those of Sam and Wildcat, who alone
could plead, that in case of meeting with Yaha-
Lusty's men there was no reason to apprehend an
attempt upon their lives. With great reluctance
and with some misgiving Dr. Gordon saw them
depart, taking the longer but safer route by the
seaward side of the island.

While they were gone, the others pressed on
assiduously with the work of getting the mast in
place and the rigging in order. Late in the afternoon, while the sun was nearing his bed in the
western waters, all on board the pilot boat were
filled with anxiety by seeing a dark smoke roll up
from the southeast, stretch across the island, and
stream far out to sea.

"Look! look!" suddenly exclaimed Harold,
who happened to have his eyes turned in that
direction. The others looked with him, and saw
an immense volume of whitish vapor, intermixed
with dark objects of various sizes, shoot up far into
the air and spread itself out. A quarter of a minute afterward, there was a heavy, lumbering sound,
like thunder, which made the vessel, and even the
water, vibrate.

"I very much fear some calamity has befallen
Sam and Wildcat," said Dr. Gordon anxiously.

"None to *them*, I am pretty sure, for here they come," responded Harold, pointing to the farthest visible limit of the beach.

The voyagers were soon alongside, and Wildcat's cheery voice shouted out, —

"Pirate make big smoke. She gone, now."

"Indeed! is that the smoke of the pirate wreck?" inquired Dr. Gordon.

"How came she afire?"

"*Happen* so. Sam can tell," answered Wildcat.

But Sam could tell nothing. He looked very stupid, and his tongue was suspiciously thick. On subsequent inquiry, Dr. Gordon ascertained from Wildcat that after they had completed their errand at the wreck, Sam lingered for half an hour in the hold, and at last came out with a jug, from which he imbibed during the voyage, until he became so very stupid that he could scarcely manage either oar or rudder. It was to be supposed, therefore, that while engaged in filling his jug, he probably dropped a half-extinguished match among some combustibles, or what was quite as likely, left his candle burning on a place where it finally communicated with the ship.

"Then we have seen and heard our last of the pirate wreck," observed Robert.

"*Seen*, yes," returned his father, "but I doubt if we have heard our last. The smoke and explosion must, of course, have attracted the atten-

tion of persons on the main, and they must be
very lacking in the usual attributes of human
nature if some of them do not come pretty soon to
ascertain the cause."

The countenances of the boys exhibited some
anxiety as Dr. Gordon uttered these prophetic
words; perceiving which he went on to say,—

"We have so nearly completed our work of refitting, that I hope to weigh anchor and spread
sail sometime to-morrow, for our return home.
We will, therefore, keep watch and ward again,
as we did last night; then get to work early in the
morning, and prepare to leave Yaha-Lusty's territory before another sunset."

The next morning's sun found the last-appointed
sentinel at his post, glass in hand, watching a suspicious movement in a clump of mangroves far
across the river. One of the canoes now went to
the spring for a new supply of water and oysters,
and the other went to obtain wood for the stove,
and forage for the brute pets. On their return
there was the tinkle of a little bell, calling them
first to prayer, and then to breakfast; soon after
which, they were engaged in their shipwork, and
three hours afterward they hoisted their mainsail,
and saw their jib flutter in the breeze.

"Now, boys," said Dr. Gordon, "before we
begin our voyage home, we must take a turn or
two in the river to try our rigging, and to prove

that we have perfect command of our little Sea Bird. Then we can anchor at the spring, take in our supply of wood and water, and set our bow for Tampa."

This announcement the boys received with a cheer, in which Mary and Frank united with all their powers, and to which Frank added,—

"Hurra for Bellevue!"

A few turns of the capstan brought up the anchor The mainsail was hauled around to catch the breeze, the jib fluttered, then filled, and the Sea Bird, with her head to sea, was joyously dashing the water from her bows. A dozen shiplengths revealed a defect, which caused them to return to their former anchorage and spend a few minutes in correcting it. In her next trial the head of the vessel was set against the wind, to try her power of tacking. The river at that point was full half a mile wide, but the part of it which they allowed themselves to use was only half that space, in order to keep out of rifle range from the other shore. They had come opposite that part of the marsh where the suspicious motion of the mangroves had been observed at sunrise. The vessel had tacked twice in a manner most satisfactory, and was now wearing around for the purpose of beginning her homeward voyage, when a sudden jet of whitish vapor darted from amidst the mangroves, followed by a roar of cannon, and in a moment afterward their beautiful mast lay upon deck, shivered by a cannon-ball.

This was a most unexpected event, for who ever associated the ideas of Indian and cannon? But here they certainly were put together. Dr. Gordon looked from the rolling smoke to the fallen mast, and exclaimed sadly, "How unfortunate!" and Robert's eye followed his father's. Harold looked fiercely from the fallen mast to the yet moving smoke, muttered something between his clenched teeth about "Redskinned villains!" He had barely uttered the words, —

"Shall we not send them a cannon-ball in return?" when Mary's voice was heard from the cabin, —

"Father, come here! Aunt is hurt."

Dr. Gordon was making a hurried move to the cabin, when Harold darted past him, reached his mother's side, and uttered a wail of distress. When Dr. Gordon came, he found her lying back in her chair, senseless, with Mrs. Gordon supporting her bloody head, and Harold kneeling by her, the picture of despair. The cannon-ball, in raking the deck, had carried into the cabin a splinter from the mast, which had torn quite a gash in Mrs. McIntosh's head.

Dr. Gordon put his finger into the wound, found that the skull was not injured, then felt her pulse, and said, —

"Rub her palms, Harold! Fan her, Mary! She is not seriously hurt; only stunned. She will soon recover. Here, let me sprinkle her face with water, then I must go on deck."

Promising to return at the first possible moment, he went up, made a hurried examination with the glass of the quarter whence the shot had come, and, while he was thus engaged, saw another jet of smoke issue from the marsh, followed by a perfect shower of spray about midway between. A canister loaded with musket-balls had been fired, and the balls had struck the water and sunk.

"Man the boats!" said he to Robert, Wildcat, and Sam, "and pull the vessel out of reach of shot."

The two boys sprang lightly in, but Sam made some excuse for tarrying until the canoes were protected by having the vessel between them and danger, when he also leaped in and pulled with great vigor.

A few minutes afterward there was another discharge from the cannon, which sent a ball dancing along the water at very safe distance from the vessel.

"I thought so, and this proves it," said Dr. Gordon; "that first shot was an accident. We need fear no other."

Harold now came from the cabin, reporting his mother recovered and doing well, though complaining of a strange feeling in her head.

"But, uncle," said he, "I am sorry to say the vessel is leaking so badly from a hole below the water-line that she will soon fill, unless we stop it."

His uncle went with him instantly into the cabin, gave a congratulatory look to his sister, then passed to examine the leak. The ball, glancing downward from the mast, had passed through the thin floor, and out of the side below, and the water was pouring in with a noise that could be distinctly heard.

It was manifest that no time was to be lost, and Dr. Gordon, passing his sister again, said, —

"I am so sorry, my dear sister, that I cannot be with you yet," went with Harold to the deck, where he hastily tore several small squares of tarred cloth, laid them together, and directed Harold to enter one of the canoes, reach down under the water and plaster these squares directly over the leak. The hole was only two feet below the water-line, and the pressure kept the pieces of tarpaulin to their place.

During the progress of this work, there was another loud explosion from the marsh, which was not followed by either ball or canister. Dr. Gordon had his eyes directed there at the moment it took place, and ere the sound reached him he saw the body of an Indian, with arms and legs ridiculously sprawling, shoot up into the air, along with some other small objects in the smoke, then

2 C

drop into the river near by; after which the Bellevue boat, manned by four paddlers, was seen hurrying away for dear life.

"'Hoist with his own petard!'" Dr. Gordon
half shouted with a laugh, as he looked upon the
ridiculous scene. Then recollecting that the boys
in the boat, not having witnessed the event, would
scarcely be able to understand the quotation, he
added, —

"One of those poor wretches, in trying to do us
a wrong, has blown himself up. Either the cannon has burst or the powder-keg has exploded —
perhaps both. We shall have no more trouble
from them to-day."

The distance between the place of anchorage,
and that from which the vessel had to be pulled
was over a mile, and the only help being from a
gentle breeze, they were more than an hour in
overpassing it.

"There are two necessary works to be done
before we can begin our voyage," said Dr. Gordon;
"one is to stop our leak more securely, and the
other is to provide a new mast. Robert, we will
leave Sam to work the pump, and Harold to attend to his mother, while I go for a few moments
with you and Wildcat to point out the tree."

To pull ashore, and point out one selected the
day before, detained him a very short time, and
Dr. Gordon used his first available moment to

return to his wounded sister. He ascertained that the singular pain complained of was caused by a portion of the splinter as large and long as his finger, which had broken off from the rest, and had buried itself beyond sight between the scalp and scull. A little cutting with his pen-knife enabled him to reach one end of it and draw it out with a pair of pliers. He then washed the wound very clean, removed the hair, brought the lips of the wound together by means of a few stitches, made with a bent needle, bound up the wounded part, and pronounced his work of surgery complete.

The mast was brought in before sunset, nicely trimmed, and ready for setting. Dr. Gordon decided as to the leak, that, as very little water now came in, they should wait until they could accomplish their carpentry with more convenience. Then, looking at the declining sun, he said, —

"Now is our time for beginning to keep the fourth commandment, which says, '*Remember* the Sabbath day to keep it holy;' that is, remember that it is coming, and prepare for it, so that no needless work remain to be done."

The preparations were made. The evening was pleasantly closed, and all retired to rest that night, except the watchers in turn, thankful that their lives had been spared through another week.

CHAPTER XXXV.

SUALLY, we can fortell the spirit in which we shall awake by observing the spirit in which we go to sleep. A poet of nature has sung —

"The child is father of the man."

This is as true of our every-day life as of our larger and longer experiences. The future seems chained to the past, like link to link. Our past begets our future.

The pleasant family circle on board the pilot-boat, that retired to rest so devoutly Saturday evening, March 4th, had reason to expect a devout waking up the next morning. The Sabbath

436

proved to them a day of rest. It could scarcely
have been otherwise, even had some of its hours
been compulsorily given to labor or to conflict.
They would have rested in spirit.

From labor and conflict, however, they were
spared. The several thicknesses of tarpaulin,
plastered first to each other, then over the small
hole in their vessel's side, acted like a valve, and
almost perfectly arrested the inflow of water.
And their dusky foes, although stealthily appearing more than once far up the river, as if reconnoitring with no friendly eye, kept themselves at
a respectful distance.

In the course of the day, Harold came with his
cousin, accompanied by Wildcat, to say to Dr.
Gordon that they had been deeply interested in
his remarks the preceding Sabbath about the
" Existence of a God," and to ask if he would not
now take up the other subject — " The Soul,
and its Immortality," and give them his views
upon it also.

"A very interesting subject, truly,' said the
Doctor, " but much more difficult than the other
to treat simply and satisfactorily, and I will show
you why. Do you believe, Harold, that you have
a soul ? "

" Most certainly, sir," was his reply.

" Then what do you suppose a soul to be ? " he
asked,—

Harold answered : —

" My mother taught me to believe it is that something within me which thinks and feels."

" A very good definition," his uncle added. ' But does not a dog also think? and does not an oyster feel?"

" Yes," he replied.

" Well, have they souls?"

Harold was silent.

" I will not press this point," his uncle said. " We will turn to another. Do you believe that you are alive?"

" Surely, sir, I should be deranged if I doubted it," Harold answered.

" What proof have you of it?" his uncle asked.

" I need no proof," he answered; " I am conscious of it."

" Then will you tell me what life is?" his uncle softly said.

Harold was about to reply, but paused. He looked at his uncle, at Robert, at Wildcat, then paused again. Robert smiled.

" I will not press this point, either," said his uncle, " but allow me to ask, Do you think you love your mother?"

" I not only think so, but I know it," said Harold, looking affectionately at her, " and she knows it, too."

" You are sure, then, that you know what love
ß," Dr. Gordon said.

" I know it, if I know anything," Harold replied, with some hesitation, however.

" Then please to tell me what it is."

Harold paused longer than before, and Robert
now laughed outright.

" I have asked you these questions," said his
uncle, " not to make you seem ridiculous, for you
have answered them nearly as well as the best
philosophers could have done, but to show you
how ignorant we are, and how difficult it is to express ourselves on some of those subjects that seem
plainest and best, on which our faith is most fully
established. You are absolutely certain that you
are alive, yet you cannot tell me what life is
You are just as certain about your love to your
mother, and about her love to you, yet you find
it difficult to tell what love is. Now do not be
surprised if we meet with difficulty in talking
about the soul."

Dr. Gordon here paused, as if gathering up his
thoughts, then said :—

" I understand you to ask, What reason have
we to believe that we have souls, and that these
souls live forever? Am I right ?"

Robert and Harold assented, and he continued :

" I understand, too, that you ask for some plain
and easy views of the subject — so plain and easy,

as I judge from the coming of our young friend
Wildcat, that he, as well as yourselves, car com-
prehend it."

The boys assented again.

"You have given me a hard task," said he
'but I will undertake it, and do the best I can.

"Three or four hundred years ago, it was not
known to our fathers, who lived on the other side
of the ocean, that there was such a country as
America. Many suspected, and a few almost believed it, some for one reason, some for another.
but no one was certain, until Columbus actually
crossed the great water, and carried back with him
as proofs some of the new people, and some of
the new fruits to be found here. So in respect to
the soul and its immortality. We may suspect it,
and feel pretty sure of it, but to be positively
certain, we must have such testimony as can be
obtained only from one who has been to that
other country. This testimony is to be found
only in the Bible, which comes to us, professedly,
from God himself, to tell us all we need to know
of ourselves and of himself, and of that other
world, from which no human traveller returns.
And I think you, Harold and Robert, will agree
with me, that if the Bible teaches anything with
clearness, it teaches that man has a spirit or soul
distinct from the body, and that this soul is
immortal."

To this Robert replied with great cordiality, in the name of the others,—

"If the Bible is not clear on these points, I think it is not clear on any. When our Saviour on the cross said to the dying man at his side, 'This day shalt thou be with me in Paradise,' he certainly did not speak of the man's body, but his soul."

"You are right," said his father, with a look of approval. "And, in view of this fact, I will say that the shortest and surest way to satisfy one's self on the subject of the soul and its immortality, is to study the Bible as a book from God.

"If, however, you ask for proof outside the Bible — proof to be obtained from what is called the light of Nature — I confess that there is little more to be had now than was had two thousand years ago, when Plato wrote his celebrated work on the subject."

Dr. Gordon mused again, and was slow to begin. But Harold said:—

"Uncle, please give us some of that little; anything that will satisfy you, will, no doubt, satisfy us."

"I am not unwilling to give it," said his uncle, "I was only thinking how unsatisfactory the light of reason is, compared with the light of revelation.

"That there is something within us that thinks

and feels, that loves and hates, that chooses and refuses, no one can doubt. We *know it*, if we know anything. That something we call *the soul*. That it is distinct from the body we know too, because mere flesh and blood can no more think and feel than can the dry dust out of which it is formed, and to which it shall return. It is this soul, more than anything else — yes, more than everything else — that we call *ourselves*."

"But, father," interrupted Robert, "will not this argument prove that birds and beasts have souls, too? For they certainly think, and feel, and love, and hate, and choose, and refuse."

Most people are unwilling to admit that brutes have souls," said Dr. Gordon, "but we cannot deny that they have something within which, if it is not soul, is so nearly akin to it that we can scarcely tell the difference. Solomon himself seemed to realize this when he asked, 'Who knoweth the *spirit* of man that goeth upward, and the *spirit* of the beast that goeth downward to the earth?' Eccles. iii. 21. By 'spirit' he no doubt meant the same that we call soul."

"But, uncle," inquired Harold, in surprise, "do you believe that the souls of brutes live forever?"

"That is a very different question," his uncle replied, "and is variously answered. I should nave no objection to answering Yes, if it could be proved either from Scripture or from reason; but

I see little in favor of it, and much against it. A soul is not necessarily immortal, any more than a body is. We are taught in the Bible that the bodies of men are in a certain sense immortal, too; that is, they shall be raised up at the last day, and shall then live forever, but this does not prove that the bodies of cows and sheep shall enjoy the same privilege."

These were new thoughts to the boys, and Dr. Gordon allowed them a moment or two to ponder before he resumed.

"Our great concern now is with the question, Is the *soul of man* immortal? That he has a soul we have just now proved to our satisfaction, but we wish to know whether that soul shall live in another state of being, after it separates from the body, or whether it shall die like the brute, and be no more. I will give the answer by piecemeal.

"We know that there is another state of being, because we know that there is a God. He is a Spirit, without body; yet he lives, and the world in which he lives is to us a hereafter, at least a *beyond*, and we properly call it a hereafter, or future life, because we cannot conceive of ourselves as entering it except by first passing through the present life. We feel as certain, therefore, that there is, what is to us, a future world, as that there is a God. We have now two points settled,—We have souls; there is another state of being.

"After that comes a third question: Does the soul outlive the body? And to this I answer, that if the soul is such as we have described it, (and I know of no better definition,) then the fleshly body can be to it only the *house* in which 't lives, or the *clothing* in which it is enrobed.

"Wildcat," he continued, turning to the young Indian, whose coal-black eye had been fixed upon him, as if searching his thought through his face, as well as by his lips, "were you to find in yonder wood a palmetto tent, without any one living in it, or were you to find on the ground a suit of buckskin clothes, such as you wear, what would you conclude about the person to whom that house or suit belonged — that he was dead or not dead?"

"Don't know," answered Wildcat. "Maybe dead ; maybe not dead ; maybe gone away."

"You are right," Dr. Gordon said. "Suppose now you were to see fresh signs of the man, not a day old, and to see at the same time that the tent he had left was no longer fit to live in, and that the clothes he had thrown aside were worn out, what would you say?"

"Man 'live; man gone away," answered Wildcat promptly.

"Right again," said Dr. Gordon, "for to be persuaded that a man is dead, we must have stronger proof than that his falling-down house has been deserted, or that his worn-out clothes

have been left behind   And just so is it with the
soul. We have no right to believe that it is dead
because it no longer inhabits its former home.   It
may have *gone away*. Oftentimes, too, it happens
that when the body comes to die, the soul is as
fresh and strong as ever. It looks through the
eyes, and talks through the lips until the eyes
glaze and the lips grow stiff in death. If it dies
at all, it seems to die *after* the body, and because
the body dies. But, as Wildcat just now decided,
it is not sufficient to prove a man dead that we
find his house empty or his garment left behind.

"Another reason for believing that the soul outlives the body is the fact that the purpose for which
man is created seems to be seldom fulfilled in this
life. Let me explain: When a tree has lived a
certain number of years, and attained a certain
growth, and shaded the ground and fertilized the
soil with its leaves, and dropped its seed to produce others of its kind, it has accomplished all
that it is fitted for, and then it dies; its work is
done. In like manner, brute animals fulfil the
purpose of their existence. The ox or the deer
goes to its feeding place in the morning, and there
browses until its hunger is appeased, after which
it takes in its supply of water, and then lies down
in some comfortable retreat, where it remains until its feeding time comes again; after which it
retires for the night, and feels that its day's duty

ıs done. This round of eating, drinking, sleeping, is repeated every day, until .ts last day closes
its career forever. Its work is then all done, and
the purpose of its life is completed. But with
man it is not so. His life is all a preparation for
something which he seldom, if ever, attains on
earth. He eats, drinks, and sleeps to fit him for
labor, and he labors to be able to eat, drink, and
sleep, with more comfort and security. But this
is not fulfilling the end of his creation. It may
suffice for a brute, but not for him. His work is
as much more noble than the brutes, as his nature
is much more exalted. Then what is it? He
never finds the end in this life, but closes his
earthly course reaching toward something yet beyond.

" These are some of the reasons, obtained outside the Bible, for believing that the soul outlives
the body. There are others which may be given,
but none which would probably be more impressive.

" And now, although you may suppose the subject ended, and although I propose here to end it,
there is one more question to be asked. We have
satisfied ourselves on three points—That we have
souls ; that there is a hereafter ; and that our souls
probably outlive our bodies. But in giving answer to the inquiry, Is the soul immortal ? we
must also ask, whether, in that hereafter, we may

expect the soul to live *forever ?* This is a ɩ ighly important query. There is nothing sweeter than life. It is so sweet that we may question whether one hour spent in the full enjoyment of our usual faculties is not worth all the pain experienced during an ordinary life-time; and it is so valuable that we may be excused if we rush past millions upon millions of years and ask, shall we live *forever ?* But this is a point upon which the light of reason can give us no satisfaction. It brightens our pathway as far as the grave—it enables us to catch a glimpse of life beyond—but on the question of real and enduring *immortality,* it sheds not a ray. It is at this stage of our inquiry where we feel the necessity not only of a revelation, but of a *Divine* revelation. No one this side of God himself can give the answer. The present dwellers in that other world are as much interested in it as we are, for if the soul of *man,* after entering that state, is liable to death, or to ending of any sort, so may be the spirit of every angel and archangel, and of all the company of heaven.

" Thanks be unto God for the Bible ! and especially for the Gospel of our Lord and Saviour Jesus Christ, ' which brings life and immortality to light !'"

With this the conference ceased, and all, ever Wildcat, seemed gratified.

As the day drew near its close, and the small

weak tide reached its lowest mark, Dr. Gordon
observed Robert lean over the vessel's side, look
toward the patch on the leak, and overheard him
say to Harold, —

"We shall have very little tide to-night."

His father, soon after that, caught his eye and
said, —

"Robert, will you let me divine your thoughts?"

"Certainly, sir, if you can," Robert replied,
with a smile of curiosity.

"If I mistake not," said his father, looking
toward the bow of the vessel, "a part of your
thought was about that *anchor*."

"You are right," he replied, much surprised.
"But I said nothing about it."

"No, nor did any one else," his father added.
"Another part of your thought was that the anchor was not in the right place."

"You surprise me," Robert returned. "How
did you know that?"

"Another part of your thought was, that that
anchor ought to be nearer in shore. And you had
some debate in your mind whether you ought not
to ask me about it."

"Father," said Robert, with a kind of bewil-
dered look, "you are a magician. How have you
been able to look so far down into my mind?"

"By using the spy-glass of human nature," his
father replied. "And you were thinking, too, of

careening the vessel on the sand, by means of to-night's tide."

Robert looked puzzled and almost alarmed.

"Father," he said, "I am not afraid of you, but this looks very strange. Will you not tell me how you have been able thus to read my thoughts?"

"Certainly," his father responded; "I used nothing more than a little knowledge of human nature, and of the laws of mind. I saw you look down toward the leak, and overheard you remark about the tide. I knew you had been anxious this morning about stopping that hole, and you gave us to understand yesterday that your plan for getting to work at it was by careening on the beach. I simply put these parts together, and drew my inferences. Two and two make four, you know."

Robert looked uneasy. He did not altogether like to be searched so thoroughly, even by his father, for every one prefers to have a privacy into which he may withdraw at will, and be free from observation. He was somewhat relieved, however, and disturbed, too, to hear his father say, —

"Instead of laying the vessel on the sand, I am disposed to draw her out further from shore. We can easily careen her sufficiently for our purpose by shifting the ballast. Let us do it at once."

Robert knew that there must be some strong

and pressing reason for this act, and therefore he asked, —

"Do you apprehend any danger?"

"I do," said his father, "although I can scarcely give good reasons for it. The truth is, I do not like the way those canoes up the river have been moving to-day. The Indians are more numerous than ever, and they are bolder, too. I am afraid that some influence is at work to lessen their dread of the island, and that they are bent on mischief."

"It seems to me," observed Harold, "that Yaha-Lusty and his men have suffered enough to keep them away. They have lost two lives already, and both of these by a kind of providence or judgment."

"I suspect," said his uncle, "that a discovery of the prize they have missed in the pirate wreck, has something to do with their present actions; and that they will not be content without attempting to regain what we have taken out of her. But however this may be, my judgment urges me to anchor in the stream out of gunshot, and also to make our bulwarks more secure by a little barricading."

This conversation was held with the boys out of hearing of everybody else. The result was, that before dark, they had drawn up the anchor, pulled the vessel into the stream, and put the deck

in good fighting condition by piling against the
bulwarks, at several places, such spars, pieces of
fire-wood, coils of rope, and other movables fitted
to resist shot as they could find, and also boring
at each of these places several auger-holes large
enough to admit the muzzle of a gun with some
degree of play.

With these precautionary measures, they closed
the evening much earlier than usual, expecting to
be up and at work long before daylight in the
morning.

CHAPTER XXXVI.

INDIAN WILES — BLOODY INTENTIONS — UNEX-
PECTED HELP.

THE half-waned moon did not rise till midnight. Not long before its level-cut face peeped over the distant mainland, Wildcat, whose watch was about to close, went softly to Harold, awoke him gently, and beckoned him aside.

"Injin in the river," said he; "Injin pulling our boat. Come see."

Harold went with all silence and dispatch, peeped over the side of the vessel through a small crevice, where he could see without being seen, and was surprised to discover one of the canoes slowly moving against the tide toward the vessel's bow.

"Moved by a fish," said he to Wildcat, in a whisper.

"No fish! no fish, but Injin," Wildcat persisted.

Leaving him in momentary charge, Harold hur-
452

ried noiselessly to his uncle, and bringing him to the companion-way, whispered to him the state of the case, and asked if the unseen mover of the boat was not probably a fish.

"I think not," said his uncle, stepping back from the vessel's side, after an examination. "I strongly suspect it is an Indian, and that he is either trying to steal our boat, which he cannot do on account of the chain, or else he is reconnoitering with a view to some plan of attack. Let us watch him."

By this time, Robert and Sam, aroused while Dr. Gordon was making his examination, had come on deck, guns in hand, ready for service. Wildcat, who continued watching, now announced, with some excitement,—

"Can *see* Injin. Four head, five head, close by ship."

Dr. Gordon peeped again, and could scarcely believe his eyes when he saw four or five black objects, like Indians' heads, upon the surface of the water, between the vessel's side and the moving canoe. The aim of this stealthy movement now flashed upon him — it was to take the vessel by surprise, and to board her by climbing the bowsprit from the canoe. He instantly decided upon his course of action. Calling the others to a pile of large cannon-balls on deck, he ordered each, in a whisper, to take two of them, and be ready when he gave the word, to throw them directly upon the heads below.

One thought produced a momentary hesitation and a slight change in his plan. It was, that *possibly* these persons might be there without hostile intent. Was he not bound to hail them first, and to give them a chance to declare themselves? It was almost certain that a call, unless very quickly followed by the blow, would permit most of them to escape. But his regard for human life was so sacred that he resolved to run the risk.

"Do as you see me do," said he to the others, who were ready with balls and loaded guns. "Lean over the bulwarks, and each select his man. I will hail, and if they make any attempt to escape, give them your balls first, and your guns afterward."

With noiseless tread they went together to the vessel's side, where each selected his mark, and stood ready with uplifted ball.

"Who's there? *Speak*, OR YOU DIE!" sounded the stern, imperative voice of Dr. Gordon.

The only answer returned was an "Ugh!" of surprise from the heads below, turned up quickly to see the threatening death, and then a splashing of the water, as each attempted to draw himself under the canoe for protection. But the motion was not quick enough.

"Let them have it!" shouted Dr. Gordon, and instantly there was a heavy splash in the water, accompanied by a crashing sound, as if some of the balls had taken effect upon some substance other than water.

"Let them have another round!" said Dr. Gordon, and again the balls flew, and of the sounds that followed, there could be distinguished more than one human voice gurgling through the water.

Ere the second discharge of balls, Harold had run toward the stern, and now called aloud, —

"Here are more of them!" and at the same instant his rifle flashed upon the darkness.

"Give them your guns wherever they appear!" was Dr. Gordon's order, and in the course of half a minute a dozen guns had been discharged from bow, stern, and vessel's side, each aimed at what in the darkness appeared to be an Indian's head.

Then all was again quiet upon the water. How many had attacked the vessel, and how many had perished, could not be determined. There were as many as eight heads counted, five at the bow, and three at the stern, and of these eight it was not certain that any got safely away; but from the known expertness of Indians in the water, and from the sound of distant voices in the dark, there was reason to believe that several had succeeded in escaping.

One suspicious circumstance remained, — something black floated upon the water just outside of the canoe. What could it be? Possibly, a poor wounded wretch, who, being too badly hurt to get away, had fastened himself there. A lantern was brought and held over the gunwale. The red light revealed no human body, but a floating log, which had been used probably to aid the assailants in swimming; at the same time there was in the canoe the glitter of something metallic.

"Let us go down and see what that is," said Harold; but as the words issued from his mouth, two rifles flashed upon the darkness fifty or sixty yards away, accompanied by the murmur of words whose *tone* was that of cursing, "not loud but deep," and the balls whizzed harmlessly by their heads.

"Boat out yonder. Can hear paddle," said Wildcat.

The others gave undivided attention, but could distinguish only a faint sound of water disturbed, which the quick ear of the young Indian had resolved into its true character.

"What a pity our guns are all empty!" exclaimed Harold, looking regretfully in the direction of the receding sounds. "We might have given them a parting volley."

"I suspect they will be satisfied with what they have received," his uncle replied; "and I am weary of taking life."

By this time, the ladies, and even little Frank, had come on deck, for although the scene has taken

pages to describe, it took but few minutes to enact.
The account which they received of their imminent peril, and of their almost miraculous deliverance, filled them with profound emotion. They
shuddered to think what might have been their
experience at that moment had not the coming of
their enemies been detected.

"What made you suspect them?" Dr. Gordon
asked Wildcat.

"Hear boat chain *clink*," returned he.

The warning, however, must have been so slight
that it would probably have escaped notice from
any other ear on board than his. Dr. Gordon
was so convinced of this that he turned to him
with much feeling and said,—

"Wildcat, we owe our lives, under God, to your
faithful watching." Then laying his hand upon
the boy's head, he added fervently,—"May he
watch over you, and reward you as we never can."

"Amen!" and "Amen!" resounded so heartily
from all around, that poor Wildcat broke away
from the presence of his friends and plunged for
refuge down the hatchway.

"We have not examined what it is that lies glit-
tering in the canoe," said Harold. "Let us go and
see," he spoke to Robert.

While they were preparing to go down, Wildcat, who conjectured the truth from the sounds of
clambering on the vessel's side, hurried from be-

low, and joined them. They used a small ladder of rope, and Dr. Gordon held a lantern as they went. Scarcely had they reached the middle of the canoe ere the boys uttered a cry of wrath and horror.

"What have you found?" asked Dr. Gordon.

"We will show you in a moment, father," Rob-art replied, his voice trembling with excitement.

He clambered back with the others, and showed a handful of butcher knives, ground very sharp at point and edge, for the double purpose of stabbing and cutting.

"These are the instruments with which they intended to take our lives," said Robert.

"And scalp too," added Wildcat.

"They put them in the canoe for safe keeping, no doubt, until they could leap on board and use them on us," remarked Harold, shuddering, as he looked at his mother and the rest.

This feature in the intended tragedy was so plainly pictured in those horrid-looking knives, that each one's blood ran cold at the sight, and each realized more vividly than ever the greatness of their deliverance.

"Let us go to work at once, and get away from this dangerous neighborhood," said Robert, looking at his father; "I am ready to begin work this minute"

"We shall, then, have to work on our mast by

candle-light," responded his father, " and I think it will not be pleasant, even if it should be safe, to work feeling that we make targets of ourselves. Two or three hours hence the moon will give us all the light we need for our work, and also to keep a good lookout upon the water. No Indian will dare attack us then."

All work was, therefore, delayed until three o'clock. The excitement, natural to scenes such as they had just passed through, kept the company on deck in animated conversation for some time. Frank at last began to show signs of weariness, and his father said to him, —

" Come, Frank, I will join you in going to bed. Others may sit up, if they please, but I shall need all the sleep I can get, to fit me for the labors I foresee to-day."

One by one, all turned in, except Harold, who was on duty, and Mrs. McIntosh, who insisted on keeping him company. Her motherly heart, which had been all aroused by his tenderness two days before, when she was wounded, had had no opportunity yet for expressing itself, and now, to-night, she felt more drawn to him than ever for doing his part in saving her once more from death.

" Do, dear mother, go in and try to sleep," he implored ; " I am used to this kind of life, and you are not."

But he implored in vain. She replied that she

preferred remaining on deck ; that she was wide awake, and that the cool, open air, was too pleasant to be exchanged for the close air of the cabin He then brought a chair and a shawl, wrapped he. up close, and seated her at a spot where his tread as sentry would bring him oftenest and nearest to her, and there, under the quiet skies, and in the light of the ascending moon, they talked freely and largely upon the past, the present, and the future.

At three o'clock in the morning, his watch expired, and that was the hour appointed by Dr. Gordon for calling all hands to work.

By this time the brilliant half moon had risen far into the heavens, and her pure beams not only afforded all the light needful for their operations on deck, but illumined the surface of the water all the way to the white beach and snowy bluff.

The work of preparing the new mast went on prosperously, and without incident, until nine o'clock, when Mary, who, with her aunt, had assumed the duties of the kitchen, came to her father with the unpleasant intelligence that the fresh water aboard was exhausted, and that until more was obtained all culinary operations were at an end. Her father was not only loth to stop the work which all were so anxious to complete, but he had conceived a real dread of going ashore, as if it were a place no longer safe. Water, however, is an indispensable of life, and must be had, cost what it may. He, therefore, made no delay, except to devise the easiest and safest mode of obtaining it.

"We must drop down stream, opposite the Live-oak Spring," said he to the boys, "and take in at once our supply for the voyage. But whatever going ashore we do now, must be done in force."

They pulled the vessel down to the appointed place, anchored her out of reach of shot from shore, took into the two canoes all the water vessels they could command, and arming themselves each with a gun and a brace of pistols, they sallied ashore, — Dr. Gordon, Harold, Wildcat, and Sam being in the boat, leaving Robert as the only guard on the vessel.

Before going, however, Dr. Gordon had the precaution to examine well the whole island and beach as far as the spy-glass could penetrate, also to load the little cannon with canister shot, and set her in position for raking the bluff, and to load all the guns and pistols left aboard, and put them at Robert's command, saying at the same time to his sister, on whose strong and steady nerves he knew he could rely, —

"I leave you, sister, as well as Robert, to watch and give me warning of the first appearance of anything suspicious. I have a presentiment of danger, without being able to assign a reason for it, except that I *scent* it.　We will take quite an armory of fighting implements in the canoes, and leave almost as large a number aboard for *you* and Robert, if you know how to use them.　Mary does," he added, looking approvingly at his daughter, "and I hope she has courage, and nerve enough too, to use them in time of need.　Eh, Mary?"

Mary replied, "I hope so, but hope, too, there will be no need."　And Mrs. McIntosh appended that although she herself could not boast of much skill, she knew both how to load and to fire a gun, and she hoped that in a time of trial she would prove herself worthy of being Harold's mother.

Dr. Gordon's words in parting were,—

"No doubt Yaha-Lusty perceives that we are almost ready to leave.　No doubt, too, he suspects that if there was anything of value on the pirate wreck, we have transferred it to this vessel.　If, therefore, he can possibly muster force enough for the purpose, I think he will make a determined effort to possess himself of our craft.　Therefore I say to you, WATCH."

Prudent though he had been, almost to the appearance of timidity, there was one spot which Dr. Gordon had neglected to examine.　That was Fish Point, whence he had just come, but which, by its projection into the water, concealed from view a narrow strip of the river, sufficient to allow boats that closely hugged the shore to come down from the bend above, and conceal themselves within half a mile of the vessel.

The two canoes went safely ashore. For nearly an hour they were occupied in replenishing their vessels from the slowly filling spring. Mrs. McIntosh aided Robert in keeping faithful watch with eye and glass. Mary and Frank, having recited their usual daily lessons to their mother, were now on deck, standing near their aunt and amusing themselves with playing watchmen. Suddenly, Frank, whose position opened to him a narrow vista on shore, not visible to the others, exclaimed,—

"Sister Mary! See yonder, behind that clump of prickly pears, what a queer thing comes moving along! What can it be?"

Mary was as much puzzled as he, for what he saw, through an opening in the cactus on shore, seemed to be a shapeless mass of brown herbage, or of dressed deerskin, she could not tell which, mysteriously moving toward the bluff, with a kind of rolling motion.

"Aunt," said she quickly, and in a tone of alarm, "what can it be? It does look very queer."

Her aunt, who was using the spy-glass, looked for a moment only through the opening, and exclaimed in terror,–

"Robert, halloo as loud as you can, and raise the red flag! Quick! quick! There's danger!"

What had puzzled Mary and Frank were the horizontal backs of a file of Indians bent almost to the ground, and marching at a half-run toward the bluff, and coming in a line so straight that the head of the first only, and the backs of the others could be seen from the vessel.

Mrs. McIntosh observed that the moment the halloos reached shore, Dr. Gordon and the rest dropped their work, seized their guns, and stood upon the defensive; though from the intervening bluff they could learn nothing of the nature, number or position of their foes. They were, however, not left long in doubt. Four of the assailants, of whom two were negroes, stopped, apparently as a reserve corps, under the large live-oak, while four others, of whom the leader was a gaudily dressed negro, fantastically painted, ran to the edge of the bluff, levelled their pieces and fired at the company at the spring, and having drawn their fire in return, retired as if to reload, but in fact to allow the reserve corps to come up and fire more deliberately.

As this was going on, Mrs. McIntosh, who seemed to have an intuitive perception of their plan, called to Robert, —

"Remember the cannon. Aim right on the party coming."

Robert was not an expert artillerist. He did not succeed in bringing his piece to bear exactly

right until the second exchange of shots was taking place, when, as his canister of bullets went
hurtling ashore, he heard his aunt give a shriek,
an l saw her fall upon the deck. Had she been
hurt? She could not have been. Then what was
the matter? He looked ashore, and saw what made
his own blood recoil with terrible force upon his
heart,—his father and Wildcat were the only persons standing,— *Harold and Sam lay prostrate on
the beach.*

"Oh, mother!" he exclaimed, clasping his
hands in agony. "Harold is down! and so is Sam!"

But a moment after he called out joyfully,—

"Aunt! aunt! wake up! Harold is not killed;
he is standing by father, strong and brave as ever."

At these words, Mrs. McIntosh slowly opened
her eyes, rose to her feet, gave one look to her son,
then another to Heaven, and was perfectly herself
once more.

That cannon-shot was most terrifying to the Indians. It was evidently unexpected, for in the
hurry of exchanging platoons, both those coming
and those going marched in a direct line with the
range of the balls; and the effect was in a high
degree disastrous, for the balls tore through the
midst of them, killing one of them outright,
wounding another, and enveloping them all in a
cloud of dust. The one killed was the gaudily
dressed negro who had opened the attack, and

2 E

whose fall seemed greatly to disconcert the rest, for they gathered round him and stood inactive, instead of reloading their pieces.

"Make haste and give them another load!" said Mrs. McIntosh to Robert, the moment her eyes could take in the scene just described; but ere his gun was loaded, the attention of all on board was forcibly called in another direction. Mrs. Gordon was on deck, her face, pale from long disease, rendered still more pallid by present excitement. She was standing near Robert, when suddenly she grasped him by the shoulder, and in speechless terror pointed up the river.

Dreadful to see, two canoes, each containing three yelling Indians, had shot from behind the concealment at Fish Point, and were urging their way with all speed to board the vessel while its defenders were occupied on shore. It was a well-laid plan. Their approach was not observed until they had gained half way to the vessel. They were still much farther off than the boats ashore, but it was manifest to all aboard that it was impossible for Dr. Gordon and the boys, beset as they were by enemies, to launch their boat, get her under headway, and reach the vessel in time to keep off these new assailants. Death certain, death terrible, from the hands of these ruthless wretches, seemed to be the fate of all on board.

But Mrs. McIntosh was not a woman to succumb so long as anything in defence of life could possibly be done. The present desperate emergency only awakened all her energies.

"Robert," said she, with a resolute smile upon her blanched face, "Mary and I can help you in this our first battle. Come ; let us move the guns forward. Each of us can aim at a man in the foremost boat, then at those in the second. And, Father of mercies," she continued, looking upward, " give us good speed this day !"

Holes for small arms had been bored the evening before through the barricaded bulwarks, and, fortunately for the present necessity, two of these barricades, with several holes each, had been prepared at the bows, which headed toward the coming foe. Robert put a loaded musket through each of these holes. and seating himself at the barricade, quietly awaited the approach of the hostile canoes.

Engrossed as they were with the prospect of speedy and of deadly conflict, their attention was attracted by another discharge of firearms on shore. Turning a hasty glance in that direction, the scene that met their eyes baffled conjecture. All was commotion. Dr. Gordon and the boys having just become aware of the danger threatening the vessel, were making frantic efforts to launch one of the boats and to push off. The firing did not come from them, nor from the Indians on the bluff.

A whitish cloud of moving smoke showed that the discharge had proceeded from amid the branches of the live-oak. The Indians under the tree, strange to say, were hurrying away from it as fast as they could run, while shot after shot from the branches above, dropped them in their tracks. Two of those under the tree had thus fallen, and also one of those upon the bluff.

These last, seeing one of their number fall by a shot from an unexpected source, hastily turned to see whence it came. This was the moment when Dr. Gordon and the boys, not knowing what was going on above, but only that their loved ones were threatened, rushed to the nearest canoe, leaped into it, and pulled with all their might toward the vessel.

For what reason, Mrs. McIntosh and the others on the deck could not imagine, the Indians on the bluff leaped thence to the beach, ran to the other canoe, shoved off, and, using the oars for paddles, hurried from shore, as if having less fear of Dr. Gordon and his guns than of some object of terror behind.

To those who approached from Fish Point, the two boats shoving off simultaneously from the live-oak spring, must have appeared as if engaged in a race for the vessel, for on seeing them thus engaged, the new-comers raised a yell, and pulled more vigorously than ever toward the prize.

When the assailing canoes came within ordinary musket range, Mrs. McIntosh urged Robert to shoot; but he answered with surprising coolness,—

"No, aunt; they think there's nobody aboard but women and children, and I do not wish them to know better until they are near enough for me to be sure of one or two in each boat. I think you and Mary can manage all that will try to get on deck."

The savages, secure of their prey, came on with whoop and yell until their high cheek-bones and the stripes of paint upon their cheeks could be distinctly seen. Then a cloud of smoke was projected from the larboard bow of the little vessel. Robert had discharged his musket with deadly aim at the foremost canoe, and without waiting for the smoke to clear away, was hurrying to the other bow to repeat his shot, when he heard the sound of a musket just over his head. His aunt, unknown to him, had rested her piece for support on the gunwale, and had pulled trigger as soon as she heard the click of his gunlock.

When the smoke rose sufficiently for them to see, the two canoes were pausing side by side in noisy conference, each containing one dead man. That pause was fatal to another of their number, leaving but two in one boat and one in the other.

"Spare them now, Robert," cried Mrs. McIntosh, "they are turning away as fast as they can."

"Yes, aunt!" said Robert, snatching up another musket, and running to the vessel's side, "I'll spare them all as soon as they get beyond the reach of shot," and with that he aimed at the hindmost canoe, having but one man, and the next moment it was floating quietly on the tide, without any one to propel or control it. The other boat moved through the water as seldom a boat has moved, driven only by two paddlers, yet it went not fast enough to outgo the bullets. Robert's aim, however, was not so precise as before, or else his guns were not so true, for his first ball struck the water beyond the boat, and his second shattered the paddle of one of the men, who was a negro; upon which the frightened wretch dropped the useless fragments, and raised his hands toward the vessel in supplicating attitude.

"I cannot resist that," said Robert; "it is a cry for quarter; and, moreover, the man is a negro."

CHAPTER XXXVII.

OW were you hurt, Harold?" Mrs.
McIntosh anxiously inquired, the mo-
ment the canoe came alongside.

"Not hurt at all, dear mother," he replied. "I was only knocked down. A rifle-ball
hit something in my side-pocket, and stopped
there. I am as well now as ever."

The quick eyes of the mother detected, as he
spoke, a small hole in the bosom of his deerskin
tunic, and he was no sooner on deck, and welcomed, than she thrust her hand into his side-
pocket, and drew thence his beautiful little Testament pierced and ruined by a rifle-ball.

The warm congratulations between the parties
on board and the parties from shore, had not

471

ceased, ere Mrs. Gordon called her husband's attention to the fact that the Indians on the bluff were beckoning to them.

"Will you trust yourself to them, after all this hostility?" she inquired.

"*They* have not been hostile," was his reply. "They have fought for us and saved our lives. Surely they may be trusted."

"Be careful what you do, brother," added Mrs. McIntosh, in a warning tone. "Remember how treacherous most Indians are. How do you know that this party have not fought the other only to possess themselves of you and your vessel?"

"I admire your prudence," responded her brother, "and certainly shall not trust myself in their hands without first knowing who they are."

He took the spy-glass, directed it ashore, and instantly his face lighted up with pleasure.

"No fear of *them*," said he. "I recognize Torgah, Somassee, Riley, and, I think, Chinnobee and his son, Moheta. Besides, there are several strangers, of whom one is an old man, singularly attired, and another is a negro, the image of our poor Sam, having his face all streaming with blood!"

He handed the glass to Wildcat, who joyfully exclaimed, "Mahinlo! and my uncle Tiger-tail!"

"We'll go ashore, boys, and thank our deliverers," said Dr. Gordon. Then turning to his sister

and to Mary, he added, " As little as we can do after all they have done for us, will be to invite them
aboard and give them something to eat. No doubt
they are hungry by this time, or soon will be.
Provide the best Indian dinner you can ; and remember it has been said by a very wise man, ' the
shortest way to most people's hearts is *down their
throats.*' "

" If we are to get them aboard, we must have
another boat. Suppose we catch that one floating
out there," suggested Robert, pointing to the canoe freighted with dead men.

His father consented. The boys went, captured
the drifting canoe, with its cargo of Indians, one
of whom still showed signs of life, and then returned to the vessel, saying, with great pleasure,—

" We have made another important discovery.
Our Bellevue boat lies moored at Fish Point."

Dr. Gordon's eyes brightened too, and he replied, " We will first go ashore, as in duty bound.
Then, as soon after as you please, you may go and
bring back our boat."

They pulled quickly to land, towing the captured canoe by its painter of twisted deerskin.
Torgah met them at the water's edge, and joyful
was the greeting between him and his young friend
Harold. The same was true of Tiger-tail and
Wildcat. Riley and Somassee, also, came to meet
them ; and so did the bloody-faced negro. The

others remained on the bluff above, with **Maninlo.**

To the surprise, as well as delight, of all in the boat, the negro proved to be Sam himself, " Come to life," he said, " only to tell them Huddie and Goodby," for he was shot clean through the head and was bound to die. They were exceedingly sorry to see the poor fellow mortally wounded, as he appeared to be, for the ball had entered the forehead, and was plainly to be felt under the scalp, at the back part of the head. But they were astonished that a person shot thus, squarely through the brain, had not died at once. During their stay upon the beach, Sam several times bade them farewell, saying that his time had come, and leaving divers messages for his wife and children in Georgia. But somehow death delayed to carry off its victim, and Dr. Gordon suspecting, at last, the truth, made a surgical examination, and ascertained that the ball had struck the frontal bone, which in some skulls is very thick and hard, and had glanced around the head, between scalp and skull, without penetrating the brain. After this discovery, Sam's only complaint was of a little headache, and before many days he was as well as ever.

Passing up the bluff from the beach, Dr. Gordon's first attentions were shown to Mahinlo, who was, beyond comparison, the principal personage of the group. It was observed, by the keen-eyed lookers-on, that they approached each other with measured, stately step, as if there were a meaning in their motion, and when their hands met and grasped there was a kindling of the eye.

" My *brother*, Mahinlo!" said Dr. Gordon, with great animation, "I come to thank you for my life, and for the lives of my people."

" Mahinlo only did his duty," the other replied, still continuing the grasp and looking Dr. Gordon in the eye.

" Glad to see you! glad to know you!" Dr. Gordon said ; then turning to the others he asked, " Are any of these brothers, too ? "

" All brothers, for my sake," he replied.

On a motion of his hand the others approached, and exchanged greetings too ; but it was observed that, however cordial these were, they seemed to lack the charm which had animated the meeting of the first.

" Glad to see Chinnobee, too ! How came he here ? " said Dr. Gordon to his former patient.

" Chinnobee come to pay debt to Medicine-man," he answered with a smile.

" More than paid it now," Dr. Gordon responded. " Medicine-man now in debt to Chinnobee."

And thus he passed from one to another, having a pleasant word to say, appropriate to each, until having completed the round, he came again to Mahinlo, whose face he observed to be overspread with a deadly pallor, while in his garments there was the evidence of blood from the coat to the moccasin.

"Mahinlo is hurt," said he; "tell me where?"

The old man pointed to his neck, saying as he did so, — "Not much," but at the same time he reeled and sank to the earth.

Dr. Gordon instantly opened the clothing and discovered, under cover of the tunic, or hunting-shirt, as it is called by our western hunters, a wound in the neck, caused evidently by a canister-shot. The wound itself was very slight, scarcely penetrating below the skin; but what perplexed and alarmed Dr. Gordon was the fact that most of the blood which issued was of a light-red color, and came in jets or pulsations, showing that an artery had been cut. Yet what artery could it be? He knew of none in the neighborhood capable of supplying such a flow, except that which conveys the blood from the heart to the brain, known as the carotid; yet that lay too deep to be reached by a skin-wound, and, moreover, is so large that a wound in it ought usually to result in death in three or four minutes. The mystery, however, was soon explained. A large button of amethyst, on the neck of the prophet's robe, had been shattered by the shot, and a sharp fragment had been driven with force sufficient to *puncture* this important vessel.

"I very much fear," said he to Robert, who assisted in the examination, "that the hours of good Mahinlo are numbered. The result may be delayed, but cannot be averted."

Ascertaining by experiment where, and how, a pressure upon the bleeding orifice was most effective in reducing the hemorrhage, and pouring cold water plentifully upon the bleeding part, it was not long before Mahinlo opened his eyes, and seemed surprised to find himself lying on the ground.

"My brother is badly hurt," said Dr. Gordon, taking him by the hand.

"Mahinlo will soon be with his fathers," he languidly replied.

"I can tie that bleeding artery, and add many hours, even days, to your life. Shall I do it?" Dr. Gordon asked.

"Mahinlo old. Time he lie down," replied the venerable man. "Bury me by my father."

In the meantime, Riley, who had made a visit to the waterside, and had discovered that the captured canoe was his own, lost some months before, came now to announce that the Indian in it, giving signs of life, was no other than Yaha-Lusty, who, on learning that Mahinlo was on shore, begged earnestly to see him before he died.

The old prophet at once made an effort to rise

and being supported by a friend on each side, walked down the bluff, where Yaha-Lusty awaited him in the canoe drawn up on the beach. Here Dr. Gordon examined the nature of his wounds, and declared that he would scarcely survive an hour. The conversation that ensued was conducted in the Indian language, but was afterward reported in English, to the following effect, —

Yaha-Lusty professed great penitence for having rebelled against Mahinlo. He said that he had been deceived by Yobly, (or Gullah-Jim, as he was called,) a negro, who boasted great powers of witchcraft, and who, upon hearing of the rich prize to be expected in the capture of the pilot boat, had promised Yaha-Lusty and his men perfect success, if they would place themselves under his guidance and command. He spoke very contemptuously of Mahinlo and his powers of enchantment, saying that the Gullah negroes excelled all the world in witchcraft, and that he was greatest among the Gullahs. But Yobly was now to be seen from the canoe, lying dead upon the bluff. This proved him to be a deceiver; and Yaha-Lusty, convinced of his error, herewith returned to his allegiance.

"You know," said he, addressing the red-men around, "that my people owned all this coast, and that I am the last of my people. I have no child nor kinsman. The last blood of the Caloosas is

growing cold in my veins. Now hear, all of you!
I give to Mahinlo all that is mine, to be his forever, especially this island. Do you hear?"

They answered, "Yes, we hear. You give to
Mahinlo all that is yours, especially this island."

The strength of the dying man, which seemed
to have been unnaturally aroused to perform this
act, here gave way, and he fell back in a swoon.

Then Mahinlo, addressing the same company,
said, —

"Hear, all of you! This island is mine. Bury
me here by the side of my father. A grave is all
I want. The remainder, I give to my young friend,
Wildcat, if he will promise, before you all, to see
me buried, and to watch over my grave. Hear, all
of you, what Wildcat says."

The weeping boy, thus suddenly and singularly
distinguished, fell at the feet of his benefactor, and
grasping his knees, said, —

"Mahinlo is my father; I will be his son forever."

The old prophet was deeply moved. He had
long and tenderly loved the boy. He wished now
to do for him the best he could. But what could
he do during the few hours of life remaining?
Turning to Dr. Gordon, and speaking in English,
with his hand still resting on Wildcat's head, he
said with emphasis, —

"*My brother!* I give this boy to you to teach

for me. Teach him as Mahinlo's son. Teach him about the Great Spirit. Teach him to be a good man. Does my brother hear?"

"I do," replied the Doctor, drawing a long breath, and answering slowly, — "I take Wildcat under my care, from this day, as Mahinlo's son, and I promise to teach him, to the best of my ability, all that is needful for his happiness in this life, and for his happiness in the life to come. Is my brother satisfied?"

"That is enough," said Mahinlo, and with that he placed Wildcat's right hand in that of his future guardian.

Meanwhile, Harold had beckoned Robert aside, and they had gone together to Fish Point, and brought around the Bellevue boat, just in time to witness the deed of gift to Wildcat, and now the last moments of Yaha-Lusty.

Among savages, the act of burial is usually not long delayed — sometimes, not long enough among the civilized. Scarcely had Yaha-Lusty's breath left the body, ere Tiger-tail invited the other red-men to unite with him in preparing for the burial. Two of them went to the woods, where they selected a tree of suitable size, girdled it in two places, six feet apart; then by inserting their knives and hatchets at an incision on one side, they removed the bark in one unbroken piece. In this bark-coffin they enclosed the body, and buried it in a shallow grave, dug in the soft sand of the bluff. The other dead bodies were buried with it, but without a coffin, and over them all was raised a mound of earth.

While this was in progress, Dr. Gordon begged Mahinlo to take up his abode on the pilot boat, where the friends whose lives he had saved might nurse him. To which he replied, that his hours were few, and that he wished to be carried at once to the prairie, where he might die by the grave of his father.

Dr. Gordon then called Wildcat and Tiger-tail, and assigned to them the duty of transporting the dying prophet to the place selected, while he prepared to join them at the earliest possible moment. After they left, he invited the others to the vessel to obtain something to eat, and to aid him in completing the almost finished work on the mast and rigging. Both these were speedily dispatched, and then, taking in their supply of water from the spring, they sailed, by a light breeze, up the north river and down the east, to the prairie landing, which they reached a little past the middle of the afternoon. The ladies remained aboard, but the tent was taken ashore and pitched upon the same spot from which it had been so recently removed. Efforts were made to persuade Mahinlo to occupy it; but he preferred the more familiar shelter of a palmetto tent erected near the ruinous house, and the other red-men provided themselves similar accommodation close in his neighborhood.

Dr. Gordon was grieved at the thought of losing the remarkable old man, Mahinlo, just as he had made his acquaintance, and his distress was painfully aggravated by the conviction that the fatal wound had been caused by a shot from the vessel. This fact he carefully kept from his sister, and gladly would he have kept it from Robert, too, but, unfortunately, Robert was present during the examination of the wound, and he was too intelligent not to surmise its character and history. Poor fellow! his frequently starting tears and choking voice attested the depth of his sorrow. Mahinlo, perceiving this, took occasion to say to Dr. Gordon, in his hearing, —

"Did not mean to hurt me. Did not know I was in the tree." Then fixing his eye full upon Robert's, he added: "Good Spirit send that ball. You could not help it. My time come."

The degree of refinement and of religious sentiment displayed in this remark was far beyond the ordinary attainment of Indians, and Dr. Gordon was so much gratified with it that he felt encouraged to make further inquiry.

"May I talk like a brother?" he asked.

"Yes!" the other replied, with emphasis.

"I hear that Mahinlo loves the Great Spirit, and loves to pray. Is this so?" asked Dr Gordon.

" Yes! yes!" he replied as before.

" May I ask what are the prayers that Mahinlo loves most to offer ?"

"Our Father who in heaven," said the old man, looking upward; then, with emotion, " And—and, Be merciful to me a sinner."

Dr. Gordon was strongly moved. Accustomed to look below the surface of words and actions for their real origin, he said to himself, in rapid thought, "Is Mahinlo a heathen? for these prayers are eminently Christian. How did he learn them? May he not be like Cornelius, the centurion,* taught to some extent both by God and man, and only waiting to know the way of life more fully? I will inquire, —

"How did you learn these prayers?" he asked.

Mahinlo informed him that in early life he had lived with a good man, who had taught him these things, and many others now forgotten. Also, that a few years since he had become attached to William Morgan, the father of Wildcat, and had been much with him during the protracted illness of which he died, and that Morgan often used these prayers, and talked with him and others about what his pious mother had taught him in childhood.

"These prayers are from the Bible, —God's book, that teaches us all we know of him, and of

* Acts of the Apostles, tenth chapter.

our duty to him," said Dr. Gordon. "Would you like to hear more from that book?"

"Glad! glad!" the old man replied.

"The Bible teaches a great deal of what we are to believe and of what we are to do," Dr. Gordon went on to say. "But of all this, I can tell you very little.

"Of what we are to *believe*, it teaches: That all men are sinners; that the Son of God, known as Jesus Christ, came into the world to save sinners; and that all sinners who believe in him shall be saved. This is what we believe when we offer the prayer, *God be merciful to me a sinner.*

"Then as to what we are to *do*, it teaches: That God is Love; that his love for us exceeds that of father or mother; and that, as he has so loved us, we ought to love him, and to love one another, and to do the works suitable to such a love. This is what we believe when we come to him with the prayer, *Our Father who art in Heaven.*"

Mahinlo listened with profound attention, drinking in every word, then said, —

"Say again."

Dr. Gordon repeated, with some explanations, what had just then been declared, then opened his Bible to the third chapter of John, in which Jesus Christ instructs the inquiring Nicodemus. Mahinlo was deeply interested. He listened without remark or inquiry until Dr. Gordon came to the passage, " *God so loved the world that he gave his only begotten Son, that whosoever believeth on him should not perish, but have everlasting life,*" when he asked, —

" What this mean ? "

Dr. Gordon explained as well as he could, and was going on with the next verse, when Mahinlo interrupted him with, —

" Read that more."

He read it again, and was going on, when Mahinlo repeated his request, " Read that more," and on its being read the third time, he said, —

" Stop now ! Let me say. *God so love, — give his Son, — believe on him, — have everlasting life.* Shut up book. That enough for Mahinlo."

Late in the evening, Dr. Gordon repeated his visit. His patient lay peacefully still, and replied to all inquiries, that he needed nothing more. The light-red blood continued to jet in tiny pulsations from the wound, and the pulse was hourly becoming weaker ; still his strength was such as to warrant the hope that his life would be prolonged through the night, and perhaps far into the coming day.

Leaving him now in the hands of the two faithful watchers, Dr. Gordon wished him " Good night and God bless you ! " Mahinlo turned quickly upon his side, seized the Doctor's hand, and, with a significant pressure, said to him, —

" Remember my boy ! Teach him what you teach me, and *more !* "

Early next morning, the Doctor called **again.**
Tiger-tail and Wildcat were at their post, and Mahinlo lay quietly upon the ship-mattress that had
been spread for him. He had spent a very comfortable night, the nurses said, and had not for
hours uttered a word, until just before daylight,
when he folded his hands together and said, as if
half dreaming, "God *so* love." The hands were
still folded, and the old man seemed to be asleep,
but when Dr. Gordon came to examine the pulse,
he found that it had ceased to beat, and that the
body was becoming stiff in death.

The announcement of this fact soon brought
together all persons on the island. Tiger-tail, as
highest in rank of the red-men, and Wildcat, as
son, by adoption, of the deceased prophet, assumed
control of the preparations made, though all that
was resolved upon was, by courtesy, first referred
to Dr. Gordon. A substantial coffin was prepared of the best materials within reach, and lined
by the hands of the ladies, with a white linen
sheet, and a neat grave was dug so close beside
that of the prophet's father, that the muzzle of
what had once been a superb rifle, and the bowl
of a costly tobacco-pipe were visible at the crumbling side. But the burial was postponed to the
middle of the next day, to give opportunity for
the attendance of persons upon the main, and
Tiger-tail, with his companion, went each in a

canoe, to give information at the prophet's recent home, and to invite his friends and retainers to the funeral.

At the appointed hour next day, quite a respectable number assembled around the grave. The funeral services were conducted by Dr. Gordon, who took occasion to speak of Mahinlo's well-known love for the Lord's Prayer, and who persuaded the attendants, in respect to the prophet, to unite with him in repeating it aloud, as a part of the burial service. He did not feel authorized to announce Mahinlo's conversion to the Christian faith, and his earnest commendation of it, during the night, to those who were in attendance; but he said that Mahinlo was his brother, dearly beloved, and that he hoped to meet him in the country of the Great Spirit.

After the services, Tiger-tail detained the company to proclaim that Yaha-Lusty, in dying, had formally bequeathed all his possessions, and especially this island, to Mahinlo; and that Mahinlo, who had no children nor kinsmen, had, in like manner, bequeathed his possessions to Wildcat, whom he had named his son. Therefore, that, in behalf of Yaha-Lusty first and of Mahinlo next, (to both of whom he had fallen heir,) Wildcat was owner of this island, and was by right Tustenuggee, or Chief, of the Caloosa territory.

Late in the day the persons in attendance from

the main returned home. Chinnobee, also, and his sons, were about to go, but Dr. Gordon requested them to remain till the next day, saying he had a word for them. They did so, and early the next morning he called them all together to the tent, where was a table on which lay a number of small canvas bags that appeared to be full of something heavy.

"You remember, Chinnobee," said he, "that I begged you and your sons to look for my lost children; and I promised that if you brought them to me, safe and sound, I would give you your hat full of silver. Now you may say that you did not find them, and are not entitled to the reward; but you, and these other friends here, have saved them a second time, when if it had not been for you and dear old Mahinlo, we should all have been murdered. Here are some bags — they are full of silver dollars. Come, each of you in turn, according to rank, Tiger-tail first, Chinnobee next, then the others as Tiger-tail and Chinnobee shall appoint, and take one of these bags. The Medicine-man thanks you for your help."

At this invitation, all except Torgah and Wild-cat came promptly forward and took the proffered bags, delighted with the unexpected munificence.

Dr. Gordon looked at these two with a smile, and said, —

"What! is this not enough?"

To this, Torgah returned not a word ; but Wildcat replied, with rather a hurt look, —

"Did not come here for money."

"Well, well, I can see *you* both some other time," said Dr. Gordon ; "for the present, I will give Wildcat's portion to his uncle Tiger-tail, and Torgah's to Riley, who has already suffered so much in my service."

This disposal of the surplus seemed to be perfectly satisfactory to all parties, and they separated from the tent in fine humor with each other, with Dr. Gordon, and with themselves. Chinnobee and his sons embarked within an hour for the main. Tiger-tail and his companion remained with Wildcat to repair the ruinous lodge, and to construct a better enclosure around the graves.

The sojourn of the Marooning party had now reached its close. Nothing remained to detain them. The Sea-Bird lay with folded wing at the waterside, swaying hither and thither with the tide, waiting their command to bear them all to Tampa. But the Marooners were in no haste to embark. Many a farewell was to be taken after every preparation had been made for departure. Mary must drink once more from her beautiful spring, and carry with her a bottle of its water as a remembrancer. Frank must go with hook and pole to the orange-tree, and obtain a bag-full of the fruit to eat on the way and for a present to

Maum Judy and to William. As for Robert and Harold, they *originated* no delays, but they sympathized in all that were created, and did nothing to curtail them.

The Sea-Bird did not leave her anchorage before high noon, nor until after Dr. Gordon's voice had several times been heard calling all who were bound for Tampa to come aboard. Wildcat went with them to the northern end of the island, where he bade them adieu, hoping soon to rejoin them at Bellevue. He was put ashore by Riley, whose boat was towed astern.

The voyage home was accomplished without accident or misfortune. In passing Riley's Island, they sailed close in shore, and had the pleasure of seeing Pancheta, with a chubby boy at her side, coming fast to meet her husband. At the Bellevue landing, they had scarcely cast anchor, ere the faithful Judy was at the waterside, with arms stretched out to receive them; and when they met, she threw her arms around Mary and Frank in an ecstacy of joy, saying, —

"Huddie! huddie! a tousan' huddie to my dear little missis and mossa!"

Then grasping a hand of Robert and Harold in each of hers, she said, —

"A tousan tankie to de good Lord, too, fuh bring you all safe home. Mossa!" said she, turning with energy to Dr. Gordon, "enty I bin tell you all along de Lord nebber gwine trow' way his own ?" *

After passing from one to another, and welcoming Sam, her brother-in-law, she looked as if for some one else who was slow to appear. No one spoke. All were desirous to keep from her as long as possible the knowledge of her bereavement. But Sam's tell-tale face was too expressive of the truth, and poor Judy went back to the house a widow.

Poor Judy, in truth! All sympathized with her, and all were ready to do for her what they could. But there are some sorrows which can only be let alone; and this was one of them. Frank's oranges, and the others' words of kindness, served somewhat to alleviate, but the sorrow was long there.

Soon as he could be spared, Torgah was dispatched to Fort Brooke, with a note to Major Burke, announcing the arrival; and the next day not only the Major came to welcome them, and the Surgeon of the post, but also Tomkins, and Wheeler, and Jones, and Thompson, and Magruder, who requested the privilege of manning the boat.

By this time it was near the middle of March. The weather was becoming very warm, and had it

---

* Have n't I been telling you, all along, that the Lord is never going to throw away his own.

not been for the breezes from sea and land, alter-
nating with but few minutes' interval, early in the
morning and late in the evening, the heat would
nave been oppressive. Dr. Gordon began to think
of returning to his home in Georgia. Before
leaving Tampa, however, he made special inquiries
through the commandant of the post, concerning
the pirate wreck, and ascertained that she was indeed a piratical vessel that had left Vera Cruz the
preceding summer, under the command of De
Rosa, and after committing several acts of depre-
dation, had suddenly disappeared. The prize being thus left in his hands without a legal claimant,
Dr. Gordon reserved to himself enough to defray
the expenses of his costly Marooning expedition,
and divided the remainder among the young people, giving to Harold much the larger share as
first discoverer; to Wildcat the next largest, as
Lord of the Island; and to Robert, and Mary,
and Frank, each a comfortable portion. These
shares he converted, in due time, into a more
available form, and placed them in the care of
suitable trustees.

After spending together at Bellevue a few pleasant weeks, during which Mrs. Gordon's health
was perfectly restored, the whole company returned
by pilot boat to Mobile, where Dr. Gordon looked
up the family of Dunbar, to whom he paid all
dues, and made them, in addition, a handsome

present. Thence they went to Montgomery to
spend a short time with Mrs. McIntosh; after
which, Dr. Gordon and his immediate family returned to their own home, thankful, as they never
before had been, for the quiet enjoyments of ordinary life.